Songs

of

IRIE

ALSO BY ASHA ASHANTI BROMFIELD

Hurricane Summer

Songs

of

IRIE

ASHA ASHANTI BROMFIELD

W

WEDNESDAY BOOKS
NEW YORK

First published in the United States by Wednesday Books, an imprint of St. Martin's Publishing Group

SONGS OF IRIE. Copyright © 2023 by Asha Ashanti Bromfield. All rights reserved. Printed in the United States of America. For information, address St. Martin's Publishing Group, 120 Broadway, New York, NY 10271.

www.wednesdaybooks.com

The Library of Congress Cataloging-in-Publication data is available upon request.

ISBN 978-1-250-84680-8 (hardcover)
ISBN 978-1-250-84681-5 (ebook)

Our books may be purchased in bulk for promotional, educational, or business use. Please contact your local bookseller or the Macmillan Corporate and Premium Sales Department at 1-800-221-7945, extension 5442, or by email at MacmillanSpecialMarkets@macmillan.com.

First Edition: 2023

10 9 8 7 6 5 4 3 2 1

For my grandfather, Daddy Burge
The original Don-dada
who owned the boddest record store in Kingston
Thank you for putting the music in my heart
And the vibes in my soul
I am so proud to be
Your Stargirl

Mummy & Father,
The first freedom fighters I've ever known
Your love is my legacy
I am so proud to be
Your Rasta child

Makeda,
My best friend in the universe
You shine brighter than any star
I am so lucky to be
Your sister

All praises to the Most High

Ever living
Ever faithful
Ever sure

May your Love unlock
Compassion
In all of creation

Ashé

Emancipate yourselves from mental slavery
None but ourselves can free our minds.

—Bob Marley

The political war that happened in Jamaica in the 1970s was the direct result of colonization by the British. The murder and senseless violence that occurred was the result of a broken system—one built off the suffering that had been inflicted onto African people for centuries. The enslavement, rape, murder, and torture by colonial powers resulted in a broken and politically divided Jamaica after they received independence from the British in the 1960s. Africans were stolen from their native land, brought to another, separated from their families and their native tongue, and then forced to put the pieces back together after centuries of brutality.

But when independence came in 1962, the island was divided. Political greed, corruption, and class division ignited a civil war in the streets of Jamaica.

Rastafarianism, a spiritual approach to being African in the new world, emerged in Jamaica in the 1930s under Marcus Garvey's Pan-African movement. The Rastafari revolution was spread out of a cry for emancipation, peace, and liberation for the Black race. The spiritual resistance and back-to-Africa identity gave birth to the music that spread the beliefs of Rastafarianism around the world.

The teachings of Rastafari tell us we are One Eternal Love. And in the slums of Jamaica, a new sound was born in rebellion to the political violence and centuries of oppression.

Reggae music became the cry for freedom.

If ah nuh so, ah nearly so.

—A Jamaican proverb

1

———

Irie

There is a war in the streets, and I live on the front line.

I glance over at Jilly, silently wondering if she understands the battle I must face the moment we part ways. We go in separate directions when we get to the schoolyard gates.

I go east, and she goes north.

Just like always.

I watch as she tucks a loc of her loose brown curls behind her ear. She shoves a compact mirror into her bright pink backpack, completely oblivious to my gaze. There's a sense of relief to her demeanor as she takes in one final deep breath of this place. She looks out at the schoolyard, grinning so wide it covers her entire face. As the sun grazes her fair, freckled skin, I can feel her anticipation of everything that awaits her in the summer that lies ahead. But even though her excitement is magnetic—it makes me feel invisible.

I find myself trying to read her thoughts—*longing* to get lost in her world.

Trying my best to *feel* what Jilly must right now.

As the hot sun beats down, I can't help but wonder what it must be like to have the world as your oyster—to have *so much control* over the direction of your life that you could hold your future in the palm of your hand. And at the very least, I wonder what it must feel like to not have to contemplate Life and Death every day on your way home from school.

Because those are not worries for girls who live on Jacks Hill.

"Irie, this is *mod*!" Jilly laughs as she takes in the excitement around us.

Our classmates rush through the doors as she waves good-bye, blowing kisses and calling out to a few of the girls from our form. She's closer to a lot more of them than I am.

Popular, even.

I'm just the poor girl who was lucky enough to be called her friend.

For the most part, I kept my head down these past four years at Arthen. And the truth is, none of these girls are going to miss me. I'm just Jillian's friend—and acquaintances with everybody else by association. But it never bothered me what they think.

Jillian's always had my back.

As I watch her say her goodbyes, I know she has no aware-ness of my angst—and if she does, she is seldom to acknowledge it. We've done this dance every day for the past few years—the same pretense steps, as if we both don't know what awaits once I cross the gates. I often wonder how much she understands about my life beyond this school—beyond the time I spent here with her—but I don't dare ask the question out loud. I keep it buried at the back of my throat and swallow it with every bated breath. Today is our last day of high school, and I've already made it this far.

I must do this walk one final time.

The hot sun electrifies the madness as girls run left and right with their schoolbags flung over their shoulders. I watch as a girl with two tight, permed pigtails pulls out an old cloth jump rope. She and a few girls from our form swing it with all their might, giving it one last go as they take turns jumping in and out. Their chanting fills the air, pulling me out of my angst.

Two, four, six, eight . . .

Dem bod, I think as I watch a girl do tricks with her feet. I fight the urge to jump in when Jilly grabs my hand, pulling me back to reality. Her palms are soft, effortlessly melting into mine—just like they always have.

I dread the moment that she'll let go.

Just like I always do.

"I cyaan believe dis is it, Irie. It's *all* ova." Her uptown Patois accent coats her tongue as she uses her hand to shield herself from the scorching Kingstonian sun. Her curls fall effortlessly around her face as a surge of laughter spills from her pink lips. Even in this midday heat—*she glows.* But Jilly has always been pretty. And not just your average pretty, either. The kind that captivates you a bit.

The kind that makes you forget yourself.

"We're freeee, Irie!" she squeals, throwing our hands up to the sky. "Can you believe it? *Finally.*"

My body tenses.

"Yeah, it's pretty surreal."

But I couldn't think of a bigger lie.

The truth is, *Jilly* is free—she has a future mapped out far beyond this summer. Her parents can afford to send her to university, and when this summer is over, she'll be off to one of her prestigious options abroad.

I, however, will never have the opportunity to set foot in a classroom again.

"Guess I betta start enjoying my last two months in Jamaica." Jilly sighs. "I swear, you're *so* lucky your fada is letting you take the year off fi decide wha' yuh wan' fi do."

She repeats the lie back to me with envy in her tone.

"Yeah, thank goodness." I shift, ashamed for bending the truth. But after four years together at Arthen, there was no way

I could admit to her or any of the girls here that I can't afford my future.

That my whole education was a waste.

"Jilly, yuh nah come?" A girl named Keisha rushes by us. "They're doing di final singing battle!" She beckons Jilly over as she sprints toward a huddle in the distance.

"*Ouu*, Irie—" Jilly pulls on my hand. "This is *all* you. Come mash it up, nuh—"

"Can't we jus' watch this time?" I whine. "I *really* don't feel like singing right now."

And for me, that's a rare feeling.

"*Please?*" Jilly persists. "Me haffi see di look pon Stacey-Ann sour face *one last time*."

I laugh, tempted at the idea. Stacey-Ann *swears* she's the best singer at our school, but the truth is she's always off-key. She's one of the cockier rich girls we go to school with—and considering most of these girls are cocky and rich, that's really saying something.

Arthen High is *filled* with the foreign daughters of elite businessmen, musicians, and investors who have all taken up residence on the island. Most of these girls aren't even originally from Jamaica—I'm one of the few girls in our form who happens to be fully Black. Girls come from all over the island to attend Arthen, and most of our houses are far from the school and one another. Stacey-Ann's parents own one of the biggest food-export businesses on the island, and if she's not bragging about her latest venture around the world, she's boasting about being half-Chinese.

Every now and then, I like to put her in her place.

"Come, nuh!" Jilly jumps up and down.

I give in as we rush through the yard toward the huddle.

We arrive just as Tasha-Kaye—another girl from our form—speaks to the crowd.

"All right, all right, who's up next?" She holds up two man-goes. "We ah play fi *juiciest* mangoes pon di tree."

"Gimme my prize!" Stacey-Ann is braggadocious as she takes her place in the center. The girls hype her up as Jilly and I shove through the crowd to get a good look.

"Unu gimme a beat, nuh!" Stacey-Ann calls.

We all begin to snap as she catches the riddim.

Last day ah school, feeling real cool
Sun ah get hot, time fi act a fool

I roll my eyes at her lyrics.
Weak.

Work all year, but we ready fi some fun
Time to tell the world summer cyaan done

"Okay, okay!" The girls applaud as Stacey-Ann takes an overly embellished bow.

Jilly gives me a look, just as unimpressed as I am.

"Anyone else?" Tasha-Kaye calls out to the circle.

I throw my hand up.

Ready.

"You got this, Irie." Jilly nudges me toward the center. "Show dem wha' gwaan!"

"Gimme a beat," I call out to the girls that surround me. They reluctantly start to snap.

"Suh'um a likkle slower," I say as I begin to rocksteady. I move slowly, rolling my chest as a melodic riddim fills my head. The words leave me before I can even think about it.

Simmer down, simmer down down down
Simmer down, simmer down down down

My voice glides as I fall in perfect tempo.

Sun hot, but Irie nah stop
Feel di vibes, mek di beat drop
Show di world who deh pon top
Let di music make yuh soul rock

"Wohhh!" The girls cheer as I continue to jam out with my eyes closed.

Simmer down, simmer down down down
Simmer down, simmer down down down
Irie alone wear di crown crown crown
Irie alone wear di crown crown crown

As I come to a close, even I have to admit—I sound damn good.

I open my eyes to find Jillian rushing toward me with a giant smile on her face. She pulls me into a hug as the girls around us cheer, hyping me up.

"Once again, Irie is the winner." Tasha-Kaye rolls her eyes as she tosses me the mangoes. "Congrats, girl."

I catch the fruit, ignoring the resentment in her tone. I'm used to the girls at this school not thinking I belong here. I got in on a scholarship, after all.

"Thanks, *girl*." I smile cockily as I toss one of the mangoes to Jilly.

We hold hands, laughing as we skip back toward the gate.

"You're a *star*, Irie," Jilly says matter-of-factly. "I still don't know how you do it."

I blush as she puts the fruit into her bag.

"The melodies just come to yuh?"

"Yeah." I shrug. "The words . . . the flow . . . everyting."

"Well, you just let me know when you're ready fi a manager.

Now that school's done, I'll be lookin' work," she teases. "I'm tellin' you, we *have* to get you onstage at Reggae Jamz, Irie. That's the next step. If DJ SupaCat ever heard yuh sing, you'd go platinum—"

"Nuh badda get my hopes up." I grow nervous at the mere mention.

Reggae Jamz is *the* biggest dance hall in Kingston for undiscovered talent. Artists go their entire careers just hopeful to get onstage and perform in front of the island's biggest reggae deejays, and that includes the iconic DJ SupaCat. He's broken some of the island's most major artists, and despite the political war going on in Jamaica, Reggae Jamz is one of the few dance halls that still happens every month uninterrupted.

It's also the hardest to get into.

"A few of the promoters came by the shop again last week." I refer to my father's record store. "They were passing out the Reggae Jamz flyers. I think it's happening next Saturday."

"Can you *imagine* if we could get you on that stage, Irie?" Jilly bursts at the mere idea. "SupaCat would sign yuh in a *heartbeat*. You'd be the youngest female artist in Jamaica with a record."

My stomach knots.

"You're sweet, Jilly." I smile, brushing her off. "But you know how many artists would *kill* to get on that stage? I overheard at the shop that the wait list is longer than a year."

"Please." Jilly kisses her teeth. "I'm *sure* we could figure suh'um out."

"It's like a one-in-a-million chance, Jilly."

"Then it's a good thing you're a one-in-a-million *talent*." Jilly does a twirl around me, and I giggle. "I believe in you, Irie. Yuh have what it takes."

I blush.

"I appreciate you. Fa real." I smile. "But even if I wanted to, Reggae Jamz is twenty-one and over. There's no way I could get in, much less onstage."

Jilly sulks.

"Well, one day soon, then." Her tone is still hopeful. "People *need* to hear your voice, Irie. Yuh have too much talent to waste."

I bite down, knowing full well she's right.

"I still don't undastand why yuh nuh just apply at Jamaica School of Music?" Jilly continues. "If you started in the fall, you could gain some real connections."

I freeze, unsure of how to respond.

I could never afford it.

"Don't worry about me." I try to brush it off. "I'm going to take the year off to relax. Figure everything out."

Jilly nods as if she understands.

She never could.

"Well, take all the time you need." She reaches for my hand as the sun grazes her rose-colored cheeks. "'Cause we *neva* haffi set foot inna dis yah place again."

I muster up a smile, trying to remind myself of my responsibilities at the shop.

Trying hard not to compare my life to hers.

"I want you to know . . . I'm going to miss you *so much,* Irie." Jilly's tone becomes sullen as she gazes into my eyes. "It's going to be tough going from seeing you every day to hardly at all. I'm sad we only started gettin' close the past two years, but our friendship is really special to me. I'm going to miss you. A lot."

I feel a flutter in my chest.

The noise around us fades as the schoolyard empties out.

"Me too," I whisper nervously.

I have to tell her how I feel.

"I want yuh to know . . ." I search myself for the words. "I'm *really* grateful for you, Jilly. I'm grateful for everything we shared together. Here at Arthen . . ."

Jilly's eyes go sad as she listens intensely.

"All of the memories we created at this school . . . skipping classes . . . trading vinyls in the bathroom . . ." I can't help but smile at the memories. "I've never had a friend like you before. Someone who believes in me so much."

I pause as the truth leaves me.

"You're my best friend, Jilly."

"*Oh, Irie*—" She beams, batting her long eyelashes. "You're mine."

Butterflies dance in my tummy as she pulls me in for a hug.

"Which *actually* reminds me," she says as she pulls away. "I almost forgot that I got you suh'um." She's sly as she reaches into her book bag and pulls out a ribbon-wrapped box.

I'm confused when she hands it to me.

"Wait," I make a face. "You *got* me suh'um?"

"Of course, bighead," she teases. "It's our last day. Yuh know I had to commemorate it."

"Jillian . . ." I'm shocked as I stare down at the box. Humbled, I pull on the ribbon.

"You *really* didn't have to get me anyth—"

My heart drops.

As I pull off the top, staring back at me are two sparkly pinkish-red bracelets that glitter like diamonds in the midday sun. My mouth falls open.

"*Jilly*—"

"They're rubies." She beams. "Pretty, nuh true?"

"I . . . How did you—"

"Daddy gave me money for a graduation gift," she boasts. "So I got two."

"Jilly." Tears instantly well in my eyes as I try to comprehend what I'm holding. I've never held anything so expensive in my life, and I'm so stunned I almost drop the box. "Jilly, there's no way I could ever accept this."

"Don't be foolish, Irie." She rolls her eyes as if bored of me playing coy. "*Of course* you can. It's a small token of my appreciation." She takes the box from my hand and pulls out the bracelets. I'm still in awe as she takes my wrist.

"Besides, they're best-friend bracelets. *A matching set.* So, if you don't wear yours, there's no point in me havin' mine." She winks before clasping the bracelet around my wrist. "See? Look how good it looks with your complexion."

I stare at my wrist, speechless.

"Yuh nah go say nuttin'?" she asks.

"I . . . *Thank you.*" I blink back the tears. "I've never owned anything so nice in my entire life. I can't imagine what this must have cost you—"

"Nuh badda concern yourself wit' the price, Irie." She fans me off. "You can't put a price on friendship. And anyways, Mummy and Daddy owed me something nice, with all the work I put in this year. What they *really* should have done is bought me a car."

I smile, unsure if she's joking as she clips hers around her wrist.

She holds her hand up to the sun, admiring the rubies as they glisten.

"Thank you, Jilly." I hold my warm brown hand up beside hers. Next to her pale skin, our complexions juxtapose each other as the matching ruby bracelets glitter in the sun.

"You're *so* welcome." Jilly smiles softly before looking over at me. We turn to each other as she takes my hand in hers. "I really meant what I said, Irie. Spending time with you every day . . . it's been so special. And it's changed me in a lot of ways." Her eyes dance as they search mine. "I really love you, Irie."

I feel time stop as the words leave her lips.

I've never had a friend tell me that before.

"Jilly, I . . ." I squirm. "I *really* love you too. A lot."

I grow hot as I bite down, nervous she might receive it weirdly—but she doesn't.

Instead, she pulls me into the sweetest embrace.

I melt into her arms.

"Come over. *Please,*" she whispers into my ear. "To my house. You *still* haven't been as yet. I could ask my parents tonight—"

"I can't, Jill." I pull away as the shame creeps up. "I already told yuh, my fada's not really di type for that sorta ting. He nuh really like me going to people's houses if he doesn't know their parents, especially not so far away."

Jilly sulks as I look away from her.

It's only a half-lie.

Even though Daddy probably wouldn't let me travel so far during such a heated time, the real truth is I'm nervous to go up into the hills. Mummy used to clean the houses up there, and when I was younger, I would hear countless stories about how extravagantly the people up there lived. The stories always made Mummy feel small, and deep down, I'm afraid to feel the same.

Even more out of place.

"I get that." Jilly sighs, giving in. "Well, maybe I could come by the shop?"

She's referring to my father's record store. Located in the heart of Papine Square—a bustling market—it's one of the most popular places in Kingston to buy music. Not too many places proudly sell reggae vinyls in Jamaica, but Daddy's shop is known for it. Famous local musicians are known to pass through, and despite its shabby appearance, Ricky's Records has quite the reputation.

"Sure. I'll be there every day," I reply. "Daddy has me working weekdays for the entire summer."

"*The entire summer?*" Jilly raises an eyebrow. "I'm sure yuh likkle work friend must be *very* excited about that." She giggles. "Wha' him name, again?"

"Junior." I smile, referring to the ten-year-old boy who sweeps up around my father's shop. He's had a crush on me for as long as I can remember, and even though Jilly's only seen him once before, she knows his infatuation with me is my daily comedy.

"Riiight, Junior." Jilly laughs as she remembers. "I'm sure he'll be *very* happy to have you to himself all day."

"Happy is an understatement. He's been waiting to hold me

hostage so he can sing me *all* those love songs he's been writing for me. One for every week we've worked together."

"Sounds like I have some competition."

I flush as Jilly laughs through a dimpled smile.

Did she just say that?

"By the way"—she changes the subject, flipping her curly hair to the side—"Mummy's birthday is coming up next week. I'm going to need help choosing a good record. Can you keep an eye out?"

"Yeah, of course. What are you looking for?"

"Anything without soul or rhythm." Jilly rolls her eyes. "She's a *very* conservative woman. Wouldn't know good music if *Bob himself* wrote her a song."

"I'll keep an eye out for anything American or top forty, then." I relax as the thought of Jilly coming to look for me at the shop brings me a small feeling of relief.

Not everything is changing, I try to remind myself.

Our love of music is what brought us together in the first place. When the other girls at Arthen turned up their noses at me for not living in the affluent parts of the island like they did, Jilly didn't care. She would catch me humming old tunes I picked up from Daddy's shop, and she was eager to learn every note. Our love for reggae music became our own little revolution.

And now, I run all the songs I write by Jillian.

I watch as she squints, searching past the gate for her driver as she gathers herself to go.

"Yuh ready?" She grows impatient as she glances back at the almost-empty schoolyard.

"You're so eager to leave," I say reluctantly.

"Should I be eager to stay?"

"Me nuh know. It's just—" I pause. "You're not going to miss it?"

Jilly thinks for a moment as if considering the question for the first time.

"Some parts . . ." She shrugs. "But there's more out there, Irie. High school is only five percent of our lives." She gives my hand a gentle squeeze. "It doesn't end here."

I nod, never having considered it as I take in the yard one final time. Lush mango trees surround the building like a shield, and bright red hibiscus flowers decorate the yard as butterflies hover low. The entire place is enchanted, a complete contrast from the dirt, cement, and zinc I'm used to seeing back home. I ache at the idea of never returning here.

Of never being a part of something so magical again.

"But what if it does?" I turn to meet Jilly's hazel gaze.

"What?"

"End here."

Jilly smiles.

"We still have *all* summer, Irie. I don't leave Jamaica for another two months."

I take a deep breath as she pulls me in for one final hug. She smells like expensive perfume, and her silky curls feel like they're still bathed in the finest of hair conditioner.

Everything about being in Jilly's arms feels like home.

My real home.

"Our lives are just beginning, Irie." Her whisper tickles my skin. I exhale as my body responds to her. "There's *so* much more out there for us, I can feel it." Her lips press softly against my earlobe as goose bumps flare down my spine. "You *sure* yuh nuh want a ride?" she asks the inevitable question as she pulls away from me. She already knows the answer, but I know she means well.

"Yeah," I say firmly. "I'm sure."

"Irie," she starts, going into the same speech I've heard a million times before. "You *know* Lloyd doesn't mind givin' you a ride. Plus, it's di *last day.* Yuh last chance fi ride inna style." She gestures to the black limo, trying her best to convince me.

"It's all right, Jilly. I swear. I have to pass by the shop, anyway.

Daddy wants me to organize some of the crates. Papine isn't too far from here."

"Yuh mod? Irie, Papine is a *forty-five-minute walk*!"

It's really an hour and a half, but I don't correct her.

"Yuh mustn't always be so proud. It's *really* not a problem for Lloyd to drop you—"

"It's *fine,* Jillian." I stress. "I promise. I like di walkin'."

Jilly rolls her eyes. She knows there will be no changing my mind. "All right, fine." She reluctantly drops my hand. "But stay safe, *Iriene.*" She smirks, sticking out her tongue. It's not even my real name, but she laughs, anyway.

"I'll come look for you next Thursday."

With that, she saunters off through the gates toward the tinted black car that has never once been late. Her driver, Lloyd, stands obediently, opening the limo door. With one final wave, Jilly slides onto the black leather and disappears into the back seat.

I wave goodbye, pretending to busy myself as I watch her go.

Our dance is routine, but the objective remains the same.

Jilly cannot see where I live.

If you asked Jilly, she would tell you that I lived somewhere in the not-so-nice parts of Kingston. But that's putting it lightly. Our school used to be the safe haven in which our worlds could collide, but Jilly has no idea how bad it's gotten out there. She comes from a well-to-do family up in the hills who are fairly complected, mixed race, and *extremely* wealthy.

Jilly only hears rumors about neighborhoods like mine.

My reality is the low hum of the evening news in the background at dinnertime. Jilly has no idea what it's like to come from Kintyre because she's protected by the tinted black windows on her driver's car. Up on the giant green hills with posh white mansions and tall iron gates, she is sheltered off from the reality I am forced to face every single day. There are flowers in her backyard.

Not bodies.

Once her car disappears down the road, I quickly clip off the bracelet and tuck it into the bottom of my book bag. There's no way I could wear it on the walk home.

It would be a death wish.

I take one last glance at the school. The girls are gone, their drivers completely cleared out. I force one foot in front of the other as I head out through the gates, walking briskly down the dirt pathway that leads me to the main road. A few more steps, and it all goes silent all around me.

I am completely alone.

I'm on edge as my shoes crunch against the gravel. The truth is, the walk home never used to feel so daunting. When Jilly and I first started at Arthen, our realities were different, but never so severed. The PLM and JCG were not yet factors in our equation.

We were innocent back then.

And maybe in some ways, Jilly still is. But ignorance isn't a luxury I can afford to have when blood is shed every day in Kingston.

When Jamaica is under a tribal war.

Darkness has always danced in our political landscape. Once the island got its independence from the British in 1962, Jamaican people had conflicting ideas on what direction the island should take. That's when two cousins from an upper-class, mixed-raced family founded two separate parties—the PLM—the People's Liberation Movement, and the JCG—the Jamaican Conservative Group. When the JCG took office, Jamaica had its first elected prime minister, but the victory was short-lived because it only took a few years for the opposing cousin to be voted in. Shortly after, Joshua Morris, his son, was voted in on a promise that he would take better care of the poorer-class Jamaican people.

And that's exactly how I ended up at Arthen.

Jamaica has been run by the PLM for the past four years, and Joshua's challenged a classist system left behind by the British and the ghost of colonization. The PLM wants to give poor people like me a fighting chance.

But not everyone is happy about the island's new direction.

Despite their push for democratic socialism, Joshua and the PLM are being accused of being a communist-leaning party, out to dismantle the class structures on which Jamaica was founded. And traditionally, a lot more people tend to vote JCG—that includes Jilly's family and all the wealthy girls I go to school with.

But down in the ghettos, it's a mix.

Depending on which street you walk down, or which gully you have the misfortune of turning onto, turf wars are everywhere in Jamaica. The PLM and JCG Dons take hold of the garrisons—and the Dons are considered the *baddest* gangsters in their area. Places like Trenchtown and Tivoli Gardens are strongholds that are fighting each other for the soul of the island, and the bodies of Blacks are the casualties of that war.

But mass murder is not a problem for the rich.

The war only happens in the ghettos, and down in the shantytowns, no one really knows why they're fighting or who they're fighting for. A lot of people in my area vote JCG because that's the party their family traditionally voted for. Daddy says that's what happens when poor people don't get an education—they just do what the politicians tell them to. He says the people of the ghetto are brainwashed by the JCG because they never learned to think for themselves.

That's why he sent me here—for a better education.

But Daddy doesn't dare thank the PLM too loud. Because in Jamaica, talking about politics can easily get you killed. And maybe that's why no matter how bad it's gotten out there, I never bring any of it up to Jilly.

Politics just isn't something we talk about.

Daddy says Joshua Morris is going to give us a new Jamaica, one in which Black people can *finally* be in charge of their own destinies. No longer under the white man's rule, the PLM fights *for* the people—and not just people with light eyes and fair skin. But poor people.

People like me.

But all the rising talk of freedom has only made opposing forces grow stronger. The JCG are fighting for a capitalist economy, and they have a corporate agenda that Daddy says only benefits the elite few.

People like Jilly.

Her father works in politics under the JCG, but she seldom talks about it except when she complains about how strict her parents are. From what I've heard, the man running against Joshua Morris—Winston Kelly—believes that a Jamaica free from the support of the United States is a poor man's dream. The JCG doesn't believe a small Black island can stand alone. And now, people in the ghettos are killing each other on behalf of the politicians.

With guns.

And knives.

And machetes.

Because just like Daddy always says, politics doesn't divide the rich—it divides the people who are already suffering.

The privilege of safety does not extend to the houses at the bottom of the hills, and in communities like mine—ghettos, gullies, and shantytowns—tribal lines have been drawn. Depending on what area you walk through, they will slice you into pieces for uttering a word of the opposing party on their turf. They will stone you for speculation of opposing allegiance and beat you until your body surfaces in a ditch. But I wouldn't dare mention that to Jilly.

I wouldn't even question if she knows.

I keep it buried behind my lips, because that is the truth that would uncloak the veil of the nonchalant *Irie* that I have worn to school every day for the past four years. These are the stories that would reveal that although I go to school with girls like Jilly, I am not *like* girls like Jilly.

I am from the ghetto.

AND when the school bell rings, I must make my way back home.

2

———

Irie

"P*sst! Yow!* Sexy gyal!"

I jump from my skin when I hear the bass approaching from behind.

My heart picks up speed as a beaten-down dark blue car pulls up beside me. A young man hangs out of the passenger side with a purple bandanna tied around his mouth.

JCG colors.

I feel every hair on my body stand up.

"Ay, gyal!" he calls out again as the car rolls beside me. In a split second, he hoists himself through the passenger window, taking a seat on the ledge.

I'm shot with fear, but I keep my focus straight ahead.

"Slow down nuh!" he barks as his friends laugh along. "Fuckin' gyal! Yuh nuh see say we ah talk?" He gulps back the rest of his beer before launching the glass at the pavement. I jump out of the way just as the bottle shatters in front of me.

In a reflex, I start to run for my life.

The boys holler, keeping up the pace as the car lingers beside me.

"Where yuh ah run to, gyal?" he slurs drunkenly as he hangs off the window.

Fuck. My eyes fill with tears.

"Yuh deaf?" He lunges toward me, grabbing for my arm.

"Stop it!" I yell out, shaky, as I trip over my two feet. I land with a hard thud onto the hot ground as I wince in pain. My hands scrape across the dirty gravel as the boys laugh, blaring their horn before speeding off down the road.

"*You're okay, Irie,*" I whisper to myself as I examine the blood on my hands. I close my eyes and silently pray for the breath to come back to my body. "*It's the last walk.*"

The last time.

But it's days like today I wish it were acceptable to just ride my bicycle to school.

Fuck being ladylike.

I just want to get home.

Months ago, the gangs didn't run the streets the way they do now—but that's all changed with the upcoming election. I glance down the road, ensuring the coast is clear before peeking into my book bag to check on the ruby bracelet.

Still there.

I take a sigh of relief before hoisting my bag onto my shoulder.

And then I keep going.

To calm my nerves, I hum one of my favorite Barrington Levy songs—"*Too Experienced.*" I repeat the words with each stride until I start to relax, and forty-five minutes later, I've hit the main road.

But an eerie feeling fills the empty streets.

Just then, I notice two women coming up the road with scandal bags in their hands. I wait until they pass by, and then I fall in line a few steps behind them.

"The shelves were completely empty." One woman leads the conversation. "Not a drop of nuttin' left."

I zone out to their murmurs for another twenty minutes, passing zinc houses and abandoned storefronts. Decaying wood and rusting zinc set the tone as the sun scorches the vegetation. Just looking around feels depressing.

Even the palm trees are sad.

I continue toward Papine as the women disperse. As long as I keep my head down, my feet quick, and my thoughts busy, I'll reach the market pretty quickly from here.

No woman, no cry . . .

Bob's lyrics come to me, and I'm reminded of the first time my dad played it at the shop. Bob's known to pass by every once in a blue moon, but this time in particular, he and a few others gathered around the record player as my father spun his new record. The room was on pins and needles as Daddy listened carefully, and I sat at the back, shuffling through a crate of lovers' rock. After a few beats, Daddy turned to me.

"Wha' yuh tink, Irie?" His commanding voice filled the store.

I fought down a smile as all the important men looked over at me.

I paused, pretending to listen in for the first time.

I had to win their respect.

"I love di vibes." I slowly nodded, moving my head back and forth to the breezy riddim. "The rawness in his voice. It feels different from his other records."

"Wha' yuh mean?" Bob looked over at me.

"Kinda like . . . I can hear the honesty comin' from yuh soul."

All the men nodded in agreement as Bob kept a contemplative hand on his mouth. But even with his massive success, it was my father who commanded the room.

It was his opinion on the music that would matter the most.

"I like it," Daddy agreed.

The memory takes me to the shop door.

RICKY'S RECORDS sits above my head in chipped red letters as I breathe a sigh of relief. Papine Square bustles behind me as I pull the door open and make my way inside.

The bell chimes as I walk in.

The shop is empty at first glance, but I hear voices coming from the back hallway. I make my way toward the front counter where a small radio plays on low.

"*We see the PLM linking arms with communist organizations and we ask ourselves why?*" the bombastic voice of Winston Kelly, the JCG party leader rumbles throughout the shop. "*This country is facing bankruptcy! If Morris wins again, he will turn Jamaica into a communist sta—*"

I turn it off, not in the mood.

I place my book bag down just as Junior runs up to greet me.

"Irie!" He beams wide with a dimpled smile, running into the shop from the back hall. "We get a new shipment today! Di Junior Murvin record *jus'* reach!"

"That's exciting." I can't help but smile at Junior's infectious enthusiasm. He has smooth, dark black skin and bright brown eyes that always seem one step ahead of him. Although he's only ten years old, he gets more excited than anyone I know over new music.

Junior's been working for my father since he was seven years old, ever since Daddy found him outside the shop three years ago. He hadn't eaten in days when Daddy brought him in, cleaned him up, and fed him. And although Daddy couldn't afford to send him to school, he *could* give him a job—so that's exactly what he did.

Daddy said there was something special about Junior.

And it didn't take long to see exactly what that was: Junior has the voice of a *literal angel,* and he can sing circles around any new artist coming up. Ever since he's been working here, I've taught him how to read and write—and sometimes when Daddy leaves me to mind the shop, I'll spin an instrumental riddim and help him write his own music. Despite not going to school, he's the brightest kid I know.

The most talented too.

"Yuh all right?" Junior's big brown eyes read my energy as he makes his way closer to me. "Suh'um happen? Who trouble yuh?"

"I'm fine." I muster a smile. "Just a long walk home, is all."

"Yuh *sure now,* Irie?" He raises an eyebrow, skeptical.

"I promise. Besides, you shouldn't concern yourself wit' big-people problems." I playfully pull him in for a hug. "So, the new record finally reach? Daddy spin it yet?"

"Not just yet." Junior smiles. "He's out back talking to Miss Claudette. Her nephew jus' recorded a song, and she's *beggin'* yuh fada to play it in di store." Junior makes a sour face. "Seems like everyone's an artist nowadays."

"Tell me about it." I look toward the stack of tapes that rest on the counter. People from all over the community have dropped them off, just hopeful that Daddy might give them a platform—hopeful that he might give them a *voice.*

The thing about Daddy is, it doesn't matter how controversial the music is. He's going to play it if he thinks it has a message—and that includes artists who speak out against the violence and police brutality. Reggae is considered rebellion here in Jamaica, and most people would prefer to listen to American music or ska. But Daddy's fearless playlist is what makes Ricky's Records the *boddest* place in town to buy music.

He's a rebel.

I've worked at the shop since I was old enough to beg, but it took me *years* to prove to my father that a girl could understand music the way he could. "*Just because you can sing doesn't mean you understand business,*" he would tell me. But I proved him wrong every single time. The truth is, Daddy never wanted girls.

Instead, he got three.

Siarah, me, and Tandi—in that order. That doesn't include our older half brother, Kojo, but he's not our father's child—we only share the same mother. Out of all of Daddy's daughters, I'm the only one who loves music enough to take a *real* interest in the shop. Daddy always says I was born with the gift of song, just like his mother. She used to sing to him all the time growing up, and according to him, her voice is what taught him the true meaning of *irie*.

So that's exactly what he named me.

"Have you seen these yet?" Junior makes his way over to the front counter, picking up a stack of papers. He hands them to me—the Reggae Jamz flyers.

My stomach knots.

"I have." I hand them back to him, not wanting to think about it. "They've been dropping them off here lately."

"Wha' yuh want me to do wit' dem?"

"Put them up at the front." I gesture to the wall. "No sense in wastin' all that paper."

Junior follows instructions.

"By the way!" He beams. "I've been workin' on suh'um' fi you." He places down the broom and runs to the back of the shop.

I smile, already knowing what it is.

"See it yah!" Junior lights up as he races back over, holding a crumpled piece of paper in his hands. "I wrote a new song fi yuh, Irie." He blushes, flashing the dimples in his smooth black skin. "I've been workin' on it fi a while now. Promise yuh nah go laugh?"

"And why on earth would I do that?" I giggle. "You know I love your songs."

"So wha' you ah skin yuh teeth fa?"

"I *only* smile because of how cute you are." I laugh. "I can't help it if I get excited."

Junior kisses his teeth.

"I'm not *cute*, Irie," he reminds me for the millionth time this week. "And stop laughin'. I'm *handsome*. I'm becoming a man now, rememba? My birthday's in three months."

"Sorry. Handsome," I correct. "*Very* handsome."

I try my best not to giggle as he unfolds the paper, serious as day. Junior's been crushing on me from the first day he saw me walk in. I offered him a bag juice, and he fell in love right then, right there. And according to him, cute is for *baby pickney*.

Not future boyfriends.

He clears his throat as he nervously grips the paper.

"It's a love song," he says, his demeanor becoming shy. "It's called 'Say You'll Be Mine.'"

"Wow. Big title."

"It's guna be a big song."

"I love di confidence." I giggle. "But yuh nuh think you're too young to have a girlfriend, Junior? I mean, you do have your *whole* life ahead of you."

"I'm not asking you to be my *girlfriend,* Irie." He rolls his eyes, fighting down the embarrassment. "It's jus' a song. To show yuh how much I appreciate yuh kindness."

"All right, all right." I smile. "Sorry. Let's hear it."

He clears his throat, and soon his soft, buttery voice fills the shop.

Girrlll, you set my heart on fiyahh
I cyaan wait until your miiiiiine,
You fill my soul wit' desiiire
I want to love you all di tiiiime—

"Who yuh a sing 'bout, bwoy?" Daddy's deep voice interrupts him as he steps down into the shop. Junior jumps, startled as he races for the broom.

"Sound like yuh in love." Daddy takes a swig of Red Stripe. "I hope not wit' my daughta."

"No, sa—I was jus'—" Junior stammers. "I was just showin' Irie a new song that I wrote."

"Me nuh pay yuh fi stand up and sing, likkle bwoy." Daddy makes his way to the register, gesturing to the tiles. "The floor nah go sweep itself."

"Yes, sa." Junior nods, hastily getting back to work.

"Well, *I* thought it was *beautiful,* Junior." I smile, ignoring my father. "Yuh song."

"Tanks, Irie." Junior blushes.

Daddy flips through some papers, easing up. "Maybe when yuh finish, Irie can help yuh find an instrumental riddim to sing along to."

Junior's face lights up. "*Really? Fi true?*"

Daddy nods. "But me haffi approve it first."

"Of course." Junior jumps for joy. "Tank yuh, sa!"

I grab a Chubby from the cooler behind the cash register as my father moves through the store at a relaxed pace. Everything about Daddy demands respect, and I exhale, grateful to be in his presence and off the chaotic streets.

Being his daughter has always been my safe haven.

When I was growing up, people in our community knew they couldn't mess with me or my sisters because we were *Ricky's daughters*. And in a community where most kids don't grow up with their fathers, that counted for something.

It afforded us respect.

"So, how's my favorite daughta?" Daddy finally asks. He wears a short-sleeved cotton white button-down and brown trousers, and in this heat, his dark skin glows. He keeps his hair picked low and a signature gold chain on his chest.

"Nuh badda say that too loud, Daddy." I smile. "Siarah and Tandi soon come."

"I can have more than one favorite." He takes another sip from the dark, icy beer bottle. "How was yuh last day of school?"

I shrug, not wanting to get into it. "Bittersweet."

He nods, contemplative as if he understands. I take a sip of the bubbly drink, fighting back the lump that creeps its way up my throat as Daddy moves toward the record player. He puts down Toots and the Maytals' "54–46 That's My Number."

A classic.

The beat blares through the walls as my worries melt away.

I said yeah . . .

I sing along to the breezy melody as Daddy nods and Junior sways as he sweeps. Records line the walls, and crates fill the aisles as we all begin to jam.

We surrender to the rhythm as we wait for the beat to drop.

I can't help but imagine what these walls would say if they could talk back. As the drums explode, the laughter involuntarily pours out of me. The song is *so good*. I watch as Junior grooves in the corner. The speakers vibrate just as Daddy goes to turn it down.

"All right, all right." He turns around. "Irie, I need yuh to listen to suh'um fi me."

"Sure." I nod a little too eagerly. I can't help it.

I get my love of reggae music from my father.

Daddy was raised by my freethinking grandmother, Mama Winnie—a radical Hebrew woman who died before I was born. From what my older sister, Siarah, tells me, Mama Winnie was raised on a compound in Constitution Hill, where she practiced ancient African medicine. Known for her mystical abilities and tinctures, she was an herbalist who worked as a midwife in the emerging Rastafarian villages. But most impressively, she was known for her horse-riding abilities.

Mama Winnie was a warrior.

Daddy says that's why I love to ride my bicycle so much. "*Yuh ride like a mon, just like yuh grandmada!*" he always jokes. According to him, she rode faster than any man in the district. But living in the 1920s, it made her a threat.

She was pregnant with twins when two men in the community purposefully startled her horse. After she lost the pregnancy,

Daddy was the first and only child she was able to have again. Years later, she married a preacher who raised Daddy as his own, and although Daddy never talks about him, his stepfather was an abusive man of the Lord. Music was Daddy's only form of rebellion against his strict, God-fearing stepfather, who would beat Daddy on Saturdays and then go up to preach on Sundays.

So, when Daddy was old enough to run, he did.

He had no education when he came to Papine, but he used all his money from odd jobs to open the record store. He fell in love with the power of radical sound, and soon—my Mother. But after they had my sisters and me, Mummy moved abroad with the family she cleaned for in the hills.

And now, we barely hear from her.

When our mother abandoned us, Daddy made it his priority to raise us to have minds of our own—to *never* accept a belief that doesn't belong to us. Compared to most Jamaican girls, we haven't been raised in the most traditional or conservative sense. While most people on the island look down on Rastas and reggae music, deeming them drugged-out and dirty—our father believes the total opposite. He's empowered my sisters and me with the messages of Rastafarianism, solely through the music he chooses to play at the shop. And although Daddy might not fully identify as a Rastaman, over time, reggae music became his religion.

Just like it became mine.

On an island where most people identify with the Christian church, Daddy taught us to *listen* for God in the music. To hear him in the *sound* and seek him in the *vibrations*.

He raised his girls as rebels.

Daddy places a box down onto the wooden counter and pulls out a handful of new vinyls.

Just then, the door swings open, and in walk my sisters, Siarah and Tandi.

"*Wha'ppen,* bighead girl!" my older sister, Siarah, sings, a huge smile on her golden-brown face. She saunters in as her long braids sway back and forth down her back.

"Sooooo . . ." Siarah beams, her doe-like eyes bright. "Tell us all about it, nuh? How was yuh last day, girl?" Her tone is *way* too eager.

"It was fine, Sisi." I shrug off her excitement. "Sad it's over."

"Well, don't be *too* sad, Irie." She eyes me. "This just means you get to spend some more time wit' me."

What she *really* means is I get to spend more time helping her around the house. She prances over to our father, handing him the same wrapped plate of food she prepares for him every day.

"Welcome to di real world, gyal. Where women have *responsibilities.*"

I flip her off when Daddy's not looking.

She giggles as she twirls back over to me, settling onto the stool beside me.

"Seriously, though, I'm happy that you're *finally* done with that school, Irie." Siarah continues her weak attempt at consoling me. "I know you liked going there, but nuh badda get amnesia—Arthen took its toll on you. Being around all those *pretentious, rich girls* all day . . . it wasn't good for yuh spirit, Irie. Look how many days you used to come home miserable."

"I guess." I consider it. "Just feels like I was starting to find my place . . . the last two years, at least." I shrug. "I got close with people."

"*People?*" Siarah raises a brow. "You mean that one light-skinned girl?"

"Her name is *Jilly,*" I say defensively. "And yes, I mean Jilly. She made my whole experience at Arthen . . . *comfortable.* It was starting to feel worthwhile."

"Well, just remember it wasn't always sunshine and rainbows," Siarah's quick to remind me. "And at the very least, now that it's over, you don't have to worry about affording that silly uniform every year. Those fees were so ridiculous."

She kisses her teeth as I recall the stress.

Unlike me, Siarah and my older brother, Kojo, didn't have the luxury of attending a fancy school because Joshua Morris wasn't in office at the time. And although they would never admit it out loud, I know they resent me for it—but I try not to blame them.

My siblings wanted a higher education too.

Siarah had dreams of becoming a teacher, but Daddy couldn't afford her school fees. So after she graduated two years ago, her dreams died just like everyone else's in our community. Opportunities are limited in Jamaica, and being the oldest girl, Siarah's new role now consists of cooking and cleaning and minding the house.

And that includes preparing Daddy's daily meals.

"Either way, I'm sure it wasn't an easy day for Irie," my sister Tandi says, offering me some empathy as she makes her way over. "Yuh all right, girl?"

"Thanks, Tandi. I'm okay." I slump, giving her a hug. "Just trying not to think about it—or too far ahead, for that matter."

"Take it *one* day at a time. Yuh life isn't over just because high school is."

I smile, grateful for the reminder.

Tandi's only a year younger than I am, but despite being book smart, she didn't pass the entry exam. With her short, coily hair and deep brown skin, there's a mousiness to Tandi that makes her a mystery to most of the family. But I've always understood her.

"Besides, Siarah," Tandi continues, "not everyone is *excited* by cleaning. Irie's a superstar, yuh know. She has big dreams."

"So wha, me nuh have dreams too?" Siarah says, faux offended. "And I'm not excited by *cleanin'*, Tandi." She playfully drapes her arm around my neck. "I'm just excited to have some company, is all. Is it a crime fi wan' spend time wit' my likkle sista?"

"Yes." I toss her arm off me. "*Especially* if that time includes washin' dishes."

"It builds *character,* Irie." Siarah plants a wet kiss on my cheek. "Yuh soon find out."

"Nuh badda get too excited," Daddy tempers Siarah's laughter as he unwraps his lunch. "Cooking and cleaning is the job of the *eldest girl child.* Irie has duties to fulfill around the shop."

I hide my smirk. What Daddy says, goes.

Siarah rolls her eyes before calling across the shop, "Yow, Junior! Yuh nuh know nobody?"

"Wha'ppen, Siarah!" Junior lights up, making his way over. "Hey, Tandi."

"Wha' gwaan, likkle mon?" Tandi smiles. "I brought you some cheese puffs."

"Fi true?" Junior jumps for joy.

"Don't distract my workers," Daddy warns. "He's in di middle of suh'um."

"Workers haffi *eat* as well, Daddy," Siarah says. "Yuh cyaan be the only one in here wit' ah full belly."

Junior makes his way over as Tandi hands him the cheese puffs.

Just then, Daddy gestures for us to come over.

"Unu come just in time," he says as we all crowd around the record player.

"That's di Junior Murvin record?" Junior's eyes light up. "Di one everyone ah talk 'bout?" He can barely sit still as Daddy pulls the vinyl from the funky blue case.

"Wha' it name, Daddy?" I ask.

"*Police and Thieves,*" he reads on the front.

"Lawd, God—*another* political record?" Siarah slumps. "Do Jamaican artists even know how to sing about anything else?"

"Is there anything else that's *important*?" I eye her.

"It's not about *importance,* Irie. Music is supposed to be *fun.* An escape from our day-to-day lives—"

"Reggae *is* an escape. A conscious one."

"Reggae is *depressing,*" Siarah says firmly. "We live in darkness every day, and now we haffi listen to it when we get home? Dat nuh mek nuh sense."

"It's called *catharsis,* Siarah. People need to know they're not alone—"

"It's called *confusion,* Irie," she fires back. "People need to hear songs that make them *feel good* right now . . . songs that make them wanna dance." She pouts. "And just because you use big words doesn't make you right."

I bite my tongue, not in the mood to argue with my sister. The truth is, reggae makes Siarah nervous.

Just like everyone else.

The songs coming out of Jamaica are more politically charged than ever right now. There was a time when lovers' rock dominated the charts, but gone are the days where artists can turn a blind eye to the war outside our door.

"*I think* havin' a political message can be fun." Junior shrugs as Daddy places the record down onto the player. "After all, Bob Marley's records are fun. People dance."

"Junior has a point." Tandi nods. "Plus, we don't even know if it's political yet."

"It's called *Police and Thieves,* Tandi," Siarah defends. "What else could it be about?"

"All right, all right." Daddy drops the pin. "Everyone just relax."

We all inch a little closer as a smooth, vibey sound serenades the shop. Staccato chords play on the offbeat as a seductive bass line moves through the room.

Police and thieves in the streets . . .

No one says a word as the lyrics play on for a few minutes. The artist speaks about how the peacemakers have turned to war officers. How the very people assigned to protect us are doing the opposite. A chill moves down my spine.

"Yeah, mon! Call dem out!" Junior's small voice belts over

the music. "About time, nuh true, Irie?" He looks to me for validation.

"Yeah." I laugh, nervously pulling him into my arms.

His excitement makes me feel brave.

"I can't wait until you grow up and yuh records are spinnin'," I whisper into his ear as the song continues. "You're guna sing with purpose, *just like that*."

Junior's smile is bright as he hugs me tighter.

"Well, what yuh think, Daddy?" I look up at my father, who turns down the music.

"I love it," he says without hesitation. "It's time fi di revolution. A Black man has to know his purpose in a changin' world."

"See?" Junior teases Siarah. "Me tell yuh! *That* is wha' yuh call *real music*!"

"Rebellion is the only way," Daddy agrees. "It's time for Jamaicans to wake up. Shake off di chains of colonization. Just because we get independence does *not* mek us free. Not if our minds are still in bondage."

"I agree wit' Daddy," I say proudly. "As Black people, we haffi be responsible for our *own fate*. And the only way to do that is through di music."

"Reggae ah di *only* sound weh ah go last! Nuh true, Irie?" Junior jumps for joy. "Promise me yaah go *always* sing from yuh soul. When yuh get on stage, yuh haffi tell di truth, jus' like di Rastaman dem."

"I promise." I giggle, pulling him in closer.

"You guys have all gone mad." Siarah can't help but laugh. "And you sound like a bunch of nationalists."

"I'm kinda wit' Siarah on this one," Tandi says nervously. "Unu nuh think it's too . . . *much*?" Her voice is weary as she looks to my father. "It's so . . . *direct*."

"Reggae music can never be too much," Daddy corrects her. "It can be *real*. But never be too much."

I nod in agreement, grateful for my father's wisdom.

"The whole point of the genre is about telling the truth, Siarah . . . opening people's eyes to di oppression. And the truth is, yuh cyaan tell di gangsters from di police. They're upholding the values of Babylon—"

"Well, *maybe* if Jamaica didn't let America export so many Mafia movies to us, we wouldn't think this is the Wild, Wild West." Tandi makes a face. "Everywhere you turn, *guns and cowboys*—"

"No offense, Daddy," Siarah interrupts, clearly not feeling the conversation. "I get that 'reggae music' isn't fully *my thing* . . . but what happened to the days when records made yuh feel *good* about life? A likkle ska or lovers' rock?" She dramatically throws her hands up. "I mean, *lawd*. Those lyrics are so . . . *heavy*. It's way too political."

"Reggae music *is* political, Siarah," I interject, annoyed. "That was my whole point—"

"You're wrong, Irie," Daddy scolds.

"But everyting he said was about politics—"

"Everything he *said* was about di *revolution*." Daddy looks at me sternly. "The Rastaman wants *peace*. Freedom. An end to the war and corruption."

"Well, not everyone feels the same way," Siarah mumbles under her breath.

"But yuh cyaan be afraid to speak up, Siarah," Junior's small voice interrupts. "What's di point of havin' a voice if yuh nah go use it?"

"Junior, yuh nuh jus' turn ten?" Siarah clowns. "Wha' yuh know 'bout usin' yuh voice?"

"That it can mek a difference."

"Tell her nuh, Junior." I laugh, encouraging him. "Even di likkle yute understand."

Siarah rolls her eyes as she gets up from the stool. "Well, then, let me not rain on this reggae parade. I have some cleaning to finish up at the house. Enjoy yuh dinna, Daddy," she says as she makes her way toward the door.

"Gone before the five-o'clock rush?" I tease.

"Sorry, Irie, but it was my last day too." Tandi grabs her bag. "Summer vacation is only two months long, and I plan to catch up on some *sleep.*"

Daddy reaches into his pocket and pulls out his wallet.

"Junior, follow dem down ah shop." He hands him a few crumbled hundred-dollar bills. "Pick me up two pack of Red Stripe."

"Yes, sa." Junior places the broom down before taking the money from my father. He folds it carefully before following my sisters out the door. "Soon come back, Irie," he calls over his shoulder. "And don't forget yuh still haffi tell me wha' yuh think about my song in *detail*. I wanna hear if yuh have any notes. I'll sing it again when I get back so it's fresh in yuh mind." He blushes. "Maybe you could even feature on di second verse?"

"I like the sound of that." I smile.

He beams one last toothy grin before heading through the door.

"See yuh tonight, Irie." Siarah waves, calling back. "Hold off on di revolution until then."

I stick out my tongue as they saunter through the door.

Daddy turns the music back up before heading to grab some more boxes. "Start sorting these fi me." He hands me a crate.

I grab the pile of records, placing them down on the table. As I start to sort them, one of the vinyl casings catches my eye. It's a black cover that reads, "*DON'T YOU CUT OFF YOUR DREADLOCKS,*" in big black-and-yellow lettering—definitely a revolution song.

"Daddy, have yuh played this one yet?" I hold it up to him.

"Ah who sing dat?" He squints.

"Uhh . . ." I scan the back. "Linval Thompson. Looks like it jus' came out—"

POP. POP. POP. POP.

The piercing sound stops me midsentence.

POP. POP. POP. POP. POP. POP.

"Get down!" Daddy screams.

But I'm frozen.

"*Irie!*" He lunges toward me and yanks me by the wrist, pulling me to my knees. I hit the hard tiles with a thud, and for a second, I swear my bones have shattered. I wince in pain as the records spill out onto the floor.

POP. POP. POP. POP. POP.

I try to scream, but nothing leaves my lips.

POP. POP. POP.

"*Daddy!*" I cry as he grips me tighter. He pushes my body into the floor, using his weight like a shield. The record spins in the background, juxtaposing the wailing and screaming.

I'm not sure if minutes pass by or merely seconds.

"Daddy!" I whimper. "*What's happening?*"

I can't breathe under the weight of his body. It feels like my skin is peeling from the bone under the force of his grip. As he jumps up from off the ground, my body goes to stone.

For the first time in my father's eyes, I see fear.

"*Don't move!*"

He leaps up from the hot orange tile floor.

"Daddy! *Wait—*"

But it's too late. He scrambles toward the door, slipping on one of the vinyls on his way out. Daylight flashes through the shop and then darkness as the door swings shut.

"*Please!*" I scream out, my own voice giving me chills.

But no one responds.

It's just me, and the walls that will never talk back.

Me, and the record that spins round and round.

Police and thieves in the street . . .

The music swallows me as I woozily rise to my feet. I almost buckle at the knees as I make my way toward the shop door. I use all my strength to push it open.

And just as the record comes to a stop, so does my world.

Chaos and mayhem take over the square as people run in all directions, stampeding one another. In the middle of the disaster, Siarah and Tandi cry out to the heavens.

To the Gods.

A sea of people surround the body as Daddy doubles over. Junior's small frame scattered out on the floor. Blood. *Everywhere.*

Junior is dead.

"*Noooo!*" It rips out of me. "*No! No! No!*"

My heart collapses in my chest.

It is a chorus of chaos as I sprint toward the body. It's not just Junior's blood that stains the concrete. There are more.

A woman. A child. A man.

Four people shot dead in Papine Square in broad daylight.

"*Oh my god,*" I bawl as I collapse onto the ground next to my father. Daddy holds Junior's body as I reach for his small, lifeless hand. Still warm. His dark skin. *Still smooth.*

My soul rips from my chest.

Tandi and Siarah grab onto me, a dark reality consuming us. You won't hear about this on the news. How we sat in our own sorrow in the heart of the ghetto, drinking disaster as the sun beats into our black skin. For us, living in paradise means we are forced to digest its poisons. There is nowhere to run, because this is our home.

A concrete jungle.

And in the ghetto, the devil lives behind the palm trees. Always watching.

Always waiting.

As Junior's small body bleeds out with the crumpled song in his pants pocket, I realize that the sun only shines up where Jilly lives. In the hills with gated houses and freshly cut grass. God doesn't live in the ghetto.

This is the devil's playground.

And with ten weeks to go before the upcoming election, I am haunted by the darkness that cloaks my side of town.

I am haunted by how much darker it will get for neighborhoods like mine.

FOR *girls like me.*

3

———

Jilly

"*Stay still,* Jillian. For crying out loud."

MUMMY'S reflection scolds me as I stand on top of the wooden stool in front of the full-length mirror. In the reflection, she sits at my vanity flipping through one of her new hair magazines. Sun streams in through the large windows of my bedroom as Amala wraps a measuring tape around my waist.

"I'm *trying,* Mummy." I fight the urge to roll my eyes. I can feel her piercing green eyes examining my every move. "It's not easy standing still for so long. I haven't even eaten since I got home."

"All the better." She flips the page. "I keep telling you, you don't need to eat every second of the day. The appetite on you young girls nowadays is *astounding.*"

"We're almost done, Miss Jillian," Amala says kindly, trying to ease the tension.

"And don't forget to take in the shoulders, Amala. Jillian's been looking rather broad up top. Bring it in as much as you can."

I bite down, used to her antagonizing comments.

Amala's brown eyes are focused as a bead of sweat rolls down her dark black skin. I feel for her. Mummy's had her running errands all day long, and I can see the exhaustion on her face. Even with the AC, the evening heat feels torturous.

I grimace as Amala pulls the pink material tighter before carefully sticking the pins through the fabric. She bends down to adjust the seams, and my eyes trace her fluffy black hair. I admire the tight coils that adorn her head like a crown. She raises back up, startled by my gaze.

"Sorry," I utter, lost in my thoughts.

"Would you *stay still, Jillian*? For the love of God." Mummy looks up from her magazine again, eyeing my tanned skin. "And I keep telling you not to stand around after school. You're ruining your complexion."

"I don't *stand around,* Mummy. I go straight into the car."

"Well, you need to be more mindful. You only have two months before you go off to school. You come from *good stock,* and it's time you took pride in looking like it—"

"Mummy," I stop her, my shoulders tensing.

I hate it when she talks like this—especially in front of Amala.

"I don't make the rules, Jillian." She waves me off as if I were the one being ridiculous.

"I don't get why I can't wear one of my other dresses," I whine as Amala grips the fabric around my waist. "They fit me just fine."

"Because you're getting *older,* darling. It's time you wore something a bit more *shapely.*" She eyes me. "Besides, Amala went all the way into town for that fabric."

I cringe.

"Don't give me a hard time, Jillian. It's a big night for your father, and I already have enough to think about."

"It was a big day for me as well, but no one seems to be concerned."

Mummy looks up from her magazine, raising an eyebrow. "I beg your pardon?"

"It was my last day of school," I sulk. "I don't see how that's any less important."

"You want a *cookie* for graduating *high school*?" She scowls. "Please, Jillian. Don't be daft." She resumes reading the magazine. "Graduating school is the *least* you could do with all the money your father and I spend putting you through it. Not to mention tutoring and all your extracurriculars." She shakes her head, disgusted by my audacity. "We'll celebrate when you get your acceptance letter to Cambridge."

My stomach knots.

"Your father has worked *incredibly* hard for this promotion. The least you can do is hold still and put on a nice dress."

I clench my jaw as Amala pulls the fabric tighter.

No one in this family has *ever* cared about what I want.

How I *feel* or what I *need*. I've worked my ass off to maintain my grades at Arthen, putting in countless hours and sleepless nights—and all I want is just one day to rest. But Mummy and Daddy couldn't care less about my efforts.

If it doesn't bring honor to them, it doesn't matter.

I'm fidgety as Amala cuts and measures, trying her best to keep me comfortable while appeasing my mother. I dread the idea of a night alone with my parents and their politician friends. But this is my life—and politics *always* takes priority.

Daddy's worked in Jamaican politics my entire life.

He's the senior advisor to the Jamaican Conservative Group— otherwise known as the JCG—and now that Winston Kelly is running for prime minister, Daddy's moved up even higher in the ranks. Winston and my father are longtime friends, and as of yesterday, he picked my father to be his right-hand man on the campaign trail—a role that comes with a lot of power.

And even more money.

"Did you hear that Tanya-Marie got into Yale?" Mummy pulls me out of my thoughts. "Her parents wouldn't stop bragging about it at the luncheon last week. As if getting into a General Arts program is anything to boast about." She scoffs. "Have you checked the mail?"

I nod. "Nothing's come as yet."

"Ridiculous." She shakes her head. "I'll ask your father to have one of his contact's reach out to the administrative board next week. I'm sure there's nothing to worry about."

"I'm not worrie—*OW!*" I jump as one of the pins pricks my side.

"Oh my gosh!" Amala's hands tremble as she drops the needle. "My apologies, Miss Jillian! I'm so sorry—"

"*Jesus,* Amala!" Mom jumps up from the vanity. "Would you watch what you're doing?"

"It's fine, Amala," I say softly. "Truly."

"It's *not.*" Mummy approaches us. "We don't pay her to poke us with pins."

"Yes, Mrs. Casey." Amala backs up, embarrassed.

The room goes silent as the record player Daddy got me as a graduation gift spins round on the dresser. Amala carefully gets back to work as Mummy moves to stand in front of me. She wears a flowy cream housedress, and her hair falls pin straight to her shoulders.

She places her hand on my chin.

"Don't worry, Jillian." Her voice goes soft. "Soon, you'll be sending us postcards from abroad, hm?" I stare into her green eyes before glancing at my reflection in the mirror behind her. It's the first time I can see our resemblance, and the revelation haunts me.

"I'm not worried, Mummy," I say, pulling away. "I promise."

"Good." She smiles. "Because tonight is going to be a *wonderful* time. Mr. Kelly's son will be there too . . . Christopher? I'm excited for you two to meet."

I tense at the thought as she makes her way toward the door.

"Amala, do something nice with her hair," she calls back. "And be sure to use the hot comb."

"Of course, Mrs. Casey." Amala nods, keeping busy.

And with that, my mother heads out through the door and

down the grand hall. I feel my shoulders fall from my ears as soon as she's out of sight.

"Are you all right, Miss Jillian?" Amala asks carefully.

I stare at my reflection, considering the question.

"They're trying to set me up with Mr. Kelly's son."

"The man running for prime minister?" Amala furrows her brows. "How do you know that?"

"It's the sixth time Mummy's mentioned him this week."

Amala smiles discreetly as she continues to stitch the fabric.

"What?" I ask.

Amala shrugs. "I just don't see how that's di worse ting? Is he good lookin'?"

"I haven't met him as yet. But by the looks of his father, probably not."

Amala lets out a small laugh. "He might not be so bad."

"*A well-to-do son of a politician?*"

"Sounds like you might have a lot in common." She smiles. "Give it a chance, at least."

She gives my hand a gentle squeeze before cleaning up the rest of her sewing materials. "You're all done. I'll be back in a few minutes to do yuh hair."

I examine myself in the flowy pink material. The long, soft fabric frames my body perfectly. My curls aside, I look like one of the dollies I used to play with as a child. The idea makes me nostalgic as I look over at Amala.

"Can we leave it curly?" I ask. "My hair."

Amala is taken aback by my request. "Miss Jil—"

"Please?" I beg. "I'll tell Mummy it was my idea."

She eyes me for a moment, a warmth to her brown eyes. "At least let me pin it up. I don't want to get in trouble with yuh mother."

"Thank you, Amala," I say, grateful to not have to inhale the burning smell of the hot comb.

"I'll go grab the pins," she says before making her way out of the room.

I lock the door behind her.

As her footsteps descend down the hallway, I head over to the record player where Debby Boone's "You Light Up My Life" spins around. I remove the pin and her voice comes to a screeching halt.

I'm so tired of listening to American music.

It's all my parents allow me to play in the house, but today, the act feels exhausting. It's my last day of high school, and the only thing I want is to hear the smooth bass of reggae blasting through the walls of my room.

True freedom sound.

I lean down to unlock the bottom drawer where I keep all my reggae records. I scan the hidden stash of albums, pulling out the Mighty Diamonds latest song, "Shame and Pride." I place the vinyl down on the player, mindful to keep the volume down low. I take a deep breath, allowing the music to fill my chest. And then I move the record player to the side.

I'm relieved to find the white envelope still there.

Untouched and unopened.

MISS JILLIAN CASEY is written on the front in black ink. My chest tightens as I study the stamps that came all the way from England. It's now or never.

"*God, if you are real—then, please,*" I whisper.

I rip it open, pulling out the white paper and unfolding it.

Dear Miss Jillian Casey, Thank you for your interest in attending the University of Cambridge . . . It takes only a millisecond for me to see the words stamped in black ink.

We regret to inform you . . .

My heart sinks.

"No . . ." My eyes instantly well with tears.

We will not be able to accept your application at this time.

"No . . . *please.*"

My tears smudge the ink as I stare down at the letter in shock.

How is this happening?

Not getting in is *not* an option.

What will I tell Mummy? How will I explain this to Daddy?

All the girls in my form got into their first options. They all have prestigious futures guaranteed abroad. I'm in shock as the inevitable truth stuns me:

I will be the first person in my family to not attend university.

The first who didn't get into *all four* of her options.

What about Daddy's political circles? How will he explain this?

Tears stream down my face as my breathing intensifies.

Cambridge was my last chance.

Knock, knock, knock.

I jump from my skin as I fold the letter back up and stuff it into the envelope.

"Coming!" I call, quickly wiping the tears from my cheeks.

I rush to take the record off the player and shove it back into its case. I pull open the drawer, tucking the letter into the corner next to the three other rejection letters I received this week. Four rejections total. I nearly collapse as I slam the drawer shut.

As I run to the door, my mother's words crawl all over my skin:

I want them to know that you come from good stock.

But it's a lie.

I'm still not good enough.

I push down the despair as I let Amala in. She greets me with a distracted smile.

"Okay." She surveys the bottles in her hands. "I brought all di products I could find—"

"I've changed my mind," I say promptly. "I want to wear my hair straight tonight."

A few hours later, Daddy comes home and we take the car to Mr. Kelly's house.

Lloyd drives us through the mountains of Jacks Hill as I

stare aimlessly out the window. Mummy and Daddy go back and forth, fussing over how my father should wear his tie. He's nervous for tonight, but would never admit to it.

Instead, he plays backseat driver, criticizing Lloyd for taking the long way.

"I told you this route would take longer," Daddy says, growing frustrated. "We would've been there by now if you got off at the last exit like I told you."

"Darling, we still have twenty-five minutes." Mummy tries to calm him back down. "And we're only about five minutes away. We'll be there any minute."

"It's the *principle,* Hilary. For Christ's sake," he says, annoyed. "You don't show up with a minute to spare for your own dinner. It's classless."

I clench my jaw, nervous for Daddy's critical attention to fall onto me. My mind is everywhere else but in this car.

"My apologies, sir," Lloyd calls from the other side of the partition. "It won't happen again."

"You bet your ass it won't," Daddy mutters.

The car goes awkwardly silent as Mummy leans forward. "Lloyd, turn on RJR."

Lloyd reaches to turn up the dial.

"Turn it off." Daddy's sharp voice fills the car. "I can't hear myself think."

I cringe, resuming my attention out the window. Daddy always gets cold when he has meetings with Mr. Kelly. But I guess that's what happens when everyone wants power, and Jamaica is the prize.

Five minutes later, we arrive at large gates that block off a stream of forestry. Lloyd buzzes in, and we continue down a long road that takes us up a steep hill. When we reach the top, we pull up to a massive estate—it's double the size of our home. Lloyd brings the car to a park, and after a few hasty moments, we make our way up to the massive double doors.

Even I have to admit I'm impressed.

I adjust the tight straps on my dress as Mummy rings the doorbell. Seconds later, Mr. Kelly, his wife, and a young man around my age—who I presume to be their son, Christopher—greet us at the door. Daddy stands up straighter.

"Winston!" He smiles wide as they shake hands.

"Good to see you, Calvin." Mr. Kelly looks a bit more informal in dress pants and a short-sleeved button-down. "The family looks wonderful, as usual."

"Oh, you're a dear, Winston," my mother fawns. "So good to see you, Marie." Mummy and Mrs. Kelly cheek kiss before exchanging pleasantries. "I had our maid prepare some banana bread."

"You are too sweet, Hilary." Mrs. Kelly beams as she takes it from her hands. "And Jillian! Look at you. So grown up from the last time I saw you."

I smile politely. It was only a few months ago at a political luncheon. "Thank you for having us, Mrs. Kelly."

"It's wonderful to see you again, Jillian." Mr. Kelly shakes my hand. "This is our son, Christopher. You two haven't met, right?"

I shake my head. Christopher is tall with bright blue eyes and an overtly cool demeanor. To my surprise, there's a handsomeness to him. He's much lighter than his father, and if it weren't for a few distinct features, I would almost swear he was a white man.

"Nice to meet you, Jillian." He extends his hand.

His voice is deeper than I'd thought.

"You as well." I nod politely.

"How about we take this party inside?" Mrs. Kelly beams. She hands the banana bread to a dark-skinned lady who sheepishly approaches, standing dutifully.

"Shelly-Anne, put this down and finish preparing the table." Mrs. Kelly ushers her inside. "I'm sure our guests are hungry. Let's not keep them waiting now."

"Yes, Mrs. Kelly." The young lady nods, scurrying inside.

We follow behind as Mr. Kelly leads the way.

About an hour later, we all sit around the long dinner table as my father and Mr. Kelly go back and forth. The discussion heats up quickly as they discuss Mr. Kelly's campaign.

I look up from my plate just as Mrs. Kelly chimes in.

"I'm telling you, if you gentlemen don't get Jamaica under control, Morris is going to single-handedly destroy this island," she drunkenly complains. "All this talk about a revolution makes my head spin."

"He's spewing communist propaganda." My father shakes his head. "And it stops now."

"The only revolution that's going to be happening in Jamaica is *capitalism.*" Mr. Kelly's drunken voice is bashful and firm. "Morris can only brainwash the people of the ghetto for so long. But mark my words—there *will* be a reckoning. And it starts with this campaign."

He takes a sip of his whiskey on ice.

"I couldn't agree more." My father nods eagerly.

"I'm excited to be working closer with you, Calvin," Mr. Kelly says. "Your policy suggestions have been the backbone of this campaign. I can tell we share the same values—*family being the first and foremost.* I've seen it in you from the first day."

"Well, I'm thankful for this promotion, Winston." Daddy raises his glass of whiskey. "And I want to assure you that I will be doing *everything* in my power to ensure this campaign is a success. We're going to create a better economic landscape for our children. With *you* as Jamaica's next leader, of course."

"I'll drink to that." Mrs. Kelly raises her glass, and everyone else follows suit. My mother gives me a scolding look, and I quickly raise my glass of sorrel alongside them.

But I feel sick to my stomach.

"You haven't touched your plate, Jillian," Mrs. Kelly remarks, pulling me out of my daze. I look down at the plate of chicken and rice. "Would you like Shelly-Anne to prepare you something else?"

"Oh no," I say, picking up my fork. "Sorry. I guess I haven't had much of an appetite."

"Jillian's watching her figure," my mother interjects. "She's got a lot to prepare for with Cambridge in the fall."

My chest tightens as the attention falls onto me.

"Is that so?" Mr. Kelly looks over at me. "How promising."

I clutch my napkin tighter under the table.

"Yes, sir. That's the plan."

"That's remarkably impressive, Jillian. Cambridge is a very tough school to get into."

"Indeed." I smile. "I'm looking forward to it."

"What will you be studying?" Christopher asks from across the table.

"English linguistics," my father answers for me. "She plans to teach English abroad."

"That's incredible." Mrs. Kelly looks at me with adoration. "Beautiful *and* intelligent. With a humanitarian heart. It takes a special soul to teach."

"We're very proud of her," my mother interjects. "Jillian's always been *so* ahead of her years. And so passionate about knowledge, ever since she was a little girl."

"You like to read?" Mr. Kelly asks.

"And write," I say anxiously. "Mostly write."

"And what do you like about language?" Christopher interjects. His blue eyes are curious, as if challenging me. I feel our parents analyzing our interaction.

"I, um . . ." I search my brain for my routine answer. "I love the bending of words, I guess. The way language can be used in so many different and colorful ways. The way it can have so many different . . . meanings."

"Meanings?" Christopher raises an eyebrow.

"Yeah. Depending on who's using it or how it's being used. Language is a medium."

"A medium?" he challenges me. "I would think it's a message."

"A lot of people do."

"And? Are a lot of people wrong?" His eyes are playful, clearly finding this entertaining.

"It's a *medium*. Not a message. Language is a vehicle for connection, but not the connection itself."

"Elaborate." He puts down his fork. "Please. I'd love to hear more."

The table goes quiet as the adults watch on, amused.

I clear my throat.

"Well, words are merely a *representative* for emotion. There's no right or wrong. They're just a compilation of sounds and vocal inflections. That's why there can be no hierarchy in language."

"Well, surely you don't believe that." He scoffs.

"I do," I say firmly.

"Christopher. Be nice—" his mother starts.

"Let the children debate," Mr. Kelly interjects.

"With all due respect, it's not really a debate, Mr. Kelly," I say boldly. "It's solely rooted in facts." I lock eyes with Christopher's blue ones. "There's no more hierarchy to your speech than to the speech of a child in the slums of the ghetto. You're both using tonal inflections to emote deeper feelings. Words are quite a barbaric practice, when you really consider it."

"Barbaric?"

"Precisely."

"So, what do you propose instead?"

"Nothing. I just find our obsession with language fascinating. The hierarchy we inherit just because our speech sounds different than others'. After all, we did inherit English from the monarchy . . . the very ones who brutally colonized Jamaica."

"Jillian," my mother stops me.

"No, please—" Christopher stops her. "I want to hear."

The table falls silent as I awkwardly clear my throat.

"I just . . . think it's interesting. Our lack of ability to convey our feelings with the language we have. It's all very coded. And archaic."

"Fascinating." Christopher nods, a smirk creeping onto his face. "If that's the case, then why don't you speak in your native tongue?"

"My *native tongue?*" I eye him. "Are you trying to be funny?"

"Not at all." He takes a sip of his drink. "I just find it amusing. You're so passionate about language, yet you don't speak your own."

"And what language is that?"

"Broken English." He laughs. "The gibberish that Blacks speak on this island."

"*Excuse me?*"

"Oh, come on, there must be *some* part of you that doesn't believe what you're saying. You haven't uttered a word in Patois all night, despite it being the language of *your people,* correct? I would hate to know it's because you actually believe you're above it."

"Above what?"

"*The marginalized.*" He looks me dead in the eyes.

The look on his face is so pompous it makes my blood boil.

"We don't encourage Jillian to use that type of language," my father says as he shifts in his seat. "Make no mistake, there's no prouder Jamaican than myself. But there's nothing *becoming* about a young lady speaking *Patois.*"

"It's a low-class language." My mother nods.

"It's a *colorful* language," I timidly correct her. "Filled with expression and great nuance. And with all due respect, Daddy, if it wasn't spoken in the ghettos, you probably wouldn't feel so strongly—"

"Jillian," Daddy scolds. "Stop."

"I think Jillian may have a point," Christopher concedes, fascinated as he watches me. "Or at the very least, an amusing perspective."

I clutch my napkin as the silence grows strained.

"I think it's stunning," Christopher says after a moment. "I like it. A lot." His eyes trace me with palpable charm, and I look away, unsure if he's referring to me or the debate.

"Well done, Jillian." Mr. Kelly claps. "You've left Christopher speechless. I don't think I've ever seen that."

The table laughs, and I smile awkwardly.

"What about you, Christopher?" my father asks. "What are your passions?"

"Politics," he boasts. I almost scoff. "I want to lead, just like my father. I'll be studying policy at Oxford this fall."

"That's marvelous." Mummy's tone is little too eager. I fight the urge to roll my eyes. "It takes deep vision to want to lead a society."

"And what exactly makes *you* a leader?" I ask.

He pauses, mid-sip.

I smirk.

Two can play that game.

"I beg your pardon?"

"You said you intend to lead. I'm wondering what *qualifies* your leadership?"

He laughs, amused. Clearly enjoying this game of back-and-forth. "I was born to lead, Jillian."

"By what standards?" I raise an eyebrow.

"Well, for one, just look at my father. Some could say it was destined. A birthright."

"A *birthright*? That's rather pompous—"

"*Jillian*—" my mother scolds.

"It's fine, Mrs. Casey," Christopher stops her. "I want to answer the question."

He puts down his glass and leans closer into the table.

"I would say I've been groomed from a young age to understand what great leadership takes. I've had the privilege of watching my father my entire life. The information has been seeped into me since I've been in diapers—so some would say, politics has become an instinct through my conditioning. Does that make sense?"

"To you."

"I beg your pardon?"

"Well, if those are the *words* you're using to convince yourself of your entitlement, then it makes sense. *For you.* But I guess that's the beauty of language—we can convince ourselves of anything."

Christopher smiles, mesmerized. "I'm convinced."

"Then it makes sense."

The table goes quiet.

"Well then." Mr. Kelly clears his throat, breaking the tension. "You've clearly raised an impeccable young woman," he says to my parents. "Deeply smart. Very well spoken. And I can tell you have a passionate soul, Jillian. I have no doubt that you have a bright future ahead of you, just like our son."

"Thank you, Mr. Kelly." I nod. I feel myself growing anxious, desperate to leave this dinner and to return to the comfort of my room.

"Your parents have spoken so highly of you, and they did not disappoint."

I offer him a small smile, unsure of when this dinner became all about me.

"As you can imagine, it's been hard for us to find a quality match for Christopher. A young lady with wit and a bright future. One who isn't after Christopher for our money or political gain. And not to mention whose head isn't filled with propaganda about 'the revolution.'" He scoffs. "Christopher needs a young woman who can challenge him. That can match his intellect and keep him grounded."

I nod, unsure of what he's getting at.

"I don't think it's by any coincidence that you both are attending school in England this fall. If you ask me, it almost seems fated."

"I said the same thing to Calvin," my mother chimes in, elated. "Destiny."

"We appreciate this dinner, Winston," my father says. "You've also raised a determined son. With deep vision. Christopher has a strong head on his shoulders, and I think our children would have an incredibly bright future together. To unite the Kellys and the Caseys . . . it would be rather historic."

Confusion takes over as I look to my father.

"What do you mean?" My eyes dart from my father to Christopher and back again.

"You're a special girl, Jillian," Mr. Kelly says firmly. "Truly." He places down his glass and folds his hands together. And then his tone grows more serious. "I think you and my son would make a great match. Perfect, even."

I freeze. All at once, it hits me why we are here.

And it is not because of Daddy's promotion.

"When your father told me about you, I had high hopes. But tonight, I can say that even those have been exceeded. You're a brilliant young lady."

"And we're *so* thrilled." Mrs. Kelly beams as she downs her wine.

"The honor is ours," Daddy interjects. "Truly."

With a big smile on his face, he reaches across the table and shakes hands with Mr. Kelly. I feel all the blood drain from my body. The Kellys are powerful.

And together, our families could take over the political landscape of Jamaica.

"So, it's settled, then." Daddy nods.

Mr. Kelly raises his glass.

I think I might pass out right here at this table.

"**WELCOME** to the family, Jillian."

4

Irie

"Dem *still* nuh know who did it."

MY older brother, Kojo, breaks the silence as we sit around the old wooden dinner table. It's been two nights since the shooting, and I stare down at my plate as I sit next to Tandi, who barely touches her food. My father sits at the head of the table as Kojo places a spoonful of rice into his mouth. He looks up at my father, waiting for him to speak.

He doesn't.

After a moment of strained silence, Kojo continues. "They're thinking it might have been a shoot-out," he says, matter-of-factly. "A turf war between PLM and JCG. Junior happened to just be a casualty that got caught in the cross fire."

"*Just a casualty?*" It leaves my mouth as the carelessness of his words rip through me.

"Yuh know what I mean, Irie." Kojo brushes me off. "Junior wasn't the *intended* target. It was a shoot-out between the PLM and JCG gang."

"I doubt that," Tandi mutters, her jaw resting on her palm. "I only saw bullets coming from *one* direction. Intended target or not, there was only one shooter."

"Tings can happen quick in those situations, Tandi." Kojo's tone is condescending. "Yuh probably miss suh'um."

"*She didn't.*" Siarah marches in from the kitchen, a pot of rice in her hand. The lines on her face make her look tired as she spoons extra rice onto Daddy's plate. "We both watched them fire bullets from a blacked-out car. There was only one clear shooter, and it *had* to have been the Tower Posse. The JCG gang has been terrorizing Papine for weeks—"

"You *saw* the shooter?" Kojo eyes her quizzically.

"No," Siarah says defensively. "But who else could it have been?"

"Siarah's right." I nod in agreement. "No PLM supporter would just shoot up Papine Square like that, Kojo. That's not what the People's Liberation Movement stands for—"

"That's not true, Irie." Kojo shakes his head. "You can't take sides. People get reckless around election time. It's important not to rule anybody out."

"So, what are you saying, then?" I look at him. "That *the PLM killed Junior?*"

"It's a possibility."

I dig my nails into my palm.

Kojo loves to play devil's advocate.

"That doesn't make any sense. Why in the hell would they *do* that?"

"I neva said they *did*, Irie. I'm just sayin' we nuh know yet."

I roll my eyes.

By *we,* he's referring to the Jamaican police force. He's been shadowing them for the past year, and to say that it's gone to his head would be a huge understatement. There was a time when you couldn't even *pay* Kojo to utter a bad word about the PLM or their role in the tribal war. But now, he prides himself in seeing "all sides."

"*Joshua is our only real chance at freedom,*" he used to preach to us. "*He was sent here by God to free the people. To lead us to the promise land of true independence.*"

But Kojo's views changed once he started working for the force.

And clearly, so has his allegiance.

His involvement with the Jamaican police force started when he and his friends formed a neighborhood watch group to protect the people of Kintyre from gun violence at nighttime. It wasn't long until the police took notice of how Kojo and his friends fearlessly guarded our neighborhood from tribal gangs, and soon, they recruited them in exchange for better weapons. But everyone in Kintyre knows that making a deal with the police is equivalent to making a deal with the *very same darkness* that terrorizes the ghetto. The police may monitor political violence at nighttime, but by day, they wreak their own havoc and unleash their own personal kind of hell.

Including killing Rastas dead in the streets.

If you ask me, the police are just as dangerous as the gangsters. If not for their own corruption and political biases, then for the colonial values and prejudices that they brutally enforce over the people of the ghetto. The soldiers in Jamaica take pride in upholding the outdated values of colonization, beating and jailing anyone who shows alliance with the rise of Rastafari culture. Here on our island, the rebellion against the old system where the few control the many has created massive division. Instead of championing peace, police persecute Rastas in the streets, shaving their dreadlocks and throwing them in jail for their free thought and alignment with African consciousness. The sad truth is, just like everyone else, the police serve the rich.

And the rich do not want a revolution.

Daddy says the police only recruit the neighborhood boys for their nighttime missions because they'd rather put the youth in harm's way than their own soldiers. But it doesn't really matter what Daddy thinks, because Kojo isn't my father's son—Mummy had him a few years before she met Daddy, with another man. And so when Kojo turned eighteen, the decision to work for the force became his own. In Kojo's mind, going out every night from sunset to sunrise to defend his community is noble.

In mine, it's stupid.

"You're so brainwashed," I mutter, annoyed by Kojo's false sense of importance.

"Wha' dat supposed fi mean?" He screws up his face.

"It *means* you used to think for yourself. I know you love playing soldier, but the police's word isn't law, Kojo."

"Wha' yah talk 'bout, Irie?" Kojo shakes his head, pompous. "All I'm saying is, it wouldn't *mek sense* for the JCG to target their own area. Think about it. Papine Square is a mix of JCG and PLM supporters, but most people vote JCG. Why would they target their own *voters*?"

"Because they're *cowards*." The words leave my mouth with force. "And you used to think the same thing before you started following the police around like a puppy dog—"

"Irie." Daddy's firm voice shakes the room. "Stop."

He scans the table, making it clear he's not asking.

I bite my tongue, sinking deeper into my chair.

He knows I'm right.

"It's not like it matters," Tandi mutters after a strained moment of silence. Daddy gives her a stern look, warning her not to push it. "I'm sorry, Daddy, but it's true. There's no point taking sides and getting all upset." Her voice breaks. "We're never going to find out who killed Junior, anyway."

Her words gut me.

"Just yesterday, there was another shooting in Hope Gardens." Kojo nods in agreement, his tone is flat. "Fourteen people dead in six seconds." Kojo's tone is grim. "The police cyaan do their job properly wit' so much goin' on. It's too much to keep up wit'—"

"Me say *no more talk about it at di table*," Daddy orders, returning to his plate. "Now unu stop di noise and eat yuh food."

The table goes silent. It takes everything I have to hold back the tears that rage inside of me. The grief that I cannot give back.

"Can I be excused?" Kojo asks. "My shift soon start."

Daddy nods, giving Kojo permission to leave.

"I'll be back in di mawnin'," he says before backing up his seat and heading toward the front door. I watch from the corner of my eye as he slides into his only pair of shoes—battered brown sandals passed down from Daddy.

"Tek care," Daddy calls.

"Bye, Kojo," Tandi calls back to him, her voice sullen. "Please be safe."

"I will." He nods.

"And for the love of God," Siarah musters, wiping a tear from her puffy cheeks, "*please* walk good."

I swallow my pride despite the disdain I feel toward my brother.

"Bye, Kojo," I mutter. I can't help but feel nervous every time he leaves to go out.

"Likkle more, Irie," he says, turning the handle. "See unu tomorrow."

With one final wave, he makes his way through the door.

LATER that night, my thoughts race as I stare up at our rusting zinc roof. I lie on the single bed I share with my sisters, as Siarah and Tandi sit across from me at the edge. Our house is small, the walls dreary and gray, made from zinc and cement. I usually dread the idea of cramming onto the small mattress with my sisters, but ever since the shooting, it's felt comforting.

I glance over at Tandi who fiddles with the radio, her head gently tucked between Siarah's thighs as she braids it into cornrows for bed. The night air is humid and hot, and the three of us sit in silence to the sound of the rain as it patters against the zinc. Tandi tunes the radio to the nightly news as Prime Minister Morris's voice breaks through the silence.

"The United States is *not* going to tell me what relationship I can have with Fidel Castro!" His commanding bravado immediately captures our attention, as the muffled static fills the room. "We are a part of an alliance of third-world nations that are fighting for justice for *poor people* in the world!"

The crowd roars, and the ferocity of support sends feedback through the tiny radio.

Tandi moves to turn it down.

"Wait," I stop her, sitting up on the bed. "I wanna hear."

The crowd dies down as Joshua Morris continues.

"As long as the PLM is in power, we intend to walk through the world on our feet, and *not. On. Our. Knees!*"

The crowd erupts.

"Whoa," Siarah says. "Talk about intense."

A surge of adrenaline moves through me. The feedback from the crowd pierces through the radio as Joshua's words light me up. I reach over toward the nightstand drawer and pull out my songbook. Gifted to me by Daddy, it's the only place I write down all my music. I flip it open onto a fresh page, curling up in the corner of the bed. As the rain continues to fall in the background, the words flow from me and onto the page:

> *I won't back down from this holy war*
> *The spirit of love will fight on and I will roar*
> *Peace will reign and wash away the sins of my brother*
> *Because I have faith that we will hold hands and one day*
> *   come home to each other*
> *For there has to be a better way, love has to know a*
> *   brighter day*

I'm stunned as I stare down at my own words.

They pour out of me, as if by no doing of my own.

We are the children of love who seem to have forgot
The truth of all we are, and all we are not
May peace reign throughout the nation, may love cover the
*   land*
And when I am weak, may Jah the Almighty take my hand
Free me from the chains of my mind, help me to see the
*   truth clear*
That wherever I go, freedom is near

"Have you seen Joshua Morris's wife in the papers?" Tandi breaks me out of my thoughts as she holds up a newspaper. It's a much-needed distraction from our gloom as she shows Siarah and me a photo of his wife, Beatrice Morris—a brown-skinned Jamaican woman who wears an African headwrap around her Afro. "She's *so* beautiful. And she looks so . . . I don't know—"

"*Black?*" Siarah looks at us. "It's about time we see people who *actually look like us* representing Jamaica."

I nod, woeful as we study the photo, the image striking us all. Despite the backlash for not looking like a "traditional politician's wife," Beatrice Morris is a portrait of the everyday Jamaican woman—something we'd had yet to see reflected back to us before.

"She kinda reminds me of Mummy." Tandi's voice goes sad. "Yuh hear from her yet, Irie?"

Her question takes me by surprise as she turns off the radio. Being the youngest, Tandi's also filled with the most hope—no matter how naive.

I shake my head, although I know she already knows the answer.

"We could be dead, and that woman would have no clue," Siarah chimes in.

"Please don' start, Siarah." Tandi sighs. "I was askin' Irie."

"I'm not startin' anything, Tandi," Siarah says defensively. "I'm jus' *saying* I'm not surprised she hasn't called. I mean, it's not like she ever does. Why would now be any different? It's not like she knew Junior."

"Siarah's right," I say, sullen as I meet Tandi's gaze. "I wouldn't hold yuh breath, Tandi. The whole of Kintyre could be burning to the ground for all Mummy knows."

"The whole of Kintyre *is* burning to the ground," Siarah says, not taking her eyes off Tandi's hair. "And Mummy *does* know. But she left us to burn, anyway."

The grim reality sets in.

The truth is, I understand Siarah's resentment just as much as I understand Tandi's hope.

Mummy can go years without calling. When we do speak, it's a two-minute call, with not much to say, and only when she has access to a phone. Some days I hate her for leaving, but more often than that, I barely remember what it felt like to have her around at all. I was only five years old when she left to work abroad, fleeing our family in the middle of the night. Daddy gifted me my songbook shortly after she left, and soon, the longing I felt for her inspired me to start writing songs about love and loss.

My mother was my first muse.

What I remember most are how sad her brown eyes were. She wasn't happy in her marriage to Daddy, but even as a child, I couldn't blame her, the way he used to put his hands on her. The memories of the abuse are distant, but on nights like tonight, when the humid air feels suffocating—*unsafe*—the memories creep up again. Because even I know that the past can never be outrun.

But still, Mummy ran, anyway.

She fled Kintyre as soon as the opportunity came up to clean houses abroad, leaving all four of her children behind. And now, I hate her as much as I miss her. I resent her, just as much as I could never blame her. My father was abusive—just like most men are to their wives. And the unsettling truth is, although he brings joy to me and my sisters—he brought our mother's life just as much misery. The perfect father and yet the worst husband.

Two realities fighting each other in one man.

Most of my memories of Mummy are foggy, and the older I get, the further away they fade. She left us for a better life, but here in Kintyre, our lives without her have not been better.

They have been destroyed.

"Yuh think she ever thinks about us?" Tandi's voice disrupts the silence.

"No," Siarah answers before I have a chance to think about it. "Now can we *please* stop talking about her?"

I try to bury the sadness that creeps up. When Mummy left, we all had to live with the shame of being motherless children, and the rumors in our community were insidious.

Why would she come back when he beat her like that?

How Ricky ah go raise all dem gyal pickney?

Everyone in the community had something to say, and Kojo got the worst of it.

Everyone called him a *jacket* because he wasn't our father's child, and they would gossip about whether Daddy would still accept him in the house as his own. But Daddy proved them all wrong by allowing Kojo to stay after Mummy left.

He raised us, and we raised each other.

Tandi closes her eyes as Siarah finishes up, and I rest back onto the pillow, tucking my songbook beside me. All I want to do is be able to sleep through the night. But the grief feels like a black hole that threatens to consume me. It's not sleeping that I'm afraid of.

It's waking up and remembering.

"Yuh think Junior went to heaven?" My voice is a whisper as I turn to face my sisters.

"Yeah," Siarah says softly. "I do."

"He *was* a real-life angel." Tandi smiles. "Yuh nuh think he's in heaven, Irie?"

Tears begin to form in the backs of my eyes.

"I do, I just . . ." My voice breaks. "I guess I just hope he made it there safely."

"Trust me." Siarah looks at me. "Junior's up there writing music as we speak."

"Siarah's right. The only thing Junior loved more than writing music was you, Irie."

My heart flutters.

"He was *so* talented," I whisper. "He knew every song. Every record by heart. Sometimes I swear he loved music more than I do."

"I wouldn't be surprised with all the love songs he wrote to you." Siarah smiles.

The moment is tender as the revelation dawns on me.

"If he were still here right now, the *first thing* he would do is write a song about all of this injustice. He would be inspired to tell the truth about what's happening out there."

"It would probably be one of the *boddest records* too." Tandi giggles.

"Tough," I say, a laugh escaping me. "*Sell off.*"

We laugh to keep from crying as Siarah gazes at me, her brown eyes remorseful. "I'm sorry I didn't undastand, Irie." She's tender as she reaches for my hand. "What you were sayin' before. About di music."

"Siarah—"

"I'm serious." She looks me straight in the eyes as hers begin to water. "I jus' didn't understand. But I do now. We have to speak up against the violence."

Her words bring me peace.

"I guess sometimes I just don't like to talk about all the violence going on. There's so much pain." Her voice grows shaky as she continues to explain. "But I want you to *always* sing those revolutionary songs, Irie. I want you to *always* use your voice and tell the truth about what's happening out there. For Junior."

A tear escapes me as I explode with love for my big sister.

"Siarah," I whisper as I bury myself into her thick brown braids.

She squeezes me back, her embrace loving and warm.

"I love you . . . *so much*," I say.

"I love you too, Irie," she says before pulling away.

"I just . . . I want *change*," I say to my sisters. My voice is hollow as I speak from what feels like the depths of my soul. "And I'm sorry for earlier. At dinner. I didn't mean to get so upset with Kojo. I just—" I search myself for the truth. "I'm just *so angry*."

My sisters gaze at me as my words hang in the humidity of the hot night.

"I'm angry too," Siarah says. "We all are. But go easy on Kojo. He doesn't mean any harm."

"But he's *causing* harm," I say defensively. "All di police are doing is terrorizing the ghetto. All this killing . . . it's senseless."

"I get that." Siarah nods. "But Kojo's just trying to protect the community in di best way he knows how, Irie. And I'm not sayin' di police are doing the best job, but let's be real—we *need* di police. Especially right now." She shrugs. "Kojo takes pride in helping keep us safe. It gives him purpose. He wants to serve just as much as you want to sing."

"*What?*" I slowly grow annoyed. "Those are two completely different things—"

"What about your friendship with Jillian?" Tandi asks. "Yuh friend from school?"

I screw up my face, suddenly feeling attacked. "Wha' that haffi do wit' nuttin'?"

"I just mean . . . it nuh really seem fair to criticize Kojo if you're friends with all those rich girls, Irie. The wealthy are *the very ones* driving fear into every poor Jamaican citizen."

"And how is that Jilly's fault?"

"Didn't you mention her father worked in politics?" Siarah asks sheepishly.

"So? It's not like she *chose* her family, just like we didn't *choose* to live in the ghetto," I say, my tone defensive. "Jilly doesn't have a say in what her father does for work."

"We're not *sayin'* she does," Siarah says calmly. "We're just sayin', yuh cyaan mek an exception for her and not for Kojo. Jillian might be yuh friend, but she's still a rich girl from uptown. The *only people* in Jamaica benefiting from this war."

My body grows tense. "Jilly doesn't *align* wit' di values of the JCG, Siarah. She wants change just as much as I do." I look at my sisters, trying to get them to understand. "She loves listening to reggae music just like I do. She's different."

My sisters are quiet as they stare back at me.

"Yuh have to know her," I mutter, my voice low.

But I'm not sure if I'm trying to convince them or myself.

"I don't have anything against her." Siarah shrugs. "But from how you describe her, she just seems a likkle far removed from reality."

"Which way is she voting in di election?" Tandi asks.

"We nuh talk about politics." I shrug them off. "We focus on the music."

But the truth comes out shamefully. As the nights in Kintyre grow haunting, it dawns on me—my friendship with Jilly does, in fact, make me a hypocrite.

"Well, just be careful," Siarah warns. "Girls like that will come inna yuh life and bring you crosses."

HER words send a chill right through me.

5

—

Jilly

Many *rivers to cross . . .*

THE sun streams through my white curtains as the soulful but tortured sound of Jimmy Cliff's voice spills from my record player. The song is one of Irie's and my favorites, and to soothe the gaping hole in my heart, I've had it on repeat all morning.

How is this my life?

I shove my face into my silk pillow, drowning deeper in despair. The fabric is damp to the touch, drenched from my tears.

But my pillow's used to my sorrow.

The music is the only thing that takes the pain away. I would give *anything* to be able to break free from my mind. From the thoughts that torment me and threaten to swallow me whole.

All I want is a life where I get a say.

But the sad truth is, I wouldn't even know what to do with it if I had one. I don't even trust myself to make my own decisions. I have no idea who I am—*what I really want.* How could I even begin to know what that is, when I'm not even allowed to decide who I *marry?*

The person who I love?

My mind is a tornado as the thoughts build strength, demanding answers.

But this is how my life has always been—controlled by my parents. They make all the decisions for me, because just like me, they don't trust me to make my own.

And how could I blame them?

I wasn't even smart enough to get into school.

Ever since I was a little girl, my choices, my interests, my education, and my extracurriculars have all been chosen for me. *Tennis. Horseback riding. Swimming. Chess. Ballet. Polo.* Honor roll year after year. Captain of a million different teams and clubs that don't even interest me. *Their perfect little award-winning daughter.*

But this year, I was so burned out.

It just also happened to be the year where it mattered the most.

I've worked my ass off for *years* just to prove that I was good enough. Just so my parents could brag at the country clubs to all their upper-echelon friends that they've raised a *good, polite, smart young lady,* whose gleaming success *almost* makes up for the fact that Mummy couldn't give Daddy a boy.

Too bad almost doesn't count.

I pay for it every day—the fact that my mother couldn't get pregnant after me. There's an undercurrent of disappointment that lingers no matter how high I achieve. *No matter how perfect I am.* In my mother's eyes, she wasn't able to give my father an heir to his throne—but she *could* prepare a good wife in the hopes that I might one day marry a man who made up for it.

My soul doesn't matter unless there's a powerful man standing next to me. And now that I'm promised to Christopher, the story of my life has been written without me ever having held a pen.

Bam, bam, bam.

A sharp knock at the door jolts me out of my thoughts. I shove my face into my pillow as the door handle turns, and in walks my mother. The sound of kitten heels against the hardwood floor sends a shiver up my spine.

She stops the record player abruptly.

I peek out to find her staring at me, in a white blouse and long cream skirt, her Coco Chanel purse draped over her pointy shoulder.

"Your father would like to speak with you," she says through pink lipstick. "Have you been in here all morning, Jillian? It's filthy."

I bite my tongue, not saying a word as I stare out at my room. Barely anything out of place.

"I'm *speaking* to you, Jillian Casey."

"I just woke up, Mummy," I mutter. "I'll be downstairs soon."

"It's nearly *twelve o'clock,* Jillian. You should've been out of bed hours ago. It's irresponsible, and quite frankly, it's lazy. I don't know where you're picking up these nasty habits . . ."

She makes her way toward me, scanning my room for something else to criticize.

"Just because it's summer break doesn't mean you're going to spend your last summer in Jamaica wasting away in your room. You still have Cambridge to prepare for in the fall."

My stomach knots.

"Okay," I muster.

"And you left the breakfast Amala prepared for you to get cold," she says as she inspects my room. "It's sitting downstairs, untouched."

"I don't want it, Mummy," I say, swallowing my frustration. "I'm not hungry."

"All the better," she says. "Look, I understand you're not pleased about this arrangement." Her tone is empty—chastising. "But throwing yourself a pity party will not negate your responsibilities to Christopher or to this family. Your father and I worked tirelessly to secure this proposal for you, Jillian. And you might not see it now, but what's happened for you is a good thing."

"What's happened for *me* or for Daddy?"

Mummy takes a step closer. "What did you just say?"

"I don't want to *marry him*, Mummy!" I explode. "I barely know anything about him, and . . . and you didn't even ask me! You didn't even ask if that's what I wanted—"

"*Cut it out*," she says sharply. "Now."

I look away.

"You sound ungrateful, and you should be ashamed. Do you understand that there are *hundreds* of young women who would literally *kill* to be in your position?" She glares at me. "We all have a part to play, Jillian. And it's time you smarten up and play yours. Do you think you're the only one who's made sacrifices?"

Tears sting the backs of my eyes.

"Your father has worked incredibly hard to provide us this life. And you need *not* to take it for granted—do I make myself clear? We're almost at the end of this campaign, and I will not let you ruin this for your father."

I clench my jaw tightly.

"It's your duty—"

"To bring honor to this family. I know."

I cringe as the words leave my mouth.

"Good. Now, make yourself presentable. Your father is waiting for you in the library." She gathers herself to go. "I'm meeting your aunt Louise at the country club. When I get back, I'd better not see you still lying there."

I hate her.

I watch in contempt as she picks up a Jackson Five vinyl casing from off the ground. "And if you continue to leave these lying around, Jillian, I'm going to start tossing them." She puts the casing on my desk and makes her way through the door.

I want to scream.

Throughout the years, my parents have gotten countless proposals from political affiliates who have wanted to set me up with their sons. Wealth means nothing without power, and both are something that my father has plenty of. He's been a major player in the JCG party since its inception, and in the world of Jamaican politics, who you're connected to has an invisible hand in how the island is run. Over the years, people would do anything to get close to my father.

Including asking for my hand in marriage.

Daddy always said no, but evidently, he was waiting for the right family.

The right creed.

The right class.

The right *caste*.

And the right amount of power.

I'm anxious as I use all my will to pull myself out of bed. I dread the thought of facing my father. I've spent the last few days avoiding him, and with the busy demands of his campaign schedule, it's worked for me up until now. I head into my closet and change out of my pajamas, slipping into a housedress.

And then I make my way to the office.

The housekeepers bustle about below me as I descend the long flight of stairs. I pass by the kitchen and head down to the end of the hall, landing at the door of my father's study. I take a deep breath, ball my sweaty palm into a fist, and knock.

A few seconds pass before he answers.

"Come in." His deep voice penetrates through the door. I push it open to find him in his usual position—behind his desk, reviewing papers.

I step inside.

He focuses in deep contemplation, his reading glasses on the brim of his nose as I make my way toward him. I pass the display of plaques and family photos that sit on the polished shelves, on edge as I approach his desk.

"Mummy said you wanted to see me," I say indirectly.

"Have a seat," he orders, still not looking up at me.

I take a seat across from him in the brown leather chair.

"Did you enjoy meeting the Kellys?" He places down the papers and looks up at me. His tone is void of any real emotion.

I look at him as though he's insane.

"A heads-up would have been nice, Daddy," I say bitterly. "Courtesy, even—"

"Don't be smart with me, Jillian," he says sharply. "I understand it's a lot to process. But your mother and I are confident in the decision we made for you. Christopher is an incredibly decorated young man. I have no doubt you'll be taken care of—"

"But I don't want to be *taken care of, Daddy*!" Frustration bursts out of me. "I'm not *ready* to get married. It's not what I want—"

"I didn't ask *what you want*," he says firmly. "It's what's *best*."

I'm betrayed by the words that come out of his mouth.

I can't believe this is happening.

"It's a privilege to be in your position, Jillian," he scolds. "Your mother and I have a responsibility to you, just like our parents had to us. *You are our business*." He holds my gaze. "You might not understand it now, but one day, you will. And you will thank me for it."

I want to explode.

"I understand you've had a lot going on in the last seventy-two hours, with graduating high school, and university in the fall. But it doesn't negate your responsibilities to this household." His tone goes firm. "You *will* marry that young man."

"But, Daddy," I cry. "I didn't even get a say."

He goes quiet, sitting back in his chair.

"Let me help you understand something." His tone is cold. "You cannot have a *legacy* off a *literature degree*. Do you understand me? I work *very* hard to afford you this life, and when your mother and I are gone from this world, what's most important to us is that you're able to maintain it. So when you *marry*—you will not marry for *love*, Jillian." His eyes search mine. "*Who* the person is—where they come from. Those are the things that matter in this life. Those are the things that guarantee your position."

His words make me feel sick.

"You have an obligation." His eyes shoot through me like daggers. "And you will do what you are told. Do I make myself clear?"

A tear rolls down my cheek as I slump deeper into the leather chair.

"Crystal," I whisper.

"Good." He nods, resuming the papers on his desk. "Now where are you at with Cambridge? We'll need to start making arrangements for your boarding."

"It hasn't come as yet," I lie, wiping the tears from my cheeks. "I'm still waiting, but so are most of the other girls in my form. I imagine I should hear soon."

He looks up at me over his glasses.

"I'm not playing with you, Jillian. This had better not fall back on your grades—"

"My grades were some of the best in my class—"

"They were *passable*," he corrects. "And the fact that you didn't get early acceptance was proof of that. The last thing I need is you playing with the Casey name—"

"I'm not, Daddy," I say obediently. "I promise. I got in."

His green eyes go dark as he resumes his work.

"Prepare yourself for the day," he orders. "You have two weeks to show me an acceptance letter."

"Okay." My voice is small as he dismisses me.

I rise from my seat.

"And don't forget you have French lessons after piano at four. I'll send Amala up to your room to help you prepare . . . and have her do something with your hair. It could use a press."

I grimace as I walk away.

"Daddy?" I stop in my tracks as he looks up from his papers. "Mummy's birthday dinner is approaching . . ." I nervously fiddle with my bracelet. "Will Christopher be there? At the dinner?"

"The Kellys will be in attendance," Daddy says distractedly. "And so will Monica. She's back in town." He refers to my older, pretty-much-perfect cousin who studies abroad. "You'll have plenty of company your own age."

"Okay." I nod, considering. "Well, I was just hoping to make some arrangements for Mummy's gift," I say, secretly hopeful that I might be able to go and see Irie. "I really want to get Mummy something nice this year, maybe a nice Elvis record."

"I'll arrange the car for you this week." Daddy resumes his work. "Lloyd can take you to the plaza. Take what you need from the kitchen drawer."

"Okay." I'm somber as I make my way back through the office doors. I shut them behind me, grateful to be out of my father's sight.

THE thought of seeing Irie my only saving grace.

6

———

Irie

"*It is a great tragedy of our history that the masses are predominately Black, but the privileged classes are predominately fair-skinned.*"

JOSHUA Morris's looming voice comes through the speakers of the shop radio as I kneel behind the counter with Siarah, sorting through a new shipment of records. The morning is exceptionally hot, and I wipe a bead of sweat from my forehead as the sun beams through the windows. It's the third shift I'm working without Junior, and everything about it feels draining.

My ears are fixated on Morris as he continues to speak.

"*It is our responsibility to assault the economic system that perpetuates disadvantages and break the delusion that race is the enemy, when poverty is the true obstacle to overcome—*"

"Daddy!" Siarah calls out over the sound of the radio. "Yuh know what time we ah go close today?"

Daddy ignores her as Siarah exhaustedly stuffs a fallen coil into her scrunchie.

"We nuh jus' start?" I look at her. "We've been here thirty minutes, Siarah."

"Hush, Irie." She fights a smile, fanning me off as she realizes the ridiculousness of her question. "I was askin' *Daddy*." She pokes her head out from behind the counter, trying again. "Een, Daddy?" She uses her best baby voice. "Yuh nuh need me here all day, do you?"

"Yes!" Daddy and I call out in unison.

Siarah rolls her eyes, and I can't help but smile, used to her antics.

As beautiful as Siarah is, she makes for an awful employee. Tandi always says it's a "waste of Siarah's pretty"—and she's not wrong. On Saturdays when Daddy forces Siarah to work the busier shifts with us, she can easily sell *double* the amount than Tandi and I can—but all that talent goes to waste because Siarah hates to work. Daddy always jokes that her lack of interest in the store means there's no way she's his child.

Siarah never found that one too funny.

"Some ah dese songs have di strangest titles." Siarah shakes her head, examining the record in her hand as she flips through the stack. "'Guava Jelly' . . . 'Tenement Yard'?" She giggles, amusing herself. "'I Shot the Sheriff'? Dem cyaan be serious."

"Why not?" I ask, turning down the radio. "Music is a form of expression, remember?"

"'I Love Marijuana'?" She holds up a Linval Thompson record, scrunching up her face.

"A classic," I say, snatching it from her hands. "Yuh know Rastafarians believe ganja is medicine, right? Kinda like an herb that comes from God . . . it can give you visions and stuff."

"Right." Siarah rolls her eyes. "All those drugs do is mash up yuh head, Irie. Don't listen to the propaganda. There's a difference between *visions* and *hallucinations*."

"Like you've ever tried it to know?"

"Yuh jus' mind Daddy hear yuh." Her eyes go wide at the suggestion. We peer over our shoulders just as Daddy disappears into the back hall. Siarah turns back to me, her voice a whisper. "For real, though, you nuh think Daddy is kinda mod for keepin' some of these records?" She passes me a Bob Marley record called "Burnin' and Lootin'."

"Yuh nuh 'fraid police raid di shop?"

"And who ah go arrest us?" I kiss my teeth. "*Kojo?*"

Siarah fights a smile. "Yuh wrong fi that one."

"Music isn't *illegal,* Siarah. And plus, artists haffi be controversial when they're coming up with record titles. It's how they capture people's attention."

"I guess so," Siarah considers, holding up another record— Junior Byles's *Beat Down Babylon.* "So, what's your song title going to be, then? The one you were workin' on the other night before bed."

My heart sinks.

"I haven't really thought about it." I shift, considering the weight of the question as I grab another pile of records from the counter. "I have to finish writing it first."

"What's it about, anyway?"

"Junior . . . and the revolution."

Siarah nods, empathetic.

"Well, you just let me know if yuh need help coming up with suh'um. I'm no songwriter, but I could definitely help yuh come up wit' suh'um catchier than these."

She drops the pile of records into the bin just as Daddy reenters.

"Daddy! It's *so* stuffy in here," Siarah whines. "I'm burnin' up."

"Ace soon come," Daddy mutters. "I hired him to fix the fan. It stop work from last week." He gestures to the tall fan that sits at the back of the store.

"*Ace?*" I make a face, looking up from the bins. "Miss Salvie's godson?"

Daddy nods.

Ace is a few years older than I am, and he lives a town over from Kintyre. He and Kojo went to school together, and when we were younger, he used to come by and do odd jobs around the shop for Daddy. At the time, he lived with his godmother, Miss Salvie—a regular patron of the store.

But one summer, he just stopped coming around.

"I haven't seen that bwoy in four years," Siarah says. "Last time I heard, he was still causin' trouble."

"I didn't know he was in town," I say, my curiosity piqued. "He came by the shop?"

Daddy nods. "Ah look work. Him ah go repair some tings fi me around the store."

Siarah and I take in the news. Just then, we watch as Daddy makes his way to the front of the store with a folded sheet of paper in his hands. He holds a staple gun, stopping in front of the wall covered in flyers. He picks the spot next to the Reggae Jamz flyers and unfolds the poster in his hand to reveal bright yellow lettering.

PLM colors.

Terror shoots through me.

"What are you doing, Daddy?" I whip over toward him. He doesn't answer as he staples the poster to the wall. A bright yellow sun stares back at me with the words *PLM* in bold letters. Underneath, it reads, *"TAKING THE POWER IN OUR HANDS."*

I'm stunned as Daddy smoothens out the edges of the poster. The gold ring on his pinkie glistens in the morning light as he takes one final look, before turning to face us.

The look on his face is righteous.

"Daddy," I say in disbelief. "Yuh *cyaan* be serious—"

"As day," he responds precisely. "Ah nuh my shop?"

My eyes dart from the poster to him.

"But you're going to put a target on our back—"

"The record store is still a *business*, Daddy." Siarah approaches.

"Siarah's right," I say nervously. "I think we should jus' cool it for now—"

"Unu stop talk," Daddy commands. The lines on his face are creased as his eyes hold ours. "We nah go cool *nuttin'*. Yuh undastand? We always keep it burnin'."

The intensity of his stare drills into us.

"Me wan' unu fi undastand suh'um. And me nah go say it again," he warns. "*Neva* back down from fear. Yuh undastand wha' me ah say? You look it *straight inna di eye* and you *fight* fi yuh *bloodclaat right.*" His tone drips with conviction. "As Black people, it's our *duty* to stand up fi our own liberation. Free ourselves from di chains of mental slavery."

Siarah and I are speechless.

"Never run away. Yuh always stand strong in who you are."

A chill passes through me as his brown eyes grow intense.

"If Morris and di PLM are the only ones fighting for our liberation, then me nuh business what nobody wan' say—me ah go show my support fi di PLM."

The conviction in his tone emboldens me.

"Never let someone come inna yuh yawd and try frighten yuh." Daddy moves closer as his eyes go back and forth. "And when me say *yuh yawd,* me ah talk 'bout *yuh mind.* Don't mek nobody plant fear inna yuh head. Yuh undastand?"

Apprehensive, Siarah and I nod as the magnitude of his words land.

"Good." Daddy nods, satisfied.

Just then, the door swings open, and our first customer of the day walks in. An older lady makes her way in, a little boy trailing behind her. My chest tightens.

He looks just like Junior.

"Mawnin', Ricky," the lady calls.

"Mawnin', Pearl." Daddy nods.

"Sorry fi hear 'bout wha' happened last week. Glad to see yuh keepin' yuh doors open."

"Duppy know who fi frighten," Daddy says, bravado in his

tone. "But dem cyaan stop di music." He turns to me. "Irie—grab me di Peter Tosh album. 'Bout time we turn up di sound."

"Okay," I say nervously as I head to the back. I make my way up the steps and into the hallway toward the outer nook of the shop where Daddy keeps all the extra crates.

The phone rings as I pass by Daddy's office door.

I make my way inside the small space and dash over toward it. "Hello? Ricky's Records."

"Irie?"

My heart drops.

"*Jilly?*"

"Yeah, hey . . ." I can hear her smiling through the phone. "How have you been? I've been trying to get ahold of you, but no one's been answerin' when I call di shop."

My stomach sinks.

"There's so much I have to update you on." She sighs into the phone. "But tell me about you, first. How have you been?"

The question almost makes me drop to my knees.

"Can I call yuh right back?" I grip the phone tightly in my hands. "I was just in di middle of doin' suh'um fi Daddy. I . . . I have to go."

"Oh. Okay, bu—"

I hang up before she can say anything else.

I take a breath, suddenly feeling more anxious than before. I can't tell her about Junior right now. The last thing I need is Jillian's pity. I don't want her to see me as *poor little Irie.*

The girl from the ghetto with the sad life.

I can't afford for Jillian to think less of me.

I gather myself, ashamed as I make my way back into the hall. I head toward the nook where Daddy keeps new shipments, taking down the stack of crates. It takes me two minutes to find the Peter Tosh record before putting the crate back and spinning around.

I nearly lose my balance when I lock eyes with Ace.

"Oh my gosh." I stumble backward.

"Careful." He towers over me as he helps me steady my balance.

"Sorry," I say, flustered. "You frightened me. No one ever comes back here."

He smiles to reveal beautiful white teeth, dimples on either side.

He's so handsome.

"Wha'ppen, Irie?" He smiles, his brown eyes warm as he takes me in. "Long time."

"Yeah, fa real." I blush. "I was surprised when Daddy said you were comin' by the shop today. I didn't realize you were back in town."

"I'll be around fi di summa." He watches me squirm. "My godmada's not doing too well. Sickle cell. She needs someone fi help her mind di house."

"Oh, wow. I'm really sorry to hear."

He nods, his brown eyes penetrating mine. His dark skin radiates under the midday sun, and he stands tall in a black marina and blue jean shorts.

"Yuh fada said yuh would know where di toolbox was?"

"Oh, yeah," I say awkwardly as I turn around to the shelves.

Ace spots it before I do. He reaches for the toolbox, brushing my hand in the process.

My stomach flutters.

"Thanks." He smiles, tracing my silhouette with his eyes. "You look good, Irie. Older."

"Older?"

"Grown up."

"Thanks." I flush. "You too."

I heat up as he takes me in.

"So, yuh wan' show me to dis fan?"

"Yeah, sure." I squeeze by him through the small space and

make my way back through the hallway and down the steps. When we enter the shop, about ten people walk around the store. I head to the front, where Daddy talks with a young man.

"Here you go, Daddy." I hand him the record.

"Tanks." He puts it down on the record player.

In seconds, Peter Tosh's *Legalize It* comes through the shop speakers.

"Wha'ppen, Ace?" Siarah approaches with a sly smile. "Trench-town deport yuh?"

Ace laughs. "Always good to see you too, Siarah. Wha'ppen?"

"Nuttin'. I didn't know you were back in town. Yuh still causin' trouble?"

"I could ask you di same ting." Ace smiles as he hails my sister. Just then, his eyes fall onto the freshly placed PLM poster.

"Power . . ." He admires the sign. "Me like yuh sign, boss!" he calls across the shop to my father. I tense as new customers start to look on.

"Yeah, mon," Daddy calls back. "Me ah try teach these girls yuh haffi stand tall. Cyaan lose yuh mind to di war."

"All he's going *lose* is business," Siarah whispers under her breath. "But him cyaan say me never warn him."

"Nah, I disagree." Ace shakes his head, examining the sign. "This is bold. Besides, someone haffi take a stand against the JCG." He looks back at me. "Nuh true, Irie?"

"Evidently so," I say through a deep breath. "The fan is just over yesso," I add as I make my way back up the aisle. Ace watches me with sharp eyes as I turn around.

I do my best walk as I lead him toward the back corner of the shop.

"It hasn't been working fi di last two weeks." I try to keep my cool as we approach the fan. "It stopped rotating a few months ago, and then it just shut down."

Ace immediately begins to toy with it.

"Hold dis up fi me." Ace turns the fan onto its side. His voice is deep and direct, and I'm caught off guard by his assertive energy. He's a natural leader, and it makes me want to listen. I can't help but notice the size of his hands as he grips and maneuvers the fan with ease. He's focused as he effortlessly pulls it apart.

I look away, feeling slightly flushed.

"I heard di likkle bwoy weh dem kill outta road used to work here." Ace looks at me with intense brown eyes, his tone casual. "Ah true?"

"Yeah," I say timidly. "He did."

"*Bwoy* . . ." He shakes his head in disgust. "How long him work here?"

"Just shy of a year."

Ace takes it in, quiet for a moment.

"Sorry fi hear dat, still."

I nod, looking away from him. "Thanks."

"I'll keep an ear out if I hear anything."

I'm quiet, unsure of what exactly he means. Just then, another record begins to spin. The smooth, silky rhythm of Burning Spear's *Marcus Garvey* fills the shop.

"Yuh still ah sing?" Ace makes conversation.

"Yeah," I say softly. "Not that it really matters. A good voice nuh mean nuttin' if yuh cyaan do nuttin' wit' it."

"Then do suh'um wit' it." He looks me in the eye. "You used to love singing around di shop. I rememba yuh voice was *wicked*."

"I'm surprised yuh even remember that." I smile.

"I remember everything about you, Irie."

I blush.

"Yuh still in school?" Ace asks me over his shoulder.

"Jus' graduated," I say. "Last week. It was my final year."

"That's riiight." He nods, just remembering. "Last time I saw you, you were keepin' up wit' di Joneses."

"All thanks to Prime Minister Morris." I shrug. "I got to pretend for a likkle bit, I guess."

"Still, you should be proud."

"Of what? A piece ah paper nuh mean nuttin'."

"That's not true." He eyes me. "Yuh smart, Irie. That's worth suh'um."

His words make me feel really good.

"So, what about you?" I change the subject. "Yuh neva want fi go back ah school?"

"Yeah, right." He kisses his teeth, laughing as he turns the screwdriver. "I realized a piece a paper cyaan do much fi me a long time ago. Bwoy and girl ah two different ting."

"I hear that." I nod, genuinely understanding his perspective. The sad reality is that there are no opportunities for boys like Ace—not when you grow up in the garrisons. He and Kojo dropped out of school around the same time.

"How's yuh bredda? Still ah work fi Babylon?" Ace refers to the corrupt Jamaican police force.

"Every night from sunfall to sunrise." I sigh, grateful that someone shares my perspective.

"Still cyaan believe he got caught up in all that. All the police do is terrorize di yout' dem. Not to mention di brutalize di Rastas. Yuh see wha' dem do up ah Coral Gardens?" The look on his face is tense as he refers to the bloody massacre that happened just a few years ago. The JCG government at the time told the military to bring in all Rastas—dead or alive.

"Yeah." I nod, feeling ashamed of my brother's alliance. "It's pure madness, Ace. But Kojo won't listen to me. He's too committed to his responsibility to 'protect and serve.'"

"Poppyshow." Ace kisses his teeth. "And yuh fada nuh say nuttin'?"

"Not really." I shrug. "Kojo's of age now. And him nuh really pass him place wit' Daddy. But if you ask me, the soldiers have the blood of the Rastafari on their hands."

Ace considers my words and for a moment, I feel vulnerable revealing my thoughts.

But something about Ace makes me feel understood.

"I like the way you think, Irie," Ace says. "You're different. Always were. Even when yuh was likkle."

"Blame it on Daddy." I shrug. "He plays so much conscious music around the shop, I didn't really have a choice in who I became."

"We always have a choice." Ace holds my gaze.

I smile, grateful to be understood.

"So where have yuh been, anyway?" I ask. "Yuh used to come around di shop when we were smaller, and then yuh jus' . . . stopped comin'."

"Life." He shrugs. "I got anotha job."

"Congratulations," I say genuinely. "You were always great at fixing things."

Ace laughs as if I were naive.

"It's not that kinda job, Irie. I stopped workin' trade jobs a long time ago. I need some extra cash to help Miss Salvie right now, but I'm only doin' repairs fi di short term."

"Oh. So what do you—"

"I run fi di Power Posse." He refers to the PLM street gang as his eyes meet mine. "You know. Grassroots stuff."

"Oh." I freeze.

In the ghetto, that's code for working for the Don.

I search for the right words.

"Wow, I . . . I never thought you to be the type."

"The type?"

"For violence."

It slips out.

"Irie!" Daddy calls from the front of the shop. He stands mid-conversation with the same gentleman as earlier. "Come cash dem out." He gestures to the small line that starts to form.

"Coming!" I turn back toward Ace. "I'll catch yuh lata."

I head to the front, making my way through the semi-crowded shop.

Later that afternoon, I sweep the orange tiles after the morning rush has died down. Siarah sits at the front register, aimlessly flipping through a newspaper as a charged rhythm fills the store. Daddy and Ace work out back on a busted pipe as Max Romeo's latest record comes through the speakers.

Step out of Babylon . . .

I nod to the rhythm as the thick drums flood the store, dizzying me like a mantra. The song speaks of the curse that Babylon left on Jamaica, and I meditate on the words as it hits me all at once. Babylon describes the terror.

The system.

The mass *mental* slavery that taught us we could not be free. The words of the song remedy my aching heart as thoughts swirl in my mind, overtaking me.

Why am I being forced to accept a life that I did. Not. Choose?

My heart races as grief transforms to fire. For the first time, I start to feel like God might have a purpose for me. Or at the very least, something that he really, really wants me to do. I drop the broom and zip across the store to my book bag as Siarah looks over at me.

"Where are you going, girl?"

"Soon come!" I'm laser focused as I pull out my songbook and pencil. I flip it open to the page of Junior's song and walk briskly to the back.

I have to use my voice.

I run into the small office and close the door, hoisting myself up onto the stool in the corner. I place the book onto my lap before pressing the pencil to the page. And then the second half of the song comes flowing out of me, all at once.

Tear down the institutions
Reevaluate the Constitution
We have to fight if we want to be free
We can't fear the power of who we could be
There's nothing to lose when you remember, my sister

That we are never alone, love comes in a whisper
There's nothing to lose when you remember, my brother
That creation is alive, we are all one another

I jump just as the door swings open. Ace stands in the doorway, toolbox in hand.

I freeze, caught off guard as he stares back at me.

"You should knock," I say, flustered. "I was in di middle of suh'um."

"My bad." He nods. "I'm all done fi di day. Yuh fada sent me fi put dis in here." He holds up the toolbox.

"Oh—sorry." I snap out of it, feeling guilty for my reaction. "Yuh can put it over there." I gesture to the tall cabinet in the corner.

"Cool." Ace nods calmly. He walks past, and I immediately heat up. For whatever reason, being so alone with him makes me self-conscious.

Nervous, even.

"Sorry, again. I shouldn't have reacted like that," I say awkwardly as I close my songbook. "I was jus' in the zone."

"It's all right. You're an artist, Irie. I understand." He brushes it off, placing the toolbox inside the drawer before turning around. "What were yuh writin' about?"

"Just this song." I shrug. "I sometimes sneak back here to work on music . . . you know, when di shop's not too busy."

Ace studies me, unsatisfied with my answer.

"As a matter of fact"—I begin to rise from the stool—"I should probably head back out there. Siarah freaks out when I leave her fi too long—"

"What were you *writin' about,* Irie?" Ace stops me in my tracks. "Don't run from me."

I pause, looking down at the yellow book in my hands. "Junior," I say softly. "The likkle boy who passed away."

"Big topic." Ace nods, taking me in. "Why?"

"*Why?*" I ask, unsure if he's being condescending. "Because Junior was my friend—"

"*And?*"

"And . . . and what happened to him was *wrong,* Ace. I want to use my voice."

"But *why?*" he drills into me, his brown eyes cutting. "*Why are you writin'?*"

"Ace—"

"I'm being serious," he challenges me. "*Why are yuh writing di song?*"

I'm overwhelmed as I stare back at him. "I'm *writing* because Junior's life *mattered.* I'm writing because . . . because I'm sick and *tired* of the war outside. I'm tired of di senseless killing and murder *every fucking day in Kingston.*" I'm passionate as I search myself for the truth. "I'm *writin'* because I have suh'um to say."

Ace is silent as he takes me in.

"Lemme hear it."

He's not asking.

"It's not finished—"

"Lemme *hear it,* Irie."

His eyes hold on to mine, and everything in me wants to rise to the occasion. As if by no doing of my own, I open my songbook.

In seconds, the melody pours out of me in real time.

I won't back down from this holy war
The spirit of love will fight on, and I will roar
Peace will reign and wash the sins of my brother
I have faith that we will hold hands and one day come
    home to each other

My voice curls, falling in tune with the smooth bass that bleeds through the shop walls.

For there has to be a better way, and love has to know a
  brighter day
We are the children of love who seem to have forgot
The truth of all we are and all we are not
So may peace reign throughout the nation, may love cover
  the land
And when I am weak, may Jah the Almighty take my hand
Free me from the chains of my mind and help me to see the
  truth clear
That wherever I go, freedom is near

Chills cover my body at the sound of my own cry. I'm transported back to the present moment, and as I open my eyes, I lock them on Ace. I'm nervous as I try to read the expression on his face.

"Wha' yuh think?"

"Irie . . ." His deep voice is stunned. "That was *so* powerful."

"Really?" I ask, lighting up.

"*Yuh mod?*" His mouth goes agape. "Irie, that was *wicked.*"

I blush, feeling vulnerable to have sung it out loud for the first time.

"Fuck. Yuh have a *real* gift." He looks at me in amazement. "Wha' yuh ah go do wit' it? The song?"

I shrug. "No idea."

"Yuh ever thought of performin' it?" He moves closer to me. "I have a link. I can get you in at Reggae Jamz if yuh want. They get a full crowd—"

"Wait, *what?*" My heart drops as his proposal rocks me from my seat. "*The* Reggae Jamz? The dance hall party?"

"The one and only." Ace nods. "Hosted by DJ SupaCat in Kingston."

"You're kidding me, Ace." I shake my head. "*You* can get me in there? *Fa real?*"

"I know a lot of people, Irie. It pays to be connected in di streets."

I'm stunned as his offer hangs in the air.

"It's a hard lineup to get into, but my bredjin works the doors. I can get you onstage no problem. All yuh need is an instrumental record fi go wit' yuh lyrics. Suh'um to complement di roots reggae vibes."

"But what about the age limit? Reggae Jamz is twenty-one and over."

"Nuh worry yuhself. Like I said. I got you."

I'm floored.

"Show starts around two o'clock."

"In di *mawnin'*?" My face drops. "Ace, there's no way Daddy would let me outta di house so late." The sad reality dawns on me. "Not wit' everything goin' on."

"So, don' tell him." Ace steps even closer. "You're a *grown woman*, Irie. Ah nuh like say yuh deh inna high school anymore." His eyes trace me as he lingers close. "Yuh can mek yuh own decisions now—"

"I'm in."

It bursts out of me. There's no way I could ever pass this up—not in a million years.

Ace smiles, watching me as I fight between two realities. Daddy would never let me out into the streets of Kingston at night, much less to an underground dance hall party. If the police raided the event, I could get arrested for just *being* in an environment like that.

Murdered, for being in the wrong place at the wrong time.

But what if this is my only shot?

"I'm in, Ace." The words leave my mouth again. "Me nuh know *how* me ah go get out ah di house, but I'll figure it out somehow."

Ace nods, his gaze enchanting as he makes his way toward the door.

"I knew you'd make the right choice." His tone is low, drawing me in. "Meet me out front of the venue Saturday night. But come alone. Reggae Jamz is an *exclusive* ting. Me nuh want no-body fi find out I have a connect."

"Of course not. I won't say a word." I nod, grateful. "Where is it located?"

"Old Kingston. Right down ah Lindell Street 'cross from di roundabout shop."

I tense, recalling the darker garrison.

The possibility of the danger that lurks in the night.

"Meet me out front fi two o'clock *sharp.*" He looks back at me one final time. "Zeen?"

"Yeah." I nod, nervous as ever. "Cool."

Ace makes his way through the door, closing it behind him.

I can't believe this.

All I want to do is make music that changes the world.

Music that puts an end to the pain and suffering.

Performing at Reggae Jamz is a once-in-a-lifetime opportunity. And as Jillian's words come back to me, I realize this is my chance to prove that I'm a one-in-a-million talent.

THIS is my only shot at freedom.

7

———

Jilly

"It's *poor people* music. Plain and simple."

MY mother's red lips are pursed and judgmental as we make our way through the breezy Caribbean Sea on our family yacht. She holds her big yellow sun hat, placing her drink down beside her as she sits up straighter in the wicker lounge chair. I sit on the other side of the yacht deck with my older cousin Monica as my mother continues, oblivious to my peering eyes.

"The fact is, reggae is *designed* for the poorest of the poor. Why do you think all those Rastafarians don't comb their hair?" She laughs with pompous disgust. "Complete lack of education. I tell Calvin all the time."

"But isn't that what it will always come down to?" my uncle Vincent agrees, his tone filled with self-importance. He takes a sip of his drink before addressing my father. "The lack of education will *always be* the fundamental downfall of Jamaica. Morris is capitalizing on the poor. *The weak.* The music reflects a broken system."

"Well, I don't care how many songs Bob and his little 'dread-headed friends' want to sing." His wife, my aunt Louise, scoffs. "That music can stay in the ghetto where it belongs."

"Have you seen the mockery Morris's wife is making in the papers?" Mummy asks Aunt Louise. "Afros, dreadlocks, and *turbans* on the front page of *The Gleaner*?" She refers to the Jamaican newspaper. "She should be ashamed—"

"As far as I'm concerned, Beatrice needs to keep her mouth shut, kiss babies, and cut ribbons. Not propose handouts and free education." Aunt Louise rolls her eyes. "She needs to stay out of her husband's business affairs. That's not a woman's place—"

"They're trying to brainwash our children," my father says firmly, pulling back his shades. "The whole lot of them. Tourists don't even want to come to Jamaica because the entire world knows we're headed toward a communist regime! Foreigners take Jamaicans for a joke. A *poor Black island too proud* to accept the white man's help. Tell me this, Vincent." He points his finger toward my uncle's chest. "*How the hell* can we compete on a global scale when the rest of the world sees us as a bunch of nappy-headed n—"

"Darling." My mother puts her hand on his thigh, giving it a rub. "Language."

"It's the truth!" Daddy explodes, impassioned off the dark liquid in his glass. "He's ruined our relationship with the United States!"

"A nation can *only* be as good as its leadership." Uncle Vincent nods, pacifying my father. "It's no wonder we have all these weed-smoking *lunatics* running around."

"*Ha!*" Aunt Louise cackles, tipsy off the spiked lemonade. "And the dreads are certainly *dreadful*. They look homeless!"

"They *are* homeless, Louise," my mother says as she ushers one of the maids for a refill. "I'm telling you. *Education . . .*"

Their words make me sick to my stomach.

My family is beyond ignorant and their thoughts are harmful and vile.

I can't wait to get the fuck out of here.

I bite down hard, desperate to be anywhere else as I decide

to tune them out. They have no idea what they're talking about, and truth is, none of them would know good music if it bit them in the ass. They're so out of touch it's embarrassing.

I sigh, miserable.

The hot sun blazes down as I lie out next to Monica, who sits daintily as she picks from a bowl of cascading fruit. Her bathing suit is slinkier than mine, but she drapes a pool towel around her shoulders to get away with it in front of our parents.

"*Jesus,* you would think they would tire of talking music and politics," she pouts. "It's all they've been going on about since I landed. I want my time back."

"I don't think they know how to talk about anything else, Mon," I say bitterly, shielding myself from the sun's piercing rays. "It's a little sickening."

"Can I get you ladies some more?" a deep voice interrupts.

We turn to find Monica's family butler, an older, skinny, dark-skinned man with big brown eyes, hovering over us. He smiles dutifully with a large pitcher of icy lemonade in his hands.

"The lemonade, madam."

"Oh, sure." I hold my glass up for him. "Please."

"You don't have anything else, Thomas?" Monica whines. "It's *so* not strong enough."

"This is all your parents had me prepare for you, Miss Casey."

"Ugh, fine. Pour it in." Monica flips through a colorful magazine. Her sandy-brown waves fall perfectly from her pony-tail, and the freckles that dust her porcelain skin bronze under the midday sun. "But *do not* go above the brim, Thomas," she threatens, her voice stern. "Last time you poured way too high, and I nearly spilled on myself."

Thomas nods regretfully before doing what he's told and scurrying away.

"It's like you have to spell it out for these people sometimes." Monica rolls her eyes.

I bite down, not in the mood to listen to Monica complain.

It's her first weekend back from school abroad, and my attendance this morning was mandatory. We spend most Sundays on the yacht with her family—my uncle Vincent and aunt Louise. Uncle Vincent is my father's only brother, and on Sundays, his and Daddy's favorite thing to do is talk politics and current affairs. Uncle Vincent works in the bauxite industry—Jamaica's biggest export and the Casey family's main source of wealth. It was passed down by my great-grandfather, a white British man who exported Jamaica's biggest natural resource before the island got its independence. The bauxite industry—the world's main source of aluminum—has afforded us to be one of the wealthiest families on the island—and it's how we became a household name in Jamaica.

"*God*, your parents are *so* cute," Monica interrupts my daze.

"What?" I turn to her as she gazes out.

"Your parents. Just look at them." She pushes her shades up before gesturing across the deck. My mother strokes my father's arm with palpable desperation, and it makes my skin crawl.

"Your mother is *so* loving toward your father," Monica continues. "That's exactly how I want my relationship with Charlie to be."

I look out at my parents and then back at Monica. "You're delusional. Be careful what you wish for."

"It's true, Jillian!" She laughs, clearly finding my discomfort amusing. "My parents barely show each other affection. At least your mum makes an effort. Relationships are hard work, you know," Monica says in a know-it-all tone as she flaunts her engagement ring to the sun. "I made a vow to myself that I would *always* keep the romance alive with Charlie. It's a woman's role, you know? To keep her husband happy."

She gives me a wink before naughtily sucking on a strawberry.

"Definitely didn't need that visual." I screw my face behind my shades. "And I thought you and Charlie were waiting until marriage?"

"We *were* . . ." Monica smiles coyly. "But our plans changed."

I glance over at her.

"What?" She giggles. "You try living on the same campus as your fiancé."

"Do your parents know?"

"Do I *look* insane?" A mischievous grin spreads across her face. "It's not a big deal, Jillian. Everyone's *already* doing it at school. Those foreign kids start screwing the *minute* they're out of their parents' sight. Most of the first-years aren't even virgins."

"*Really?*" I raise my eyebrows.

"Mm-hmm." Monica's green eyes lock with mine. "They do it all up in London. Drugs too. I've even tried some stuff with a few of the girls from my dormitory."

I stare back at her in disbelief. "*Monica Casey—*"

"Relax. You'll become more experimental the second you step foot on campus too. It's like you're finally free, you know? To try the things you want."

My stomach tightens as my curiosity piques. "What did you try?"

"Weed," she whispers. "And I even tried a little cocaine this one time at a party."

"*No way.*" I'm stunned as I process.

Monica smiles as she bites down, enjoying my reaction. "I'm telling you, Jill." She leans into me, her voice a whisper. "The whole purity thing is a complete myth. Sex is good, and drugs are even better . . . and when you mix them." She dramatically rolls her eyes back. "*It's a combustion of pleasure.*"

I'm speechless as she resumes her bowl of fruit.

Monica never fails to surprise me.

Growing up, she was the closest thing that I had to a sister, and being the only child, I idolized *everything* about her. She and her older brother, Eric, grew up in Jacks Hill alongside me, and I used to spend a lot of time at her family's estate. Monica always had the coolest things—the prettiest dresses, the best lipsticks, and the most interesting friends from all over the world.

She's the most popular girl I know.

If her striking looks didn't hook you, then her charismatic personality would. Her perfectly thin frame is one that Mummy is always quick to compare mine to, and her soft green eyes have a tinge of blue that everyone says looks just like the Caribbean Sea. With bright pink lips and fair freckled skin, Monica has managed to turn a lot of heads in Jamaica, simply because she can pass for a white girl. And my entire life, my parents have constantly compared me to her.

"*Stay out of the sun*," Mummy would scold when I was a child. "*You don't see Monica hanging around outside like that. Why do you think she has such a nice complexion?*"

I tense at the memories.

Monica graduated with triple honors, and now, she's off living a luxurious life abroad. We used to hang out a lot more when she lived in Jamaica, but now that she and Eric have both gone away to school, I only see her in the summertime when she comes home to visit. She attends Oxford in London with her fiancé, Charlie, and it just so happens that her first weekend back, my life blew up in my face.

"So, when are yuh headed back to London?" I ask her, making conversation.

"I just got here, and you're trying to ship me back already?" Monica takes a sip of her drink. "And since when is your accent so strong, Jillian? I go away for a few months and you sound like a full-blown yard girl."

I shrug, not in the mood.

I'm so tired of being picked apart.

"I think I might stay for the summer." Monica delicately nibbles down on a strawberry. "Charlie's working for his father this summer, so there's really no sense in me rushing back to England."

"So you'll be in town for Mummy's birthday dinner this weekend?"

"Didn't say all that." Monica makes a face. "I'll be in Negril for Tiffany's birthday. She's home from Europe, and she's having her twenty-second on the beach—"

"*Mon,*" I whine.

"*What?* Her father rented out all of Seven Mile Beach, Jill. There's no way I'm missing that to attend some stuffy political dinner with our parents' friends."

I sulk, suddenly feeling even more bummed out.

The last thing I want to do is face this night alone.

"Cheer up. You've been to a million political dinners. This one should be no different." Monica barely takes me in, checking her engagement ring for the millionth time before gesturing to the bowl of fruit in front of her. "Want some?"

"I don't have much of an appetite."

"I hope this isn't about the whole weight thing, Jillian." She looks over her shades as if she's onto me. "I think a few extra pounds look good on you."

"What?"

"I was eavesdropping." She shrugs. "Our mothers were talking on the phone last night. Something about you needing to prepare for Cambridge?" She examines my stomach. "But if you ask me, I think you look just fine."

I burn up as the insecurity crawls its way up my skin. I pull my towel up just as Mummy calls to me from across the deck.

"Jillian, I hope you're wearing sunscreen, young lady!" Her voice cuts through the wind. I roll my eyes as she turns back to my aunt and uncle. "She never listens, that girl. I keep telling her she's going to get *too dark.*"

"Those who don't listen must feel," Aunt Shirley agrees before calling over to us. "Monica, you girls stop lying around in the hot sun!"

"*Jesus Christ*. They're *so* overbearing," Monica mutters under her breath. "Come. Let's get lunch. I've been home all of five minutes and the sound of my mother's voice is already driving me *insane*." She pops up from her chair before reaching for my hand.

I peel myself up and follow her off the boat terrace.

We walk around the large wraparound deck and make our way down onto the first floor where the workers bustle about. One of the yacht maids hands us both a towel, and I trail behind Monica as she prances her way into the main-floor dining room. A giant chandelier hangs in the center, hovering above a large seating area with plush couches. The heated marble floors and wooden cabinets have all been updated, and inside, the maids prepare a buffet-style meal down a long, glass table covered in floral arrangements.

"We came down early," Monica announces to the room, pulling her shades from her hair. "I'm too hungry to wait on Daddy to stop talking." She places her shades down at the bar before strolling over to the television. The voice of a news anchor fills the room.

"*The Tivoli Gardens murders will bring the death toll to one hundred twenty casualties this week alone. Political tensions are at an all-time high, and Morris says all options are on the table as the PLM considers a state of emergenc—*"

Monica abruptly shuts it off.

"I swear to God, if I hear *one* more thing about politics—" She rolls her eyes before grabbing a piece of fried dumpling. "All the news does is focus on the negative. As if Jamaica is some poor, war-torn island."

"I guess things have been heating up with the election."

"That doesn't mean I have to spend my entire vacation *concerned* with it, Jillian," she says, annoyed. "It's all fearmongering.

They want you to think Jamaica is some ravished island to scare tourists off. It's just simply not true. Need I remind you, we're on a yacht right now."

"Touché." I take her in.

Thomas prepares us both a plate of ackee and saltfish as we settle down at the marble high-top bar underneath the massive chandelier. A gentle breeze moves through the dining room as the crystals glimmer in the afternoon sun.

"So, anyways, what's been going on with you?" Monica asks. "You've been in a strange mood all morning. I thought you would've been thrilled to be done with school."

"I am," I say awkwardly. "Just processing. The last few weeks have been a lot."

"Have you heard back from anywhere yet?"

I shake my head as my stomach knots. "Still waiting."

"*So far out?*" Monica makes a face. "You didn't get *any* early acceptance?"

"They put me on a list." I bend the truth. "So hopefully I'll know soon."

"Like, a *waiting* list?"

"Yes, Monica. A waiting list," I say frustratedly. "I'm planning for Cambridge. I imagine it won't be much longer before I find out."

"So *that* explains why you've been sulking around all morning like some kind of puppy dog." She takes another bite of dumpling. "Your face has been as sour as Mummy's lemonade."

"Sorry," I say genuinely. "I don't mean to ruin your first weekend back. I'm happy to see you." I look at her. "Really."

She smiles, grabbing my hand. "Keep your head up, Jill. The bigger schools usually take a longer time."

"Coming from the girl who got into all her top choices early."

"That's only because I graduated top of my class." Her tone is firm. "I kept telling you, if you'd studied as much as you listened to those records—"

"I was better this year," I say defensively. "I even took up extra classes, joined two more clubs. Mummy had me working with *three* tutors."

"What were your grades like?"

"They were good," I say modestly. "But with everyone applying abroad . . . the acceptance rates have gotten even more competitive."

"I wouldn't stress." Monica squeezes my hand empathetically. "You're a *Casey*—you could get into those schools off your looks alone, Jillian. What you *really* should be concerned about is who you're going to be cuddled up with at Cambridge." She giggles. "Those London boys go *mad* for us Jamaican girls, you know. Bob Marley's all the rage over there."

"I don't think I'll have to worry about that," I say dryly. "Apparently, I'm already spoken for."

"*What?*" Monica drops her dumpling mid-bite.

I nod.

"Daddy auctioned me off to the highest bidder last week," I say resentfully. "In a matter of seconds over a round of cocktails and a plate of chicken and rice."

Monica's mouth drops. "Are you kidding me, Jillian? Why didn't you say anything?"

"Because I'm not exactly *thrilled,* Monica."

"Who did they promise you to?"

"Winston Kelly's son."

"*Christopher?*" Monica's eyes go wide. "No way. He's like, the most *eligible bachelor* in Jamaica right now. Do you know how many of my girlfriends have had their eye on him?"

"Looks like I'm the lucky winner."

"Jillian, I am *so* happy for you!" Monica's eyes light up, completely missing the point. "The Kellys are *rich.* Like, *rich, rich.* That's a powerful move."

"My life isn't a chess game, Monica," I say bitterly.

"Oh, come on, it's not like you didn't know it was coming."

Monica laughs excitedly. "Your mother's been trying to marry you off since diapers—"

"I don't want to marry my *father's boss's son*," I say, my tone grim. "I mean, does it get any more *cliché*? Politics has already consumed my entire life."

"But if Christopher's father wins this election, the Kellys will be running this *entire island,* Jillian." She lights up at the idea. "And if you're looking to climb ahead in your career abroad . . . *wife of a politician* doesn't sound too bad on a résumé. Do you know how hard it is to get hired in those prestigious positions overseas?"

I slump, knowing full well she's right. "I don't want my accomplishments to be based off a man—"

"You mustn't be so proud. There's nothing wrong with accepting a little help." Monica makes a face. "Besides, you're the pickiest girl I know. You barely give boys the time of day."

"That's not true. Samuel was charming," I say, recalling the boy I dated at Christian summer camp a few years back. He's the only guy I've ever let touch me below the waist.

"The Kellys are protecting the fundamental rights of the upper class," Monica is quick to remind me. "They're going to win, and when they do, you'll want to be hanging off Christopher's arm. Trust me on that."

I sigh as I stare out the window, silently wondering if Monica could be right.

When she got promised to Charlie Thompson, the heir to a multimillion-dollar hotel chain of resorts throughout the Caribbean—it was easily the happiest day of her life. Monica never had to worry about marrying the wrong person or not getting into the best school.

The plan for her life has always been as perfect as she is.

"No more sulking," Monica orders as she makes her way behind the bar. She grabs two crystal flutes from the cabinet. "We should be *celebrating,* Jill! Your last summer in Jamaica and my first weekend back." She grabs a bottle of champagne and pops it open as the maids carry on around us—they're familiar with our routine, and it's above their pay grade to say anything about it. Monica's sea-blue eyes light up as she holds up her flute.

"To a life-changing summer."

"Cheers."

Our glasses clink.

Later that afternoon, I try calling Irie from the main-floor storage room. The line rings three times and goes without an answer. Frustrated, I make my way back into the main room, where one of the maids finishes off Monica's afternoon pedicure.

She looks up at me as I enter.

"Do you have any music, Mon?" I ask, hopeful to change my sullen mood.

"Depends on what you want to hear," she says distractedly. "I think Eric may have left some vinyls downstairs. You might be in luck."

When she finishes up, we head to the lower level.

"What type of music does Eric listen to?"

"Mostly Frank Sinatra, cabaret stuff. Popular American songs."

"He doesn't listen to reggae?" I ask as we step down to the bottom floor.

"Are you *joking*? He wouldn't be caught dead." Monica scoffs. "Especially with how political these songs are getting. Don't tell me you're still listening to that stuff?"

"From time to time." I shrug defensively. I bend down to a pile of records that sits on the floor, and I begin to sift through. "I just don't see why everyone makes it such a big deal. It's just music."

"It's the *devil's* music, Jillian," Monica says with conviction. "I draw the line at the whole Rastafarian thing. It goes against the church, and I praise Jesus. Not *Jah*."

I roll my eyes. Monica's always been a Bible thumper. "I thought you said everyone loved reggae at your school."

"Doesn't mean I follow the crowd. Bob played a concert in Brixton, and everyone went *nuts* trying to get tickets. But I don't support how reggae is riling everyone up. Especially in the ghettos. The last thing Jamaica needs is an uprising."

I consider her words, unsure of how I feel about them.

"Besides, the only thing Bob and I have in common is our love for ganja. Which reminds me." She perks up, walking across the room toward a storage closet as I scan through the vinyls in my hand—Elvis Presley, Frank Sinatra—nothing that interests me.

"Where do you hear that stuff, anyway?" Monica asks me over her shoulder. "Reggae music? RJR and JBC and the only two stations in Jamaica, and they don't play any of that garbage."

"I *buy it,* Monica," I say, cringing at her disrespect for the genre. "From one of my good friends at school . . . Irie."

"You're *still* hanging out with that girl?" Monica makes a disapproving face. "Isn't she that same brown-skinned girl you were telling me about from the ghetto? The one whose father pumps all that propaganda into Papine?"

"Mon."

"What?" Monica shrugs. "Look, I know you want to play hero to your less fortunate friends, but this is still a *white man's world,* Jillian." Monica's tone goes serious. "People like that . . . they're pawns in the game. You and I are fortunate to look . . . *a certain way.*" She shrugs, clearly alluding to our fair complexion. "Reggae music is for *poor people.* Not people like us. Honestly, it's just not our battle to fight."

"How can you even say that?" I shift, feeling uncomfortable.

"*Because* I've seen it happen at school *so* many times. Foreign kids sticking their noses in things that don't concern them. All these white kids from wealthy families turn into these radical, hippie types after one semester of pumping that propaganda into their ears." She shakes her head as she rummages through the storage closet, speaking to me from across the room. "They drop off halfway through the semester in the name of 'the revolution' *as if* capitalism doesn't make the world go round." Monica smirks as she pulls something from the storage closet and makes her way back over to me. "It's complete brainwashing."

I tense as she steps toward me and holds out her hand.

"What's that?"

"Something to help you relax. Take your mind off university admissions." She smiles coyly, opening her hand to reveal a tiny plastic baggie.

I'm immediately hit with a strong, musky smell. "*Ganja?*" I take it from her and peel the bag open. A small spliff stares back at me as my mouth drops. "How did you even *get* this?"

"I told you. They inhale it like oxygen at school." She smiles. "I've only done it a few times at parties, but it certainly makes for a good time."

I stare down at the spliff. "You expect me to smoke this?"

"Have I ever led you astray? Just put it somewhere safe. And if your parents find it, you *did not* get it from me."

I nod in disbelief.

"Come." Monica waltzes back across the room. "Let's go swim."

I roll the bag up in my towel as my pulse starts to race.

Daddy would kill me if he found it.

But somehow, my inhibitions fall away as I follow behind Monica. Rebellion sneaks its way up my spine, turning fear to excitement. For the first time ever, I *feel* something.

Something exciting.

We make our way back up to the deck, and I quickly run to hide it in my bag. I shove it down deep, zip it closed, and tuck it away before making my way across the deck to where Daddy sits with Uncle Vincent.

I interrupt them mid-conversation as Daddy puffs his cigar.

"Daddy . . . Sorry to interrupt. But I wanted to tell you I spoke to Monica about Saturday," I say politely as he looks up at me over his shades. "She just informed me she won't be able to make it . . . to Mummy's dinner."

"Ah yes." Uncle Vincent nods. "She has a friend's birthday party to attend."

"I was wondering if I might be able to invite a friend in her absence?" I keep my tone respectful as I address my father. "To celebrate Mummy, of course."

"I don't think so, Jillian—"

"Why not?" Uncle Vincent interjects. "Let the girl bring a friend her own age. I think that's a marvelous idea." He leans back in the chair, taking a sip of his drink. "It's always good to have young people engaged in the political discourse. The future of this island is in their hands, after all."

"All right. Fine." Daddy nods, giving in. "You can invite one of your school friends, Jillian. But I expect you both to be on your *best behavior*. We have a lot of important people attending . . . some of the campaign's biggest donors."

"Of course, Daddy." I beam, trying my best to hold back my excitement. "*Thank you.*"

Careful not to push my luck, I turn on my heel and head across the deck toward Monica, who prepares for a swim in the yacht pool. I bite back the smile that creeps onto my face.

Two can play my parents' silly little game.

If they want to treat me like a child, then maybe it's time I make a scene. I'm tired of being their *good little princess*. I should be able to invite whoever I choose over to the house—no matter how embarrassed they might be in front of their stuffy political friends.

IT'S time for downtown to make its way uptown.

8

Jilly

"*Jamaica's relationship with Cuba has been the strain of our relationship with the United States. But I do not believe that a small country must determine its policy based on what some powerful neighbor feels. Jamaica will not cower to the United Sta—*"

LLOYD switches off the muffled radio, interrupting Prime Minister Morris's interview. I shift in my seat, knowing full well that Daddy would never approve of him playing a PLM message in the car.

I mind my business, nonetheless.

We drive through the mountains of Jacks Hill until the lush hills become dirt roads, and soon, they turn to paved ones. The midday heat blazes through the blacked-out windows, but I say a silent prayer, just thankful to be out of the house and on my way.

Thankful that I *finally* get to see Irie today.

It's been almost two weeks, yet so much has changed. *So much has transpired in my life.* I've missed her energy more than words, and my heart races, wondering where I'll even begin. How I'll even bring myself to tell her about what's happened since the last day of school.

The car bounces, and my stomach drops.

There's no way I can tell her that I didn't get into school. It's too embarrassing, and it's not a secret I'm willing to unearth yet—to *anyone*.

Not until I figure out what to do.

And the truth is, Irie would never fully understand my situation. Her father didn't even make her apply to university at all. From what I've seen of her father, Ricky, he's way more laid-back than my parents could ever dream to be. Our realities are different. And as mine sinks in, I grow anxious about what a life in Jamaica could even hold for me beyond this summer.

I can't afford to get left behind.

Irie doesn't need a fancy degree to impress her family or a prestigious career to maintain the family name. And she most *certainly* doesn't have to deal with people telling her who she's *supposed* to be. My only hope is that I can confide in her about the engagement. And maybe, just maybe, she'll accept my invitation to Mummy's party this Saturday.

Perhaps I won't have to face the Kellys alone.

"Thank you for bringing me down, Lloyd. Truly." I'm on pins and needles as we make our way through the square. "It really means a lot."

"Don't mention it, Miss Jillian." Lloyd nods. I know he means it literally. Lloyd could lose his job if my parents knew he occasionally drove me to this part of town. Mummy and Daddy assume I get my American records from a plaza in the hills. I don't dare mention Irie. And I most certainly don't mention her father's record store.

Lloyd rounds into the back of the store as I gaze out the window at the wilted palm trees.

"I'll wait here." Lloyd looks back at me, his gray hair poking from the sides of his hat.

"Thanks, Lloyd," I say nervously. "I shouldn't be more than thirty minutes."

My hands tremble as I check my reflection in the window.
Why am I so nervous?

I dig for courage as Lloyd hops out and opens my door.

"Thanks," I say as he helps me out. I begin to make my way around to the front of the store when I notice that the back door to the shop is halfway open. I pivot, carefully making my way up the concrete steps before poking my head inside. I'm immediately hit with a heavy bass, putting me at ease as I make my way down the tight hallway.

I'm *so* grateful to be back.

I feel so free whenever I step foot into Ricky's Records, even though I've only been here a couple of times.

I'm so jealous Irie gets to experience this every single day.

"Jilly?" I spin on my heel to find Irie standing in the small hallway, shock covering her face. I beam, a rumble of laughter pouring out of me the moment we lock eyes.

"*IRIE!*" I squeal as I dash toward her.

I nearly knock us both over into a pile of boxes as I pull her in for a hug.

She feels so good.

Her brown skin glows as I pull away from her, making me envious. I joyously twirl her long braids around my fingers—she looks like an *absolute goddess.*

But everything about Irie is divine.

"Wait, Jilly . . . What . . . *what are you doing here?*"

"I told you I was comin' by, rememba?" I laugh as I stare into her brown eyes. "I kept calling the shop, but no one was picking up."

Irie stares at me, stunned.

"*Gosh,* I'm so happy to see you." I light up. "I could barely hold still in di car."

Irie's face drops, and she says nothing.

"What?"

"Nothing . . . I jus' . . . I must've forgotten." She shakes her head. "I guess I just wasn't expecting to see yuh today. That's all . . ."

"Well, I hope you're *happy* to see me at least," I say, feeling unsure.

"Of course, Jilly." Irie half smiles. "My mind's just been all ova di place—"

"*Tell* me about it." I exhale. "I wouldn't even know where to begin." I try my best to hide my awkwardness. "I meant to come earlier in the day, but Mummy *insisted* that I finish up the chess lesson she had planned fi me dis mawnin'." I roll my eyes, trying to lighten the mood. "She still thinks I have a chance to go pro. Can you believe it?"

Irie musters a smile. She looks radiant in a peach spaghetti-strap shirt and shorts that perfectly hug her body—*and I notice she's not wearing a bra.*

I flush, looking away as Bob Marley's "Satisfy My Soul" echoes through the walls.

"Cyaan lie, I love how loud yuh fada plays his music," I say nervously. "It's like it goes right through you."

"I don't think he knows any other way to play it." Irie smiles, warming up. "Yuh wan' go fi a ride?" She shifts, moving in closer. "Somewhere where it's more quiet?"

"Sure." I'm drawn into her as the music blares. "That would be really, really cool."

Ten minutes later, I sit propped up on the handlebars as Irie skillfully weaves through the streets of Papine. She glides in and out of cars like a pro as we dash through the market. Eyes are glued to us as we ride by.

As she navigates, I close my eyes and imagine what it must feel like to be her.

Free.

Unbound.

She masters every turn, anticipating every passerby. And soon, we pull up to an open patch of grass that sits just outside the square. Irie slows down before bringing the bicycle to a stop. We hop off, and I regain my balance, smoothing out my dress as Irie rests the bicycle against a large palm tree that sits off in the distance. She walks confidently, and I can't fight my smile as I follow behind her.

"That was *everything*, Irie," I say as we take a seat on the grass. "I didn't even know bicycles could go that fast."

"Really?" Irie makes a face. "That's funny. I didn't even think I was going that fast."

"Well, Mummy would've had a heart attack if she saw me. She doesn't think bicycles are for girls." I roll my eyes. "Yuh fada really doesn't mind that you ride?"

Irie shakes her head. "He was di one who taught me."

"Wow," I say, envious. "Yuh really lucky, then. I had one of the groundskeepers try to teach me once. Until Mummy decided it wasn't very ladylike."

"I could teach you sometime." Irie looks at me, her brown eyes sincere. "If yuh want."

"Really?" I ask as it occurs to me. "Maybe we could start this weekend, then? I was actually hoping to invite you to my mada's birthday party this Saturday. Daddy said I could bring a friend, and *of course* you're di first person I thought of."

The look on Irie's face is hesitant. "Me nuh know, Jilly." Irie shrugs. "I have a lot goin' on right now."

"So do I," I say adamantly. "Which is *exactly* why I need you there. Lloyd could pick yuh up and everything. I know your fada doesn't like you sleeping out, but maybe he'll make an exception this time."

Irie looks away from me.

"Come nuh, Irie." I try my best to convince her. "I need you there. I mean, what could you *possibly* have to do on a Saturday night?"

Irie pauses before looking at me. "Reggae Jamz."

My mouth falls to the ground. "Wait, *what?*" I stare at her, stunned. "Did you just say *Reggae Jamz*?"

Irie nods, fighting a nervous smile.

"Like, *the* Reggae Jamz?"

"Hosted by DJ SupaCat in Kingston." She beams, quoting the party slogan. "I got in, Jilly. *On the lineup.* A friend of mine—Ace, he does repairs at the shop—he knows one of the guys who works the doors. He said he can get me in."

"*Are you serious?*" My mouth goes agape. "Irie, this is insane."

"I know." The look on her face tells me she can hardly believe it herself.

"How did this all come about?"

"I sang him this new song I've been working on, and he thinks I have a shot. He thinks I could *actually* get a deal with SupaCat." Her eyes go wide. "But yuh cyaan say nuttin' to anyone. Ace doesn't want word getting out that he has a link—"

"Hold up, yuh wrote a new song?" I ask, overwhelmed by all the information. "When? I'm used to you running all of your new stuff by me."

"It was a spur-of-the-moment ting." She shrugs. "Ace asked me to sing for him."

"Oh." I push down a trace of envy. "Well, I'm really happy for you. This is major."

"Thanks, Jillian." Her brown eyes glisten. "I just haffi figure out how the hell I'm going to get out of the house. The show starts at 2:00 a.m., and there's no way Daddy would ever let me out into Kingston so late at night—"

"Sleep over, then." The idea dawns on me, leaving my mouth before I have time to think about it. "We could leave out from my place. Sneak out after the dinner."

The idea stuns us both.

"Jillian . . ."

"Think about it," I say, my adrenaline pumping as the plan takes me over. "You could teach me how to ride. I have two bicycles in the shed at home. After the dinner, when Mummy and Daddy have gone to bed, we could ride them to Reggae Jamz—together."

"I . . . Jilly," Irie starts. "Ace already told me not to tell anyone—"

"But it's been a *dream* of mine to watch you perform there, Irie," I say adamantly. "I can't miss it. For anything. And I also need you at this dinner."

Irie pulls on the grass, deep in thought as she considers. I place my hand on top of hers.

We lock eyes, and my stomach flutters.

"*Please.*" I stare into her dreamy brown eyes. "I really want to come with you, and I *really* need your support at Mummy's dinner."

Her brows crease, confused as I muster up the courage to tell her the truth.

"My parents arranged my marriage." The inevitable leaves me void of emotion. "To the son of a politician."

"*What?*" Shock covers Irie's face. "They set you up wit' someone?"

I nod, biting back the shame. "His name is Christopher. I found out di las' day ah school. That's why I was calling you that day."

Irie sinks. "Oh my god. Jilly, I—"

"It's fine," I say, brushing it off. "It's a common thing in political circles."

"And you can't say *no*? You should have a choice in who yuh marry."

"I wish, but that's not exactly how it works. It's my responsibility to honor my parents. What they say, goes." I lock eyes with her. "I haven't even told yuh di best part. They promised me to Winston Kelly's son—the prime minister–elect that's running against Joshua Morris."

"Wait—*what?*" Irie's entire face drops. "Stop lie—"

"Swear. Ah di truth."

"You're joking." Irie's baffled as she stares at me. "You're telling me you're engaged to *Winston Kelly's son?*"

I nod, ashamed.

"How in di *hell* did that happen?"

"My father got a promotion, and evidently, I'm di reason why." I give her a faint smile. I'm devastated as I come to grips with my reality all over again. "It's probably for the best, anyway." I sigh, the sad reality dawning on me. "Daddy's right. I would have no idea how to run the family estate on my own. I don't know the first thing about business or finances."

I couldn't even get into university, much less carry a legacy.

"Jillian. That's terrible." She shakes her head. "I'm *so* sorry." Her tone is gentle as she wraps her hand around mine and squeezes it tightly. "That's so awful. I-I don' even know what to say."

"You can start wit' sayin' goodbye to my freedom." I take a deep breath to calm my racing thoughts. "Anyway, don't feel too bad for me. I'll figure it out."

She gazes at me with empathetic eyes, and for the first time since we've sat down, I notice the bags that crease under them. I immediately feel insensitive for not noticing.

"Is everything okay?" I ask softly. "With you? Yuh eyes look . . . kinda sad."

Irie pauses, staring out at the market.

"Irie?" I ask again.

She takes a deep breath. "Yeah . . . it's just . . . there's been a lot going on in my world too."

"I'm sorry," I whisper. "How selfish of me. I hadn't even asked. How have things been for you?" I ask curiously. "I mean, besides

Reggae Jamz, of course. Clearly, yuh life hasn't blown up in yuh face like mine." I smile, trying to make light.

She's silent.

"Irie?"

"They killed Junior." Her eyes water.

"*What?*" Disbelief rocks me. "No. The same likkle bwoy who worked at the shop?"

Irie nods as tears fill her eyes.

"But . . . but we were just talking about him di odda day." I shake my head as confusion takes over. "What happened? *When* . . . Do they know who did it?"

Irie shakes her head. "Last week. Just another random killing."

"Oh my god," I say. "Where?"

Irie's jaw tenses. "One of the garrisons." She shrugs. "I don't really know di full details."

"Wow, Irie." I'm at a loss for words. Although I didn't know Junior well, I know how close she was to him. She would always talk about their love of music.

"Irie, I am *so* sorry." I shake my head as guilt creeps up. "Here I was talking all about my problems. That's *so* terrible. I . . . I didn't realize di violence was getting so bad. I mean, I hear about it on di news and stuff, but I guess election time is really making tings heat up. Daddy says the people are out of control in the shantytowns. That's where Junior lived, right?"

Irie nods, looking away.

"Wow. I really hope they find who did it."

"They won't."

"Yuh nuh know that—"

"I do." Her pained eyes meet mine. "My brotha works for di police. They're not concerned with finding the killer."

My heart breaks for her as a tear rolls down her cheek.

"Yuh all right?" I whisper as she stares off in the distance.

"I don't know, Jilly," Irie whispers before turning her head to me. "It's like, since he died . . . *di music* . . . it's *speaking* to me. *I can hear it in everyting.* It's like . . . for the first time in my life, I *truly* get what it's trying to say." Her eyes lock with mine, focused and intent. "I understand the message that's trying to come through. *From Rastafari.* And I feel like . . . I feel like I'm *finally* understanding my purpose." Irie's eyes hold mine as her tone drips with conviction. "I'm understanding what Jah sent me here to do."

Her eyes are desperate, as if needing me to understand.

"It's the *words,* Jillian . . . the words of reggae music. The Rastas are singing about the unification of mankind. The music has di power fi *transform* people. To change *consciousness.* To make things better on this island."

I can feel her intensity as we sit under the blazing sun.

"I have a voice, and I *need* to use it," she says softly. "For Junior."

I'm drawn into her as her passion radiates. I'm reminded that my favorite thing about Irie has always been her *fire*. She's not like me or any of the girls we went to school with.

Irie's always been a star.

She has the courage I wish that I were brave enough to have. And as I watch her light up, I've never wanted to be a part of her world—of her dreams—more than I have right now.

"I believe in you, Irie," I say softly as I take her hand in mine. "You're a star. I knew it from the moment we met at Arthen, and I can't wait for the rest of Jamaica to know it too."

Irie's eyes twinkle with hope as she takes me in.

"Sleep over." I gaze into her eyes. "On Saturday."

"Jilly—"

"Don't overthink it," I say boldly as I search her face. "I'm tired of following the rules. I want to do something that *matters.* I want to help you get your voice out there. And this way, yuh fada will never have to know. There's no way you'll get caught."

Irie considers, a smile creeping onto her face. "Okay. Fine." She beams. "I'll tell Ace."

And then she pulls me in for a giant hug. "I can't believe this." She laughs, excited as she buries herself into my neck. "I can't believe you're coming with me."

My body instantly rejoices as gratitude takes over.

"I love you, Jillian."

"I love you *more.*" I'm lit up as I hold her close.

Being there for Irie means everything to me. And now, I won't have to suffer through the dinner on Saturday alone. If sneaking out of the house means freedom, I'm willing to take my chances.

I would bet on Irie any day.

"I don't know what I'd do without you, Jilly."

Her words make me tingle.

For the first time in months, I'm not worried about my parents, or school, or applications, or expectations. Irie feels *so* good in my arms, and adrenaline rushes through me at the audacity of our plans. We hold each other for a moment longer before letting go.

But every part of me wants to pull her back in close.

"So, what does this make you? My manager?" Irie's whole face is radiant. My entire body heats up as her brown eyes buzz with gratitude.

"Or yuh groupie." I laugh coyly.

I start to grow nervous as my feelings for her heat up. And suddenly, I understand what she means about feeling purposeful.

"Thank yuh, Jilly . . . for doing this wit' me."

I shiver as she wraps her fingers around mine. I bring her hand to my jaw. Everything goes quiet as she strokes me, her touch

gentle and loving. I graze my lips across the center of her palm.
By accident.

Or maybe on purpose.

I feel her so deeply it lights me on fire.

"**WHAT** are friends for?" I whisper softly.

9

———

Irie

D*addy said yes.*

I'M overwhelmed by my emotions as I stand in front of an old broken mirror, adjusting the material on a yellow dress Siarah made by hand. It's almost 6:00 a.m., and she and Tandi lie on the bed behind me, dressed and ready for their day at the shop. The morning sun streams in through our bedroom window as my reflection stares back at me, in awe of Siarah's masterful craftsmanship.

Reggae Jamz is less than twenty-four hours away.

"I told yuh it would fit!" Siarah beams from the bed, even more excited than I am. "Yuh ah go look *so* good tonight, Irie. Me ah start get jealous."

"Me too." Tandi stares in amazement.

My stomach knots.

"Yuh *sure say* we cyaan come?" Tandi kids. "I'm tired of eating dry beans."

"Yuh betta be grateful." Siarah screws her face. "I'll have you know I had to fight off a lady at the market last week *just* to get my hands on that." She props herself up in the bed. "Gyal nearly tried fi tek me out ova a can of beans. There's nothing left on the shelves."

"No wonder people are so upset." I sigh. "They're hungry."

"Can yuh bring us back a slice of cake, Irie?" Tandi pouts. "The one wit' di frostin' preferably. Me hear say rich people *love* nyam dat one."

"I'll do my best, Tan," I say, already feeling the pressure to please my sisters. But I can't make them any promises. I don't want to do anything that's going to make me feel out of place tonight. The last thing I want is to be judged as some *poor girl from Kintyre* who only came for the food.

Tonight is about the music.

Under usual circumstances, Daddy would never have let me sleep out. But letting me go to Jacks Hill means one less daughter to protect from a stray bullet in the night. He knows I'll be safe—and that I'll be fed, too. I told him it was a "going-away gathering for a friend from school"—one I'd never have the chance to see again if I didn't go tonight.

Only a tiny lie.

"Do a twirl, nuh!" Tandi breaks me out of my thoughts.

I spin as they scan me up and down.

"*Wow.*" Siarah's face drops. "Irie, it's *perfect.*"

"*More* than perfect." Tandi beams. "Yuh look stunnin', girl."

I blush. "Yuh did such a great job, Siarah. Truly. I don't know what I would've done—"

"Don't mention it." Siarah leaps up from the bed to unzip me. "We're just excited for you, Irie. Yuh *deserve* to get away fi di night. It's been so hard to sleep wit' all di shooting weh ah gwaan ah nighttime."

"For real." I sigh.

"Are yuh excited?" Tandi asks.

The question sparks a wave of nerves.

I'm the worst at lying to my sisters.

"I'm jus' . . . nervous, I guess." I shrug. "I've never been up to that part of town. Or been in those type of houses. And I guess no matter how many years I went to school wit' all those rich girls, it can still mek me feel kinda small."

"Well, you're not below *anybody*, Irie." Siarah's words bring me comfort. "Don't overthink it. Dem ah go love you." She wraps her arms around me. "If anyone's got this, it's you."

"Thanks, Sisi."

But the anticipation makes my heart race.

Riding through Kingston in the middle of the night puts me at the cross of danger.

And I know I have to tell my sisters.

"I'm supposed to meet up with Ace tonight."

Siarah and Tandi stare at me in confusion.

"Wha' yuh mean?" Tandi asks.

"Ace," I say again, this time more firmly. "He's going to get me on stage . . . at Reggae Jamz."

"*What?*" Siarah's face drops. "What about Jilly's?"

"I'm going to the dinner, yes, but I'm also planning to sneak out when it's time fi bed."

My sisters' eyes go wide.

"Wait—*Reggae Jamz?*" Siarah asks. "That dancehall sound clash they promote in the shop? Isn't that, like, impossible to get into? Much less onstage—"

"Ace has connections. I spoke to him di other day at the shop. He said he can get me on the mic tonight. And if I leave out from Jilly's, Daddy won't even kno—"

"Are you *mod*?" Tandi stares at me in disbelief. "*Seriously*, Irie? *Ace*? Do yuh hear yuhself? What connections could he possibly have?"

"And how exactly do you plan fi leave outta Jilly's house?" Siarah asks.

"Jilly has a bicycle," I say, feeling attacked. "*Two*. And Kingston is only a thirty-minute ride."

"Yuh know di roads?" Siarah asks.

"Jilly does." I squirm. "And once we get out of Jacks Hill, I'll know my way from there."

I still have no idea how I'm going to tell Ace that Jilly is coming tonight.

"Lawd, Irie." Tandi makes a disapproving face. "Use yuh head, nuh. It's dangerous out there. If Daddy ever find out—"

"He *won't*, Tandi," I say sternly. "Because no one is going to tell him."

My sisters exchange a look.

"Please. I *really* need yuh support on this." I try to read the expression on Siarah's face. "Reggae Jamz is a once-in-a-lifetime opportunity. I *cyaan* pass dis up. Performing there could change my life," I try to reason with my sisters. "I really think it's my chance to be heard."

"I think yuh should do it," Siarah says.

"*Seriously?*" Tandi raises her eyebrows.

Siarah shrugs. "Think about it. There's only one way for Irie to get her voice out there. She has to start performing her material sometime."

"And you think that time is *right before an election*? It's dangerous—"

"It's *necessary*," Siarah defends. "And Reggae Jamz—that's a huge platform. Irie could get discovered."

Her words take me by surprise.

"Unu jus' mind Daddy find out—"

"I have to sing di *truth*, Tandi," I say boldly. "I can't just sit back anymore. I have to be honest about di violence. *About how it's killing all of us on the inside.*" Tears start to creep up, and I fight to push them back down. "I know it might not make sense to you. Sometimes it doesn't even make sense to me. But this opportunity . . . it feels like Junior sent it to me. It feels like he wants me to use my voice for suh'um *bigger*."

I stop, choked up by the mere thought. "I *haffi* sing what's on my heart." A tear escapes down my cheek. "I *haffi* believe in my purpose."

"But yuh already have a purpose, Irie," Tandi's eyes water. "*Being our sister*. And we can't afford to lose you. Not to this war."

Her words crawl up my skin as the room goes silent.

"She's going," Siarah says firmly, looking me straight in the eye. "If anyone has a chance at makin' a change, it's Irie."

"Siarah." I feel my nerves subside as relief washes over me.

"The world needs yuh voice, Irie. So jus' go and sing. Don' worry about Daddy or *Tandi*." She playfully nudges our little sister. "I'll tek care of everything, jus' . . . jus' *sing yuh heart out tonight*. And head straight back to Jilly's when yuh done."

I sink into relief as a smile takes over my face.

"I promise," I whisper.

ELEVEN hours later, Lloyd pulls up out back of the shop.

I say a quick goodbye to Daddy and my sisters before heading outside to find Lloyd already waiting in an all-black suit. His dark skin glows as he greets me with a warm smile. I try my best to shove my insecurities down.

The shiny black limo looks out of place.

"Good evening, madam." He tips his hat.

"Hello, Lloyd," I say awkwardly. "It's really nice to meet yuh . . . *officially*, I mean."

"The pleasure is mine, dear." He smiles politely, opening the door. I slide onto the warm black interior, smooth and luxurious to the touch.

Wow.

I fiddle with my dress as Lloyd makes his way into the front seat. I reach into my handbag and pull out the ruby bracelet

Jillian gave me, clipping it on for the evening as Lloyd hops in the front seat.

"All set?" he asks, glancing at me in the rearview.

"Sure." I smile politely.

I try my best to relax as we drive out of Papine Square.

Lloyd doesn't say much, and neither do I. After a few minutes pass, he turns up the radio and dials it to the news channel. Joshua Morris's voice moves through the car.

"Three hundred years of slavery and colonialism have left Jamaica a nation of very few haves and many have-nots. For a long time, Jamaica has permitted a small, privileged group to have a really good time in life. But the PLM is going to change that by laying the foundations of an egalitarian society."

I look out the window to distract myself. I'm surprised to hear him listening to such a radical message, and my mind starts to wonder what he really thinks of Jilly's family and their politics. But soon, he changes the station to RJR, and Teddy Pendergrass's voice comes through the car speakers.

Wake up, everybody . . .

I turn my gaze out the window as we begin the trek into the tropical and robust forested mountains of Jamaica. The roads bend and curve the higher up we get, and as I gaze out, I realize I've never been so high up in the hills before. Everything looks so different compared to down below.

The blood doesn't stain the leaves like in Papine.

Forty minutes into the drive, it's clear we've entered some type of rural community. Lloyd makes a right turn at a traffic light, and my mouth falls open.

Giant mansions are *everywhere.*

They scatter along the sides of the hills, all nestled behind bushes, each one bigger and more luxurious than the last. I shift to get a better look, and my mouth falls agape.

The estates are pristine white and immaculate.

My heart begins to race.

"This is her area?" I reluctantly ask Lloyd.

"Yes, madam," Lloyd says dutifully. He makes a right up a long, winding driveway surrounded by luscious palm trees. Lloyd approaches the giant iron gates, winds down the window, and presses the buzzer. My eyes dart from Lloyd, to the house, and back again.

There's no way in hell this is Jillian's house.

"Welcome to the Casey estate," Lloyd says calmly, pulling through the gates as they slowly open. My eyes instantly water as we drive down another long, winding path. I've never seen anything like it in my life.

Nothing even close.

The all-white estate is majestic, with brown roofing and more windows than I've ever seen on a house before. It's nestled by a handful of looming and lush palm trees that decorate the front yard. Four giant pillars sit out front of a large stairway and an even bigger veranda.

The front steps alone are two times the size of my house.

Breathe, Irie. I try to calm my nerves. *This doesn't change anything.*

But in a split second, I can feel my courage disappear. I'm insecure as I look down at Siarah's handwoven dress.

Relax, I tell myself as we drive through the front yard—it's an entire forest in and of itself. I notice a few men with dark black skin working vigorously, cutting and watering the perfectly green grass—*that continues for miles.*

Sweat drips down my thigh.

"We've arrived," Lloyd says as if it weren't already obvious.

But I can't pick my mouth up off the car floor.

I always imagined Jilly's house being big, but never in a million years did I think it was going to be this . . . *regal.*

The mansion sits nestled right at the edge of the mountain, with other mansions tucked off in the mountains in the distance. From where Jilly's house is positioned, I can see a panoramic view of the island. I push down panic as Lloyd hops out and makes his way to the trunk to grab my bag. I take a deep breath.

And then another one.

You can do this, Irie.

But the sight of Jilly's estate confirms exactly why it's taken me so long to come up here. In the shadows of her massive, looming estate, I feel completely small and out of place.

Just like how I felt at Arthen.

I say a silent prayer as Lloyd opens my door and offers me his hand.

"Thank you." I tremble as my feet touch the walkway. I reach for my bag in his hands.

"Don't worry," he says kindly, clearly detecting my angst. "I'll bring it up to the room for you, madam. You just focus on having a good time."

I nod as we make our way up the steps.

Just before Lloyd can reach for the door, it swings open, and there stands Jilly—bubbly and radiant as ever. She's effortlessly beautiful in a white flowy housedress as she jumps for joy, her soft-pink toenails freshly painted.

"*OHMYGOSH*, Irieee! You're here!" she squeals, throwing herself into my arms. She smells incredible—*like warm vanilla and fresh fruit.* "I cyaan believe yuh *actually* reach!"

Jilly squeezes me tight as Lloyd makes his way inside.

"Hey, Jilly." I'm relieved as I hug her back. I try my best to relax as I breathe her in.

"You look *really* good," she whispers into my ear.

"You too." My stomach flutters. "You look really beautiful."

She slowly peels away and takes another look at me, and for a second, I'm taken aback by her beauty. Her eyes sparkle, and her skin glows under the evening sun. Her long brown curls fall down her back and the majestic palm trees blow softly in the wind behind her, framing her body like a photograph.

Suddenly, I feel peaceful.

Relaxed.

"Yuh wearing di bracelet." She lights up when she looks down at my wrist. "It looks *so* good on you, Irie, especially against your skin," she tells me for the second time.

"Thanks." I giggle as she takes me in. "My best friend has great taste."

"How was di ride?"

"It was nice. Lloyd was lovely, and he played really nice music."

"He's the best, nuh true?" Jilly beams as we stand in the doorway. I can't help but notice how different it feels to see her in her own environment.

Almost as if I'm seeing all of her for the first time.

"I couldn't sleep all night." She shakes her head and her curls tousle. "I thought *for sure* yuh might cancel las' minute. I even thought of calling di shop again." Her smile is infectious, and it bubbles through my entire body. "But I'm so glad yuh came."

"I'm so glad yuh invited me."

There's a spark between us, and somehow, deep down, I know she feels it too. Just the sight of Jilly lights me up. Just the *feel* of her breaks me down. I lock eyes with my best friend, and somehow all is right in the world.

"Come." She grabs onto my hand. "I'll show yuh inside."

I muster up all the courage I have and follow behind her.

10

———

Irie

"Holy—"

IT escapes me in a whisper as I enter through the double doors.

I'm in awe as my sandals touch down on the shiny, all-white marble floors. I've never been inside a house this big in my entire life. It takes everything I have to push down the anxiety that threatens to take me under—that screams I don't fit in.

Jillian Casey is more than just rich.

She's wealthy.

The gleaming white floors *sparkle* for miles, and the entrance-way is nothing short of grandiose. Giant white walls surround me, and as I scan the massive space, Jilly closes the door behind me. A long flight of oak stairs winds in front of us, and I glance in both directions to find spotless white cream carpet—the *plushest* carpet I've ever laid eyes on.

I make a mental note to tell Siarah and Tandi.

They're never going to believe this.

"Amala just cleaned up for the party," Jilly says as I tuck my shoes into the corner. "So everything's extra shiny."

"Who's Amala?"

"Our maid."

I cringe, put off by the term. When Morris was elected prime minister, one of the first things he did was implement that housekeepers in Jamaica were no longer to be called *maids* but *domestic workers.*

I guess Jillian didn't get the memo.

I follow her down the long hall, glancing into rooms to find more domestic workers running about and preparing for the evening. As we continue down, my eyes graze the portraits that hang on the big white walls. I stop to analyze the array of family photos, and it dawns on me how little I know about Jillian outside of Arthen.

Outside of the world we built together within those four walls.

"Mummy's always changing the photos. She redecorates. That's her thing." Jilly gestures to the tropical oil paintings that line the opposite side of the wall. "She thinks she has a good eye." Jilly smirks as I take in the fruit painting. "And if she asks you, you think so too."

"It's beautiful." I try to shrug off my anxious thoughts. I could only imagine the look on her mother's face if she knew I lived in a zinc-roof home off a dirt road in Kintyre.

"It's *imported,*" Jilly corrects. "I keep trying to tell her the importance of supporting local artists. Jamaicans will pay *millions* for art that comes from halfway around the world, but they won't pay a dollar for the art that comes from the Rasta on the roadside."

"Oh." I nod, trying my best to wrap my head about her reality. "Yeah. That's true."

"Come. I'll bring yuh to meet Mummy dearest." She continues, whispering as I trail behind her, "And when yuh say happy birt'day, nuh badda ask how old she turn. It's forty-three, but she always ah put suh'um different pon di cake."

"I'll be sure not to ask." I smile.

We enter a giant, bright kitchen with oak cupboards and

marble floors. For the third time, I'm forced to pick my mouth up off the floor. Just like the front, everything is tiled and gleaming. Balloons are everywhere, and at the back of the kitchen are floor-to-ceiling windows that overlook a *massive* backyard where green grass continues for *miles*.

Standing over the table with her back to us is Jillian's mother. She fiddles with a bouquet of flowers as we make our way into the kitchen. Her skin is even fairer than Jilly's, and her dark curls have been permed pin straight. She wears a soft-pink lipstick, and her green eyes instantly fall on me as she turns around.

"Mummy, this is—"

"Irie," she says through tight lips. "So you're the one always calling the house during the school year."

I freeze. Her English is formal, and I instantly stand up straighter.

"You're the only one of Jillian's school friends I haven't met as yet."

"It's really nice to meet yuh, Mrs. Casey." I smile eagerly. "Happy birthday."

She scans me up and down, a disapproving look on her face. I fight the urge to shrink as her eyes run along the stitching of my handmade dress.

"I suspect you had a nice drive up?"

"Yes, thank you. I did," I say, trying my best to shove down my accent. "Lloyd was great. The drive didn't feel too long or anyting."

"Hm." Her eyebrows furrow. "And where are you from again, exactly?"

"Papine." I bend the truth. "Near the market."

"Papine?" Her tone is short as she looks to Jilly. "I didn't realize you had Lloyd driving all the way out there, Jillian?"

"I told you it was Kingston—"

"But you didn't say *Papine*," she scolds.

Her eyes are cutting as she turns back to me.

"Has Jillian shown you around as yet?"

"No. Not as yet, but I'm looking forward to it," I say awkwardly. "Yuh home is so beautiful. I've neva seen anything like it."

"I imagine." She smiles, patronizing, before turning to Jillian. "Guests will be arriving around seven-thirty, Jillian, so hurry up and get ready. Your father and I expect you girls downstairs on time tonight, am I understood?"

"Of course, Mummy," Jilly says begrudgingly as she grabs onto my arm, turning to go. "I'm going to change and show Irie to the garden. We'll be waiting out back."

Her mother opens her mouth to respond just as the phone rings. She turns to answer it, and Jilly uses the opportunity to lead me across the kitchen. We make our way to the big white fridge, where Jilly grabs two bottles of Ting. As the fridge lights up, a colorful array of options stare back at us.

It's fully stocked, with more food than the supermarket.

"If you'll excuse us, Mummy." Jilly closes the fridge as I catch my breath. Mrs. Casey gives us a dismissive wave as I follow Jilly out of the kitchen.

"Yuh all right?" she whispers to me.

"Yeah. Of course." I try to shake it off, not wanting to overthink the interaction as I trail behind her. We reach the entryway and begin to make our way up the winding carpet stairs. In the center, a massive chandelier dangles from the top-floor ceiling. The iridescent crystals rattle gently from the evening breeze as I round the steps behind Jillian.

I can't even imagine what something like that is worth.

"I'm really sorry about her," Jilly says remorsefully, keeping her voice low. "Mummy can be kinda cold sometimes. She hates gettin' old. She cyaan *stand* the idea of Daddy looking at younger women. I've been to enough parties wit' dem to know."

I smile, trying my best to be polite.

"Just try not to tek anything personally tonight."

"Okay." I breathe deeply. "Sure."

Jilly approaches a large wooden double door at the end of the hallway, and using one hand to balance the drinks, she pushes it open.

"Welcome to ma room."

There's no way.

I enter the space first as she closes the doors behind us.

"*Jilly . . .*" Her name falls out of my mouth. I can't believe my eyes.

Her room is a dolly house brought to life.

I step onto her plush cream carpet as I take in the entirety of the space. The walls are soft white, and light pours into the room through a floor-to-ceiling window that overlooks the enormous front yard. Her bed is decorated with frilly cream sheets, and it's bigger than any bed I've ever slept on. A flash of envy passes through me as I take in the entirety of the space.

Jillian stands in the center with the two icy bottles of Ting in her hand.

"Yuh like it?" she asks, her voice hopeful.

She can't be serious.

"Jilly . . ." I'm genuinely at a loss for words. "It's *stunning.* All of it." I glance around the room at her childhood photos, trophies, and medals that line the shelves. Over her bed is a cursive sign of Jamaica's National motto—"*Out of Many, One People.*"

I'm floored.

"I had no idea yuh room was so nice . . . or so *big.*"

"Thanks, Irie." She lights up. "I'm not really used to havin' people over."

"Seriously?" I look at her, surprised. "I would think yuh had lots of people come by. What about the girls from school?"

"Not really." She shrugs. "No one really comes ova to my house, except for my cousin Monica. The one I told yuh about."

"Who goes to school in London?" I remember briefly.

Jilly nods. "And she's gone for most of the year, so I'm usually here alone."

"Wow." It dawns on me. "So, it's really just you and yuh parents in this big house?"

"And Amala. Our maid I was tellin' yuh about earlier." Jilly repeats the term as she smiles faintly. "Downside of being an only child, I guess. Most days I make my own fun." Her eyes are sad as she looks to me. "Yuh lucky yuh have so many sisters."

"Yeah." I nod empathetically as she passes me one of the icy green bottles. "Thanks."

I crack it open, admiring her freshly made bed behind her. Long white curtains drape down either side—a giant princess canopy. I tinge with jealousy as Jilly pops open her Ting.

"Cheers, Irie," she says as our eyes meet. "To yuh big break tonight. And all yuh dreams comin' true."

My stomach flutters. "Cheers," I repeat softly.

Our bottles clink. I'm brought back to the present moment as we hold each other's gaze.

A feeling of giddiness rushes through me, and I look away, unsure if my nerves are because of her or the fact that I'm performing at Reggae Jamz tonight.

"It's kinda strange seeing each other outside of school, isn't it?" She blushes. "Or even seeing you outside of di shop. It's like I'm seeing a different side of you. I really like it."

"I like it too." I blush, knowing exactly what she means.

We're both quiet as we take each other in.

I break the moment as I turn to gaze at an array of photos that sit over her dresser.

"Where was this?" I make my way over a group photo of girls in lavish debutante dresses—all of them fair-skinned of different races, none of them full Black.

They sit in a row with wide smiles on their faces.

"Church camp," she says, a trace of disdain in her face. "It's where I got most of these silly awards." She refers to the trophies that line the shelves. "Mummy and Daddy used to make me go every summer."

"Wow. Church camp? I've neva even heard of that. What would you do there?"

"Praise di Lord." Jilly giggles. "Learn about Jesus and how he died for our sins . . . practice proper etiquette, like how to hold a knife and fork. How to be properly courted by a boy . . . yuh nuh—pretty much just grooming on how to be a lady."

"Sounds dreadful," I say earnestly. "Daddy wouldn't let me or my sisters within two miles of a church."

"*Really?* He nuh believe in God?"

"He does, but he subscribes to his own teachings. Mostly musical ones."

"Wow. So, you've never been to church?"

"Only a few times. But we were a lot younger; Mummy used to bring us when we were small. But I don't think Daddy appreciated it very much. He always said she was brainwashing us with the tools the colonizers left behind."

"Lawd. Strong words." Jilly takes it in. "Yuh neva talk about her much . . . yuh mada."

"Not much to say." I shrug. "She left us when we were really small."

"I'm sorry—"

"Nuttin' fi sorry about." I cut her short, not in the mood for anyone's pity. "I have my fada, so it worked out." I shrug off the conversation as I walk over toward the window.

I never discuss Mummy with anyone but my sisters.

"Well, I'm here if yuh eva want to talk about it—"

"I don't, Jilly," I say quietly out the window. "She's been gone for a while, so we're all used to it. It's old news."

Jilly nods, taking the hint.

"I'm really sorry I took so long to come up here, though," I say, eager to change the subject. "I know you've been wanting me to come ova fi ah likkle while now."

"I'm just happy yuh finally made it up." She smiles, her tone becoming shy. "It really means a lot to me to have yuh in my space. I was starting to think maybe yuh didn't want to hang around me outside of school or suh'um."

"Yuh felt that way fa real?" I ask her, stepping closer.

"After a while." She shrugs. "I wondered if maybe it was me, if maybe yuh didn't value di friendship the same way I did." She shrugs awkwardly. "It was hard not to take it personally, yuh know? All the rejection."

"I'm really sorry," I say softly. "I didn't mean to make you feel that way. Truly. I just . . . I guess I was just afraid."

"Afraid?"

"Me nuh know." I shrug as I look around her room. "To feel out of place or suh'um. Yuh house is *beautiful,* Jilly, and your world here . . . it's just so different than mine." I choose my words carefully, hoping she understands. "But it's really nice to finally be here. To see yuh room and . . . where yuh live."

Jilly's eyes dance at my admission.

"I understand that." Jilly's eyes hold mine with empathy. "I know our lives might be a likkle different, Irie, but I'm just glad that yuh finally came." She moves in closer. "It feels really good to spend some time alone with you for once." Her eyes search mine. "And I'm sorry again about my mada . . ." She shakes her head, embarrassed. "Hopefully now yuh see why I needed yuh support tonight."

"Nuh worry yuhself," I say delicately, not wanting to harp on it. "I'm here for you, Jillian. Always will be."

Her eyes trace my lips as my body tingles.

Whoa.

I push the feeling back down.

"By the way." She smiles as she makes her way across the room. "I have suh'um fi you."

She reaches into her closet and pulls out a long, flowy white dress. "Yuh look *beautiful,* of course," she says as she holds it up.

"But I thought maybe you could wear this tonight. There'll be a lot of eyes on us. Yuh might feel more comfortable."

I'm stunned as I look down at my dress. "There's suh'um wrong with what I have on?"

"No, no—not at all, Irie." Her eyes are apologetic. "You look radiant . . . *truly*. It's just, I know how Mummy and Daddy stay. And these dinners can be a likkle . . . *extra*."

"Oh." My stomach drops. "Okay. Yeah, sure."

I take the fancy dress from her hands, trying my best not to take it personally. "You sure you don't mind me wearing yuh dress? It's so fancy."

"Are you kidding?" She looks at me. "I'd be honored, Irie."

"Okay." I place the bottle of Ting on her dresser. "Can you unzip me?"

"Of course." She makes her way over to me, and I turn around. Her hands are cold from the bottle as she undoes the zipper. I can feel her fingers linger, and it sends a shiver up my spine.

The dress falls to my ankles as Jilly watches me change.

"So, how yuh feelin'?" She pulls me out of my daze. "Are yuh ready fi tonight?"

Reality sinks in.

"As I'll ever be," I say earnestly. "I found an old instrumental riddim at the shop to perform to last night. I think it fits nice wit' di lyrics I have, but me nuh know," I confess. "I'm jus' feelin' a likkle nervous, I guess. About di whole sneaking-out ting. And lyin' to my fada . . . and performing in front of an audience for the first time." I unravel as the thoughts overwhelm me. "I just want my lyrics to be right, yuh nuh? I want it to resonate wit' people. I was up all night, tossin' and turnin'—I couldn't stop thinkin' about the words and whether or not they were ready." I slip into the dress as I turn to look her in the eyes. "Whether or not *I* was ready."

"*Yuh bawn ready, Irie.*" Jilly smiles as she grabs my hand. A rush of energy shoots through my entire body. "It's normal to be nervous. It just means that yuh care. The best artists do." She gives my hand a gentle squeeze.

I turn around, my back facing her.

"You're not in this alone," she reassures me, speaking softly into my ear as she takes the zipper in her hand. "You're going to be *amazing* tonight. I have no doubt everyone is going to love yuh music just as much as I do."

Her words bring me peace.

"Just mek sure yuh rememba me after yuh become a superstar." She's giddy as she zips me up.

I turn toward the mirror, mesmerized by my own reflection.

The dress looks exquisite.

"Wow." Jillian admires me in the mirror. "You're so gorgeous."

My tummy flutters. "It's your dress—"

"But it looks *way* better on you." Her eyes light up. "You're so beautiful, Irie. I don't even think you realize."

We lock eyes in the mirror as Jilly's hand lingers on my shoulder.

"I betta get cleaned up." Jilly moves her hand, and my heart sinks. "Yuh haffi teach me how fi ride that bicycle before the dinner guests arrive."

"You'll learn fast, I'm sure," I say as I watch her move about the room. I turn to examine her shelves, immediately making my way over to her record collection. I'm like a kid in a candy store as I approach, but I'm surprised when I find that all the vinyls are mainly Christian records and Top 40 American music.

"Since when yuh listen to so much worship music?"

"It's the only way Daddy would agree to getting me a new record player." Jilly gestures to her other dresser. I'm at a loss for words when I spot the sparkly record player.

I rush toward it. "May I?"

"Of course." She smiles.

I run my fingers along the smooth oak—a much newer version

than the one Daddy has. "I didn't even know they sold this model in Jamaica."

"They don't. Mummy and Daddy got it on a trip overseas. As an early graduation gift."

"That's really nice of them," I say, pushing down my envy. "How come yuh nuh seem too excited about it?"

"Because all their gifts come wit' a *contingency*. My hand in marriage being one." Jilly shrugs, her tone deflated. "Besides, it's not like I can even play di songs me wan' fi play."

"They don't let yuh play reggae music?"

"Yuh mussi mod." She looks at me as if I'm crazy. "Daddy and Mummy are *devout Christians,* Irie. Jah is not exactly their cup of tea."

I'm confused as she reaches under the dresser and pulls out a key. She proceeds to unlock the bottom cupboard, opening the door to reveal mountains of vinyls stacked on top of each other. Every record she's ever bought from Daddy's shop.

Piles of reggae classics, all tucked away.

"Wait—yuh keep them all *down there*?" I'm shocked as I move closer.

"It's a crime. I know." Jilly slumps as we sit down on the carpet. I pull out the records, in shock as I sift through them.

"I'm not allowed to play reggae when my parents are home," Jilly explains. "Daddy says him nuh want that type of sound blastin' through di house."

"That's silly—"

"That's *politics*," she corrects. "To my fada, reggae might as well be PLM music."

"What?" I make a face, looking up from the Burning Spear record in my hand. "How can reggae be PLM? Music is universal—"

"It promotes *communism*, Irie," she says in a matter-of-fact tone, and it takes me off guard. "Yuh know—freedom of di people, emancipation from the government . . . Daddy *hates* that type of stuff. Especially since it aligns wit' Morris's whole socialist propaganda."

"Socialist propaganda?"

"You know, poor people wanting to rise up." She shrugs as if it were obvious. "Daddy works in *government.* He's not exactly thrilled about poor people wanting to overthrow it."

Her words jolt me.

"The PLM is trying to make things *equal* for people, Jilly . . . give everyone a fighting chance. And reggae music isn't about *socialism or communism*—" I feel myself growing defensive. "It's about peace and . . . love consciousness. *Our purpose as a Black race.* It's about unity for all of mankind—"

"Of course I know that, Irie." Jilly's tone grows defensive. "But try tellin' that to my parents. To them, it's pretty much the devil's music."

"Wow." Her words rattle me. "That's *so* foolish. They're missing the whole point of the revolution." I shake my head. "We learned Christianity from our colonizers, Jilly—and they *enslaved* Black people. Daddy says the entire monarchy made trillions off the slave trade." The mere thought infuriates me as I repeat what Daddy's taught me over the years. "Reggae music is about *freeing ourselves* from mental bondage. *Remembering* who we are as African people."

"I guess so." Jilly shrugs, clearly not wanting to get into it. "But some people see it differently, Irie. Yuh cyaan convince everybody."

Her dismissive response takes me aback. "So yuh cyaan play *anyting* conscious?"

"Not unless it's imported from the United States."

"What about Bob?"

"Yuh mod? *Especially* not Bob Marley."

Her words stun me. I knew Jilly's parents were Christians,

but I had no idea they would be so against reggae—especially since Jilly buys so many conscious records from the shop.

"It just all seems silly. Reggae music is about *love*," I say to her, still not fully understanding. "When the Rastaman sings, that's what they're singing about. That's *who* they're singing to. Jah is Love—"

"Irie." Jilly looks at me as if I couldn't be serious. "Daddy nuh business wit' *none* ah dat. According to him, reggae is nuttin' more than poison for poor people to ingest."

Her words gut me.

"Not everyone is as lucky as you." She offers me a half smile. "Yuh fada teaches yuh a lot about all that stuff . . . *African consciousness*. I can only listen to that type of music when my parents go off to bed." Her eyes lock with mine. "I usually just fall asleep with it playin' on low."

I nod, resentful as I take in how far my reality is from hers. While Jilly's drifting off to the sweet sounds of reggae music from her princess canopy bed, I'm awake listening out for the sound of stray bullets.

I glance down at the records in my lap, and on top of the pile, Max Romeo's latest release—"Uptown Babies Don't Cry"—stares back at me.

The irony of the title is haunting.

I sift through the pile, burying the title with another record.

"Well, at least you have options." I muster a smile as I continue to flip through her stash. It's not lost on me that *a whole world of reggae classics*—emotion, activism, pain, and immense suffering—have just been locked away in the bottom of her chest of drawers.

Played in secret only when she's ready to be sung to sleep.

I glance up at Jilly, who begins to put the records back. I'm captivated as I watch her. Her world is *so* different from mine, her reality so far away. She's unaware of my gaze the same way she's unaware of the polarity of our lives. But I'm mesmerized at how she can exist so far beyond me.

Only an hour's drive away.

Her light eyes and fair skin shield her, like a cloak, from the war terrorizing my home. Even on the surface, Jillian and I are worlds apart. I stare up at the *Out of Many, One People* sign over her bed—suddenly unsure of how the national motto *actually* makes me feel.

"Yuh all right?" Jilly looks back before moving in closer to me.

It feels too close.

Or maybe not close enough.

"Yeah." I breathe slowly, trying to make sense of all the things I feel for her at once. I'm overwhelmed by resentment, anger, envy . . .

Lust.

They all swirl around inside my chest as Jillian reaches for my hand. Her fingers linger, and she gives me a tender smile before she moves to stand back up. She makes her way over to the closet and pulls out a beautiful yellow party gown that sits on a hanger. And then she casually slips out of her housedress. My breathing intensifies as the cotton fabric hits the floor. She stands half naked, in a fitted satin bra and matching panties.

I flush as my eyes trail along her breasts.

"Mek yuhself at home. I'm going to have a quick shower." She bats her lashes before turning around. "And then we can head out back to the garden before di guests arrive."

"Yeah, cool." I tremble. "Sounds like a plan."

"Oh, and Irie—" She pauses. "Tonight at dinner, do you mind not mentioning yuh fada's store?" Her tone is apologetic as she turns back to me. "I don't want my parents knowing I drive so far out . . . you know, to buy my music."

"Oh. Sure," I say, taken aback. "No problem."

She smiles, making her way into the private all-white bathroom.

Play it cool, Irie.

But as I sit alone in her massive bedroom, surrounded by her trophies and pictures of her perfectly crafted life, I can't help but wonder what other secrets Jilly keeps hidden at the bottom of her drawers.

WHAT other parts of herself she hides away.

11

———

Jilly

I'm overly aware of myself.

MY every word. My every move. I've daydreamed about having Irie over for so long, and I wrestle with my excitement as my feelings toward her grow muddled. *Complicated.*

Irie makes me nervous, kind of.

Butterflies dance in my tummy. I've always thought she was beautiful, but somehow seeing her all dressed up does something different to me. It makes me feel things.

Things that I know a best friend shouldn't feel.

"Yuh ready?" I ask casually as I lead her out of my bedroom. We go back down the hallway toward the kitchen, our fingers wrapped around each other's. We swing hands like friends, but it feels so much better than that.

It feels like so much more.

Irie's presence calms the anxiety I have around seeing the Kellys tonight. I feel more protected with her by my side. We're stronger together—a united front. And our plan to go to Reggae Jamz tonight gives me something else to think about—something other than Christopher or how I'm going to tell my parents I didn't get into university.

Right now, I have Irie's attention.

And she has mine.

I slowly peel my fingers from hers as we approach the kitchen, unsure of who could be around the corner. The maids run to and fro, preparing for the party as the smell of food fills the air. I guide Irie toward the back doors to outside.

"This is the backyard," I say as I slide open the glass door.

Irie steps out, and I trail behind her onto the vast, green grass. I watch as she marvels at the stream of coconut trees that line the landscape. As the evening sun sets over the hills, I'm reminded that my backyard is the only part of my house that brings me *true irie*.

I smile at the irony.

"Oh my god, *Jillian.*" Irie's face lights up. She spins around on the grass, her braids flying as she twirls. "Yuh have *so* much space to run up and down!" She laughs, her dress swaying as she stumbles. "I would neva want to leave!"

"You'd be surprised." I give her a small smile. "Come. I'll show yuh di garden."

I lead her across the yard and toward the garden entryway.

Once we're out of sight from the house, our fingers lock again.

I keep my gaze focused ahead, praying she doesn't notice my heart beating faster than usual. I try to reason with the arousal that drifts its way up my evening dress.

But I can't fight it.

I pulse against my will as my body starts to crave more of her. The setting sun hovers over us as we walk in a delicate silence, both of our breaths bated. My heart beats so loud I'm almost sure she can hear it, and soon, her soft brown fingers fondle mine.

I turn my attention to the rustling trees.

It's all I can do to keep from combusting. Irie's energy is a spell that draws me in, making me feel small and seen, both at the same time. As the birds chirp sweetly in the distance, I start to wonder if there could be more between us.

If she could possibly be feeling what I am right now.

I look up to Irie so much.

Her confidence.

Her courage.

Her talent.

And it makes me feel good that she's impressed by me—by the seeming mundanity of my life. Irie makes me feel important. *Desired.* And as her hands hold mine, I feel invigorated.

Made anew.

Far from the house, we approach the large fountain where the bicycles rests. A flutter ripples through me as our hands peel away from each other's.

Neither of us wanted to let go.

"So, this is it." I smile humbly as I gesture toward the pink bicycles that lean next to the fountain. "The bicycles I could neva manage to ride." I flush, slightly embarrassed.

Irie examines them, ringing the gold bell.

"The spare was for Monica." I gesture to the other bicycle.

"They're perfect." She looks at me. "You'll learn in no time."

"Here's to hope." I make my way over, carefully hoisting up my dress before draping one leg over. Irie watches me as I sit down onto the warm leather seat.

I glance back at her.

"Yuh *sure* it's a good idea to learn in yuh pawty dress?" she asks me, a doubtful look on her face. "I don't know if yuh mada would appreciate that too much."

"Mummy doesn't appreciate a lot of things." I roll my eyes. "And if I took inventory, there'd be no life left to live."

"Okay." She reluctantly braces the bicycle for me. "But if yuh drop down, *please* don' tell yuh mada this was my idea."

"Ye of likkle faith." I giggle.

Irie leans in closer, steadying me on the bicycle. "Yuh ready?"

I nod, suddenly a fit of nerves. I haven't tried to ride in years.

I pedal my feet in slow strokes, keeping my focus on the hibiscus bush in the distance as Irie walks beside me. She holds the seat as we move farther down the path and deeper into the garden.

"Riding is really all about balance." Irie's focus is locked in as we disappear into the garden. "Which is really and truly an internal ting. Yuh just have to feel into it." Her breathing becomes slow and rhythmic as she walks beside me. "That unknown space inside yuhself. Allow it to become bigger." Irie starts to ease her grip on the handlebars, and I immediately start to shake.

"I'm telling yuh, Irie." I brace my feet on the ground. "I'm no good."

"Lie yah tell." She steadies the bicycle again. We lock eyes for a moment, and a flutter moves through my entire body. I feel hot as I refocus on the task at hand.

"You're doing amazing, Jilly," she whispers. "You got this."

I try again, and soon, I start to get the hang of it.

Her hand holds the back of the seat as I push back into it.

Irie's hand grazes me. I become bold in her company as I reposition once again, gliding on her hand—she doesn't seem to mind. A ripple of pleasure moves through me.

"Yuh doin' great." Her breathing is soft, and her voice is silky as we round the forested garden. Surrounded by hibiscus flowers and tall walls of greenery, the garden feels hidden and enchanted as Irie presses into me. We're more alone than we've ever been.

On the edge.

As her fingers linger, I know it's a touch that blurs the line of what best friends are allowed to do. What best friends are allowed to *feel*. But as I melt deeper, I realize it's a line I am very much willing to cross. Hidden behind hibiscus walls, only we can feel it.

And only we can pretend it never happened at all.

We toe the line between lovers and friends as she steadies the handlebars, her fingers wrapped around mine. "Yuh have really good form, Jilly . . ." Irie's voice trails. "Relax into it a likkle bit more."

So, I do.

Irie picks up the pace, walking briskly as I pedal fast.

And just as she lets go, I take off.

Laughter spills from me as my curls go flying in the evening breeze. The sweet smell of coconut fills the air, and I can taste the tropical fruit as I soar through the garden. Irie beams, racing to keep up as we go even deeper into the forest.

I taste freedom on my tongue.

"Yuh doin' so good!" Irie calls out. We fly through the hidden oasis until Irie begins to lose steam, slowing her pace as I continue to do circles around the garden.

"I knew yuh could do it!" She laughs.

All I can do is join in.

I round the garden for another fifteen minutes, until I start to grow tired. Eventually, I come to a natural stop. Irie stands across from me, elated. Far from my house, the garden engulfs us into our own private wonderland.

Our own little piece of nirvana.

"That was *amazin', Jillian.*" Irie glows as I catch my breath. "Yuh picked it up so fast."

"I had a great teacher." I grin. I make my way off the bicycle as we take a seat on the grass.

"You'll have no problem tonight." Irie smiles as she watches me. "It should be a smooth ride once we hit the main roads. And we can go slow. Take our time . . ."

"Cool." I blush, feeling proud of myself for once.

We sit in silence for a moment, staring out at the setting sun. I watch as Irie delicately runs her fingers through the grass, clearly deep in thought.

"What is it?" I trace my fingers along her knee.

She looks up at me, and suddenly, her eyes are contemplative.

"It's just . . . yuh *sure* tonight is a good idea? The sneaking-out part. Yuh not afraid to get caught?"

"No." The lie falls from my lips. But my desperation to experience freedom surmounts my fear. "I believe in you, Irie." I study her brown eyes. "Reggae Jamz is a once-in-a-lifetime chance. I really think tonight is going to be special . . . for both of us."

"And yuh *sure* yuh parents won't find out?"

"I promise. Mummy and Daddy will be distracted wit' di party. By the time we leave out around one o'clock, they'll be fas' asleep."

Nerves erupt as the plan begins to sink in.

"Okay." Irie nods, biting down. "I trust you." Her brown eyes sparkle as she squeezes my hand tightly.

I bite down, feeling fuzzy inside. When I'm with Irie, I don't have to face the dooming reality of my life—because if only for a few hours, I can lose myself in hers.

"Tonight is about *you*, Irie. This is your shot."

She smiles, stroking my hand as the rubies on her bracelet glimmer under the sunset. We sit in silence, gazing out at the orange hue that falls over the yard. The sound of crickets takes over, and from afar, party guests bustle inside the house. Irie looks to me, a sweetness to her pecan-brown eyes as the sun reflects off them. Just looking into them does something to me.

Something special.

I push down the nerves that swim beneath the surface of my skin.

"I still cyaan believe it's our last summa together, Jilly. It doesn't feel real," Irie says delicately. "Just nuh badda forget me when you make all yuh *fancy new foreign friends*. I'm still yuh best friend. No matta what."

"Of course, Irie," I whisper, giving her a small smile. "No matta what."

Guilt creeps in, feeding off my omission.

How could I ever admit to her that I have no future?

That my life is a façade.

Tell her the truth. The thought swirls in my brain. *She's your best friend.*

"Irie, there's—"

"Miss Jillian!"

I stop midsentence just as Amala rounds the bend of the garden. I quickly snatch my hand away from Irie's grip, shoving it into my lap. I sit at attention, snapped back to reality. Amala makes her way toward us, her apron folded over a cream dress.

"Apologies, Miss Jillian," she calls out regretfully. "But yuh mother is calling you girls inside now. The guests have started arriving, and dinner will be served momentarily."

"Thanks, Amala," I say promptly. "This is my friend, Irie, by the way. Irie, this is Amala. She's been with our family forever."

"It's nice to meet you." Irie smiles politely.

"The pleasure is mine." Amala does a small bow. "Jillian, if you ladies will follow me inside?" she asks kindly. "Your mother has instructed you walk in through the front doors, with the other guests."

We both stand, following behind Amala to the front of the house.

As we walk away from the sunset and toward the fully lit estate, the inevitable feeling of doom drops to the pit of my stomach. If Mummy wants me to make a formal entrance, it's because the Kellys are inside.

You can do this, Jilly.

I take a deep breath, calming my nerves as we round the yard to the front doors and make our way up the steps. I glance at Irie, who looks just as nervous as I am.

Just as we make our way inside, Mummy stops us at the door.

"Uh-uh." She stops Amala in her tracks, pursing her pink lips. "You know the rules, Amala. Through the back. We have company."

"*Oh*—yes, Mrs. Casey." Amala nods apologetically, scurrying back down the steps as Mummy turns to us. The look on her face is neurotic.

"Come, come." Her voice is stern as she ushers us inside. "Hurry up, Jillian. Your father's about to make his speech." She heads into the grand entryway, flashing fake smiles to the dinner guests who litter the house.

We trail in behind her.

The house is lit up as people move about in their fanciest suits, ties, and dresses. I glance over at Irie, who's mood seems to be different.

"You okay?" I whisper through clenched teeth as we weave in and out of the commotion.

"Fine," Irie whispers.

But I can tell something's wrong. She looks to me.

"It's just . . . how come she's not allowed through the front doors?"

"Who?" I whisper back. "*Amala?*"

"Yeah." Irie shifts, clearly uncomfortable. "Why couldn't she come inside with us?"

I shrug, unsure of how to answer as Mummy and Daddy's friends look on. "It's just the way things are, Irie." I keep my voice low, distracted as I try my best to show face. "Everything is about keepin' up appearances. That includes hidin' the help."

Irie wilts as we round the corner, but there's no time to take it on. Because just as we enter the living room, I lock eyes with the Kellys.

AND I realize that a distraction, is only that.

12

———

Irie

"I want to thank all of you for joining us tonight."

I'M on pins and needles as Jillian's father speaks to the roomful of guests with a commanding bravado. He stands at the head of a long oak table as he poignantly addresses the crowd. His green eyes are penetrating, and there's a militance to him that commands the room.

He is all business.

"We're so thrilled to have you here with us to celebrate Hilary's birthday. We have some *generous* donors in the room, and on behalf of my wife and I, we want to thank you for your support. It's been *critical* to the growing success of this year's JCG campaign."

I watch him closely as I stand next to Jilly, still coming to terms with the fact that I'm in the same room with what appears to be the majority of the JCG party. Dozens of people stand in their finest attire, hooked on Jillian's father's every word. Not a trace of melanin covers his skin.

Just like everyone else in the room.

His hair is silky and low, and he addresses the room in a fitted black suit. Next to him stands Jilly's mother, who wears a floor-length cocktail dress that cinches her tightly at the waist. She beams a polished, rehearsed smile with a glass of red wine in her hand.

I've never felt so out of place.

"We have no doubt that the JCG will be victorious in this election with your backing," Jillian's father continues. "Winston and I have some great things on the horizon." He nods to a slender, fair-skinned man. My heart drops as it dawns on me.

That's Winston Kelly.

Up until now, Winston Kelly has only been a name I've heard around the shop—a name cursed or praised in passing, depending on who you ask. But seeing him in person feels like an urban legend has been brought to life right before my eyes.

I can't believe we're in the same room.

I glance over at Jilly, doing my best to read her expression as I fight to play it cool. Besides the housekeepers, I'm the only brown-skinned girl in the entire room.

Stay focused, Irie. I remind myself. *Tonight is about Reggae Jamz.*

It's about the music.

"Before we begin, we have some exciting news to share," Jilly's father breaks through my thoughts as he glances at his wife. "Hilary received her birthday gift early this year. In the form of an engagement. But not from me, of course. That deal is already sealed."

The audience chuckles as they glance around the room. Everyone's eyes land on Jilly as I watch the blood drain from her face. She keeps her smile tight, and her eyes focused ahead.

Poised.

"If you know Hilary, you know how excited she's been to find the best match for Jillian. And this year, she finally got her wish." He smiles proudly as he gestures to a stalky man who stands next to Winston Kelly. "We're delighted to be welcoming the Kellys into the family. Christopher will be formally asking for Jillian's hand in marriage next week."

The guests clap in delight as Jillian's face goes pale.

"We are just as thrilled." Winston Kelly addresses the room as the applause settles. "We're delighted to be welcoming Jillian into the family. She's a wonderfully bright young lady. I'm sure there'll be plenty to discuss tonight."

Jilly's father nods.

"Cheers to a great evening, great discourse, and an even better dinner, hm?"

He raises his glass in a toast, and everyone follows before a light applause. The room disperses to their seats just as Jillian grabs my hand, bringing me back. I'm a fit of nerves as she leads me through the room of people. Jilly smiles politely, saying quick thank-yous to the adults that congratulate her as we make our way to our seats. The long table is decorated in fancy bouquets of lush white roses and long candles.

I've never seen anything so extravagant in my life.

We find our seats just a few chairs down from the head of the table. Just before we can sit down, an older woman with dark-brown skin hurries over to us.

"Madam," she says dutifully before pulling out Jilly's chair. I stand perplexed as Jilly nods kindly, taking a second to adjust her dress before sitting down.

Before I can even process it, the lady pulls out my chair.

"Oh, thank yuh." I settle into the fancy white chair, although the gesture makes me feel uncomfortable. I look down the table; it spans the entire room, and thirty or so of Jilly's parents' friends fill the chairs. The domestic workers run about, placing steaming-hot food onto the plates. I'm in disbelief at how expensive everything seems.

I always knew Jilly's father worked in politics.

But I never imagined how high up.

Jilly lifts a white cloth from the table, a smile on her face as she keeps her composure. Across from us, Winston's son takes a seat next to his father and a woman who I presume to be his mother.

What. The. Hell.

I am quite literally sitting across from the man who could be the next leader of our nation.

And my best friend is set to marry his son.

I glance over at Jilly, whose casual demeanor is well rehearsed. Any trace of Patois that lingered on her tongue has vanished, and she plays the role of a politician's perfect daughter with ease, keeping herself humble and charming. It's clear she's done this a million times before.

"Wine, madam?" One of the housekeepers approaches us, holding up a bottle.

"Oh, um—" I turn to Jilly, unsure.

"She'll have some." She nods on my behalf.

The lady leans over my shoulder and pours the red wine into my glass before moving onto Jilly's. I look at the crystal, excited to try it.

"Yuh drink in front of yuh parents?" I ask, slightly surprised.

"They don't care enough to notice." Jilly whispers under her breath. "They're too busy getting drunk themselves. One of di small perks of attending Mummy's parties."

"Oh. Okay." I pick up the crystal glass and take a sip.

The red liquid lands harshly on my tongue as I swallow.

Interesting.

"Irie," Jilly whispers, taking up the white cloth that rests next to my plate. "Don't forget the napkin." She carefully unfolds the cloth and passes it back to me. I'm not sure what to do until I spot hers on her lap. Just then, Amala approaches us.

"Good evening, ladies," she says. "Would you like some stew chicken?"

"Oh yes, please." I smile kindly as she places a spoonful onto my plate. "Thank you."

"Thanks, Amala," Jilly echoes.

Amala proceeds as another housekeeper follows behind her, spooning rice onto my plate. The smell of fresh Jamaican spices fills the room, and I'm overcome as the robust flavors tickle my senses. With the food shortage in Kintyre, I haven't had a meal like this in years.

Nothing even close.

I lift my hand to reach for the bread when Jilly stops me mid-reach.

"Not yet," she whispers to me. "We have to pray first."

"Oh, sorry," I say, slightly embarrassed.

"Let us bow our heads and pray." Her father's deep voice cuts through the table chatter. Everyone falls silent, and in a few seconds, our heads are bowed.

Please, God, get me through this dinner and onto that stage.

"Heavenly father, we thank you for this day. We thank you for your mercy and your grace tonight, and we ask that you cover this meal in your blood, Jesus—"

Just then, I freeze dead in my seat.

I look down to find Jilly's hand sliding into my lap. With her eyes still closed, she traces her way up my thigh, her hands hidden by the long skirt of the table. Her fingers are soft as she carefully weaves them with mine. I close my eyes shut once again as her father continues.

Goose bumps race up my spine.

"So we thank you, Jesus Lord, for this day. You are the almighty God, and in your heavenly name, we pray. Amen."

"Amen," the long row of people echo.

As if on cue, Jilly snatches her hand away as everyone opens their eyes. The table bustles as everyone dives in.

"You've done *such* a phenomenal job, Hilary," a woman who sits a few seats down from me in a pink dress calls to Jillian's mother. "You're a lucky man, Calvin. I can't imagine Hilary has you lifting a finger around here."

"Only when she needs me to sign the check."

The table laughs in unison as everyone picks up their forks and knives. I follow suit.

"That one," Jilly whispers to me, pointing to the other fork that rests beside my plate. "The other one's a salad fork, and the smaller one is for dessert."

"Oh, *tanks.*" I fumble as I reach for it.

"Your birthday came early this year," a fair-skinned woman cuts through the noise as she beams at Jillian's mom. "You've been talking about finding a match for Jillian for *months,* Hilary. It's so wonderful to see it *finally* happening. And with *such* a fine young man."

"We're delighted," Jilly's mother gushes.

"You're not the only ones." Winston Kelly's voice is deep. "We're excited to welcome you into the family, Jillian." Mr. Kelly looks down the table at Jillian with sharp blue eyes. "Christopher certainly had his pick of the litter. But Jillian was by far the most impressive."

I cringe as Christopher nods pompously.

"So, tell me, Jillian, what campus will you be attending in the fall?" Mr. Kelly asks as he takes a sip of the icy brown liquid in front of him.

"I'm still waiting to hear, sir," Jilly says modestly. "But I should know soon, I trust."

"They haven't given you your schedule?" Christopher asks from across the table.

"Not as yet."

"It'll be important for you two to find a good balance if you want to maintain your grades, " Mr. Kelly continues, focusing his gaze on Christopher and Jilly. "These next four years are some of the most important of a young man's life."

Christopher nods, maintaining his self-righteous demeanor.

"And who's this?" Winston Kelly asks.

I freeze, pulled from my thoughts as the eyes of the dinner guests land on me. "Me? Oh, uh—"

"*Irie*," Jilly and I answer at the same time.

"One of Jillian's school friends." Mrs. Casey's tone is apologetic as she explains to the table. "The girls went to Arthen together."

"*Irie?* What a peculiar name." Christopher's mother screws up her face as she takes a sip of wine. "Irie, like the *Patois word*?"

"Yes, ma'am." I smile awkwardly. "Irie, like 'all is well' or 'eternal peace.'"

"Ah. I see." She smirks. "And where are you from, dear?"

"Pa—" Jilly starts.

"Kintyre."

Shit.

It slips out. Jilly looks at me, confused as I start to grow hot.

"It's near Papine," I clarify to Jilly. "Yuh just have to cross a bridge to get there, but it's pretty much di same place."

"Oh." Jilly nods. "I didn't know that."

The truth is she's never cared to ask.

"I'm not too familiar with where that is," Christopher's mother says. "Which part of the island did you say?"

"The ghetto," Winston Kelly boldly interjects. "The exact place Morris is failing."

I start to burn up as the table falls silent. Christopher fights a smile as Jilly opens her mouth to change the subject.

Her father beats her to it. "So, Irie, tonight must be a treat, then?"

"Pardon me?"

"I said it must be a *treat*," he emphasizes. "I imagine they don't have this kind of food in Kintyre. Not with Morris leaving all those shipments at the pier."

"Dad—" Jillian starts.

"It's okay," I say respectfully. "He's right. There hasn't been a lot of food comin' into the supermarkets as of late," I say awkwardly to the table. "There's been a huge shortage in my area."

"Really?" Jilly looks to me. "I didn't know that."

"Yeah." I smile, battling my beating heart. "But it's not a big deal; it's sort of normal now." I try to brush it off as I look to Jillian's mother. "I definitely haven't had anything this good in a long while. Di food is delicious, Mrs. Casey."

But as my accent slips out, every part of me feels caught. *Exposed.*

"*The,*" her mother corrects me. "*The* food is delicious."

"Mummy—" Jilly starts.

"Morris is failing you," Winston Kelly interrupts. His tone is pointed, and he looks me straight in the eye with his razor-blue ones. "And I hope you realize the importance of voting in this election, Irie. You have more power than you think to change how things are being run in your community."

"Of course, sir." I nod respectfully.

"That rhetoric means nothing to the people of the ghetto," Jilly's father scoffs. "They're not smart enough to understand. They lack the education."

I'm stunned silent as the words leave his lips.

"And to think, all Morris had to do was tell them that 'socialism is love.'" Christopher laughs, joining in. "He's selling poor Blacks a pipe dream."

"The poor are Joshua Morris's easiest targets." Jilly's father's eyes land on me. "And it's important not to be a pawn."

I look down at my plate, fighting the urge to stick up for Joshua Morris.

For all he has done for me and the people of the ghetto.

"He's got them all wrapped around his finger," Christopher continues. "And then you throw in the message of the Rastaman . . . it's no wonder their heads are so convoluted. It's not just the ganja messing them up, it's the social programming." Christopher's eyes lock with mine. "Isn't that right, Irie?" he challenges me from across the table. "I mean, correct me if I'm wrong, but I imagine you can't go anywhere nowadays without hearing the message of the 'Revolution' in your neighborhood." He smirks. "All that *exodus* propaganda infiltrating the ghetto, convincing the poor they actually have a fighting chance at true wealth."

My blood boils as he stares at me. "I actually love reggae music," I say boldly.

The table falls dead silent as Jilly glares at me. Her eyes go wide.

"My father owns a record store. We play a lot of music, but reggae is definitely ma favorite genre," I continue, my heart racing. "I find it a really beautiful, honest means of expression."

"Oh, don't be foolish." Jillian's mother laughs out loud. "You went to *Arthen,* Irie. I would hope they educated you better than that, or it would be a waste of your parents' money."

"It's not a *waste* if she got in on scholarship," Jilly's father mutters as he looks up at me. "What are your thoughts on the PLM administration, Irie? Surely you must have some."

"I . . ." I dig for courage as the entire table watches on. "I, um, I actually think Morris is rather progressive." I search myself for the right words. "Uplifting the masses, trying to ensure everyone's basic needs are met, like education."

"She can't be serious," Jilly's mother starts.

"Let the girl speak," Winston Kelly says. "I want to hear it."

My heart beats from my chest. "I just . . . I don't think it's such a bad thing. What he's trying to do. Social class and race seem to be the two biggest problems affecting the island right now, so I think it's a good thing that he's bringing attention to it."

"*Right.*" Christopher laughs out loud. "Clearly, the music has gotten the best of you."

"I actually think what the Rastas are doing is quite remarkable. And incredibly revolutionary." My voice tremors as I stand up to him. "They're freedom fighters; music is their activism. And their hair . . . it's a symbol of rebellion to conformity. Rebellion against Eurocentric ideals that go against our true Afrocentric identity." My palms grow sweaty. "Their dreadlocks are like receptors. To God, almost."

"*Surely* you can't believe that nonsense." Winston stares me down, clearly offended.

"What's the old saying?" Christopher smirks. "You can take a girl out of the ghetto . . ."

"Tell me something, Irie, are you a *Christian*?" Winston glares.

"I—no, sir, not officially," I say awkwardly. "I believe in God, but I don't go to church. I did when I was likkle, with my mada. But she's gone to foreign."

"And what exactly does your mother *do*?"

"She's a domestic worker."

"A *maid*?" Jillian's mother raises her brow.

My cheeks begin to burn up under everyone's gaze.

"Irie's father's store is actually a very popular one," Jilly interjects, charming the table with a smile as she tries to quell the tension. "And it's Irie's job to be familiar wit' all kinds of music."

"I hope that's not where you've been spending all my money."

"No, sir." I jump to her defense. "Jilly's never been to my fada's shop."

"What did you say the name of it was?" Christopher's mother asks from across the table, clearly enjoying this. "Your father's store."

"Ricky's," I say clearly. "Ricky's Records."

"He's a *big* deal in Kingston," Jilly says proudly. "People love him, right, Irie?"

I give her a tempered look.

"I would hate to know that your father is promoting a

communist agenda in his store," Winston grills me. "Not with such a big platform. Who does he vote for?"

A bead of sweat rolls down my stomach as I look to Jilly for support.

"Can we change the subject?" Jilly smiles.

"Where exactly is the store located?" Mr. Kelly asks, not willing to drop the issue.

"Papine Square," I say, my voice small. "In the market."

"Wasn't there a shooting there last week?" the gentleman beside me asks. "Four or five people shot dead in broad daylight?"

"God, I *swear* those people never learn," Jilly's mother says. "Complete wasted life."

Breathe, Irie.

"Your father has a lot of influence owning a record store. Especially in an impoverished area like Papine," Winston Kelly continues. "It's a dangerous agenda to give those revolution artists a platform, especially so close to the election."

"Yes, sir," I muster. But my throat is so dry I nearly choke.

"Look around this room, Irie," Jillian's father says, his voice stern. "How do you think people like us were able to build a life like this?"

I'm speechless.

"It certainly wasn't from handouts," Jillian's mother says mid-sip.

"My point exactly." Winston scoffs. "We've all worked incredibly hard to build what we have. And now here comes Morris wanting to take from the rich and give to the poor as if he's some kind of Robin Hood."

The table chuckles as my face goes red.

"Life isn't a *fable,* Irie." Winston looks me directly in the eye. "It's important you get clear on the future you want for Jamaica. And it's important you work *hard* for it. Voting is a privilege, and people like *you* need to use it wisely."

Jilly's father nods. "The last thing you want to do is throw your vote away to the PLM."

"All right, Daddy," Jilly interrupts, annoyance in her tone. "No one's voting for the PLM. Now can we *please* eat in peace without being grilled on politics?"

"*Jillian,*" her mother starts.

"Would anyone like some more wine?" Amala enters from the kitchen. She cuts the tension as she rounds the table.

"*Oh,* I thought you'd never ask. Right here, darling." Christopher's mother points to her glass as Amala begins to fill it up. I quickly grab mine, taking a giant gulp. Just then, Mrs. Kelly reaches for her glass and knocks Amala's hand.

Red wine spills everywhere.

"*Jesus!*" Mrs. Kelly yells as the red liquid hits the table.

"Amala!" Jillian's mother screams. "What in *God's name* is wrong with you?"

"Come on, Amala," Jilly's father scolds. "Get it together."

"I am *so* sorry." Amala uses her hand to pick up the glass shards.

"Well, don't just *stand there,* Amala!" Mrs. Casey yells. "Go and get something to clean it up!"

"Of course, Mrs. Casey. My sincerest apologies." Amala obediently scurries out of the room.

I'm shocked as I look to Jilly. She says nothing, as if she's seen it happen a million times before. But I'm completely floored as I watch the scene play out.

It wasn't even her fault.

I lose all appetite as I stare down at my untouched plate. This entire evening has made me feel sick. I feel poked at. Prodded.

Humiliated.

Mrs. Kelly wipes where the wine hit her dress as Mr. Kelly moves to help. I drown out the table banter, trying my best to focus on Reggae Jamz—*the real reason why I'm here tonight.* But anger rises in my chest. I feel like a chess piece in a really weird and delusional game.

As Jilly takes her last sip of wine, she looks to me. "I am *so* sorry, Irie. We soon finish."

Her green eyes are apologetic as she whispers softly.

"IT'S almost time for cake."

13

———

Jilly

"*Are you an idiot?*"

MUMMY'S tone is cutting as we stand in the side hallway, a few doors down from Daddy's study. The clock above her head reads quarter to nine as Irie waits for me up in my room. The evening has mostly winded down except for the Kellys and a few others, and as the sound of the guests drowns out, Mummy cuts into me like a knife.

"How *dare* you bring that stray into this house, Jillian! On my birthday of all days? *Have you lost your mind?*" Her eyes go wide. "In front of the Kellys?"

"Mummy."

"You embarrassed your father in front of some *very important company tonight*. And what for? *Hm?* To make some kind of statement? You're lucky Mr. Kelly didn't think to call off the whole engagement!"

I sink, remorseful it didn't work. "Daddy was the one who told me I could bring a friend."

"And tonight is your *last night* hanging around her. Do I make myself clear?"

My heart plummets.

"The *last thing* I need is you being brainwashed by some *ghetto girl* from the wrong side of the tracks. Filling your head with propaganda and devil's music . . . *Jesus, Jillian.* It's bad enough we're still waiting on your acceptance letter. If I find out she's been filling your head with that garbage—"

"Reggae music isn't *garbage.*"

"Watch it." She yanks my jaw, and I yelp in shock.

"You're walking a *thin line,* Jillian Casey." Her voice goes cold. "And I'm telling you *right now* it's one that you don't want to cross. Because once you do, there's no going back. Do I make myself clear?"

I nod, pushing down the tears that well in my eyes as she drops her hand from my jaw.

"You're acting out. And it *stops now.*" Her eyes are chilling. "You should be embarrassed the way you handled yourself in front of Christopher tonight. That's *no way* for a young woman to behave in front of her future husband."

She digs into her purse and pulls out a gold tube of lipstick.

I'm so angry I could burst.

"Christopher's waiting for you in your father's study." Her words are a clear order as she puts the gold tube in my hand. "Now smooth out your dress and put this on your lips."

I swallow my rage as I take the cap off the tube. I apply a thin layer of pink onto my lips, reluctantly rubbing them together.

"I expect you to be on your best behavior in there. And when he's finished speaking with you, you and Irie go *straight* to bed." Her eyes are scolding as she takes the tube. "I want her gone by morning, Jillian. Understood?"

"Yes," I whisper, silently shooting daggers into her cold heart.

"You don't invite girls like that into your home. It's a wonder nothing's gone missing." She takes a deep breath, regaining control. "Now head in there and *be good.*"

I'm fuming as I make my way past her.

I grab onto the door handle, bracing myself.

"Now," Mummy says.

I wince, turning the knob and slipping inside of Daddy's study.

I enter the dimly lit space to find Christopher standing in the center of the room, waiting for me by my father's desk. He stands confident and tall, placing down an old family photo as I enter the room. His eyes twinkle in the moody light.

"Look who it is." He smiles, picking up his drink from the desk. "I thought I'd never get some time alone with you."

"Dreams come true," I say sarcastically. "What do you want?"

"Wow." He laughs, taking a sip of the scotch in his glass. "That's how we're starting off? You're about to be my fiancée, you know."

"What do you *want*, Christopher?" I demand. "Was it not enough for your father to buy me at auction? Or you want to terrorize your shiny new toy too?"

"You look gorgeous, Jillian," he says, clearly enthralled with me. "I've been wanting to tell you that all night." I tense as his eyes scan my white dress. "You know, contrary to what you might think, most girls would pay to be my future wife."

"I'm not most girls," I say bitterly. "You can't buy my love."

"Don't be foolish." He laughs. "Of course I can."

He steps closer to me, looking into my eyes before reaching into his pocket. His cologne is musky as he pulls a small box out of his pocket and hands it to me.

"I know the official engagement party isn't until next week, but I wanted to get you something. As a token of my appreciation— you know, since we started off on the wrong foot."

I pull off the bow and open it to reveal a diamond tennis bracelet. A row of diamonds fill the small chain, glittering in the shadows of the room.

"Diamonds," he says cockily. "Rough around the edges. Piercing, but so beautifully worth it. Just like you."

I look down at the bracelet and then back up at Christopher. "You must be joking," I say, handing the box back to him. "I don't want it."

"I beg your pardon?" he asks me.

"*I said* I don't want it." I look him straight in the eye. "Just because my father can be bought doesn't mean I can."

"Come on, Jillian," he interrupts as if bored of me playing coy. "Even a spoiled girl like you shouldn't be so proud. It cometh before the fall, you know."

He steps closer to me, his deep voice low. "Look, I like you. *A lot.* You're scrappy. It's one of the things that I told my father I wanted in a future wife, and I'd say he over-delivered."

"I beg your pardon?"

"Bringing a girl from the ghetto into your parents' home on the night of one of Jamaica's most important political dinners? In front of campaign donors, Jamaica's *wealthiest* elite *and* the future prime minister?" He laughs, taking a sip of scotch. "Well played. You've definitely got some guts."

"You have no idea what you're talking about," I say defensively. "Irie's my best friend."

"If you say so." Christopher shrugs. "But just so you know, your little plan is backfiring. You just keep impressing my father. He likes that you have a mind of your own. It's a rare find in young women nowadays."

"Are we done here?"

Christopher ignores me. "I *do* find it odd that you call her your best friend, yet you didn't know she doesn't eat three square meals a day." He laughs, challenging me as guilt takes over. "Seems like something a best friend would know."

"Irie didn't tell me that."

"But your father should have," he says, smug. "He's responsible, after all."

"*What?*" I stare at him in confusion. "What are you talking about? Daddy's not in control of what the Morris government does."

"Never underestimate a Casey, right?"

I freeze.

"There are a lot of ways to sabotage a campaign, Jillian," he continues. "Block shipments. Pay people off so all those boats of food stay docked at the wharf . . ." He looks at me as if my innocence were cute. "You *really* thought that was Morris?"

"I—" But I don't even know what to say. "My father would never—"

"Your *father* proposed it the first day he signed on to my father's campaign. There's only one way to the top, whether you like it or not." He looks at me, his eyes pointed. "*Sabotage.*"

I'm stunned, unsure of whether to believe him.

"Politics is a dirty game."

"How do you know all of this?"

"I know a lot of things." He shrugs. "Especially when it comes to my father's business dealings. Contrary to your assumptions, I'm not just a pretty face."

There's no way. He's just trying to mess with my head.

"You're smart, Jillian. The only difference between us is you don't know it yet, so you surround yourself with ghetto girls to feel better about who you are. You distract yourself from your power with people who are below you. But you can't run from yourself." His eyes search mine, intense and focused. "You can't be afraid of your own destiny."

His words crawl their way up my skin like a snake.

"Your parents have sheltered you *tremendously* from the real world. It's a shame. But I can help you." His deep voice goes quiet as he eyes my evening gown. "I can show you what to do with all that intelligence."

The moment between us grows heavy.

I pull myself out of it, shaking my head in disbelief. "Wow."

I laugh out loud at his audacity. "I didn't know it was humanly possible for someone to be so vain."

"There's a difference between *vanity* and *truth*, Jillian. And when someone respects you enough, they'll give you the latter."

He inches closer, bringing his fingers to my chin.

"You're not the delicate little flower they make you out to be. You're a *woman* . . . strong . . . *smart*. You're worthy of respect."

I pull away. Fed up, I turn on my heel and march toward the door.

"I know that you're lying about Cambridge."

His words stop me dead in my tracks.

"*What?*" My heart catapults as I spin back around.

"Come on, Jillian. Don't play dunce." He laughs. "It's a wonder your parents believe you."

"*I told you*, I'm still waiting on my letter."

"Bullshit." He eyes me. "You got it already, didn't you?"

I panic as he watches me sweat.

"I knew it." He laughs. "You're lying. You didn't get in."

Terror rings through me as I look to the floor.

"Just . . . *Please* don't say anything to my parents."

"And why on earth would I do that?" Christopher steps closer to me. "You're my future *wife*." He reaches down and takes my hand. "I've been picky for a *very long* time about the woman I marry. My father is a powerful man, and it means I have a lot to protect. It also means that I get whatever I need. And the woman I choose to marry will as well."

He gently caresses my hand, and for a moment, I let him.

"Just say the word. I'll have my father arrange for your acceptance within seventy-two hours."

No way.

"My father is incredibly connected. I'll bring the letter to our engagement party, and I'll ensure he doesn't say a word to your parents. It'll just be between us . . . our little secret."

I'm taken aback as his offer buzzes around in my head.

"How . . . how could you guarantee that?" I say nervously. "That he wouldn't say anything?"

"Because ensuring my happiness is more important to my father than maintaining any allegiance he has to your father," he says, matter-of-factly. "*I am* my father's biggest investment. And by default, that means that the woman I choose to marry would be as well."

The energy between us grows thick.

As I debate how to respond, Christopher takes the tennis bracelet from the box, gently taking my wrist in his hand. "I noticed your bracelet at dinner." His touch is intense as he unclips my ruby bracelet. "Rubies are nice, but diamonds are a girl's best friend."

I hold my breath as he raises my hand and clasps the diamonds around my wrist. The string of diamonds sparkle, eerily glittering in the dimly lit room.

It's breathtaking.

AND despite my better judgment, I leave it on.

14

———

Irie

What the fuck just happened?

I'M on edge as I wait for Jilly to come through the bedroom door. It's been over thirty minutes since I've been alone in her room, marinating on the night and the hellish conversation at dinner. My worst nightmare came true, right before my eyes.

The *Out of Many, One People* sign stares back at me as I replay the horrific events over and over again. I can't believe they picked me apart on the *biggest* night of my life. I can't believe how they spoke to Amala, the darkest-skinned woman in the room.

Snap out of it, Irie. I pull myself together.

I'm a ball of anxiety, but I don't have time to be consumed. Not with so much on the line. In just a few hours, I'll be faced with the biggest opportunity of my life.

And I can't afford to lose sight.

The reminder is humbling as I scan Jilly's array of prestigious awards. *There are so many of them.* I walk across the fluffy white carpet, taking in trophies that date back to primary school— medals for netball, chess, ballet, and spelling bees.

My curiosity gets the best of me as I mull over her things like a kid in a candy store. I flip through the books on her shelves and play around in fancy lotions, pretending—if only for a moment—that they were mine. I'm overcome with an urge to know more.

To see life through her eyes.

I take a seat at the vanity, impressed by the bundle of lipsticks and perfumes that are sprawled out in front of me. I glance up at my reflection in the mirror, taking in the long braids that fall down my back. My brown skin glows under the soft yellow bulbs that line her vanity, and for a split second, I get a glimpse into what Jilly must feel like every morning.

Enough.

I stare at my reflection, carefully spraying the perfume onto my wrist. The scent instantly calms me down as I rise from the vanity and continue around the room.

What could her mother be talking to her about for so long?

I make my way across the room toward her wooden dresser, admiring the record player that rests on the counter. And then I mindlessly pull the top drawer open.

Inside, her underwear is folded neatly, her bras and frilly socks carefully piled on top of each other. I'm about to close it back when I notice a white letter sticking out. I reach for it and pull it out, and on the front in bold black letters, it reads, THE UNIVERSITY OF CAMBRIDGE.

"Wow," I whisper as I admire it. I've never held an acceptance letter before.

Just as I go to open it, I hear footsteps on the other side of the door.

Shit.

I fumble, quickly stuffing it back into the drawer as the door handle turns. I spin around the same second that Jilly enters the room.

Caught.

"Hi," I say. "I—"

"*I'm so sorry* I took so long, Irie," she says, an apologetic look on her face. She balances a bottle of red wine in her hand as she makes her way into the room. "The conversation wit' Mummy ran a likkle longer than expected. But I brought suh'um to mek up for it." She holds up the bottle of wine. "Hopefully, it'll take some ah di edge off for your performance tonight."

"Oh, it's all right," I say awkwardly, gesturing to the drawers. "I was just looking fi ah T-shirt to wear to bed." The lie rolls off my tongue.

"Yuh changing already?" She gives me a peculiar look.

"For later tonight," I correct myself. "When we get back, I mean."

"Oh, yeah. Sure." She's unfazed as she makes her way toward me. "It's in di third drawer. I'll grab one fi yuh."

The bracelet on her wrist is blinding as she inches closer.

"Whoa, where did you get that?"

"I snuck it up from di kitchen," Jilly says proudly, referring to the wine bottle as she rummages through the drawer. "There must've been a dozen bokkles left ova."

"I meant di bracelet, Jilly." I stop her, gesturing to the sparkly tennis bracelet that cuffs her wrist. "It's . . . *gorgeous*. Is it real?"

"Oh." She looks at her wrist as if just noticing. "I'm not too sure. Mummy just gave it me. She *loves* to regift di tings weh she nuh like." She pulls a nightie from her drawer and passes it to me. "Is this okay?"

"Yeah, thanks." I take the satin dress from her hands. "So she gave it to you just now?" I ask, confused as I take a seat on the bed. "She seemed really upset when I came upstairs. What did she want to talk to yuh about?"

"My behavior, of course." Jilly's tone is casual. "She was upset at me for talkin' back to Daddy at dinner." She shrugs. "But honestly, it's not important. What's important is *tonight*." She smiles excitedly. "You're performing at *Reggae Jamz*, Irie. Can yuh believe it?"

Her words are oddly dismissive as she screws open the wine bottle and brings it to her mouth. She takes a big, long sip before holding the bottle out to me. "Want some?"

"Sure," I say, already feeling buzzed from earlier.

Jilly hands me the bottle, and I bring it to my lips.

"I swear my parents are trying to put me in an early grave," Jilly vents as I swallow the wine. "I hope it wasn't too much."

"It definitely was," I say abruptly. "No offense, Jilly, but they attacked me at that table." I look her in the eyes, the wine making me bold. "Yuh didn't find what they had to say . . . *insulting*?"

"*Of course* I did." Jilly reaches for the bottle. "But in my defense, Irie, I *did* ask yuh not to bring it up—yuh fada's shop. I already know how my parents are."

"But yuh certainly didn't mind telling them how *popular* di store was."

"What? Irie, I was trying to help the situation."

"But you didn't," I say firmly. "You made it worse."

"That's not fair." Jilly shakes her head. "Yuh cyaan put that on me. I mean, the entire table nearly found out I've been *driving to Papine* to buy records because *you* decided to mention it. Not me."

"And what's so wrong wit' *driving to Papine*?" I grill her.

"*Nothing.* I never said there was." She tucks her hair behind her ear. "I don't know why you're being so defensive."

"I'm not being *defensive*, Jillian, it jus'—" I pause, tempering my frustration. "It just kinda seems like you're ashamed or suh'um. Of me . . . and reggae music."

"I'm not *ashamed*, Irie. I'm not *allowed*. There's a difference." She's on edge as she looks at me. "I mean, cut me some slack. I expected you to be yourself, but you pretty much spoke out against the entire JCG campaign at dinner."

"What? They *asked me* what I thought."

"Reggae music is about *freedom*. Not politics."

"Maybe for you, Jillian." I scoff.

"And what's that supposed to mean?"

She shakes her head, growing frustrated. "Election time does this to everybody, Irie. Yuh cyaan get so caught up."

"I'm not *caught up*. I'm just *saying* that not everyone has di luxury of freedom. For some people, *who* they vote for determines how free they actually are."

"Yuh nuh tink I *know* that?" She stares at me blankly. "Where is dis comin' from, anyway? We never talk about politics."

"Well, maybe we should start."

The moment between us grows strained.

"Look, Irie, I'm sorry about tonight," Jilly says, exasperated. "But regardless of JCG or PLM, violence is happening on *both* sides. Picking a side just leads to more division. And our friendship . . . it's supposed to be an escape from all that noise."

I sink as her words hang in the air between us. I search for the courage to tell her how I really feel. To tell her that I don't agree.

But I cower.

"I just felt *so* out of place tonight."

"But who cares what they think?" she brings my hand to her heart. "*Tonight is about the music, Irie.* You're performing at Reggae Jamz, for crying out loud! For the first time in my life, I'm not concerned wit' what anybody thinks of me right now." She searches my eyes. "Not about you, and not about reggae. Not for a second."

I shift, unsure of how to process as she lets go of my hand.

"I hate living in this house most days," she confesses, looking around the room. "School was di only place I ever had a likkle bit of freedom. The time we spent talkin' about music and artists . . . Those were some of the most magical days of my life. It was the first time I started to see myself and *actually liked* what I saw," Jilly whispers softly. "Dancing away the darkness to Peter Tosh lyrics . . . You taught me so much, Irie." Her eyes linger on mine.

"I know my family is messed up, and I'm *really sorry* for how they treated you. But tonight isn't about them—it's about *us.*"

She gives my hand a gentle squeeze.

"I appreciate yuh apology," I say softly. "And I'm sorry too."

Jilly grabs the wine bottle from the floor, passing it back to me. "*Now can we please* start again?" She fake sulks. "We were havin' such a good time before everything happened."

I give in as I tipsily bring the bottle to my lips.

"I know we may have grown up differently." Jilly looks up at me. "But it was our love of reggae music that brought us together. *Freedom sound.* Always remember that."

Her words feel like silk as she inches closer.

"Tonight is your chance to show people that reggae unites. Not divides."

Goose bumps race down my spine.

I smile softly, deciding to let it go. "You're so right. No more political talk."

"Agreed." Jilly laughs. "Let's switch up this vibe."

My stomach knots as she drunkenly rises from the bed and makes her way over to the dresser. She reaches into the cupboard and pulls out Bob Marley's "Could You Be Loved." In a second's notice, a breezy, reggae beat comes over the player.

She turns it down low as she spins around. "I have suh'um fi yuh." A mischievous smile spreads across her face. "But yuh haffi close yuh eyes."

She bolts across the room to her drawer, grabbing something before making her way back over to me.

"What is it?" I laugh, intrigued as I look down at her hands.

"Yuh trust me?"

"Of course, bighead."

"Good. Now close yuh eyes. And no peekin'."

"Fine," I say softly before following instructions.

I can sense her as she moves in closer, and I grow more open with each breath. My body buzzes with the rush of the liquor, and I feel my nipples start to grow hard under the satin material of the dress. Even without touching each other, I feel Jilly's energy all over me.

"Yuh ready?" Her voice trails.

I nod.

"Keep yuh eyes closed." She giggles, stumbling over her words. "And hold out yuh hand."

I take a small breath, following instructions. My stomach flutters as she takes my hand in hers and places something inside.

"Now yuh can open."

I peel my eyes open, and I'm shocked to find a perfectly rolled spliff no bigger than the size of my pinkie staring back at me. I look at Jillian in confusion.

"*Ganja?*" I blurt drunkenly. "Where in di *worl'* did yuh get this, Jillian?"

"My cousin Monica." She beams, intoxicated as she bites down on her bottom lip. "I figured we could give it a try tonight, to celebrate you performing at Reggae Jamz."

"Yuh serious?" I look down at the spliff and back up at her.

Jillian nods, unsure of how to read my reaction.

I'm stunned but intrigued at the audacity of her request. "Yuh know dis is illegal, right?"

"So?" She laughs, her inhibitions clearly lost. "Rastafarians do it all the time. It'll help you with your performance tonight. Besides, we said tonight is about tekin' chances."

"Yuh mussi mod." I laugh, tempted.

The truth is I've always wanted to try it.

I beam at the daring look in her eyes. It doesn't take that much convincing.

"Fine." I smile, giving in. "Pass di spliff."

"*Yay!*" she squeals, wrapping her arms around me.

"But only a few puffs." I giggle, melting into her embrace. "We cyaan afford fi miss di set."

"Of course not," Jilly reassures me. "We still have a few hours left." She pulls out a matchbox. "Come. Let's get high in di bathroom." She takes my hand. "There's a window we can smoke out of that overlooks di backyard."

Adrenaline rips through me as we spring up from her bed. We're a giggling fit—young, wild, and—if only for tonight—*free* as we drunkenly dash across the room toward the secluded confines of her private bathroom. With Reggae Jamz only five hours away, I follow behind Jillian on the edge of glory.

READY, more than I've ever been, to take my chances.

15

Irie

"**W**ait here," *Jillian says as we enter the dark space.*

SHE bolts back through the door to change the record as I scan the space. *Even her bathroom is bigger than my room.* Seconds later, "Jamaica Ska" plays softly throughout Jilly's bedroom walls. The prancy pop record juxtaposes our risky behavior, sending me into a fit of giggles just as Jilly makes her way back into the bathroom.

"What's so funny?" She smiles.

"Nuttin'. I'm just excited."

"I knew yuh would be." She smiles as she closes the door behind her and turns the lock. "Just in case," she whispers.

And just like that, we're alone once again.

"Yuh look so good in the moonlight," Jilly says softly. We stand facing each other in the dark, scanning the silhouettes of each other's bodies as my heart beats wildly.

"You too," I whisper. The blood rushes to my fingertips. I'm desperate to touch her, but I hold back.

Before either of us can admit what we're feeling, she guides me toward the window on the opposite side of the bathroom. It overlooks the massive backyard, and the ledge is large enough for two. I watch in a rapture as Jilly effortlessly slides it open and props herself up onto the ledge. She holds my eye contact, positioning herself as her dress slinks from her shoulder. Her legs drape over the edge in her nylons as she holds the spliff in her hand.

"Got a light?" she slurs.

I bite down on my lip as I make my way toward her in the dark. I hike myself up beside her using the glow of the moon. Soon, we sit across from each other on the ledge as I take the matchbox and draw the match.

An instant flame.

"Yuh wan' go first?" I ask her as I hold the fire in my hands.

"Yeah." She tucks her hair behind her ear before putting the spliff in between her lips. She moves gracefully, leaning into me as I bring the match to the tip of the spliff and light it. Just as it catches flame, I softly blow it out.

Jilly leans back and takes her first draw. Like a pro, she inhales the smoke, holding her breath before blowing it out the window. The sweet smell of ganja floods the bathroom, instantly filling my lungs and relaxing my nerves. Jilly covers her mouth as she starts to cough.

"Shh." I giggle as she puts her hand over her mouth. "Yuh all right?" I touch her leg.

"It's strong." She makes a face as she passes it to me. I take it from her and hold it in my fingers the same way I watched her do it. I bring it to my lips and take a draw. The smoke fills my mouth as I try my best not to cough.

I can't hold it. I begin to choke as the smoke pours out of my mouth.

"I told yuh it was strong!" Jilly whisper-laughs. Seeing her laugh so hard makes me laugh too, and soon, we are a giggling, coughing fit. I'm overcome by an instant head rush, and in seconds, everything starts to feel a little buzzier.

"I kinda like it," I say as I come back to my breath, surrendering to the lightness of the feeling. "It feels nice . . . kinda calming, nuh true?"

Jilly nods as she takes the spliff from my fingers. I watch as she takes another pull, this time skillfully blowing a thick cloud out the window before passing it back to me.

"Yuh feel any different?" I ask her.

"Jus' a likkle hazy . . . It's nice."

I take another pull as the heavy emotions that cloud me begin to lift. "Whoa," I say as Jilly watches me exhale. "No wonder di Rastafarians are always singing about peace." I giggle as I pass the spliff back to her. "Why be angry when yuh can feel this good?"

Jilly laughs as if it were the funniest thing in the world. The smoke curls from her mouth, dancing in the night before floating out the window. Her eyes lock with mine. "Tonight is going to be *so* good, Irie. I feel it."

"Me too," I whisper. I move my braids to the side and take a longer pull. All at once, ease covers me like a blanket. I melt into myself as the events from earlier begin to feel like a distant memory. For once, I feel like I'm doing more than just surviving.

Tonight is my night.

"How come yuh didn't tell me yuh lived in Kintyre?"

I'm brought back to the present moment by the sound of Jilly's voice as I peel my eyes away from the garden. "What do you mean?" I ask, feeling caught.

"Yuh neva told me," she says again, before staring out the window. "I always imagined yuh lived in Papine. Near di record store or something."

"Technically, yuh never asked."

"I guess so." She takes in my response. "It just seems strange yuh neva mentioned it."

"It's not really strange." I shift, adjusting myself on the ledge. "They're not too far from each other. Yuh jus' haffi cross a bridge fi enter Kintyre."

"A bridge?"

"Yeah, a swinging bridge."

"Oh, wow." She looks at me. "Isn't that dangerous?" She takes another pull of the spliff before handing it back to me.

"Yeah," I say, feeling self-conscious. "But I'm used to it by now."

Jilly nods, going silent.

"What?" I ask her.

"Nuttin', just . . ." She searches herself for the words. "I just want yuh to feel like yuh can tell me these things. I don't want yuh to feel like yuh have to hide."

"I wasn't hiding," I say defensively. "It just neva really came up in conversation."

"Okay." She nods, sincere as she backs off. "Well, I'm sorry for not asking. Not only about where yuh live but di whole food situation. I had no idea there was a shortage in your area."

"It's fine, Jillian." I stop her, desperate to change the subject. In the black of night, I feel exposed. I don't want her to see me as a charity case.

I don't want her to think that I'm beneath her.

"Yuh sure yuh nuh want to talk about it?"

I look away as the ganja brings down my walls. Every part of me wants to unload myself—come undone.

"We still eat and stuff." I hand the spliff to Jilly, who puts it out. "But it's hard to get yuh hands on certain foods."

"Irie . . ."

"Don't look at me like that, Jillian."

"Like what?"

"Like yuh feel sorry fi me." I say it outward to the night. "You're always saying it . . . that *you're sorry*. But yuh don't have to be. Yuh don't have to pity me so much."

"I don't *pity you*, Irie," she says, taking my hand. "I *love* you. There's a difference."

I'm vulnerable as her words cover me like a blanket. My defenses lower as her eyes stare back at me with genuine compassion, and for the first time, I allow myself to surrender to her.

I allow her to care about me.

"I love you too, Jilly," I whisper.

And I really, *really* mean it.

My mind is a vortex, but the marijuana makes me clear. I want to burst wide open and reveal myself to her in the safety of her bedroom walls. I want her to help me carry all this pain. The pain I feel about my people, about my family and my home. About where I *come from* and the violence that punishes us. Locked away in the privacy of her bathroom, I feel the courage to finally put the load down.

I have to tell her the truth.

"Can I be honest with yuh?" I whisper. Jilly's eyes meet mine.

"Always."

"I lied to you," I say softly. "About Junior. I told yuh that he was murdered, but I lied about where it happened." My mouth is dry as I confess. "They killed him right in front ah Daddy's record store. Him and three other people."

"*What?*" Jilly's mouth goes agape. "In front of Ricky's?"

I nod. "On di last day of school." The tears begin to creep up, and I try my best to blink them back. "Siarah and Tandi both saw it . . . and my fada . . . my fada and me held him while he bled out."

"Oh my god, Irie." Jilly brings her hand to her mouth. "How come yuh neva tell me?"

I wipe the tears that stream down my face. "I didn't want you to judge me." I shake my head, looking at her. "I didn't want yuh to think less of me. For coming from an area like that."

"Irie, you're my *best friend*."

"I know, I jus'—I didn't want it to change your view on di shop. How you view *me* or . . . the music."

"Oh, Irie. Yuh *have* to know me betta than that." She raises her hand to my cheek. "I would neva judge yuh, Irie. I promise."

I take a deep breath as she wipes my tears away.

Relief.

"Seeing you and all di girls from school about to go off to these fancy colleges and universities, I felt so left behind. I never imagined my life could have purpose in di same way, but tonight . . . tonight is the beginning of that. Me having a purpose, just like you."

Jilly watches me, wiping away my tears. Even though the pain is heavy, it is not sadness that I feel.

It is love.

"I'm so proud of you, Irie," she says softly. "And I hope you know that I look up to you *so much*. You're so brave and *you're going to kill it on that stage*. Tonight is the night. I jus' feel it."

I smile as she lights up.

"Oh my gosh, that reminds me." Jilly bolts up. "There's this record I've been meaning to play fi yuh. It's called 'Tonight Is the Night' by Claudette Miller." She's excited as she jumps down. "This *must* be a sign from God."

I laugh as I watch her excitement.

"Come nuh!" she calls as she makes her way through the bathroom door.

I giggle, tipsy and high as I make my way down from the ledge. I stumble through Jilly's bathroom and into her room.

"Here it is." She makes her way over to the record player as I go to sit back down on the bed. Time seems to move slower as I look about the room, amazed by all the details I didn't notice. Stuffed animals and old trinkets. A small Bible on her nightstand table and ribbons on the shelves. "Come here, nuh." Jilly calls back over to me as she stops the record.

I raise up and make my way over to her.

"Tonight Is the Night." She puts the record onto the player and drops the pin. Just then, a smooth riddim starts to play as the sound of a woman's raspy voice quietly fills the room.

Neeeervous, tremblinnn' . . .

Jilly's face lights up as the bluesy, soulful voice fills the room. The woman's voice is romantic, and I watch as Jilly loses herself in the melody all over again.

Under the shadowy moonlight, she radiates.

Tonight is the night you make me a woman . . .

"I *loooove* dis part." She's so focused on the song it almost feels too personal to watch. "*Ughhh.*" She throws her head back.

But her excitement comes out like a moan, sending a shiver straight through me. Jilly grabs on to my hand and I swallow, my mouth wetter than usual as she pulls me in.

"It's like everything in her voice feels so . . . *bare,* yuh know? She's not worried about the song being catchy or di words rhymin'. It's just about di *feeling.*"

I lose myself as we dance drunkenly, twirling before pulling each other close.

"I swear, Jilly, if it were up to me, I would just spend my whole life performin'. Singing all ova di place."

"Tonight is the night," Jilly sings along to the words, responding to me in the same breath. Under her gaze, I feel unfiltered.

I feel the audacity to dream.

"You would be *sooo* good, Irie," Jilly says drunkenly.

"Yuh think? Fa real?"

"*I know.* Everyone, *everywhere,* is going to know yuh songs." She stumbles over her words. "Just imagine yuh name in lights."

I'm intoxicated as the rhythm fills my chest. As I groove my hips this way and that, we come alive to the music as we dance the night away. We spin round and round like the record, lost in our own magic as we grip desperately to our youth. *To each other.*

To our final months of being teenagers.

Our last summer together in Jamaica.

I feel safe as we spin like schoolgirls, twirling in our party dresses. Dizzy and drunk with adrenaline, we collapse onto the floor, grabbing on to each other for stability. Her soft hands fall onto my brown skin as goose bumps race down my spine.

The laughter stops.

And so does time.

"Irie." She says it so softly it barely leaves her lips. "*You are so beautiful. Did you know that?*"

My mind swirls as fantasy and reality bleed together. Jilly drunkenly draws her hand up to my cheek. My heart beats heavy in my chest.

"Yuh have no idea, do you?" she whispers again as she slowly crawls on top of me. She playfully straddles me, sitting down onto my lap.

I start to pulse.

"You have no idea how beautiful you are."

I can feel her panties press into me through her stockings.

Warm and . . .

Wet.

"Irie . . . ," she slurs.

She's intoxicated, and so am I.

But there's no use in words.

I feel her already.

BAM BAM BAM.

A sharp knock makes us both jump from our skin. Euphoria turns to terror, and as Jilly stumbles to her feet, the door swings open.

And there stands her father.

Livid.

"What the hell is going on in here?" He barges into the room.

"Nothing, Daddy," Jilly says.

I quickly stand up. "Good night, Mr. Casey." My voice trembles.

"What are you two listening to?" He marches over to Jilly's record player.

"Daddy, we were just—"

"How many times do I have to tell you about playin' that blasted music?"

"It wasn't even reggae, Daddy! It was just a slow song."

"If I have to talk to you again, I'll smash this record player, Jillian. Do you understand?"

Jilly looks at the floor.

"*Do you understand me?*" he barks.

"Yes, Daddy."

He throws the needle off the record before grabbing the record off the player. I nearly die as I watch him handle it with such force.

"I want you girls in bed," he orders, his tone jolting. "*Now.*"

I keep my head down as Jilly and I scatter to the bed, quickly hopping in.

"I don't want to hear another peep from you girls, you understand?"

"Yes, Daddy," Jilly mutters.

His eyes examine the room one final time before making his way back toward the door. He flicks off the lights, and the room goes pitch-black as he slams the door shut.

Oh my God.

I try to shake the shock as I lie next to Jilly. I look at the nightstand table.

10:20 p.m.

I'm on pins and needles as we lie in silence, our backs to each other as the hum of night fills the room. All I can hear is the echo from the party downstairs and my racing heart.

Neither Jilly nor I say a word.

I'm nervous to even breathe too loud, so I hold it tightly in my lungs. To breathe would be to admit that what just happened . . . did.

We lie still in the black of night as I come crashing down from my high. After a few moments of strained silence, Jilly speaks.

"Yuh okay?" she whispers.

"Yeah."

But the truth is I'm not.

What just happened?

I want to cry.

Disappear.

Drown deeper into everything I just felt with her. *Feel it again,* just one more time.

Or forever.

I bite down, desperate for her to say something else. But she doesn't. My entire body tenses as the crickets in the distance attempt to soothe our racing hearts.

It doesn't work.

I can hear Jilly's heart beating just as loudly as mine. Even in our silence, we crash into each other. We are thinking the same thing, and we both know it.

How? And why?

And why?

And why?

I am a drunken daze of confusion as the question plays on a loop. I close my eyes, praying it will all go away. And soon, we drift off.

Alone,

BUT together.

16

Jilly

Buzz. *Buzz. Buzz.*

THE alarm goes off at 1:00 a.m. sharp.

My head throbs, woozy as I peel my eyes open to the abyss of my dark room. Everything feels like a blur. And then it comes back to me, and guilt crashes over me like a tidal wave.

What the fuck happened last night?

The question paralyzes me, holding me down with fear as I lay pinned beneath the sheets next to Irie. Flashes of pleasure erupt through my body against my better judgment. I remember it all, I feel it all, and I want it all again.

Irie setting me free.

I'm aroused all over again as I lie still in the bed. But the feeling of shame that accompanies it is corrosive. Regret crawls its way up my sheets. Because just as butterflies dance through me, the demons come out to play.

Mummy and Daddy would have killed me.

They would have me dead if they ever found out I got that close to another girl. They would ship me off to Christian camp and throw away the key. I would spend my life repenting for my sins and being force-fed holy water. And not to mention Christopher.

Fuck.

Christopher.

I'm woozy as all the events from earlier in the night come crashing back to me. The dinner. My mother. The conversation with Christopher in my father's study. The bracelet . . .

His offer.

I look down at the diamonds that glitter on my wrist as my stomach ties into knots.

What the hell am I going to do?

I try to soothe my anxiety as I peel up from the bed. I lean over Irie and reach for the small alarm clock that quietly buzzes on the nightstand table and turn it off. I watch as Irie stirs beside me, rubbing her eyes as she wakes.

"Mawnin'," I whisper, trying my best to play it cool. "How was yuh nap?"

"Hey." She smiles, her voice warm. "It was good. I have no idea when I even fell asleep. Yuh bed is so comfy, I jus' knocked out."

"That tends to happen." I smile.

The silence between us is tender as we sit side by side. In the late hours of the night, my house is dead silent. It's clear that Mummy and Daddy have long gone off to bed.

"Yuh feelin' all right?" Irie's voice cuts through the dark. "Yuh not hungova or anyting?"

"Not too bad," I say. "How about you?"

"No . . ." Her voice trails. "I'm good."

As she watches me in the dark, I can't help but wonder what exists in the words we don't speak. But as the seconds between us linger, the truth is I'm not brave enough to ask.

And it's time for us to go.

"So what's di plan?" Irie whispers as she moves from under the sheets.

"We'll go out through di front gate," I say, grateful for the shift in focus. "After we get the bicycles from the shed . . ." My nerves turn to adrenaline as I say the plan aloud. "I just have to get di key fi di gate. It should be in di kitchen."

I'm electrified as the plan starts to feel real.

All we have to do is make it through the house.

"Yuh ready?" I whisper to Irie.

"Bawn ready," she says confidently as she gets up. Even after the night we had, she looks stunning in her crumpled party dress, her braids perfectly intact as they cascade down her shoulders.

As she shimmies out of the bed, I fight the urge to pull her back in it.

We go in opposite directions, tiptoeing throughout the room to get changed. I head to my drawer just as Irie makes her way to her overnight bag. With my back to her, I pull out a pale purple spaghetti-strap top and a short flared black skirt. We move cautiously as we slip out of our party dresses and stockings with our backs to each other.

I try my best to act normally, but every part of me wants to turn around.

Every part of me wants to see Irie naked.

Stop it, Jillian, I scold myself as I slip into the black skirt.

I spin around to find Irie already dressed, checking herself out in the mirror. Songbook in hand, she wears a yellow tank top, a short flowy white skirt, and brown sandals.

She looks gorgeous.

A vision in the night, Irie stands in the shadows like a *real-life goddess.* I can feel her courage even from all the way across the room. I wish I could be as bold as she's about to be tonight. As unafraid.

As honest.

She smiles at me in the mirror when she notices me looking. I look away, flustered.

"All right." I pretend to fiddle with my skirt. "Yuh ready?"

Irie nods as she bites down on her lip. "It's now or neva."

"You were born for this, Irie," I say, wanting her to know it for herself. "Now jus' follow my lead, and whatever yuh do, *don't mek any noise.* Stay close and try fi walk light."

"Cool." Irie nods without question.

And with that, I lead the way through my bedroom door.

We walk on eggshells as we tiptoe into the dark hallway, mindful as we round down the steps. Mummy and Daddy's bedroom is at the end of the hall, and we move with haste as we descend the stairs. I'm shot with adrenaline as we head into the kitchen, carefully making our way across the tiles toward where the shed key is located. On my tippy-toes, I reach up and grab it along with the gate key. I grab Irie's hand, and we make our way toward the back door.

I unlock it, and Irie steps out into the night.

I follow behind her, careful as I gently close the door. All at once, euphoria takes over. The island feels wondrous and alive in the late hours of the night.

Irie and I instantly lock eyes, giddy and excited to have made it out of the house. I tuck the keys into my bra before grabbing on to Irie's hand again. Careful to stay close to the house, we round the estate and make our way to the bicycle shed that sits in the distance. My hands shake as the thrill of what we're doing sets in like a tornado.

I can't wait to get the fuck out of here.

We grab the bicycles from the shed, staying close to the bushes to avoid being seen through the windows by any of the staff. Once we round the bend to the front of the house, we walk even more carefully as our sandals cross the driveway.

I pull the key from my bra as we approach the gate.

Irie steadies my bicycle as I turn the lock, and then I slowly push the gate open. We check to make sure the coast is clear one final time before Irie walks through, guiding both bicycles beside her. I slink out behind her and lock the gate.

The road is dark and empty, lit up only by the few lampposts that line the street. We guide the bicycles away from the house as Irie places her songbook and the record into her basket. I grip my handlebars tightly as we both mount onto the bicycles. Irie doesn't miss a beat, effortless as she kicks off, leading the way in front of me. I follow her lead, surprised at how easily the movement comes back to me. Irie looks back at me, and I give her a silent thumbs-up.

We don't stop until we're out of sight from my house.

Eventually, the laughter comes pouring out of us like a song.

"I *cyaan* believe it." Irie laughs, keeping her voice quiet. "We *actually* did it!"

"Right?" I'm a fit of giggles, in disbelief myself. "What kind of manager would I be if I made yuh miss yuh first gig?"

Irie beams. "Yuh think you got di hang of it?"

"Yeah, I'm good." I nod. "I can lead di way out of the hills. I've driven the route with Lloyd about a million times."

"Cool. And I'll pick up when we hit di main street."

I nod, feeling slightly uneasy. "Okay." I try to mask my apprehension. "Let's do this."

And with that, we speed off into the night. *One foot after the other,* I tell myself with each stroke.

My efforts become seamless, and soon I'm riding like I've been doing it for years. I turn my face to the moon, and I feel my troubles fall like shadows behind me.

I'm finally free.

"This is incredible!" I laugh with reckless abandon as I throw my head back in the warm night breeze. Irie can't help but join in as she throws her hands to the sky.

"Wooooo!" she yells to the night. "Reggae Jamz, here we come!"

We throw caution to the wind as we speed down the mountain and out of Jacks Hill.

Once we hit the main road, Irie takes over. I follow behind

her for another ten minutes, and soon, the atmosphere changes. Every now and then, a random car passes by, but for the most part the streets are barren. *Eerie.* The exhilaration quickly fades as we enter the dark, looming streets of Kingston.

"I know a back route," Irie whispers. "But stay close."

"Okay," I say, trusting her as I trail behind.

The streets are so dark that I fight to see just a few feet in front of me. But I push through the fear. We stop for nothing.

We ride for a few more miles until soon, we approach what looks like an abandoned street. We make our way past a long strip of zinc houses, and I'm stunned to imagine that people could actually live in homes made from scrap metals. As we approach the end of the alleyway, Irie slows her bicycle.

"I think we haffi make a right," she says as she examines the street signs. So, we swing a right and continue down the road. The farther we go, the more people we begin to see littered throughout the night. After a few miles, it becomes clear we're approaching our destination.

Soon, Irie slows her legs, bringing her bicycle to a stop. I follow her lead as we begin to walk the bicycles up the road.

"We can leave them in the alleyway," Irie says.

"Yuh sure?"

"I mean, it's definitely a risk, but we don't really have another choice."

"Okay." I swallow, trying not to let fear paralyze me.

We've made it this far.

We turn down a deserted alleyway, trepid as we briskly make our way down. Irie walks for a few minutes before finding a piece of abandoned zinc and tucking the bicycle behind it. She places mine next to hers before grabbing her songbook and record from the basket.

I'm a nervous wreck as we lock eyes.

"Ready?" she asks.

I nod before pulling her in for a hug. We hold each other, both aware of the danger in front of us before pulling away. With no time to waste, we turn back in the direction we came.

We run out of the alleyway, keeping a low profile as we try our best to blend into the side streets. But the farther we go down the road, the more people watch with curious eyes as we pass. We keep our focus straight ahead as we follow in the direction that everyone seems to be going. People are dressed to the nines, smooth, clean, and ready to have a good time. There's no need to ask anyone for directions because the booming bass leads the way.

We are headed to the dance hall.

We round the corner to find the old building tucked away at the end of an abandoned street. People scatter along the roadside, and the energy is noisy, rebellious, and chaotic as people try their best to get inside. There's an exclusivity in the air that screams, *If you know, you know,* as a long line of people wait impatiently at the doors.

"So, where do we go?" I ask Irie as we approach the line.

"Ace said he'd meet me at the front."

I look at her like she's crazy. "*All di way* up there? We can't jump the line."

Irie takes a deep breath, knowing I'm right as we look at the line. Just then, she spots him. "Right there," Irie says excitedly. She's clear and focused as she takes my clammy hand, and we make our way over to her friend Ace, who stands off to the side. He's incredibly handsome and tall, with smooth black skin that glows in the hot night. There's a distinct bad-boy energy to him, and he looks like he couldn't be more than mid-twenties. He watches us, laid-back and cool in a black button-up shirt and dark black shades. As we get closer, he pulls them down to reveal glassy brown eyes.

"Irie," he slurs. "Wha' gwaan?"

"Hey, Ace," Irie says as we walk up. "This is my friend Jilly."

His eyes land on me, confused.

"She's cool," Irie says quickly.

"Me nuh tell yuh already yuh nuffi bring nobody?"

I fidget as he eyes me.

"I know. I'm sorry, Ace." Irie looks him in the eye. "But Jilly's my *best friend*. She's the only reason I could even come tonight. We snuck out from her place in Jacks Hill."

"Irie." Ace pauses, frustrated. "Me *already* tell yuh say—"

"*Please*," Irie says adamantly. "Jilly nah go say nuttin'. I swear."

Ace eyes me, and I fight the urge to squirm under his gaze.

"Wha'ppen, Ace?" I smile awkwardly, putting on my best Patois accent.

He stares at me, skeptical.

I've never felt so out of place.

"Fine," he gives in. "But if yuh tell anybody I got you in, you and me ah go have problems. Yuh understand?"

His brown eyes penetrate mine.

"Yeah." I nod, unsure of how to take his threat. "Of course not."

"Good." He eases up. "Unu bring yuh money?"

"Shoot." Irie looks at him. "I forgot I needed cash."

"Cover is ten dollars each," he says. "I can cover fi one ah yuh."

"It's cool," I interject. "I always walk wit' money on me. I'll pay for us."

"Tanks, Jilly." Irie smiles.

"All right, yuh have yuh song?" Ace turns back to Irie.

"Right here." She passes him the record. "I'm singing ova an instrumental."

"Cool." He takes it, examining the case before tucking it under his arm. "Now here's how it ah guh go. When we go inside, me ah go talk to me brejin so he can put yuh on di list. It's Saturday night, so it's competitive. They only let a few people on di mic, but I think you'll have an edge because you're a girl."

Irie nods as we take in the information.

"Tonight might jus' be yuh lucky night. U-Roy is the special guest."

"*What?*" Irie says in shock. "Daddy Roy?"

"Who name so?" I ask.

"Only the biggest, *boddest* deejay in all of Kingston," Irie says as her nerves get the best of her. "He's the godfather of dancehall. His song 'Natty Rebel' is always playing at di shop."

"Oh, wow," I say as it comes back to me. "I think I know that song."

"The man pretty much created di genre of deejaying," Ace says.

"Totally," Irie agrees. "I mean, there were others before him like Count Matchuki and King Stitt," Irie explains. "But Daddy Roy is a legend. He's known for turning di rotations into a story."

"And toasting ova di beat," Ace says.

"Toasting?" I ask, feeling insecure that I don't know.

"It's kinda like talking or chanting over the song," Irie explains. "He even has his own special sound system. *He's iconic.* One of di pioneers of reggae music."

"And he's started a lot of artists' careers," Ace says.

"Wow," I say in disbelief. "And he's here *tonight*?"

"Where else would he be?" Ace looks at me slyly. "This is *Reggae Jamz,* girl. Biggest sound clash in Kingston. Only di best of Jamaica comes out fi DJ SupaCat. Real musicians are *always* amongst di people . . . rememba' dat."

His tone is condescending, humbling me.

I glance over at Irie, whose face is filled with a mixture of excitement and shock.

"Wow, Ace," she says in amazement. "*Thank you.* I don't even know what to say."

"Don't say nuttin'." He winks. "The only thing yuh haffi do tonight is sing yuh heart out."

Irie beams, ready.

"Welcome to di dance hall, ladies. Follow back ah me," Ace says before slinking off toward the front of the line. Irie and I follow behind him like two giddy schoolgirls. I keep my head down as we push by the angsty partygoers. Ace is confident as we approach the bouncers at the front of the line.

"Wha'ppen, Reggie?" he hails up the security.

"Big mon. Wha' gwaan? Everyting chris?"

"Yeah, mon, everyting straight."

"Wha' yaah deal wit'?"

"Dem two girl yah." He gestures back to us. "They're wit' me."

"Cool." The man nods.

Ace gives us the go-ahead, and we hastily follow behind him.

"Hey!" a lady calls out from the line. "How come dem get fi bud di line?"

"Dat nuh right!" a man calls out.

And just as the crowd begins to get irate, we quickly make our way through the doors.

"Whoa." It slips from my mouth as the bass reverberates in my chest.

The music bumps, and people are littered around the entrance with drinks in their hands. I self-consciously adjust my skirt as we make our way into the party.

The vibe is *wicked*.

The smell of ganja is thick, and it covers us like a cloud as it wafts through the air. I feel my entire body start to relax as we make our way through. The energy of the dance hall hits me like nothing I've ever felt before in my life.

I can't believe we're at Reggae Jamz.

Black bodies fill every corner of the space, the energy grimy and raw as they move in time to the dancehall beat. A slow, steady dub explodes through the room as the sound system shakes the walls and blares through my chest.

"Holy—" Laughter pours from my lips as Irie and I take in

the scene. The energy is *electric* and the movements are *magnetic* as people grind back and forth, dancing on one another in perfect time. Hips sway this way and that as a deep, heavy voice comes over the sound system.

"PULLLL UP!"

"Wait here," Ace instructs. "I'm going to talk to di selecta."

He takes the record and makes his way deeper into the party. Irie and I stand near the doors as joy explodes through every inch of our bodies.

"Nuff drum and bass mek yuh whine up yuh waist!" DJ SupaCat's voice echoes through the night. *"This one's for di people!"*

"This is *mod*!" Irie laughs, calling out over the music. "I can't believe we're here!"

"Right?" I beam, grabbing hold of her hand. "I've neva seen anything like dis in my life, Irie!"

And it's true.

The rebellious vibrations are seductive as men and women groove through the space uninhibited. *Free.* There's an urgency to their movements—rough, yet tender at the same time as they dance on each other with a palpable desire. The lust is everywhere, and it's *thick* as they whine on the edge of the sound, yielding to their desires as a natural rhythm takes over. Everyone is in a complete state of surrender.

It feels like we're watching a trance.

A few seconds later, Ace emerges from the crowd and gestures for Irie and me to follow.

"We're good," he says, smooth and confident. "Come wit' me. And stay close."

We follow his instructions.

Ace's energy is dominating, and even though I don't know much about him, as we follow closely behind, I feel protected. *Like I blend in a little more.* The energy is tantalizing as the ferocious beat blasts through the room. Ace walks effortlessly cool, grooving to the music, and the farther we go, the less self-conscious I feel. All my insecurities melt away, and soon, my body moves in time with the rhythm just like everyone else's. I sway my hips from side to side as the bass moves me, and in an instant, the three of us are dancing in sync with the rest of the room.

Sweaty.

Grimy.

Raw.

Liberation crawls up my spine like a snake as I hold on to Irie's hand. She looks back at me, and joy adorns her face, her eyes lit up even in the dark. I laugh, throwing my head back in the dark space as I whine my hips this way and that. I slither and coil, giving myself permission to set my soul free. *If only for now,* I offer my pain to the music.

To the night.

I am one with the sound, and it feels *so. Damn. Good.*

For once, I don't have to worry about the music being too loud or my spirit being too free. I'm allowed to move my hips and honor my body as it rolls and curls. My breath is drowned out by the thickness of the bass line as Ace guides us to the wall and the sound takes over—an eerie, lustful, and mysterious dub. I throw my hands up as the three of us move in sync, rocking steadily to the beat. The energy is contagious.

And it controls me.

The place is packed, and the smoke from the ganja wraps itself around us as Ace moves in closer, his eyes alluring and fo-cused. I watch as he slides himself behind Irie, holding her hips as they begin to grind together to the music. Irie surrenders, and a tinge of jealousy moves through me. I look away, pretending not to notice as I continue to sway my hips to the side.

But as the minutes pass, my envy only grows.

Ace nuzzles himself into Irie's neck, his energy commanding as he moves passionately and skillfully. As he steadies her by the waist, butterflies flutter in my stomach.

I don't know if I'm more jealous of him or her.

I can't help but be turned on as I watch them rocksteady. I want to be a part of their dance. I watch lustfully as Irie closes her eyes, losing herself in the music.

I can't take my eyes off her.

She moves like a true artist—a siren in the night. There's a comfort to her, almost like she's used to being around this type of vibe. Or maybe she just belongs here a little more than I do. I start to feel self-conscious as I run my fingers through my silky hair.

I fit in, but not really.

Not truly.

I watch in a rapture as Irie grooves her body. I've never experienced her like this—so free and in her element. She glows under the cascading red lights, and when she opens her brown eyes, they instantly lock with mine.

I smile, grateful that she didn't forget about me. The entire dance hall is lit up like fire, and as the space gets tighter, everyone is lost in the rhythm of the night.

The moment is magical.

Ace leans back on the wall, pulling Irie on top of him as the deejay plays their bodies like a symphony. As I watch them, a feeling creeps up, an urge that I can't satisfy, no matter how deeply I sway my hips.

I want her.

The quiet desperation fills every inch of me as Ace pulls a spliff from his pocket and lights it just over Irie's head. He takes a long draw before passing it to her.

"Tek ah draw," he instructs.

She does so without question. I stare directly into her brown eyes, enchanted as I watch her take a pull. Both of us are aware of the things we don't say.

The feelings we don't dare speak aloud.

She turns her face away, blowing the smoke upward before passing me the spliff. "Yuh want some?" I can barely hear her over the music.

"Yeah!" I call, taking the spliff from her fingers. I draw the smoke in, allowing it to fill my lungs once again as my thoughts melt away. I exhale into the night, not missing a beat as the smoke curls in the air, wrapping itself around us like a spell.

The vibrations feel like a dream.

"Tanks," I slur as I pass the spliff back to Ace. His brown eyes hold mine as he takes it from me. I immediately look away, losing myself in the music as I whine not too far in front of them. I move to the beat like a private dancer.

And then the song comes to an end.

And the spell is broken.

"We just ah get started!" the deejay's deep voice calls over the mic. As the next song pours from the sound system, Ace gestures for us to follow him. The party is in full swing as we dance our way through the crowd toward the back corner of the room.

"That was amazin'!" Irie says as we break away from the crowd.

"Only di beginnin'," Ace says, relighting the spliff.

"Oh my gosh, Jilly." Irie grabs my hand and spins me around. "That's him right there. Daddy Roy." She gestures to a Rastaman who sits behind the deejay booth with a mic in his hand. With long dreadlocks down his back, he works the turntable with effortless precision, spinning and mixing in between hopping on the mic.

"He's a legend!" Irie calls out over the music.

"And he's in control of who touches di stage tonight," Ace says, blowing out a cloud of smoke. "My boy talked to him already. You're up first."

"*First?*" Irie's mouth drops.

"Relax." Ace puts his hands on her shoulders, calming her

down. "You're *ready, supastar.* I heard yuh lyrics, and I know yuh have what it takes. But yuh haffi believe in yuhself."

"I do, it's just . . . this is my *first* show."

"Then yuh betta mek it good."

"The crowd is going to love you, Irie!" I smile.

Irie nods, taking a deep breath.

"For Junior," I say to her, taking her hand.

Her eyes twinkle as they lock with mine. "For Junior." She takes a deep breath.

I pull her in for a hug, and I can feel her body trembling as I hold her tightly.

"You got this," I whisper into her ear.

"All right, leh we go," Ace says.

And just like that, we follow him up to the deejay booth.

We weave our way up to the front as people groove to the drums that reverberate through the space. Daddy Roy is busy on the mic as a group of men stand beside him, including the iconic DJ SupaCat. The men dig into the crate, pulling out another record and preparing it for the show. Ace moves closer to SupaCat and whispers something in his ear while Irie and I wait.

"I *cyaan* believe I'm going to sing for him tonight," Irie says to me under her breath.

"The only woman, too," I say. "And probably di youngest." I look around the room, surveying the faces. Only men surround the booth, waiting for their turn on the mic.

Just then, an older woman passes by us.

"I *love* yuh bracelet!" she calls, pointing down to the diamonds on my wrist. "Is it real?"

Shit.

I totally forgot I still had it on.

"Tanks," I say politely, doing my best to hide my wrist. "And no, it's not."

"Well, it's *gorgeous*!" the woman says, grooving to the music as she and her friend continue into the party. When Irie's not looking, I clip it off and tuck it into the side of my bra.

I don't need another reason to stick out.

"Yow!" Ace calls back to us, locking eyes with Irie as he turns around. "Yuh ready fi touch di stage?"

Irie nods, trembling as fear bathes her face. She holds her songbook tightly in her hands.

"Yeah!" I call out on her behalf. "She bawn ready."

"Cool," Ace says. "You're up after dis track."

"I can't breathe," Irie says, starting to panic.

"Yes, you can." I gaze into her eyes just as Daddy Roy's "Natty Rebel" comes over the sound system. "Not only can yuh breathe, yuh can *sing*. And afta tonight, *everyone* here's going to know it too."

Irie nods, a twinkle in her eyes as she takes me in.

I'm a rebel . . .

The energy from the bass pumps its way through the dance hall as the lyrics cover us in a final embrace. Irie flips her braids to the side, passing me her yellow songbook.

The pawty *tun up*.

"For Junior." She exhales.

AND with that, she makes her way to the stage.

17

———

Irie

"Yuh nah go tek di mic?"

DADDY Roy's deep brown eyes stare back at me as I stand in shock at the audacity of what I'm about to do. The bass thumps as I move closer to him, keeping my back to the crowd. He stands behind the booth next to SupaCat and Brigadier Jerry.

Reggae legends—Deejays known for spreading the message of Jah's love.

My knees wobble as I reach for the mic in his hands.

"Tanks." I smile, silently praying to God that I don't collapse.

"Wha' yuh say yuh name was, girl?" Brigadier Jerry asks me.

"Irie!" I call out over the music.

"Irie." He nods. "Me love it! Where yuh come from?"

"Kintyre."

"All right, well, gwaan mash it up, girl!"

"Tonight ah yuh night." SupaCat nods. "Gwaan bod!"

"Tank you." I beam as I grip the mic in my hands. "I will."

I take one final deep breath before turning around to the crowd of people who dance the night away under the moody dark red lights. Suddenly, a blinding spotlight shines down onto me. I'm overcome with fear and elation all at the same time.

Holy shit.

"Yow, yow, yow!" SupaCat calls over the riddim. "Next up on di mic, we have a young empress in di buildin'!" The crowd starts to rustle, slowing their dancing as SupaCat calls from the booth. His voice booms from the sound system as my heart slams against my chest.

"Give it up fi *Irie from Kintyre*!"

Terror shoots from the top of my head to the pit of my stomach.

One foot in front of the other, Irie.

I tremble as I make my way toward the center of the stage. All the eyes begin to fall on me, and I know that after this moment, nothing will be the same.

I got this, I tell myself as I scan the crowd for Jilly and Ace.

And just as the instrumental record comes over the speakers, I spot them. As I lock eyes with Jilly, I bring the microphone to my mouth.

"Hello and good evenin', everyone, my name is Irie . . . Irie Rivers," I say as the catchy beat takes over the room. "It's an honor to be here with all of you tonight. Dis is a song I wrote for a friend of mine; I promised him I would always tell the truth wit' my music."

And just as the beat drops, I let it all out.

I won't back down from this holy war
The spirit of love will fight on and I will roar
Peace will reign and wash away the sins of my brother
I have faith that we will hold hands and one day come
    home to each other
For there has to be a better way, and love has to know a
    brighter day

The lyrics rip out of me, full bodied and whole. I sing from the pit of my stomach to the top of my heart, not holding anything back.

Not anymore.

We are the children of Jah who have forgot
The truth of all we are and all we are not
So may peace reign through the nation, may love cover the
*   land*
And when I am weak, may Jah the Almighty take my hand
Free me from the chains of my mind, help me to see the
*   truth clear*
That wherever I go, freedom is near

I open my eyes and look out at the audience. Everyone's eyes are glued to me as they rocksteady to the horns and drums. I find confidence as I lose myself in the beat, grooving with my own lyrics as I throw my body this way and that. The sound is *infectious,* and I watch as the room comes alive. As if by no doing of my own, my body takes over as we all groove in time to the music. I let the beat ride before catching it again, belting my heart to the night.

Tear down the institutions
Reevaluate the Constitution
We have to fight if we want to be free
We can't fear the power of who we could be
There's nothing to lose when you remember, my sister
That we are never alone, love comes in a whisper

I let my voice run, playing with the notes as I whine my hips. I look to the crowd, belting the words with all my heart.

There's nothing to lose when you remember, my brother
That creation is alive, we are all one another

And just as I hit the last note, the entire place goes *crazy*.
The dance hall is alive.

The crowd erupts as Daddy Roy blares the horn over the sound system, and people start to stomp and bang on the walls in celebration. I'm swept up into my own symphony as I lose myself in their applause. My entire body buzzes with joy.

I can't believe that they're cheering for me.

BUHBUHBUHBUUUUUR!

Daddy Roy blasts the horn again, hailing me up as the beat continues to ride out. The entire place is *shot* as they cheer me on, chanting for an encore. In the front row, I lock eyes with Jilly, who jumps up and down, and I beam, bursting all over again as she gives me a thumbs-up from the crowd. I glance over at Ace, who wears a wide smile across his face, impressed under his dark shades.

SupaCat's voice fills the space once again. "Cool, cool, cool." He tries to simmer the crowd. But it's no use.

They continue to cheer, this time chanting my name. "IRIE! IRIE! IRIE!"

"Wow!" It escapes from my lips as Daddy Roy spins the record again, bobbing his head to the music.

"So nice yuh haffi play it twice!" SupaCat's deep voice comes over the mic. "Irie from Kintyre! Di people want an encore!"

AND so, I give them one.

TEN minutes later, I'm still on a high as I turn around and hand the mic to the next performer—a young Rasta who prepares to take the stage. The entire dance hall claps me offstage as Daddy Roy bleeds into another riddim. As a heavy dub fills the space, I descend into the crowd. I'm on cloud nine, at a true loss for words as my entire body buzzes. The young Rasta begins toasting on the track just as Jilly rushes up to me, a gigantic smile on her face as Ace trails behind her.

"Irie, yuh were *fantastic*!" She's a ripple of laughter as she pummels into me, taking me into a giant hug.

Home.

"Tank yuh, Jilly." I squeeze her tightly as I nuzzle into her neck. My entire body clings to her. "I couldn't have done it without yuh."

"Yes, you could," Ace interrupts as I pull away from Jillian. "That was a mod ting, Irie. Di entire dance hall loved yuh."

"Yow!" We're interrupted by a husky voice that calls out from behind. I turn around and I freeze, stunned to be standing face-to-face with Daddy Roy.

He looks down at me with a reserved smile on his face.

"Dat was wicked, young lady. Yuh very talented."

"Wow." I flush. "Thank yuh, Daddy Roy. I-I'm such a big fan."

"Yuh have a manager?" he asks me.

"No—"

"Yeah. Right here." Ace extends his hand. "Ace. My brejin is the promoter."

"Cool, bredda. Well, look, I like her sound; I think she has a real message. It's been a while since I've heard a woman tek over di dance hall like that." He reaches into his pants pocket and pulls out a battered card. "Come by my studio some time dis week. We'll work suh'um out." He passes Ace the card, and I nearly faint. "Di address deh pon di back."

"Cool." Ace nods, examining the card in his hands.

And just like that, Daddy Roy slinks off into the crowd back toward the booth.

My heart bursts wide open.

"Did that just happen?" I squeal, jumping up and down. "Daddy Roy wants to record *me* in his studio? I mus' be dreamin'."

"Play it cool nuh, Irie." Ace smiles, calming me back down. "Yuh not even leave out di venue yet."

But I can't help it. Real excitement floods through me for the first time in my life.

A future.

"Wait here." Ace trails off to grab the instrumental record as Jilly and I stand in the crowd. Her eyes dance as she watches me.

"Irie, I cyaan believe it. Yuh were *flawless*!" she exclaims. "Every note, every move, every run. Yuh had di whole place going *mad*! They loved yuh!"

"I still cyaan believe it myself." I shake my head. "Siarah and Tandi won't believe it, either. I'm going to record my *own* song!"

Tears of joy creep up into the back of my eyes. "This is a *dream come true*. I've neva even been to a studio before." I laugh as pure ecstasy spills out of me. "Do yuh know what this *means*?" I take Jilly's hand as we groove with the rest of the room to the heavy dub. "I'm going to have my *first actual* record, Jilly! Yuh haffi come with me!"

"I wouldn't miss it for the world."

A surge of bliss moves through me. "My *very own record*." I bite down on my lip as I take it in. "One I could play at di shop. Maybe even on di radio."

"Nuh badda get too far ahead of yuhself." Ace laughs as he approaches us from behind. "Yuh still haffi record di song first. And you know reggae nuh play pon radio in Jamaica." He hands me back the vinyl.

"A girl can dream, Ace." I stick out my tongue as I take the case from his hands. "Besides, yuh betta start talk to me nice. Daddy Roy say me ah star."

"Mm-hmm!" Jilly laughs. "She have *talent*, yuh nuh hear?"

We're a ball of laughter as we groove. I'm so happy that things aren't weird between us after last night, and my stomach flutters as we dance the night away.

Nothing between us has changed.

After a moment, Ace gestures for us to follow him back through the crowd. As we make our way through, people from all over the club hail me up as we go. My head is on a swivel as people call my name.

"IRIE! Yuh voice *wicked*, girl!"

"Pawty shot, gyal!"

I glow, caught in a frenzy as I take it all in. I've never had so many people hear my music. My voice. *Something so deeply personal to me.* Junior would be so proud, and the thought alone brings instant tears to my eyes.

I know he was here in spirit tonight.

Once we make it through the crowd, Ace, Jilly, and I spill out through the front doors. The nighttime breeze is intoxicating as we pass the line of latecomers who wait to get inside the dance hall. As we approach the road, I stand in between Ace and Jilly, still on a high.

"What did it feel like up there, Irie?" Jilly asks.

"Magic," I burst. "It felt like I wasn't me . . . like I was this other version of myself."

"Oh, it was you, all right," Ace says as he pulls the card from his pocket and hands it to me. "It was di version of you that I've seen all along. I'm glad yuh finally saw her too."

I blush, examining the card as we come to a stop. Ace's eyes scan me, his gaze intense as I look up at him.

"I was serious in there yuh nuh."

"About what?"

"Managin' you," he says firmly. "Yuh have a major talent, Irie. And what you're singing about is important. Di JCG are mashin' up di streets, and we have to tek a stand against it. Reggae artists have di most power because they give a voice to di truth . . . to the people."

His words are intoxicating, but the statement makes me self-conscious in front of Jilly.

"Yuh need someone to help you. Someone who believes in you and can help yuh line up some more gigs. If yuh serious, I can help yuh mek a name fi yuhself. I know all ah di promoters in di dance hall scene."

"Ace, I—" But I'm unsure of what to say as I take in his offer.

Every part of me wants to say yes.

But as Jilly stands next to me, I hesitate, feeling slightly guilty. "Me nuh know, Ace. Jilly and me—"

"Don't be foolish, Irie!" Jilly brushes me off. "Yuh know I was only joking wit' di whole manager ting. I don't know di first thing about managing you, and besides, yuh deserve a real manager. Someone who can help take yuh places." She smiles humbly, but I still feel bad. "Don' let me get in di way of that."

"All right." I take a deep breath, meeting Ace's brown eyes. "Yuh have a deal." I smile. "Managa."

"That's what I like to hear." He holds my gaze, taking my hand in his.

Before I can say anything else, he breaks us out of the moment. "I have some business fi go handle." He pulls away. "And you two should probably get going. It's not safe to be out in Kingston so late."

Shit.

"Yeah," Jilly says. "The sun's going to be up inna few hours."

"Cool. Well, tanks again, Ace," I say genuinely. "Fi everyting tonight. Yuh really came through, and I think it just changed my life. I owe you."

"Don' mention it." His voice is deep and raspy as he begins to walk away. "Jus' meet me at that address. Wednesday at one o'clock."

"I'll be there." I nod eagerly as I look to Jilly. "We both will."

"It was good to meet yuh, Ace." Jilly smiles at him. "I'll see you again soon, I'm sure."

Ace nods, saluting us as he lights a spliff. He slinks off into the night as we make our way back down the road. I silently wonder what business he could be handling this time of the night.

Taking the same route as before, Jilly and I walk for a couple of minutes before approaching the alleyway. We run down the dark space, both of us eager to see if the bicycles are still there.

I'm on pins and needles as we approach the pile of zinc, and I pull it to the side.

God is good.

I'm relieved to find them still there.

"Thank the heavens," Jilly says as she picks up her bicycle. I do the same, and we both straddle on before making our way out of the alleyway.

We ride for a few blocks until we're far away from the party and back in the dark streets of Kingston. The nighttime is eerie the farther we go, but as soon as I'm able, I take Jilly around a side street that shields us from the lone cars that drive in the night. We ride for about a mile until we soon approach an open field.

I slow down and Jilly speeds up, catching up beside me.

"Almost home." I glance over at her as I pedal. We ride alone under the moonlight, vulnerable as our silence fills the space between us.

"We still have some time," she calls, her smile bright as she looks to me through the black of night. "Yuh wan' pull ova? Chill out fi a bit?"

"*Now?*" I ask her, confused as I slowly pedal. "Yuh nuh wan' get home?"

"No." Jilly makes a face. "I want to enjoy all di time we have together. I mean, who knows when we're ever going to get to do this again."

"Me nuh know, Jilly." I look to the dark roads as we pedal side by side.

"Come nuh, Irie," she begs through a smile. "There's *nobody* around. And besides, we're on the side streets now, and we still have a few more hours before dawn."

I keep my eyes focused, tempted but unsure. Although we're far away from the noise, Kingston is still incredibly dangerous this time of night.

"This has literally been di best night of my life." Jilly faux sulks as she rides. "I don't know, I just . . . I don't want it to end."

I bite down on my lip, giving in.

I feel the exact same way.

"Follow me," I whisper.

I continue down the road, swinging a left as Jilly follows behind me. I use instinct to find a side street before taking us down a dirt road surrounded by lush bushes and wild forestry. We pass by a beautiful wall of hibiscus flowers before stumbling upon an open piece of land covered in different-size palm trees. Besides the crickets that sing to the night, the land is still and quiet. Barren.

We're completely alone.

We pedal our bicycles over to the nearest palm tree, slowly scoping out the area as we approach. As we come to a stop, a gust of courage moves through me. I say a silent thank-you to God. I'm so proud of myself, and for the first time in forever, I allow myself to just *feel good.*

What I did tonight was bold.

What started off as the worst night of my life has quickly become the best.

And I couldn't have done any of it without Jillian by my side.

I'm a flurry of emotions, and it's lost on me how I could ever have been mad at her. *Or jealous of her.* I swallow the shame back down. The truth is, I'm *so lucky* to have Jillian in my life. I'm so happy that someone like her sees *me* as worthy.

And no part of me wants to take that for granted.

Jilly's the reason I could even be here tonight, so I don't care what party her family belongs to or what they fill out on a ballot. Jillian Casey is my best friend. And tonight, all I want to do is show her how much she means to me.

I smile as I watch her straddle the pink bicycle, fumbling a little as she hops off. She's clumsy but cute, her hair falling down her shoulders as she turns back to look at me.

"Still gettin' di hang of dis ting." She smiles.

"Well, I think yuh doin' a great job," I say as I rest the bicycle on the ground.

"I guess you're not di only one who deserves a standin' ovation tonight," she teases.

I blush, her words silky and coded in the dead of night.

We take in the warm breeze before slowly making our way over to a nearby palm tree.

"This island is *so* beautiful," Jilly whispers, opening her arms to the night. "Just look at all dis land, only *two seconds* from di road." She twirls around on the grass. "Jamaica is truly paradise."

I smile as I watch her. I haven't heard someone describe Jamaica like that in such a long time. Not since all this war.

"Are yuh going to miss it?" I ask her. "When yuh leave?"

Jilly stops spinning, quiet as she thinks about it.

"A lot," she says softly, looking up at me.

A plunging sadness moves through me as the harsh reality dawns.

These moments together could be our last.

"I'm really going to miss you," I whisper. "I have no idea what I'm going to do."

Jilly is silent as she takes me in. "Let's not dwell on that right now, Irie." She changes the subject. "Tonight is about *you*. Yuh just brought down di house at yuh very first show."

"I know." I laugh as it sinks in all over again. "And I still cyaan believe I met Daddy Roy. My fada prob'ly wouldn't believe me if I told him."

"Well, in a few years, Daddy Roy will telling everyone that *he* cyaan believe he met *you*."

I blush as we slow our pace, hazily making our way through the field.

"It's so quiet out here," I whisper, a smile creeping on my face. "It's really nice."

"Yeah," Jilly agrees as the silence between us grows bigger.

Everything feels still.

Clear.

The full moon beams down over us, shielding us from real life if only for a few more hours. Jilly's soft voice cuts through the silence.

"Can I ask yuh suh'um?"

"Anything," I say as we near the palm tree.

Jilly blushes, looking away.

"Wha?" I smile, curious. "Ask me."

"Promise yuh nah go laugh?"

"Neva."

She pauses before looking up at me. "Ace . . . Yuh tink he has a crush on yuh?"

"*Ace?*" Her question takes me by surprise. I freeze, feeling slightly caught. "I'm not sure . . . maybe." I shrug it off. "Why?"

"I was jus' wonderin'." Jilly takes it in.

"Why?" I smile as I watch her.

"Nuttin'." She shrugs, looking down at her hands.

"Tell me, Jilly."

"Me nuh know." A tender smile makes its way onto her face. "I guess, jus' . . . when you guys were dancin' tonight. It felt like there was a vibe between you two. But maybe I read it wrong."

"Wait, don' tell me *you* were crushing on Ace?" I giggle. "I didn't realize he was your type."

"He's not."

Butterflies dance through me in the dead of night as she looks at me.

"Did di dance mek yuh jealous?" The question boldly leaves my lips.

"Of him, or you?" she whispers as we stand inches apart under the palm tree.

"Either, I guess."

My heart beats faster as she begins to move in closer, gently taking my hands in hers.

"Him." Her tone is soft, delicate. Her eyes glossy. "I was really jealous of him. That he got to dance with you. Like that."

I can feel her energy as it rushes through me.

I want all of her. All of her energy, her time, and her attention. Every single part of me wants to draw Jillian in closer. Wants to *merge* my body with hers. I want desperately to yield to the desires that explode inside of me. I know that it's wrong to say it out loud in Jamaica.

A crime, even.

But I want to make love to my best friend.

"Jilly." The confession leaves me in a whisper. "I . . . I love you."

Her eyes are intense, not leaving mine for a second. And then, ever so slowly, she brings her hand to my jaw and presses her forehead into mine.

"I love you too, Irie," she whispers.

And then we just stand.

Still, but . . .

Together.

I take in her energy, allowing every part of her to wrap itself around me. I let her in. *All of her.* Because for once, I'm not afraid to show her my heart.

"I love you so much, Jilly," I whisper again. "Thank yuh for being there for me tonight. Having you as a friend it's . . . it's really changed my life. And I'm *so, so* grateful."

I mean every word.

Under the glimmer of the moon, *Jilly shines*. Bright. And as her light reflects onto me, I can't fight the ripple of sensations that threaten to take me under. I'm mesmerized by her beauty as she stands in front of me, her curls draping down her back. As the moon beams down onto us, the truth couldn't be clearer.

I'm *so* in love with Jillian Casey.

Her thumb is warm as she traces it along my cheek before nuzzling herself into my neck and wrapping her arms around me. I do the same, melting into her familiar embrace. As we hold each other under the starry night sky, we stand together, at the edge.

Once again.

"Irie," she whispers into my skin like a prayer going out into the night. "Yuh mean *so much* to me, Irie . . . I . . ."

I can feel the hunger that trembles inside of her.

"I was *so* jealous tonight . . . seeing you with Ace like that."

I shudder as she rubs her nose into my neck. Goose bumps race down my spine just as she pulls away. And then our eyes lock.

And time stops.

"I was *so* jealous, Irie," she whispers again, her tone desperate. "I swear to God, I . . . I wanted yuh for myself. And I could feel it everywhere in my body. It was so unfair."

Her breath is slow and rhythmic, and I shiver as she slowly draws her hand up my arm.

"Watching you move like that on di dance floor . . . it was liked yuh *belonged* there. In di dance hall . . . And then seeing you on that stage . . . how yuh jus' *controlled* di entire crowd wit' yuh voice alone."

"Jilly," I whisper.

"Everyone loved yuh tonight, Irie, Ace included. But I was jealous. I was jealous because I wanted yuh. I wanted yuh for myself."

Her words leave me speechless.

"I'm really sorry I made yuh feel that way, Jilly," I whisper. "It was just a dance. I promise it didn't mean anything—"

"But even if it did," she stops me. "I didn't want it to stop." There's a yearning in her eyes as a sharpness moves through me. "I didn't want him to stop touching you, Irie. *I wanted to keep watching.*"

My mouth grows wet.

"Seeing you lose yourself in di music like that . . . it made me feel things. Things I shouldn't. And I . . . I know maybe that's wrong or weird to say, but that's how I felt."

"It's not wrong," I whisper. "Or weird."

Desire dances through me. We're closer than we've ever been.

"You're a *star,* Irie," she says. "I want you to know it."

My eyes begin to water as she touches the deepest parts of me.

"Jilly . . . I . . ." But I don't even know what to say. The night air is thin as her words cut through the veil, wrapping its way up my spine like a snake. I have no choice but to believe her.

To let her in.

"Can I kiss you?" she asks delicately, her tone shy. "*Please?*"

My heart pumps heavily in my chest.

Dazed and on fire, I nod.

And before I can say another word, Jillian presses her soft, warm lips into mine. We collide like two clouds that come together to create rain as she showers me with kisses. She pours into me, over and over again, quenching my thirst in the thick heat of the night.

Jamaica is hot, but Jilly is my rain.

I surrender to the storm.

Breathless, I take everything she gives me. Her mouth is soft and wet and gushy as her lips explore mine. It takes only a second to catch each other's tempo, and soon our movements are effortless as our hands glide along each other's bodies. Her tongue slips into my mouth, warm and gentle as I bring my hands up to her neck, carefully weaving my fingers into the curls of her hair. Her scalp is tender and warm in my palm as I gently massage her in my hands.

I can taste her desire as it spills into my mouth.

We melt deeper into each other as her hands fall down my body. She wastes no time, pinning me to the palm tree as she slides her hands down to the hem of my shirt. Her touch is warm, and soon her hands hold my breasts as she strokes me with her fingers.

I nearly explode.

"Does that feel good?" she whispers sincerely into my ear.

"*Too good . . . ,*" I say softly. My tone is desperate as she slowly slides her knee in between my legs, caressing the most sacred part of me. She applies a gentle but urgent pressure as I slowly start to grind into her. We move instinctively.

Hungry for one another.

The sensations overwhelm me as I search for my breath. Desperate to feel more of her, I hold up the thin material of my shirt, revealing my bare chest under the magic of the moonlight.

"Are yuh sure?" Her eyes water.

I nod, yearning.

She leans down and takes me in her mouth.

Fireworks explode through my body as I lean back against the palm tree. My fingers run wild in her hair under the starry night sky. I'm dizzy and drunk with adrenaline as she takes me to the edge of feelings I didn't even know I could have.

"Should we keep going?" I pant, on the edge of everything *good.*

Her hazel eyes look up at me.

"*Yes . . .*"

We're inches away from a moment we can't return from.

But freedom calls my name.

I search for my breath, but it's lost somewhere between me and Jilly as we merge into one. I don't know where my body ends or hers begins. And then, she carefully slips my underwear to the side.

"*Oh my god . . .*"

Tears of joy spill down my face as she watches me with a tender compassion.

I'm so in love with her. And I come alive as she plays me *deeply,* stroking rhythmically and melodically like the bass that permeated the dance hall.

Except this time, under the light of the moon—

ONLY we can hear the music.

18

———

Jilly

We search for freedom and find it in each other.

I don't want the feeling to end. We move in the shadows, feeling everything, all at once. My heart bursts for her as pure pleasure erupts inside of me.

I've never felt this good in my life.

I am Cinderella waiting for the clock to strike as my deepest fantasy plays out in front of me. I've always wanted her. *Loved her.* Since the first day we met. I'm slow and tender, and she shudders as I release her. I've never made someone feel *that* good before.

As she decompresses, I don't take my eyes off her for a second. Her beautiful brown skin and her perfect black braids. Both of our mouths are wet as we drip with anticipation.

I watch her in reverence.

We're in the throes of passion as we trade places on the palm tree. Seconds later, Irie's body holds me against the tree stump as she runs her lips down the corners of my neck. Goose bumps flare up my spine as she makes her way to my ear.

"I love you, Jilly," she says softly.

"*I love you too . . .*"

I'm broken open as her love washes me clean.

I want to spill into her.

Come undone.

The sounds that leave me are melodic as she massages me in her hands. She plants a million kisses onto my skin before sliding the straps of my top to the side. Her lips are fluffy and full as she leans down and takes me in the warmth of her mouth. I feel her love for me blast through my bones as her tongue goes round and round, and soon, she descends.

My heart races as our eyes meet.

"Do you want me to keep going?" She looks at me with compassionate brown eyes. She's so gentle with me I could cry. All I feel is love. I bite down on my lip, nodding.

And then, the warmth of her soft lips cover me.

Oh my God . . .

I'm silky and drenched as I press deeper—*free* in my own body. I feel everything *Irie* as I cave into her, surrendering as she plays every note. And then suddenly, I hear something.

A sound we don't make.

"*Did yuh . . . did jus' hear that?*"

"*Hmm?*" she moans, distracted.

But then the sound returns.

"*Irie,*" I whisper. "I heard suh'um."

"*Yuh wan' me to stop?*" she asks.

Maybe it was in my head, I tell myself.

"What's wrong?" Irie plants a gentle kiss onto my lips.

I quiver.

"A sound," I say again as we peel away from each other.

We listen closely, but the night is quiet except for the crickets.

"I don' hear anyting," Irie whispers. "But we should probably get goin'—"

And then we hear it.

A rattling sound.

This time more distinctly—like wheels turning down the road in the far-off distance.

"There's a truck comin', I think," I say as the rattling continues.

"*Shit.*" Irie hastily pulls down her top as the sound grows louder.

And closer.

"We have to go," Irie says, grabbing my hand. "*Now.*"

"Are yuh *sure*?" I retreat. "You don't think it's betta if we hide?"

"If they turn down this road, they can block us in." Concern floods Irie's face. "I don't know these roads, Jilly." She pulls me away from the tree. "Come."

"But—"

"Come nuh!" Irie panics. "*We haffi go now, Jilly!*"

In a moment's notice, we are sprinting toward the bicycles.

The sound grows louder as we hop on, pedaling as fast as we can. We make our way through the bushes, pushing past palm trees. The moon lights our way as we race our bicycles across the grass and back toward the dirt road. My mind races as I pump my legs, following behind Irie. As we approach the end of the path, she swings a left onto the main street. I do my best to keep up with her, but just as we near victory, we see them.

A pickup truck coming down the road.

We watch in terror as a group of rowdy men hang off the back, turning in our direction.

"Irie!" I panic.

"We have to keep going!" she calls back to me. "Our only option is to pass dem!"

Terror blasts through every cell of my body as the truck approaches us. The men cause a ruckus as they flash their headlights, beaming it into our eyes as they approach.

There's no doubt they've seen us.

"Hurry!" Irie calls back as we race toward them.

We have to pass them—there's no other choice and no time to turn around.

"We haffi go faster!" Irie calls back. "I'm going to speed up on di count of three, all right?"

Fuck.

"No!" I yell. "No, I don't think I can!"

"We *have* to, Jilly!" Urgency pours out of her. "One . . . two . . ."

I pray for my legs to take me faster.

"Wait, *please*!"

"Three!"

"No, *Irie*!" I yell out. "*Wait!*"

But in an instant, she takes off, ripping past the truck.

I pedal as fast as I can, but it's no use; Irie's already meters in front of me. As I fall behind, my hands begin to tremble as I wobble on the bicycle.

"*Shit, shit!*" I panic as they move in close. Just before I can give it a second attempt, they turn the truck sideways and block the road. *I'm trapped.* My heart catapults to my stomach as they create a barrier between Irie and me.

"Irie!" I cry out. But it's too late.

All the breath leaves my body.

They hold M16s and AK-47s in their hands.

I come to a screeching halt as two of the men jump off the truck and into the road with M16s flung around their shoulders.

"Jilly!" I hear Irie call from the other side of the truck barricade.

My entire body goes weak. I gasp for air—*for anything*—as the men make their way toward me. Tears well in the back of my eyes, and I don't know whether to run for my life or stay still.

I do the latter.

"Yow!" one of the men calls out just as Irie rounds the truck. She hops off her bicycle and runs toward me, stopping a few meters behind the men. The men look us up and down as the rest of the guys hang off the back. "Wha' gyal ah do outta ah road so late ah night?" He looks at my skirt. "*Ah wear short skirt . . .*"

"She mussi mod." One of the men laughs.

I tremble as I grasp on to the handles of my bicycle.

"Ay, girl, yuh nuh hear me a talk to yuh?" The man in front of me grabs hold of his M16 and points it in my direction. My heart stops dead in my chest.

"*Tower* or *power*?" He stares at me.

I almost vomit as I stare down the barrel of the gun.

"Wh-what?" My voice trembles.

"*Tower* or *power*?!" he yells again, this time more forcefully.

"I—"

"POWER!" Irie yells out from behind them. Her entire body tremors as she raises her hands up in the air. "We're power! PLM! We're voting for Morris in a few weeks."

"So wha' she ah do ah wear purple?" the man yells as he steps closer to me.

Horror blasts through my veins. I'm stunned as I look down at my light purple tank top.

The gun is pointed straight at my chest.

"*Please!*" I cry. Tears pour down my cheeks like hot lava.

"Get down pon yuh *bloodclaat* knees!" he yells.

I tremor as I throw myself to the floor. "Please," I whimper again as I press my face into the hot ground. "I didn't know."

"She's PLM!" Irie cries again. "I promise to God. We're from Kintyre. My fada is Ricky. He owns Ricky's Records in Papine!"

The man stops, turning around to face Irie.

"I promise." Irie's voice is shaky. "We're *PLM* voters. Power Posse."

Tears pour from my eyes and into the rubble as the men stare back at Irie.

He relaxes the gun in his hand as he looks back down at me. "Tek off yah *fuckin'* shirt," he orders, pointing to my top with the gun. "Fuckin' *eediot* gyal."

I'm stunned by his request.

"*Okay . . .*" My entire body convulses.

I'm terror-stricken as my fingers tremble to the hem of my shirt. In a frenzy, I hastily pull the tank top over my head. "*Please,*" I whimper again as I throw it toward him, begging for my life. "I promise I didn't know . . . I . . . I'm not even from this area."

I whimper in the night, facedown in nothing but my white bra as the man takes a step toward me in the shadows. His foot nears my head, and he kicks dirt in my face before using the barrel of the gun to scoop my purple tank top from the ground.

"*Yuh mussi fuckin' mod fi wear dis color round yesso.*" The rage in his voice is paralyzing. My skin presses into the soil as I say a silent prayer.

Ready to die.

"*Eediot gyal.*" He spits.

And then he reaches into his pocket and draws a match.

Tears blur my vision as he sparks a light, setting my tank top on fire. I flinch as he drops the burning cotton to the ground just inches away from my face. I watch in horror as my tank top goes up in flames. I can feel the heat from the fire on my skin as the burning smell of cotton fills my lungs. As my tears spill onto the hot dirt, he hovers above me, his words menacing.

"*Next time I'll kill you, dutty bitch.*" He says it clear as day.

And then, just as quickly as they hopped off the truck, they hop back on.

I squeeze my eyes shut, praying for it all to be over as I press myself into the ground. All I want is for the earth to swallow me whole. All I want to do is go back to Jacks Hill, curl up in my bed, and never disobey my parents again.

All I want to do is go home.

The rattling of the engine resumes as the men reverse the truck, continuing back down the road. I lay in shock, vulnerable and half-naked as Irie sprints to my side.

"Jillian!" she cries as she bends down to help me up. "Are yuh all right?"

She reaches for my arm, and I flinch, instinctively yanking it away. "*Don't!*" I yell, my body shot with fear. "Don't . . . *don't* touch me!" I cry.

I tremble, naked and afraid on the dirty streets.

I hoist myself up from the ground as Irie stands above me, stunned. I'm covered in dirt and rubble as we lock eyes, and all I want to do is *rage*.

All I want to do is combust.

"Why di *fuck* did yuh leave me?" I cry as the truck disappears down the road.

"I didn't mean to, Jilly. I—" she starts, her tone helpless. "I *swear* I thought yuh were right behind me."

"But I *wasn't*, Irie! Yuh know I'm still gettin' di hang of dis bicycle."

"I counted to three!" Irie's brown eyes search mine. "I told yuh we had to hurry up."

"And I *told you* we should've stayed behind!" I yell. "If we had just stayed back there like I said, *none* of this would have happened. We should have hid or done *something*." My voice is desperate, a whimper in the night as I search myself for the answers.

How could she let this happen?

"Why didn't yuh tell me?" I sob. "About di shirt . . . *the purple top*? How could yuh let me leave di house like that? I . . . I had *no* clue."

"I didn't realize."

"But you *knew*!" I say adamantly. "*Jesus*, Irie. I'm not *from here*!"

"And what's that supposed to mean?" Irie says defensively.

"I'm not *from here,* either, Jillian. I'm from *Kintyre.* I don't know this area any more than you do."

"Seriously?" I'm in disbelief as we stand in the middle of the deserted street. "*That's* what yuh want to argue about right now?" My anger only grows. "Why do yuh always have to be so difficult? Yuh know what I meant."

"No, maybe *I don't!*" Anger flashes through Irie's brown eyes. "Maybe I have *no idea* what yuh talkin' about because this isn't even my garrison, Jillian! I'm not even *from* dis part of town. But if ah *di ghetto* yuh ah talk 'bout, then fine. I'm *from here.* But that doesn't mean I would purposely put you in danger!"

The look on Irie's face is pained as her eyes well with tears. But my temper only rages—she's not about to make herself the victim.

Not again.

"I can't believe this." I shake my head. We're tense as the fire blazes in the distance, the only thing that lights the dark. Acrimony blasts through me, in need of somewhere to go. *In need of someone to blame.* I feel so violated as the shock of what just happened holds me in its grip. But just as the tears crash down, so does reality.

I have to get home.

"Ma parents . . ." My jaw trembles as I whisper. "Ma parents are going to kill me." My head spins on a swivel.

The nighttime makes me delirious as I run past Irie and toward my bicycle.

"Jillian, wait," Irie tries again. "I *really* didn't mean to leave you behind."

And the tears in her brown eyes tell me it might be true.

But even if she didn't mean to, she did.

I race to my bicycle and hop on. The smoke from the fire fills the streets as I grip down on the handlebars in nothing but my bra and battered dirty skirt. I'm exposed in the night. *More vulnerable than I've ever been in my life.* The night air is haunting as the fire continues to burn, setting our friendship ablaze. Without saying another word to Irie, I take off down the dark road toward Jacks Hill.

WE'RE worlds apart as the full moon lights the way home.

19

———

Irie

How can she blame me for this?

MY thoughts race a mile a minute as we make the final turn onto Jillian's street. The night begins to fade as the gray of morning sets in, and the smell of fruit and hibiscus fills the air. My mind is in turmoil as I replay the events, picking apart every detail.

Was she right? The question haunts me. *Is this really my fault?*

I'm sick with myself as I contemplate how such an incredible night could turn into such a nightmare. Images of her body on the ground flash through my brain. Pinned to the dirt, just like Junior. And I stood there, helpless.

She could've died.

The inevitable truth sinks to the pit of my stomach.

How did I not notice she was wearing purple?

I'm all nerves as we approach Jilly's estate. I'm anxious to get inside without getting caught. I don't know the time, but by the looks of the dusky morning, it's still early enough that her parents shouldn't be awake. We hop off the bicycles as we approach the gate, slowly walking them over. Jilly doesn't say a word to me, and I watch in silence as she unlocks the gate. I'm at a loss for words as I grip down tighter on the handlebars.

I didn't mean to leave her.

And I turned back.

She unlocks the gate and carefully pushes it open. Without so much as a glance at each other, we quietly guide the bicycles back inside. But no matter how hard I try, I can't get her out of my head. *Everything we experienced together tonight.* The way we explored each other's bodies like no one else ever has. As we make our way onto the property, my veins pulse against my will. *My body remembers her.* And she remembers me. And deep down, I can't help but wonder if that's the real reason she's so upset with me.

Because she liked it.

We make our way across the yard, sticking close to the side of the house just like we did before. Once the bicycles are back in the shed, we tiptoe around the house and through the yard to Jillian's back door. I wait patiently as she slides it open, careful not to make a sound. She takes off her sandals and I do the same, and just as the sunrise begins to peak over the backyard, we quietly make our way back inside.

The house is still dark when we enter.

Her parents haven't woken up yet.

Jilly closes the back door, and just as quietly as we'd left the house, we sneak back through it. We're fast as we tiptoe down the marble floors and creep across the hallway. But just as we approach the stairs, we stop dead in our tracks. Because across the hall, with a basket of laundry in hands, stands Amala.

Fuck.

"Morning," Amala whispers politely. I watch the blood drain from Jilly's face as she crosses her arms across her almost bare chest.

"Mornin'." Jilly nods before scurrying up the stairs. I nod

politely at Amala before bolting behind Jillian. We don't stop until we enter through her bedroom doors and Jilly closes it shut behind us.

"Jilly—" I start.

"Please." She stops me, overwhelmed. "It's been a long night, Irie. I jus' . . . I really don' want to talk about anything."

My stomach sinks.

"Okay," I whisper, unsure of what to do with myself as I make my way over to her bed. I take a seat at the edge and watch in grim silence as Jillian heads over to her drawer. She's emotional and frantic as she holds her hair in her hands, pacing the room as she looks for a shirt. I can feel her unraveling right in front of me. *She's in shock.*

She's never experienced anything like that before. She doesn't come from where I come from. Where crime happens casually.

The feeling is gutting, and everything about it feels *so* unfair. *Why does she have to be held more delicately just because she's not used to it?* I'm the one who has to deal with the realities of violence every single day. And *none* of it is by choice.

Where was she when I was holding Junior? When he was the one bleeding out?

Tucked away in the plushy pillows of her queen-size bed— *that's where.*

I seethe. *How is this my fault?* She should have known better than to wear purple. It shouldn't be my job to protect Jillian from the scary streets of Jamaica. An island we *both* call home. Why should I? Because my skin is darker?

Because I'm *poorer* than she is, I should know the ropes?

Just because she gets to leave this island behind doesn't mean she gets to take less responsibility for it. I shouldn't be the only one bearing the burden of the ghetto.

I bite down hard, trying my best to suppress my feelings. But the truth is, I'm livid.

She's not the only one who deserves to be protected.

I watch as Jilly ties her silky curls up in the mirror, digging through her drawer. Annoyance blasts through me at her entitled rich-girl behavior. I'm not going to hold her like some delicate flower just because freckles dust her face. She doesn't get a *pass* just because her skin is light and her eyes are hazel. She's not *better* than I am just because her circumstances are. I deserve to feel safe too. And as I look around her room, I realize that in her world, I never did.

Just as I open my mouth to let it all out, Jillian lets out a gasp. "Oh my god." She starts to sob, throwing herself to the floor.

I watch her shatter into pieces right in front of me.

The perfect picture, broken.

"*The bracelet.*" The whisper leaves her lips as she leans against the drawer, pressing her palm to her forehead. "*Shit! Shit, shit.*"

"Di one yuh had on?" I rise from the bed.

"It's gone." She wipes her eyes. "I lost it."

"Yuh sure yuh didn't misplace it?"

"No . . . I . . . I put it in my bra when we were at di dance." Tears fill her eyes all over again, and she cries, defeated. "It must have been stolen."

I'm unsure of what to say as she rises from the floor, turning away from me. I can't even pretend to feel sympathy for her in this moment. "Is there anything I can do?" I ask her, keeping my voice low. "To help."

"No, Irie." She shakes her head. "I needed your help *back there*. Not now."

"Why are you being so unfair?" I lose it.

"*Unfair?*" She looks at me in disbelief. "You really want to talk to me about *unfair*? Irie, I just had a gun pointed at my chest!" Tears stream down her rosy cheeks. "Or does that not matter to you because I'm not *poor*? *Hmm*? Do my tears mean *less* because I wasn't born in the *ghetto*?"

"What the hell are yuh talkin' about, Jillian?"

"Yuh made me feel awful earlier!" she cries. "Like I was some kind of *horrible person* all because my family is JCG!"

"That's because they *terrorized* me at dinner!" I defend, helpless. "They treated me like I was some sort of *wild animal.*"

"How can you even *compare* that to what just happened, Irie?" Jilly comes undone as the tears spill down her face. "Look, *I'm sorry* you didn't get the princess treatment at dinner, but you *weren't* di one lying facedown in the dirt with a gun *pointed* at yuh chest ova a friggin' *tank top!* Those were *your people,* Irie! The PLM! Tonight was *your* responsibility."

"*No, it wasn't!*" I cry as we stand face-to-face. "I'm not your *pet,* Jillian. I'm a *person.* I'm not a dolly you get to dress up and play with when you're bored of your miserable life!"

"Wow." Tears of betrayal stream down her face as she turns to walk away. "You know what? Forget it. My parents were right about you."

"*Excuse me?*"

"My family may have our flaws, but at least we don't gun people down like a bunch of *fucking savages!*" she bursts.

The words leave her mouth with force, striking me dead in my core.

"I could've *died* tonight, Irie. And *you* left *me.* Not the other way around." She shakes her head, wiping her tears from her face. "Yuh know what? Jus' forget it. This has literally been the worst night of my life and . . . and I jus' need to get some sleep."

She takes a deep breath before heading into the bathroom and shutting the door.

Just like that, I'm alone in her bedroom at the crack of dawn.

I'm a mess as the pink glow of morning fills the shadows. I quietly change into the overnight clothes that Jilly lent me and resentfully slip into her sheets, careful to stay to my side. My thoughts stir as I wait for Jilly to come back from the bathroom. After a few minutes, the door opens, and she makes her way over to the bed. I lie still as she settles into the sheets, her back to me. The sound of a morning owl coos in the distance, sending a shiver up my spine. After a strained moment of silence, she speaks.

"Irie?"

"Yeah?"

"It's probably best you go home now. Since it's morning time, I can arrange for Lloyd to take you back to Kintyre. He's usually up at this hour."

My heart sinks.

"Sure," I whisper. "Fine."

My entire body goes numb as I rise from the bed.

The feeling is foreign, but clear.

OUR friendship is over.

20

Irie

"So, what's next?"

I walk side by side with Tandi and Siarah two days later as we make our way down the hot rubble toward the studio. The sun is blazing and the walk is long, and as I drown in my thoughts, Siarah presses me about the show, eager to get the details out of me.

"Ace wants to manage me," I say to them, grateful for the change in topic. Grateful to focus on something other than Jilly.

"*Manage,* manage?" Tandi looks at me for clarity as she makes a face. "What does Ace know about that? I thought he fixed pipes."

"He knows a lot, evidently," I say as I hold my songbook in my hands. "He said he's goin' to line up some shows fi me. Help me get my name out there."

"I thought he was a *bod mon*?" Tandi asks. "Not a bookin' manager."

"He's a *repair*mon," Siarah corrects.

"Well, he needs to pick a lane," Tandi says, judgment in her tone.

"People can have more than one job, Tandi," I say defensively.

"Since when is street crime a real job?"

"Cool nuh, Tandi." Siarah kisses her teeth. "We're supposed to be supportive."

"I *am* bein' supportive." Tandi rolls her eyes at Siarah. "I just want to mek sure Irie's surroundin' herself wit' di right people. Not just people who want to leech off her talent." She looks at me. "That's what happens when yuh born wit' a gift, yuh nuh. People want to take parts of it fi themselves. Yuh haffi me be mindful."

"I appreciate yuh concern," I say, tempering her paranoia. "But I think Ace has done a *pretty* good job so far. Let's not forget I'm about to be in di studio wit' Daddy Roy."

"Irie has a point," Siarah agrees. "Which reminds me, yuh still neva really told us how the night went."

"I did," I say defensively. "They loved di song."

"It must have felt so good to be up on that stage." Tandi smiles.

"Yeah." I sigh as the memory comes back to me. "It did."

My belly tingles with anguish. Every part of me longs for that moment again.

The moment before everything went down.

"So, tell us about Jilly's, nuh!" Siarah nudges me. "Yuh neva even give us di details."

"There wasn't much to it," I lie. "It was a chill night, besides from di performance."

"But give us di *details*!" Siarah whines.

"Not right now, Sisi." I try my best to shake the subject, tempering my nerves. "It's an important day, and I really want to focus on the studio. On Junior's song."

"Oh, come on, Irie." Tandi sulks. "You've been holding out."

Because I can't stop beating myself up for what happened.

What they did to her.

"Irie?" Tandi nudges me.

"Fine," I say, giving in. "You'll neva guess who was there."

"At di dinner?" Siarah asks.

I nod.

"Who?" they ask in unison.

"The prime minister–elect."

"*WINSTON KELLY?*" My sisters stop dead in the street.

"*Shh!*" I immediately hush them back down. "*Unu mod?* Not so loud." Everyone knows you don't utter a party leader's name out loud in the streets of Kingston.

"Sorry." Siarah comes back to her senses.

"It's fine," I say promptly as I usher them along. "Unu hurry up. I cyaan afford to be late."

"But wait." Tandi shakes her head as they catch up. "You're telling us *di leader of di JCG* was at Jillian's mada's birthday pawty? Yuh cyaan be serious."

"I swear." I nod again. "I could hardly believe it myself."

"And yuh *met* him?" Siarah asks.

"More like he interrogated me." I roll my eyes.

"Whoa." Siarah takes in the information. "That's *so* Winston Kelly."

"Yuh jus' betta mek sure Daddy nuh find out he was there," Tandi warns. "I don't think Daddy would like it if he knew yuh were rubbin' noses wit' those kinds of people."

"I wasn't *rubbin' noses*, Tandi," I say, already annoyed that I brought it up. "I was just there for the dinner pawty. It was barely a few hours."

"Me nuh know, Irie. Tandi might have a point." Siarah's shock turns to concern. "Politics are *hot* right now. The election is only a few weeks away. Me nuh know how Daddy would feel if he knew Jilly's family was so politically involved."

"Or that yuh were dining with *Winston Kelly*," Tandi whispers. "If di wrong people found that out, yuh could get killed, Irie. *Murdered.*"

I'm anxious as I shrug them off.

"It was *one night*. Yuh both are overreacting," I say, pushing one foot in front of the other. "It's not like I *jus'* started spending time wit' Jillian. We've been best friends."

"You've been *school friends*," Tandi corrects me. "There's a difference, Irie."

"Can we *please* talk about suh'um else?" My stomach sinks as I bite down hard.

Tandi and Siarah recoil, giving each other a knowing look as they go silent. I know that they're just looking out for me, but the truth is I'm in no mood to be questioned by my sisters. I'm so tired of having to defend my friendship with Jillian. And after everything that happened, maybe the truth is that there's nothing to defend anymore.

I have to focus.

I have a major opportunity in front of me, and I can't afford to mess this up.

We trek on, passing by a few shops as I look down at the card in my hand. I slow my pace as we approach an old building.

"This is it." I tremble. I look down at the card and back up at the building, and then to my sisters who stand on either side of me. "This is the address he gave." I pass the card to Siarah to confirm.

She nods. "Looks so. Should we wait for Ace?"

"He might already be inside."

"Only one way to find out." Tandi takes my hand as she pulls me along. "I didn't walk two hours fi nuttin'. You're recording a *hit* today."

I'm on pins and needles as we make our way up the steps of the small redbrick building.

"And no pressure, Irie." Siarah reads my energy as we approach the doors. "No matta what happens, yuh going to be great."

"Always," Tandi says.

"Tanks." I smile, grateful for their support. I take a deep

breath and knock. We wait for a few moments when, just then, a tall man with locks opens the door.

"Wha'ppen?" he asks, his demeanor friendly as he holds a spliff.

"We're . . . we're here to see Daddy Roy," I say nervously. "I'm recordin' a song today."

"Yuh have a session booked?" He looks at me skeptically.

"Yeah." I nod. "I'm di artist, Irie, and these are my sistas, Tandi and Siarah."

"Nice to meet yuh." He says before opening the door wider. "Come in. Pretty girls like you shouldn't be walkin' alone wit' all di madness weh ah gwaan." He ushers us inside. "U-Roy deh ah di back."

Nervous but hopeful, my sisters and I make our way past him and enter through the building doors. The space is modest but undeniably cool. Reggae bleeds from the walls as ganja smoke fills the air.

"Right down di hall." The man nods coolly before slipping off into a different room. Siarah and Tandi give me a look, unsure of what to do next.

"I guess we go down di hall."

Holding my songbook by my side, I make my way down as Siarah and Tandi hesitantly trail behind me. The deep sound of dub pours through the house as we pass an array of open and closed doors. People move about the space, going in and out of different sound rooms.

As we approach the end of the hall, I spot Ace standing by the back door.

"Ace," I say as we get closer, grateful to see a familiar face. "Wha'ppen?"

"Wha' gwaan, Irie?" He pulls me in for a hug. His body is husky and warm as he takes me in a protective embrace. "Yuh found di place all right?"

"Yeah." I smile, gesturing behind. "I brought ma sisters."

"Longest walk of my life." Tandi wipes her forehead with a handkerchief.

"Good to see yuh again, Ace," Siarah says.

"Yuh brought di posse." He smiles. "I like it. Unu ready?"

Before I can answer, Ace puts his hand on the door handle and turns it. I walk in first to find Daddy Roy sitting in a chair beside a tape deck. Two men sit beside him, spliffs in hand. The bass bumps and the vibes are *electric* as they sit across from a glass window. On the other side, there's a small booth with a mic.

"Irie!" Daddy Roy calls when he sees me. "Wha'ppen, superstar?"

"Hello, Mr. Roy." I nearly faint as he calls my name. *I still can't believe he knows who I am.* The two other men nod, acknowledging me as they take another draw.

"It's a pleasure." I beam as my sisters file through the door behind me. They make their way into the space, saying a polite hello. "These are my sisters, Siarah and Tandi. They came fi di support."

"Nice to meet yuh, Mr. Roy," Siarah says kindly. "You're a legend in Jamaica. Our fada always plays yuh music at his shop."

Daddy Roy looks at me, his long locks flowing down his back. "Yuh fada owns a record store?"

"Yeah." I nod. "Ricky's Records. In Papine Square."

"*Rawtid.*" He chuckles. "Ricky's a real rebel. Music must be inna yuh blood."

"I'm hopin' so." I smile humbly.

"Yuh have di riddim?" he asks me.

"Right here." Siarah leaps up, passing me the record.

"Tanks, Siarah." I smile. I hand the record to Daddy Roy, who examines the case.

"Cool," he says after a moment. "Earl will set yuh up inside di booth."

"Tanks, Mr. Roy." I beam as one of the men rises from his seat, leading me toward the door.

"Call me U-Roy."

"U-Roy." I nod before throwing an excited smile to Siarah and Tandi. They settle in on the small couch at the back of the room as Ace stands next to them in the back corner.

I'm giddy as I wave goodbye to them.

I can't believe I'm in a real studio.

I follow the man out of the room and into the hallway. We go through a smaller door, and I'm surprised to see the booth I saw from the room right in front of me. I walk inside, and my stomach flutters when I realize everyone gathered on the other side can see me. My hands are cold as Earl passes me the headphones. He adjusts the mic and the levels as I place the headphones over my ears.

"Yuh can hear me all right?" Daddy Roy's deep voice startles me.

"Oh, yeah," I say.

"All right. We jus' ah go work on yuh levels."

"Okay." I start to tremble. Earl gives me a thumbs-up before making his way out of the booth and closing it behind him. As the rhythm pours into my ears, I hear Daddy Roy's voice again.

"Whenever yuh ready."

"Okay." My heart slams against my chest.

All eyes are on me.

I vibe with the rhythm, singing a few *oohs* and *aahs*.

"Can yuh turn me up louder?" I say into the mic.

Daddy Roy gives me a thumbs-up from the other side, and when the beat drops, I start to sing.

I won't back down from this holy war
The spirit of love will fight on and I will roar

My voice is shaky, and I don't hit the notes as smoothly as usual.

"Sorry," I say over the mic. "Can I start again?"

A few moments later, Daddy Roy restarts the track. "Yuh good, Irie. Jus' focus on feelin' di lyrics. How yuh were feeling when yuh wrote them," he says through the headphones. But the thought of focusing on Junior makes me tense.

His body on the ground.

Lifeless.

"Okay," I muster. I dig into the pit of my stomach and take a deep breath.

The track starts again.

I won't back down from this holy war
The spirit of love will fight on and I will roar
Peace will reign and—

"Sorry, I forgot di lyrics," I say apologetically.

"It's all right, Irie. Tek a few minutes." Daddy Roy's voice comes through the headphones as I watch him rise from his chair. "I'll leave di song playin' so yuh can practice some more."

"Okay." I wither, feeling ashamed.

Daddy Roy and another man leave the studio as Earl smokes a spliff, shuffling around. Siarah and Tandi wait patiently on the back couch. Just then, the studio door opens and Ace slides inside.

"Sounding great," he says, closing the door behind him.

"Nuh badda tell no lie," I say, defeated. "I cyaan get di notes right. I'm too in my head."

"Yuh jus' need a likkle bit more practice," he reassures me as he takes a seat on the stool. "It's no different from di odda night. Nothing's changed."

"You'd be surprised." I sigh, taking a seat on the stool. I pull the headphones down from my ears, embarrassed. "U-Roy's going to think I'm a fraud."

"He's not. He's going to think you're a *star*. Because that's what you are."

My eyes start to well. "Me nuh know, Ace. Maybe today just isn't a good day."

"*Really?*" He looks at me, bemused. "Yuh come *all dis way* and *now* yuh wan' lose yuh confidence? *Now*, of all times?"

I blink back tears, angry at myself for not performing the way I had hoped. "No." I cower, looking away. "I'm not losing my confidence; I jus'—I feel like I'm messin' up."

"What a gwaan wit' you, Irie? I could tell yuh energy was off the moment I saw you," he says, crossing his arms. "It's either we talk about it, or yuh can let it ruin yuh studio session. Your choice."

I sulk, not wanting to get into it.

"Lemme guess. Suh'um wit' yuh likkle rich friend? Wha' she name again?"

"Jilly," I say. "And I thought yuh liked her."

"Like and *trust* ah two different tings."

I wilt. "We got stopped by di Power Posse on our way home the other night." I meet his gaze. "Before I knew it, they had her lying in di streets wit' an M16 to her chest. All because I forgot to tell her not to wear purple."

"She neva know?"

I shake my head.

"She ah eediot. Everyone knows yuh nuffi wear dem colors around election time. Especially so late ah night." He shakes his head. "Ah dem kinda gyal yuh haffi watch. They'll get yuh in trouble and act like dem hand nuh dirty." He kisses his teeth. "The PLM gangs are doing their *job*, Irie. Where is she when the Tower Posse is terrorizing di ghettos? The Power Posse *has* to be vigilant."

"I get that, but it still didn't make it right, Ace. And it certainly doesn't mek it any easier to watch." I shudder. "All dis violence. Fi nuttin'."

"It's not *fi nuttin'*, Irie. How much time me haffi tell yuh?" Ace's gaze is intense. "That's yuh problem. Yuh nuh understand wha' yaah sing 'bout."

"How can you even say that?" I say defensively. "Yuh know this song is about Junior."

"Yuh didn't write dis song for *Junior.*" Ace loses his patience. "God rest his soul, but Junior's dead and gone. He's not di one suffering in a godless Jamaica."

His brown eyes hold mine as he takes a step closer to me. "Mek me tell yuh suh'um, Irie, and it ah go save yuh *a lot* of time inna dis life." His voice goes low as he leans down, hovering above me. "*Everyone* picks a side eventually." He searches my eyes. "Everyone has a role to play. Yuh understand?"

I'm quiet.

"If yuh wan' fi know freedom in this life, yuh haffi be willing to *die* for it. Why yuh tink all those yutes are out there are holding machine guns? Murdering each other in *cold blood* over a *fuckin'* election? Over politicians who nuh give a *shit* about dem? Een?" His gaze is locked, intense. "Because they're willing to *die fi dem freedom.* Di only difference between dem and you, is that *yuh weapon* is *yuh voice.* Yuh weapon is the music. Always rememba dat."

His words send a chill through my body.

"Yuh were *blessed wit' a gift,* Irie. And if you don't use it, God will tek it away from you." He brings his finger to my chest, his voice low. "*Use that weapon to free yuhself,* Irie. Sing from yuh *heart.* Not yuh head."

I bite back tears as his words transform me.

"All right, unu ready?" I hear Daddy Roy's voice come through the headphones.

I look out through the glass to find him and Earl settling back into their seats. I nod just as Ace heads toward the door, turning back to me one final time.

"Yuh have suh'um to say." He holds my brown eyes. "So, mek we hear it."

My stomach drops.

Seconds later, the track comes through the headphones.

I nail *every single note.*

21

Jilly

I am sick with myself.

IT'S been two days since everything happened. Two days since Irie and I were touching each other in the most sacred of places. Two days since I felt the most *freedom* I ever have in my life. Two days since I was digging my face into the dirt with an M16 pointed at my back.

"Fix your *face,* Jillian. For the love of God."

I stand waiting by the bar as my mother sneaks up behind me. Light streams in through the windows at the ceremonial JCG luncheon, and somewhere in the sea of old, pale faces, Daddy works the room. I tense as Mummy slides up next to me, her demeanor scolding. It's not even noon, and she's on her third glass of champagne. She keeps a tense smile on her face as she looks through her purse, pulling out a compact mirror to check her lipstick.

"You keep sulking like that and your face will stay that way."

I ignore her, looking away from the bar and out across the room. I don't care what my mother has to say. I'm miserable as hell, and I don't care who knows it.

Where the hell is Monica?

Anger bubbles inside of me as I watch Daddy chat up a group of investors in the distance. They laugh, jovial and nonchalant, and the sight alone makes me sick.

Forty-eight hours ago, I could have lost my life. And yet still, I'm forced to stand here and listen to people talk politics.

"Wipe that look off your face before I do it for you, Jillian Casey," Mummy scolds in a singsong voice under her breath.

I give her a faux smile before taking a sip of my drink.

"What can I grab for you, Mrs. Casey?" the bartender asks.

"Another glass of champagne. Be a doll, would you?" She passes him her empty flute. I cringe as she bats her lashes at him. "The peach undertones were *exquisite*."

"It just came in." The bartender smiles. "France."

"Ah yes." Mummy turns to me as he goes to prepare her drink. Just watching her makes me resentful that we're of the same blood.

"I didn't bring you here for you to stand around looking miserable, Jillian. Stop drawing attention to yourself."

"Cyaan you just arrange for Lloyd to bring me home?" I whine. "I don't want to be here, Mummy. I'm tired. Daddy doesn't even need me."

"I said *no*." Her eyes are sharp. "And *quit it* with that accent before I give you something really to sulk about. You're a *lady*. Act like one."

"Here you go, madam," the bartender interrupts.

"Thank you." She smiles.

I resent everything about her.

I hate that I cling on to her approval. I hate that no matter how hard I try, I still care what she thinks of me *so damn much*. I resent that against my will, her comments and snide remarks sneak their way under my skin. *Into my heart.* And even despite her disdain toward me, I still long for her kindness.

For her praise.

The feeling is gnawing, and it makes me disgusted with my-self. Even as memories of the PLM holding me at gunpoint flash through my head, I still feel like a cowering child in need of her mother. *It's so pathetic.* I'm nothing without my parents. I have no idea of how to be in the world on my own, and so I have no choice but to conform to theirs.

I take a sip of my champagne as Mummy stands next to me, watching over me like a hawk as we look out at the stream of guests. I war with myself as the events of the weekend terrorize me all over again. I belong nowhere, and in a room filled with people, it's the silent truth that makes me want to explode into a million tears.

But a Casey always keeps it together.

I stand prim and proper, the cord my mother wraps around my neck holding me in perfect place. I know she can feel me die inside every time she rejects me. And deep down, I think it makes her feel good every time she makes me feel like I'm not enough.

Every time I believe it a little bit more.

"Your father and I have put a lot on the line for you, Jillian." She takes a sip of champagne, throwing a smile to a couple of donors who pass by. Her tone is low as she continues. "I don't know what's gotten into you lately, but it ends *now.* Your time at Arthen is finished, and you need to be mindful about who occupies your time. When you hang out with trash for too long, you become it."

"Auntie Hilary!"

I turn my head to find Monica sauntering her way toward us. She wears a long cream dress as she bounces through the party, her hand raised in the air as she spots us.

"*Jillian!*" she squeals, excited. "There you are!"

Saved by the bell.

"Auntie Hilary, I was looking for you. Mummy and Daddy

just arrived. They're talking with Uncle Calvin." She pulls my mother into a hug, kissing both cheeks.

"Good to see you, darling." My mother beams. "You look radiant as always. Slim too." She smiles as Monica twirls. "We missed you at my birthday party."

"I know." Monica faux sulks. "I was *so* upset I had to miss it." *Bullshit.*

"But I'm so glad you had a good time, Auntie." Monica gives my mother puppy-dog eyes. "I *swear* you don't age. I can only hope to look as good as you one day." She moves away from my mother and toward me. "Jilly!" she squeals, extending her arms as she pulls me in.

"Hey, Mon," I muster.

"Oh my gosh, I've *missed you,* cousin," she says as she pulls away from me. "Auntie Hilary, do you mind if I borrow Jill?" Monica asks. "They've set up a paint area in the next room, and I'm *dying* to check it out."

"Sure, darling," my mother says. "But you girls don't roam too far."

"Of course, Auntie H." Monica winks before grabbing my hand. She blows my mother a kiss before sweeping me through the soirée.

We make our way through the conversative crowd, weaving in and out of men and women in their finest suits and gowns. Monica guides me through the door, and we make our way into the next room, where a gallery of art hangs from the walls. Lined across the large, open space are blank canvases, and as people mingle, others paint. I trail reluctantly behind Monica toward the back window of the space, and we take a seat in front of two large canvases and a row of paints.

"Madam." A gentleman in uniform approaches us with an array of paintbrushes.

"Oh." Monica smiles before taking them from the tray. "Here, Jilly." She collects a handful and places them down in front of us.

"Thanks," I say to the gentleman as he walks off.

"I *love* when they do stuff like this." Monica gulps back the champagne. "Interactive stuff. It makes the events so much more bearable."

"Don't know if I'd go that far," I say as I fiddle with the paint-brushes, dipping them into the glass of water that sits beside the easel.

Monica looks over me as if just noticing me. "*Why* is your face so long every time I see you?" She raises an eyebrow. "You need to come hang out with me and my friends more. Get out of St. Andrew."

"I'm just going through a lot." I shake it off, changing the subject as I stir my paintbrush in the water. "Anyway, how was Negril?"

"Yuh mean how *wasn't* Negril?" She giggles. "We partied for four days straight. I don't even remember most of it. Her father let us take the yacht, so we spent the entire weekend on the water."

"Sounds like a blast."

"Oh, come on, Jillian. Talk to me." Monica pouts, dipping her brush into the water. "What were you and your mother talking about, anyway? Something intense, from the looks of it." She looks over at me. "What'd you do this time?"

"Nothing," I say defensively. "I brought a close friend to her birthday party. She didn't like it, and now she's punishing me for it." I trail my wet brush across the canvas, not wanting to get into it.

"Hold up. *Please* don't tell me you brought that same girl from school. The scholarship stray from God knows where?"

"Her name is *Irie*, Monica." Her contempt makes me defensive. "And she's my good friend. Can you not talk about her like that?"

"Jillian, she's your *school* friend. I've never even seen her around. You've only known her for, what? The past four years?"

"And we've grown close," I retort. "Irie's the main person I hung out with at school. We spent a lot of time together, especially this last year."

"My point exactly." Monica's eyes are cutting. "*At school.*"

I shake my head, returning my attention to the painting. I trail the outline of a rose just like I've done a hundred times before in art class.

"Look, Jill." Monica's tone eases. "I'm not trying to hate on your little friend. But the people you meet in high school are usually the ones you leave behind."

"Well, not Irie," I say firmly as I drag the red across the page.

"Jeez, *touchy.*" Monica rolls her eyes, focusing on her own painting. She washes her brush and dips it into the yellow. "I'm not saying anything *bad* about the girl. I'm just saying you're *clearly* on two different levels. She's from *the ghetto,* for goodness' sake." She makes a disgusted face. "I get why your mother is upset you brought her to an important political dinner."

"It was a *birthday* dinner, Monica."

"With the entire *who's who* of Jamaica in attendance," she corrects. "Don't play daft, Jillian. You've clearly got some guts."

She modestly flips her hair behind her back. "It's election time. Everyone is on edge, and you're out here crossing the tracks in the name of friendship?" She smirks. "You like to play with fire and then wonder why you get burned."

"Whatever, Monica," I say bitterly.

"*What?*" Monica plays innocent. "Don't be so sensitive, Jill. I'm just saying if you bring home a *ragamuffin,* you must know there's going to be repercussions."

"Irie's my *friend.*"

"I *know* that. God, Jillian. It's like the more time you spend with that girl, the more she brainwashes your head. You're so sensitive about stuff now."

I close my mouth, saying nothing as I consider her words. *Is Monica right?* My mind flashes back to the feeling of my cheek pressed into the dirt, and suddenly, I feel like I'm suffocating in a room full of people.

Maybe I have taken things with Irie too far.

I dip my brush into the water as my cheeks go red. I can feel my heart rip in two different directions. Irie and I got too close.

Shared *too* much.

And as the thought grows incessant, the feeling becomes insidious. Maybe I've defended our friendship for too long. *Maybe what we did together was wrong.*

"What?" Monica looks over at me.

"Nothing."

"You sure?" She raises an eyebrow, concerned. "You look red."

"I'm fine, Mon." I shrug, refocusing on the easel as people mingle behind us. "I just—I just have a lot on my mind is all."

"Okay." She sighs. "Well, just know that I love you, Jillian, and I don't want to see you throw your future away for friends who can't do anything for you in return. People like Irie will only hold you back. Those type of people never leave the ghetto, much less Jamaica."

I wet the canvas with the brush, considering if she could truly be right. Maybe my friendship with Irie *does* hold me back.

"Yeah." I sigh, finally giving in. "Maybe you're right."

"I'm *always* right—"

"Jillian Casey."

I freeze when I hear my name called from behind me.

Christopher.

Monica and I turn around to find him standing right behind us. Hands in his pocket, he stands cool and collected as the rest of the luncheon guests mingle behind him. The sun streams onto his inquisitive blue eyes as he stares down at me.

"I'm so happy I found you," he says smoothly. "Your mother told me I would be able to find you in here."

"I-I didn't know you were coming." I sit frozen as I realize how stupid my statement sounds. *It's a JCG luncheon.*

"We just got here." He nods. "My parents are speaking to your father in the other room. Your mother said you were painting. I was fascinated to see what."

I give him an awkward smile as we all stare at the half rose on my canvas. "Um, Christopher, this is Monica." I gesture to her. "My older cousin. You'll see her at the engagement ceremony, I'm sure." I surprise myself as the words leave my lips.

"Wow." Monica's mouth falls to the floor in excitement. "*The* Christopher, huh?" She extends her hand, and, like a gentleman, he takes it. "It's nice to meet you, cousin-in-law."

"The pleasure's mine." Christopher nods as his eyes linger. "I see beauty runs in the family."

Monica bats her lashes. I feel a slight tinge of jealousy as his eyes zero in on her. Monica is stunning, and he'd be a fool not to see it. Anyone would. Still, the interaction makes me feel strange. *Weirdly territorial.*

"Is this seat taken?" Christopher points to the chair next to me. The blank easel sits next to a fresh glass of water and an array of acrylic paints.

"Yeah—"

"No," Monica finishes. "Take a seat, please." She sets down her brush. "As a matter of fact, I was *just* saying to Jillian here how thirsty I was. Why don't I go grab us all a drink?"

"Oh," Christopher stops her. "Allow me."

"No." Monica stands, gesturing to the empty seat. "I insist. Besides, I'm sure you and my cousin have some bonding to do before the big ceremony, right, Jillian?" She flashes me a smile. "I'll grab champagne for everyone."

She waltzes her way back through the sea of guests, and just like that, Christopher and I are alone in a crowded room.

"I like her," Christopher says as he sits down.

"Everyone does," I say sarcastically.

Christopher smiles. "How have you been?"

"Look, I'm really not in the mood for small talk."

"You *do* realize we're getting married, right?"

I ignore him, focusing on my rose.

"Do I make you *that* nervous?"

"It's like your head gets bigger *every time* I see you."

"You noticed that." He smiles, dipping the brush into the water. He begins to paint a sunrise on the canvas, clearly enjoying our back-and-forth. My stomach knots as I silently wonder whether there's a part of me that's beginning to enjoy it too.

"I brought your letter."

"What?" I say under my breath as my eyes zone in on him. "I thought you said—"

"I was able to get it faster than I'd thought."

I feel the blood drain from my face.

"What?" He smirks, amused. "I already told you my father was a powerful man. Here." He reaches into the inner pocket of his suit and pulls out a white envelope. "Still sealed and everything."

He hands it to me, and I nearly pass out as I take it from his hands. *Miss Jillian Casey* is written on the front in black letters, and in the return line, it reads THE UNIVERSITY OF CAMBRIDGE.

"Christopher."

"Thank me by becoming my wife." He looks at me, his blue eyes piercing. "Happily, that is. Thank me by *happily* becoming my wife."

"You really still think you can buy my love?"

"No. But it is worth a shot." He looks down at the letter. "I know it means a lot to you. Your education. And it should, especially as a young woman in the modern world. You want more for yourself, and you deserve to go there."

My hands tremble as I stare down at the letter and back up at Christopher. "What about your father?"

"I swore him to secrecy."

"And your mother?"

"My father doesn't exactly *include* my mother in any of his formal decisions. I can't see him beginning now, and especially not concerning this."

"Progressive," I say sarcastically.

"I don't make the rules." He laughs. "I told you. I just take the time to learn them. Life is political whether you like it or not."

I look down at the white envelope, still in shock. *I can't believe he got me into Cambridge.*

"Congratulations." Christopher smiles, enthralled as he watches me. A million questions swirl around in my mind as my annoyance turns to gratitude.

So much gratitude.

Everything I was worried about, *all the pressure that sat on my shoulders,* evaporates within seconds. I'm stunned as I look up at Christopher. "But how did he—"

"He spoke to the dean of admissions. Turns out, he owed my father a personal favor. It was a two-second call." Christopher shrugs casually. "It doesn't take much when you're about to be the leader of an entire island."

"Apparently not," I say, still stunned. "Wow. Well, thank you, Christopher. It means a lot. Truly." I smile politely, unsure of what to do or say as he watches me squirm. The smile on his face makes my stomach flutter a bit.

He's amused by me, and I kind of like it.

I snap back to my senses, quickly sliding the envelope into my white purse. "Well, at least I don't have to worry about my parents breathing down my back anymore." My voice is soft as I try my best to resume the painting. "I don't know how much longer I would've been able to stall my father. The election has been my only saving grace." I glance over at Christopher, who says nothing as he focuses on his painting with precision.

I take a deep breath. "Christopher, I really appreciate it. What you just did for me." I feel vulnerable as my gratitude speaks. "You didn't have to. And I want you to know that it really means a lot."

He takes the brush from the canvas and turns to me. He's handsome under the afternoon light that streams in through the windows.

"I appreciate that," he says, his demeanor smooth.

I fidget as I search myself for the right words. "I know we didn't exactly get off on the right foot. I was hard on you. But I want you to know that you're not so bad. And I don't know . . . maybe I was wrong about some things. Maybe I judged you a little."

"Wow." He laughs, taken aback. "That is the sweetest thing you've ever said to me. I'm blushing."

"Oh, shush." I smile, fanning him off. "I haven't been *that* bad."

"You've been worse."

"As if you've been any better?" I say, faux offended as he looks at me. "I mean, come on, your whole *vibe* is straight out of a bad JCG commercial."

"Ouch."

"Sorry. It's just . . . It's hard for me to see past all this political stuff. It's really not my thing. None of it."

"I get that." He nods, taking me in. "But we have a lot in common, Jillian. More than you think. I've met a lot of girls to know that you're different." His eyes lock with mine. "You're special."

I blush. "Well, I appreciate you." I smile earnestly. "What you had your father do . . ." I glance back at him. "Just . . . thank you," I say softly.

"You're welcome."

There's a moment of stillness as he holds my gaze a little

longer than he should. My stomach flutters as I turn back to the red rose in front of me.

"You're not wearing the bracelet I got you."

"I lost it," I say remorsefully.

"So quickly?" He looks at me. "Intentionally?"

"No. Of course not," I say genuinely, looking at him. "I was careless the other night."

"It's okay. There's lots more where that came from. You're to be my wife, remember? Till death do us part."

I tense.

"Relax." He smiles. "I'm not as evil as you think I am."

"I never said you were *evil*." I shift. "It's just . . . it's a lot."

"I get that. But I see you, Jillian Casey. *Clearly.* And I know that somewhere deep down, there's a part of you that wants this to work too." He holds my gaze as I hold my breath.

I'm vulnerable as he reads me, leaning in closer.

"You enjoy my company, Jillian. Maybe even more than you care to admit." He smiles slyly. "I think you're just worried you might actually *like* what Mommy and Daddy picked out for you this time."

"Can you stop?" I say abruptly, feeling fed up. "I don't need you to psychoanalyze my life. I'm so tired of everyone doing that to me." I shake my head. "You haven't even known me longer than two weeks."

"And yet still I know you better than anyone ever has." His eyes are intense. "You want *freedom*, Jillian. I can see it *all over your face*." He studies me. "I can give you that and so much more. That letter is only the beginning."

My breathing quickens as I take in his words.

The feeling he evokes is different from what I feel with Irie.

And I try to force myself to like it.

"Look, don't get me wrong." I squirm. "I appreciate what you've done. But at the end of the day, this engagement is happening *whether I want it to or not*." I keep my voice low. "It doesn't matter how I feel about *it* or *you,* because I don't have a choice in what's happening."

"You *always* have a choice, Jillian." His eyes hold mine. "How you feel about something is a choice."

I look away from him, peering over at his painting out of the corner of my eye. I'm surprised when I see orange, yellow, and red watercolors bursting across the canvas.

Jamaica at dawn stares back at me.

The portrait is stunning.

"Wow," I say. "That's beautiful."

"Just like you," he says without hesitation.

He reaches over and takes my hand in his.

Claiming me.

"I like you, Jillian." His voice grows vulnerable, honest. "I like that you're smart. You question things. You don't just take what's handed to you."

My heart races. Despite my better judgment, something about his touch quells my devastation. It picks the humiliated parts of me up from off the dirt road. Christopher sees me as *smart,* just like Irie does. Except with him, he asks for nothing in return. He sees my worth and only wants to give me more. He doesn't need me or my help—*he wants me.* And in this moment, it makes him seem a little more attractive.

"You like me too, don't you?" He moves in closer.

Where is Monica with those drinks?

"Admit it," he continues. "You feel what I feel."

"Maybe," I whisper.

My defenses lower as his thumb trails along my palm. I feel the heat from his fingers transfer to mine as he weaves his fingers in and out.

Toying with me.

Teasing me.

I don't know what it is, but I feel *something.*

"Being happy is a choice only you can make, Jillian," he says confidently, his voice low and his eyes direct. "But I *promise* your voice will always matter with me. Do you understand?"

I nod, our eyes locked in a crowded room.

For the first time ever, I allow myself to believe him.

"YEAH," I say softly. "I do."

Irie

"I *cyaan* believe yuh recorded di *entire* song!"

SIARAH beams as we rush home from the studio. I'm on cloud nine as the sun sets above us and we follow the palm trees home. *I tore it up in the studio.*

"I *cyaan* believe I'm going to *have* my own song!" I burst. "Suh'um I can *actually* play out loud and listen back to."

"It's surreal." Tandi beams.

"*You're a supastar!*" Siarah bursts. "Just wait till people hear dis record."

"Daddy's not going to believe it," Tandi says.

"Daddy's not going to *find out.*" I stop her in her tracks. "No one says a word. Are we clear?"

"Yeah, yeah." Tandi fans me off. "Long as you break me off a likkle suh'um when you reach number one."

We burst out laughing, invigorated by the mere idea.

"So, what's next?" Siarah's eyes go wide. "How we get yuh fi blow up pon di radio?"

"Radio in Jamaica doesn't play reggae music."

"Irie's going to be the first!" Siarah says. "She'll mek history."

I grin wide as my sisters go back and forth. "Yuh guys are

sweet." I smile. "Ace says U-Roy haffi get the record printed first, so it can be on vinyl."

"What are yuh goin' to tell Daddy?" Siarah probes again.

"Nuttin'." I quickly kill the topic as we make our way past the mounds of vegetation, approaching Kintyre. "I don' know how I would explain to him where I met Daddy Roy."

"Either way, he probably wouldn't believe you." Siarah laughs. "Can you imagine? *Irie—the next biggest star outta Jamaica. The female Bob Marley.*"

I'm on a high as we continue through the forest. If only for a moment, my mind drifts away from the devastation of losing Junior. For the first time in days, I'm not thinking about my fight with Jilly or that horrific night. For once, I'm focused on my future.

My sisters and I race down the hill, weaving our way in and out of branches until we reach the bottom. My palms are clammy as we approach the swinging bridge into Kintyre. It hangs over the rapids of the river, and crossing it on a good day is terrifying. I calm my nerves, preparing myself, but just as I'm about to cross, I notice a group of men standing on the other end.

They spot us instantly.

"*Bumbaclaat,*" one of them calls out. "Wha' gwaan, sexy?"

I'm stunned as I turn back to my sisters.

"Just go. Let's get it ova with." Siarah takes a deep breath. "If we stay here, they can corner us out of Kintyre. And it's getting dark. We can't run back into the streets."

"Okay." I nod, knowing full well she's right.

"Here, I'll go first." Siarah slips in front of me. "I'm di oldest."

My heart pounds. "Okay." I glance back at Tandi, whose face turns to stone.

Fear serves no use. *We have to get home.*

The bridge sways back and forth as I follow slowly behind Siarah, focusing on each step. The men hoot and holler as my heart wages a war in my chest.

I'm on the razor's edge of panic as we approach them. A young man with cornrows clutches his waist, and I almost drop to my knees.

A pistol.

"Wha'ppen, babez?" the man slurs as he inches in closer, a purple bandanna in his back pocket. *Tower Posse gang—the JCG.* He pulls out his gun just as Siarah takes the final step off the bridge.

"Ay, gyal! Yuh neva hear me ah call to yuh?"

I step down off the bridge behind Siarah, my breath caught in my lungs. The men scowl as I reach back to help Tandi off the bridge.

"*Yow, bitch!* Unu nuh hear me ah talk to yuh?" the young man barks as his friends move in from behind him. I grab hands with my sisters as we squeeze down tightly.

"It's okay," Siarah whispers to us as the men make their way over. "Let's go."

But we're outnumbered.

They laugh, blocking us in.

"*Three* pretty gyal ah road and puss have *all* ah unu tongue?" His eyes are sinister as he traps us at the end of the bridge.

"Excuse me." Siarah keeps her head low.

"Yuh deaf, bitch?"

"We hear you." The words firmly leave my lips. "Now can you *get out of our way*?"

Siarah and Tandi look at me in shock. But I can't take it anymore. I'm *tired* of fighting a war that I didn't even ask for. *Every. Single. Fucking. Day.*

"Move," I say again firmly. "We ah *try* fi pass." My entire body tremors as his eyes rip into me. But I'm *done* suffering at the hands of boys with guns.

"I said *move*!" I yell again. "*Move!* Get outta di *bloodclaat* way!"

"*Irie.*" Siarah panics.

"Yuh fuckin' mod, gyal?" He knocks the barrel straight into

my forehead. I gasp as the cold gun bucks my skin. Tandi and Siarah scream out as they grab onto me.

"Who di *fuck* yuh ah talk to? Een? Fuckin' eediot gyal." His eyes drill into me. "Yuh tink say yah *bod gyal*? Ah try play *hero*?" He laughs in my face. "I'll take yuh fuckin' life."

My life flashes before my eyes as he shoves the pistol into my head.

"Dutty fuckin'—"

"*YOW!*" A brooding voice comes from down the road. "*WHA' DI FUCK AH GWAAN?*"

I whip my head to see Kojo and a pack of boys running toward us with guns and machetes and stones—*the neighborhood watch group.*

"Tek yuh *bloodclaat* hands offa dem!" Kojo yells as the gang of boys move in closer. The man with the cornrows redirects the gun in Kojo's direction.

In a matter of seconds, it is a standoff.

Kintyre is under attack.

The JCG Posse moves to draw their guns, but it's too late. They're outnumbered as Kojo and the Kintyre boys move in closer. And just then, Kojo sends a warning shot into the air.

Siarah screams, grabbing my arm and pulling Tandi and me down into the bushes beside the bridge. We lock into each other, huddled together in terror as we watch the shoot-out from behind the branches. Kojo and the boys fling heavy stones and shoot bullets into the air as the JCG thugs scamper away. One by one, they dash down the swinging bridge as the Kintyre boys shoot after them—missing them by inches.

BLOW. BLOW. BLOW.

"Don't come back round yesso!" the boys call until the last of the men have long disappeared. My heart beats out of my chest as I huddle with my sisters. The Kintyre boys begin to scatter out, securing the premises as Kojo jogs over to us. Siarah and Tandi whimper, but I can't shake the rage.

"Unu come!" he calls out as we untangle ourselves from the bushes. "Unu all right?"

"I might be if someone wasn't too busy tryna *play hero!*" Tandi cries out, taking me by surprise. "Wha' di *hell* was dat about, Irie?" she screams.

"Wha' yuh mean? I—" I search myself for the words as she glares at me. "I . . . I had to say suh'um, Tandi!" I yell, feeling attacked. "I couldn't just *stand there!*"

"You almost got us *killed*! And fi wha? So yuh can exercise yuh pride?"

"*Relax,*" Kojo interrupts us. "Everyone calm down. It's not safe to do this out here." He ushers us down the path. Tandi shakes her head, looking away from me in disgust.

"Unu gwaan back up ah yawd," Kojo orders.

"I *cyaan* believe she ah blame me," I say in shock.

"*Because yuh should have stopped!*" Tandi turns around.

"Me say unu *gwaan back up ah yawd*!" Kojo barks, making it clear it's not up for discussion. "*Now!*"

I bite down hard as I hesitantly trail behind them, passing by Kojo. "Tanks," I mutter to him as I make my way past.

Kojo's face is grim as he continues off to secure the area. He doesn't say, "You're welcome," and it makes me feel bitter—*not grateful*—as I watch him walk off into the setting sun, a cloak of nobility around his shoulders as he goes. Rage boils in my gut like a dutch pot as I trail behind my sisters. I'm *so angry* that just because the boys hold guns, they have the power to decide whose life matters and whose doesn't. I can't fight an unfair war.

And I'm tired of running away like a scared little bitch.

I'm done being afraid in my own community.

AND the truth is, I'm not fucking sorry.

23

———

Jilly

She used me.

I stand over the pile of reggae records pulled out from my bottom drawer as the tears stream down my face. I'm a mess as the horrors of that night take everything I have left.

Irie Rivers used me, and she hasn't even called.

Not one sorry. Not one apology. No sense of remorse for putting my life on the line. She used me. All so she could sneak out and perform at her stupid fucking show.

It was never about me—*about us.*

My feelings never mattered to her, and clearly neither did my life. And in the aftermath of my devastation, it's clear our friendship didn't, either. *She hasn't even called.* And as I stare down at the mountain of records in front of me, what I need to do next becomes clear.

Burn it.

I'm scared straight by what happened that night, and it's time I go back to the safety of my own life. Because at the very least, it's a life I'm familiar with.

It's a heartbreak I can handle.

I pile the records into a cardboard box as the tears pour down my puffy cheeks. If my parents ever found out what we did together my entire life would be over. If they knew I felt that way for a *girl* . . . they would destroy me. Just like Monica said; I can't keep playing with fire and wonder why I get burned. There's no way I can keep any of this music—every single last record reminds me of Irie. Every vinyl is etched to a memory of her.

I want to set it all ablaze.

My family was right—reggae music and girls like Irie should stay in the ghetto where they belong. They should stay far away from girls like me, so they don't rip our hearts in two. So they don't tempt us with a life—*with feelings*—we could never truly have.

It's a crime for me to love a woman in Jamaica.

And I had no business sticking my nose in a revolution that never concerned me.

I pack each record away, trying my best to destroy the love I felt for her. There's no future for us, even if I wanted there to be. Even if it's all I've ever dreamed of.

I take off my ruby bracelet and put it in the box. Just before sealing it shut, I take out Bob Marley's "No Woman, No Cry" and place it on the dresser. Maybe I'll just keep one.

Just then, there's a knock on my door.

I jump up as one of the housekeepers pokes her head inside.

"Miss Jillian." She enters humbly. "I've prepared your lunch downstairs."

"Thanks." I look back at the cardboard box. "Can you get rid of that box for me?"

"Of course." She nods dutifully. She makes her way into the room and grabs the box. "Any place in particular you'd like me to put it, madam?"

"The trash." I blink back the tears that threaten to escape.

A wave of anxiety comes over me, and I feel sick to my stomach. In just a few days, I'll officially be engaged to Christopher. And if that weren't enough on my plate, I still haven't told my parents about Cambridge.

I have to do that today.

I make my way downstairs to the kitchen table, trying my best to muster up an appetite. I open the fridge to grab some water just as the telephone rings behind me.

Riiing, riiing—

"Would you *get out* of the fridge, Jillian?" Mummy takes me by surprise as she hastily walks into the kitchen. I close the fridge door just as she breezes past me. "I keep telling you you're going to put on weight this summer if you keep it up."

I hate her.

"Hello?" She answers the phone on the fourth ring. She's silent for a moment. "Jillian's busy right now."

My heart drops as she hangs up the phone. I stare at her, on edge as she turns around to face me. "Who was it?" I ask.

"You tell that girl to stop calling this house, Jillian. I'm not going to warn you again."

Fuck—Irie.

I wither, desperate to call her back immediately.

Mummy saunters by me in her long green skirt and chiffon blouse. "And smile, Jillian. Your father's home, and I don't need him seeing you pouting around the house. The next few weeks are *very* important for him."

I ball my hand into a fist as Mummy shuffles through the letters that sit on the kitchen island.

"Head upstairs and get ready," she says distractedly. "We're picking out fabrics today for your engagement dress. And, Jillian?"

I stop, turning back around.

"Your father is going to call the school this afternoon. We've been waiting long enough."

Fuck.

"Where's Amala? I'll have her check the mailbox."

"I'll go let her know," I say abruptly. "I think she should be laying out my clothes for the day." I glance up at the clock.

Noon.

Her usual time.

"Hurry up, then." Mummy resumes her attention to the letters.

I reluctantly turn on my heel.

I make my way out of the kitchen, down the long hallway, and up the windy stairs toward my room door. I'm nervous as I make my way through the house; I haven't faced Amala since the other night when she caught Irie and me sneaking in. I've managed to keep to my room and avoid her during the hours she cleans it. But now, as I turn my bedroom door handle, a sinking feeling drops to the pit of my stomach. I've never lied to Amala, but she works for me.

It's her job to keep my secrets.

I open the door to find her standing over my bed, laying out my dress and stockings.

"Good afternoon, Amala," I say politely.

"Oh, Miss Jillian." She busies herself. "So good to see you. I was just—"

"Laying out my clothes." I nod. "Thank you." There's a moment of awkward silence between us. "I know you're busy, but Mummy was wondering if you could check the mail."

"Oh yes. I checked it earlier."

"And I checked it before that," I lie.

Amala looks at me, confused as I make my way toward my chest of drawers. I pull open the top drawer and take out the sealed letter from Christopher.

"This actually came in the mail last night," I say as I turn around to face her. I feel ashamed as the lie leaves my lips. "My acceptance letter. From Cambridge."

"Oh, my goodness, *Miss Jillian*." Amala beams. "Congratulations. Yuh nuh want to give it to yuh parents yourself?" she asks, confused.

"No. She wanted you to check the mail."

"Oh." Amala's hesitant as she takes the white envelope from my hands. "Okay. I'll let her know." She smiles politely as she turns off the iron, unsure of my motives.

But either way, she goes with it.

I swallow my guilt as Amala makes her way past me.

"Oh, and Amala." I turn around as she approaches the door. "Please don't say anything about the other night. Irie and I . . . we were just hanging out in the backyard." I shrug off the lie. "Came in a little late, is all."

"Certainly," Amala says obediently, turning to go.

Just then, she stops. "Miss Jillian?"

"Hmm?"

"I don't mean to impose, I just—" She pauses with the letter in hand as she stands at the door. "You're an incredibly bright girl, Miss Casey." She smiles humbly as she looks to the ground. "I just . . . I don't want to see you throw your future away. Or get caught up wit' di wrong friends."

"Have you ever been?" The question leaves me, haunting. "Caught up? Wit' the wrong friends, or . . . caught between the life you want and . . . the life you were born into?"

Amala nods solemnly, her brown eyes distant. "Every day."

And with that, she turns on her heel and closes the door.

Her words chill me, and I'm left alone in my room to process them. I throw myself down on the bed, tucking my head under the pillow to bury my sadness. I wait with a doomed feeling in my gut for the inevitable. The clock ticks slowly, and it feels like hours pass by. I head to turn on the radio. Seconds later, an upbeat, catchy tune fills my room.

Something American. Joyful and light.

As I plop back down onto the bed, the music soothes my restless soul. Masking my broken heart, drowning out the songs I no longer wish to hear.

THIRTY minutes later, there's a knock on my door.

"Miss Jillian." One of our maids whose name I can't seem to recall pokes her head through the door. "I'm so sorry to interrupt, Miss Jillian, but your parents would like to see you in your father's study. They've requested you come down immediately."

"Okay. Sure." I swallow hard as she closes the door.

I search myself for the courage.

It's now or never.

I change into the dress Amala laid out for me before quickly checking myself in the mirror. And then I head through my bedroom door. I don't stop until I'm at the looming oak entry of my father's study.

Knock, knock, knock.

"Come in." My father's deep voice penetrates the door.

I turn the handle and enter. The study is lit up by the afternoon sun, trophies and photos on full display. I round the corner to find my mother and father sitting behind the desk.

"Have a seat, Jillian," Mummy says when she sees me. "We have some good news."

I shift, taking a seat, trying my best to keep cool. "What's going on?" I ask dumbfoundedly.

"Amala just brought in the mail." My father reads over the letter in his hands, the look on his face almost disbelieving. I dig my nails into my palm as I nervously look at the white paper. Daddy places it down in front of me. And then he smiles.

"Congratulations, Jillian." His voice is proud. "You got in."

"Really?" I use my best surprised face.

"You did it, Jillian." Mummy smiles pleasantly.

"We're so proud of you, darling," Daddy says.

I'm raw as the emotion bubbles inside of me, pouring out against my will.

They're proud.

AND it's the first time in my life I believe it.

24

———

Irie

"The Black youth are trapped in inner-city poverty, and Jamaica cannot afford to have our young succumb to cynicism."

JOSHUA Morris's voice comes through the static of the radio as I sit in the office, trying desperately to escape my racing thoughts.

"But every now and then, I say to myself—it'll all come out in the wash. History is the great leveler of artists and activists alike."

I sigh, turning it off as I decide to pick up the phone.

Riiing, riiing, riiing.

I'm a nervous wreck as I wait eagerly for someone to answer. But for another day in a row, nothing.

It's been well over a week, and still no word from Jillian.

I'm so angry that she hasn't returned any of my calls. I can't believe I ever thought we were friends. *Best friends.* Her silence makes me feel desperate and helpless.

Why is she doing this?

It's not fair that I'm forced to take all the blame. After everything we shared together, she won't even give me the respect of a phone call. I tense my jaw as resentment shoots through me.

As much as I want to speak to her—to apologize and tell her

how sorry I am for that night—a part of me feels just as angry with her as she is with me. Jilly experienced *one* night of hell.

I suffer through it every single day.

I put the phone back on the hook as I sit in the back room of the shop. Frustration builds as the thick reggae beat blasts through the walls of the store.

My eyes well with tears, and I fight to swallow them back. I'm not going to let her ruin my life. Maybe she was always planning to drop me as a friend at the end of the summer. Maybe I really was just her *school friend*.

Maybe she really does see me as below her.

I rise from the stool, wiping the tears from my cheeks.

I make my way out of the back office and into the dark shop hallway. Up front, Daddy, Siarah, and Tandi scurry about unloading a new shipment. The shop is relatively empty with only a handful of customers scanning the store. With the election only two weeks away, business has taken a hit. No one wants to be on the streets right now, but we still have bills to pay.

I step down into the store to find Daddy and a customer in mid-conversation at the register. Tandi stands nearby, making a list of the inventory. I roll my eyes, turning in the other direction. We haven't spoken since the bridge, but I refuse to feel remorse. I'm not going to pretend to be sorry.

I make my way over to Siarah, who fiddles with the shipment boxes. I grab one from the floor and begin to help her unload. A concerned look covers her face.

"What?" I ask.

Siarah sighs. "I've jus' been thinking," she whispers. "About everything that happened the other day. And . . . I don't know. Yuh think we should at least tell Daddy?"

"*Daddy?*" I furrow my brows as if she must be crazy. "Why would we do that?"

"Me nuh know." Siarah shrugs as she begins to organize the bins. "Tings are gettin' worse, Irie. What if they come back?"

"Kintyre is *filled* with gunmen, Siarah," I say diligently. "Those boys aren't special. And if we tell Daddy, it's only going to get him more worked up." I glance over at the yellow sign. "Yuh nuh see the PLM sign? The last thing we need in here is another one."

"You think that's why business has slowed down? Because of the sign?"

I'm taken aback by her question; I hadn't thought of it before. "I doubt that." I shake my head. "Election soon come. Everyone is just on edge."

"I guess." Siarah shrugs, not convinced. "I'm just scared. I mean, whoever those boys were, they *know* we live in Kintyre."

"Well, then, I guess that's for Kojo and his police friends to worry about," I say bitterly. "Isn't that why di police are paying them in weapons?"

"The same *weapons* that saved our lives, Irie."

"And the same *police* that would take them in an instant," I say defensively. "Don' let Kojo's *hero act* confuse you."

"Irie." Siarah looks at me. "Yuh *haffi* give it a rest."

"Just because I had a gun to my head doesn't mean I *deserved* it, Siarah." I keep my voice low. "And just because Kojo saved us doesn't make him a hero. *He's a part of the problem.*"

Siarah rolls her eyes. "Whatever. *I'm* talking about being honest with Daddy. For our own safety."

"Not yet," I say firmly. "I don't want to mess anything up with this record. If we tell Daddy about the boys, we'll have to tell him where we were coming from." My stomach drops at the mere idea. "Just, let me hear the record first. I'll figure out my plan from there."

"All right." Siarah sighs reluctantly. "I won't say a word. But I cyaan speak fi Tandi." She gestures to the front, where Tandi stands alone, sulking as she goes through receipts.

"I'll talk to her," I say as I put the last record into the pile.

I just need a little more time.

I stack the empty crates just as Daddy's conversation at the front grows louder.

"Yuh *need* fi tek it down!" a woman scolds him. "Yuh turnin' away customers."

"If dem nuh like it, they can buy from somewhere else."

"People are *tired* of Morris puffing up his chest, Ricky! They want *food* back on di shelves."

"My stance is my *stance*. And it *nah* go change." Daddy stubbornly dismisses her, handing her the scandal bag with her purchase inside. "Walk good."

The woman screws up her face before making her way out of the shop.

Siarah gives me a knowing look, and I ignore her, going about my duties as the Abyssinians' "Declaration of Rights" bumps throughout the shop.

Get up and fight for your rights, my brothers . . .

LATER that afternoon, I head to the back office to work on music while Siarah lulls around and Tandi cleans. I sit behind the office desk for about twenty minutes, trying my best to come up with new lyrics, but everything about my vibe feels off. *Think about Rastafari,* I tell myself. *Peace and compassion.*

But I'm the furthest from feeling any of those emotions. My optimism feels lost as I struggle to find the words. In the past week alone, I've been held at gunpoint—twice.

Write about what you felt with Jilly. The thought creeps up. But I'm a mess as our night together washes over me. Tears instantly flood the back of my eyes. *Why is she doing this to me?*

All I want is my friend back.

I hold my pencil to the page, staring down at the blank lined paper. *I'm so damn frustrated.* I just want things to be good with us again. I need to know that our friendship means more to her. That *I* mean more to her.

That everybody else wasn't right.

I turn and stare at the telephone as I contemplate what to do. My palms instantly go sweaty. I'm more than Jillian's school friend—and what we shared last weekend proved it.

I dig for courage as I reach for the phone, dialing Jillian's number one last time.

Riiing, riiing, riiing, riii—

"Hello?"

"Oh, hi, um, Mrs. Casey?"

"Yes."

"Hi. It's Irie again. I, um—I was just wondering if Jilly might be home?"

"How many times do I have to tell you, girl?" Her tone is cutting. "She's *busy*. Now *stop* calling this house."

Dial tone.

"Fuck!" I slam down the phone, bringing my hands to my temple.

The tears fall like rain.

"Whoa."

I jump, looking up to find Ace standing at the door. My heart catapults as he watches me with curiosity.

"Who ah trouble you, stargirl?" he asks me as he makes his way into the office. "Nuttin' yuh manager can't fix, I hope."

I quickly wipe the tears from my face, completely taken aback. "Sorry, I-I didn't see yuh standing there," I say, flustered. My cheeks burn, embarrassed to be caught crying by him. He stands tall and brawny in a brown T-shirt and jean shorts, his skin gleaming from the midday sun.

Handsome, just like always.

"Don't apologize." He smiles smoothly. "Every supastar is allowed at least one meltdown. Besides, yuh look cute when you're upset."

"Shut up." I fight the smile that creeps up. "Why are yuh here?"

"Yuh fada has some money fi me fi di work I did the other

day." He uses his chin to gesture to the desk. "Him say fi tell you the envelope was on di desk."

"Oh," I say, noticing the white envelope that rests on the table. I reach for it, passing it to him.

"Tanks." He nods. He stands across from me, silent for a moment. "So?"

"What?"

"Yuh nah go tell me why you're upset?" He takes a seat on the desk. "Don't tell me you're still crying over yuh likkle stush friend—"

"I don't need another lecture, Ace," I cut him off. "Not now. And I promise anything yuh haffi tell me about Jilly, my sisters have already told me twice."

"Well, maybe you should take their advice."

I slump, bitter as I look away from him. "It's not like di PLM is innocent, Ace," I say, exhausted. "Look at what they did to Jilly."

"And how much worse has di JCG done to *you*?" His deep eyes are pointed. "They *murdered* your friend, Irie. Shot him dead right at yuh front door."

"It still doesn't make it right," I say adamantly. "On both sides."

I sigh, desperate to change the subject. "Have yuh talked to Daddy Roy? Did he say when di record will be ready?"

"He'll have di vinyl ready next week. I already have a few ideas for your next show. Have yuh been writing?"

"It's kind of hard to write when you've had a Glock to your head."

"What?" Ace looks at me, confused. "Who held a Glock to yuh head?"

"The JCG." I look up at him. "My sisters and I got stopped by the Tower Posse after we left the studio. We crossed di bridge into Kintyre, and they were all just standing there." My eyes begin to water. "I spoke back to one of di yutes, and he drew a gun on me. Would've pulled the trigger if it wasn't for Kojo showing up in time."

"Yuh tell yuh fada?"

I shake my head.

"Irie."

"I *can't,* Ace. It'll just get him more riled up. I've got enough to think about right now. The last thing I need is Daddy putting up a sign that says, 'JCG Do Not Enter.'"

"All di betta." Ace's face goes cold. "They're lucky I wasn't with you. I've would've murdered off all ah dem bloodclaat."

"Cool, nuh," I say, not in the mood.

"*Fuck cool,* Irie!" Ace slams his hand down onto the desk. "What you need to do is get *angry.* Yuh need to *get upset.*"

"*You don't think I'm upset?*" I say defensively. "But what am I supposed to do? Blast them with a machine gun?" I cry, frustrated. "Yuh have *no idea* what it's like to be a *girl* growing up in these streets. Yuh nuh tink sometimes *I* want revenge *too?*"

"So *take it,* then." Ace tosses my songbook at me, his tone threatening. "Stop complain and ball fi yuh *likkle rich friend.* Tell *di truth* about *your life* in Kintyre. Tell *di truth* so that people know what's going on in Jamaica."

My heart beats out my chest as I stare down at my songbook.

"Start writing," he instructs, pounding his finger down on the book. "I'm workin' on a gig fi yuh next week. I expect a new song the next time I see you." He rises from the stool as I sit there, bitter as he walks away.

"And where exactly are you going?" I say stubbornly. "Aren't yuh supposed to be my manager? Yuh always slipping off when I need you."

Ace looks back at me as he grips the door handle. "I have things to do, Irie," he says spitefully. "I'm a part of suh'um bigger. And when you're ready to be as well, you let me know."

And with that, he closes the door.

Fuck.

Reggae music blasts through the walls as I sit alone with my thoughts. Ace is right—I have to put the truth in the music. And the truth is, I'm pissed. I open my songbook and grab my pencil. And then, it rips out of me and onto the page.

Anger.

Rage.

Fury.

As a luminous reggae dub moves throughout the shop, I catch waves of the vibration and write down the truth of what I feel. The nuance of my anger. Of being caught in the middle of a civil war. What it feels like to be a young woman growing up in Jamaica, fearing for my life every single day. An hour turns to two, and by the time I look up, the office is dark, indicating sundown. I look down at my lyrics.

Wash away the sin
Drown me, begin again
Jah Jah
They got the knife at my throat
And the gun at my door
But I and I nah go back down from di war
I is a fighter, Jah salute
Ready to do wha' me haffi do

If the war is over
Why is paradise
Only getting colder?
Why is Babylon
Only getting bolder?

Tired of peace
And we ready fi war
But when we dead and gone, Jah Jah
Who ah keep di score?

Fighting for our lives
Fighting for salvation
Tell me will the music be
The way to restoration?

Blood in Babylon
War and corruption
Have I killing for Zion
Jah deh have I killin' for Zion

Save me, holy lion
Save us, holy lion

My own words chill me. I hear the music volume in the shop lower, and the sound of my father and my sisters tidying up grows louder. I look down at the page in complete awe.

I wrote an entire song in one go.

Knock, knock, knock.

"Yeah!" I call out, distracted. I look up from my songbook to find Tandi peeking through the door. "Daddy says it's time to go."

"Oh—sorry, I didn't realize di time."

"Iz all right. It was dead, anyway." Tandi nods awkwardly, clearly still upset with me. "We're packing up now."

"I'll meet unu out front." I nod, gesturing to my songbook. "I'm jus' finishing up."

Tandi nods before closing the door.

I glance over at the phone before rising from the seat, shoving down the urge to call Jillian one final time. I close my notebook, tucking it under my arm before heading toward the office door. And then I hear a sound that brings me to my knees.

POP, POP, POP.

"*No!*" The scream rips out of me as I trip over myself, grabbing for the door handle.

POP! POP! POP! POP!

This can't be happening again.

I bolt into the hallway to find Tandi on the other side. She stands frozen in her tracks, just out of sight from the shop floor. My knees are weak as I dash down the hall, but before I can make my way past her, she pulls me to the ground. I fight as she drags me backward, frantic as she covers my mouth.

"*Stop!*" I try to peel her hand off my mouth.

"*You can't!*" she whispers, clutching me tightly.

I'm stunned in position. Because right down the hallway, I see them.

Four masked men.

And my father, *lying shot*.

Tandi digs her fingers into my skin as we huddle just out of sight. The tears pour from my eyes like lava.

We watch as our father lies in a pool of his own blood.

Time stops as the men tear through the shop, reggae still blasting through the walls.

"Daddy," I cry as I try to fight out of Tandi's grip.

"*They'll kill you, Irie!*" Tandi's eyes are desperate as the looming beat swallows us whole. I'm helpless as we watch our greatest horror play out in front of us.

POP! POP! POP!

The men hold up M16s, shooting and looting as they rummage through the shop, destroying equipment and turning over bins. Tandi and I crouch in the back of the hallway as they ravage through the store, destroying everything we love.

Taking everything we have left.

"*Where's Siarah?*" I panic, whispering to Tandi.

But then we spot her instantly.

Standing in the corner with an AK-47 held to her head.

A man who wears a mask holds Siarah in his grip. Her arms are clamped behind her back, a cloth around her mouth as she whimpers. She tries to fight her way out, but the man yanks her back, holding her by her hair. He smiles, revealing a gold tooth.

"*Aghhh!*" Siarah cries as the men drag her out of the store. And then, they grab my father from the ground and haul him through the shop doors like an unwanted dog. He wails out in pain just as they put a bag over his head. Tandi and I are stunted.

Frozen.

Shock renders me numb as they leave just as quickly as they came. Before I can think to do anything, the shop bell dings and the door closes.

Seconds later, we hear the car zoom off.

Doomsday falls upon us as the bass from the speakers shakes the shop walls.

The tiles, completely red from Daddy's blood.

"*Daddy!*" I wail in devastation.

It's the only word I can muster the strength to say. I bolt down into the shop, tripping over fallen records and broken equipment, wailing through the thick reggae bass.

BOOM, BOOM, BOOM.

And just then, I see it out of the corner of my eye.

The setting sun bursts off the page, juxtaposing the disaster. The yellow party colors are bright as the PLM poster lies in the middle of the shop floor.

A bullet hole straight through the center.

25

———

Irie

A thunderstorm roars through Kintyre for the first time this summer.

THE clock strikes 4:00 a.m. as Tandi and I cry into each other's arms. We are a sea of sadness as the storm rages, ravishing us with every dooming sound. The only thing necessary becomes clear:

Revenge.

"They're not going to get away with this, Tandi," I weep as I hold my little sister tightly. "It's guna be a *war*. They're going to *pay* for this."

A bolt of lightning crashes down just as a knock on the door jolts us from our seats. I grab the machete that's tucked nearby and creep over to the doorway, terror mounting with every step.

"Who is it?" I yell over the thunder.

"Ah me," Kojo's voice comes from the other side.

Thank God.

I unlock the row of bolts and yank it open. Kojo stands in uniform, drenched from the rain with his gun tucked into his waist.

"*Kojo,*" I bawl, surprising even myself as I fall into his arms.

"I'm *so* sorry, Irie," he whispers as he holds me.

After a few seconds, urgency floods back to me as I pull away from him. He steps into the house, locking the door.

"They have a lead on Daddy." Kojo drops a bomb. "They took him to Up Park Camp. They're holding him up there, but there's no word yet on where they took Siarah."

"Wait, *what*?" My mouth drops as I process the information. "*Up Park Camp?*"

Up Park Camp used to be the headquarters for the British army, but now it's a detention center used by Jamaican soldiers. It's where they lock up some of Jamaica's biggest crime bosses and war criminals.

"So, you're saying *the military* took Daddy?"

"I don't know who *took him,* per se," Kojo corrects me. "But I know that's where he ended up. I got word this evening they're holding him up there."

"So then where's Siarah?" Tandi asks, frantic.

Kojo shrugs. "That's all they're telling me."

"So, *it was your people*?" I stare at Kojo in disbelief. "Jamaican soldiers?"

"But they were masked men." Tandi shakes her head in disbelief. "The people who took them weren't in uniform. We saw them with our own eyes."

"They weren't *police,*" I agree. "They were gangsters."

"Depends on who's paying them," Kojo says grimly. "It could be the PLM government for all we know, but they're not telling me anything else."

"So how do we get him *back*?" I say urgently. "And what about Siarah?"

"There's no coming back from Up Park Camp, Irie. Not until they're ready to release him," Kojo says matter-of-factly. "We just have to sit tight."

I look at him as though he's insane. "Yuh can't be serious."

"Have you *been* outside? It's a *war* zone, Irie. There's nothing we can do tonight. Bodies are droppin' left, right, and center."

His words take me aback. "*I'm sorry*—do yuh even *hear yuh-self*, Kojo? *Yuh shift is over!* You're not on the clock!" I explode. "We can't just sit around! We have to get them back."

"*All* I said was be patient. Let di police work pon it."

"Fuck the police!" I yell.

"Can unu stop?" Tandi cries.

"No! They're not going to investigate this, *just* like they didn't investigate Junior!" My eyes water as I look Kojo directly in the eye. "I can't believe you're going to leave Daddy up there to rot!"

"I'm done with this conversation." Kojo shakes his head. "Yuh too hotheaded, Irie. Too hotheaded fi yuh own good."

"Whatever." I bite down as the tears pour. "You know, I should've known better. It's not like yuh ever *really* cared about Daddy. He's not yuh father, after all. And we're just yuh *half sisters* from di mother who abandoned you. This house is just yuh room and board."

"Wach yuh mout', Irie!" The words leave Kojo with force. "How could you even *fix yuh mouth* fi say suh'um like that to me?"

"Because you're *a traitor*!" I scream, coming undone. "Family should come before your allegiance to some military *soldier* bull crap."

"And what about *you*?" He storms over. "Your allegiance to yuh likkle boasty friend from school? Yuh light-skinned massa?"

"Don't talk about Jilly."

"Or what?" He stares at me. "*What?* Too hard to admit that you're a *hypocrite?*"

I bite down, balling my hands into fists. I want to punch him straight in the face.

"Don't blame me because it's too hard for *you* to let go, Irie. Yuh got to play dress-up at that school for *four years* while di rest of us had to stay in di same fuckin' place. And now you want fi come look down at di job *I do to protect my community?*"

I'm seething as he steps closer to me.

"I have news for you, Irie. There's blood on *every hand*. Purple *and* yellow. I don't pick sides, because I serve *di ghetto*. And unlike you, I'm not ashamed to admit I come from it."

"Unu cool nuh, mon!" Tandi bawls to the night.

But it's too late.

In an instant, my brother turns to a stranger right before my eyes.

"Fuck you, Kojo," I sob. "Yuh so *fuckin'* jealous and brainwashed yuh cyaan even see yuh own fault." Disgust drips from my tone as the shell of my brother stands in front of me.

Corrupted by Jamaican soldiers.

"Yuh turn soldier and yuh turn *heartless*, Kojo. Yuh turn fool."

"Well, at least I'm not trying to live a life that's *not mine*."

"I hate you."

"And I've *protected* you," he fires back. "Every night from *sunup* till *sundown*. So me nuh business whether yuh wan' *hate* me, Irie. Writing songs nah go save us from di reality of what's going on outside! We're in di middle of a *civil war*. Not a sing-off."

And with that, he brushes by me, making his way into the bathroom and slamming the door. I'm fuming as lightning rips through the night.

"*AHHHH!*" Everything inside of me erupts as thunder roars throughout the dark house, haunting as it consumes me in its doom. Tandi curls into a ball as fury sets fire to every cell inside of my body.

Fuck Kojo.

I'M going to get my family back.

26

Jilly

"Look at the size of that *ring*!"

I'M smothered by my aunt Maureen as she gushes over the rock on my finger. I haven't seen her in ages. Or any of these women, for that matter. Mummy's friends from the country club, the wives of politicians and businessmen, and a few other desperate housewives stare down at my hand as if they don't have their own blood diamonds to marvel at.

Christopher beams proudly in the distance as the crowd of guests mingle around the room. The space is grandiose, decorated in freshly cut flowers and draped in the finest of French cloth. But despite the huge display, there's an ache in the pit of my stomach.

I need a break.

"Would you ladies excuse me?" I politely wiggle my hand away. "I'm just going to run to the ladies' room."

"We're about to do the toast, Jillian," Mummy scolds. "Don't go running off."

"I just need to freshen up." I flash a tempered smile before taking off through the ballroom.

I dash through the doors into the hallway as the hotel staffers look on. They smile, greeting me as I make my way down the hallway of the Pegasus Hotel in my gown. I'm reminded they're paid to put up with people like me as I make my way to the nearest bathroom. I burst through the doors and take a deep breath, locking eyes with my reflection.

What the fuck am I doing? I grapple with myself as I weigh the future that lies ahead of me. A future without Irie.

I search for air as our night comes back to me. Her brown skin. Her beautiful brown eyes. Her angelic voice. *Her hands on my body.* Her lips on my collarbone.

Her mouth on my—

"*Stop it, Jillian,*" I scold myself in the mirror. I'm ashamed as the memory crawls its way up my skin.

We were just friends having fun, I tell myself to calm the guilt. But the idea of anyone ever finding out haunts me.

Irie better not have told anyone. What happened between us was a *one-night thing.* We were caught up in the moment. Drunk off the adrenaline and high off the vibrations.

And it will never happen again.

I have way too much on the line to throw my future away to someone who would leave me for dead in the streets. Maybe I *don't* have a choice in my life—in who I marry or what circles I'm apart of—but I've never made her feel less than for where she comes from.

And I've most certainly never put her life at risk.

Maybe Mummy was right about girls like her. She was obsessed with me. With my life. Clearly, the love she had for me had nothing to do with who I actually am. She liked me for my nice house and all my shiny things.

For all I know, she was the one who stole my bracelet. I turn on the tap, praying it takes all memory of Irie down the drain.

Knock, knock, knock.

I'm jolted by a sharp tap on the bathroom door. "I'm using it!" I call out.

"It's me," a familiar voice calls back.

Christopher.

"I'll be right out, just . . . just tell Mummy I need a few more minutes."

"Relax, Jillian. No one's looking for you. Let me in."

"It's a ladies' room."

"Well, then, it's a good thing you're my lady. And that my father rented out the entire hotel." He pauses. "No one's coming, Jillian. Just let me in."

I sigh, giving in. I make my way toward the door and open it. He stands tall and handsome, his hair slicked back as he towers over me. He wears a white button-up dress shirt, his blue eyes sharp as he zeroes in on me.

"Hey."

"Hey." He smiles, slinking into the bathroom as he closes the door behind him. "Everything all right? Looked like you really had to use the bathroom."

I smile. "You're silly." I shake my head. "No, I just . . . needed a minute, I guess." I glance up at him. "Am I missing anything out there?"

"I wouldn't exactly say that." He laughs. "They were getting ready for the toast, but then your mother started telling a story about a family trip to the South of France." He raises an eyebrow, looking at me. "Let's just say she really knows how to work a room."

"Especially after a few glasses of champagne." I roll my eyes. "She loves the attention."

"Nothing wrong with that." Christopher gazes at me. "You look beautiful, Jillian."

I flutter. "Thanks," I say softly, feeling a little awkward. I'm unsure of what to say as his kindness draws me in.

"May I kiss you, Jillian?" His eyes graze my lips. "Please?"

For some reason, I nod. Christopher moves in, gliding his hands through my hair as he gently grips me at the nape of my neck. He places his lips on mine, and to my surprise, his lips are tender.

And kind of nice.

I surrender to him and it feels different from kissing Irie . . . not as passionate or deep. But in this moment, it doesn't really matter. Because someone else soothes my sorrow.

Knock, knock, knock.

We both pull away.

"Jill?" Monica's voice calls. "You in there?"

I flush, immediately standing up. "Coming!" I call, quickly patting down my dress. I turn around and open the door, slinking into the hall to find Monica waiting for me.

"Where have y—" She stops midsentence as Christopher exits from behind me. "Okay, lovebirds." She laughs tipsily. "Couldn't wait until the wedding night, huh?"

"Hush, Monica." I blush.

"You two are missing all the excitement," Monica says, holding her glass of champagne. "Morris is calling for a state of emergency. Our parents are all freaked out."

"*What?*" I ask, confused.

"A state of *emergency*?" Christopher's face drops.

"Yup." Monica shrugs.

"Excuse me." Christopher brushes past her, scurrying down the hall. Monica and I follow behind him, unsure of what's going on. As the three of us make our way back into the ballroom, I can feel it in the air. People are *pissed*.

"He's *using* state terrorism to secure the election!" Mr. Kelly screams. "It's the oldest trick in the book. Playing hero to a war that's not even fucking happening!" Anger drips from Winston Kelly as he stands next to Daddy.

Monica, Christopher, and I watch in horror as the adults go into a frenzy.

"Fucking *moron*." Daddy shakes his head in agreement. "Joshua Morris is just trying to rile people up. Create havoc in the ghetto so it can lead to a state of panic." Daddy kisses his teeth. "Who calls a state of emergency *two weeks* before an election?"

"He really called a state of emergency?" Christopher asks.

"Twenty minutes ago," Daddy says, deflated.

"The military presence is already out of control." Concern bathes Mrs. Kelly's face as she speaks to the group of women who surround her. "We don't need more soldiers militarizing our roads. Jamaica's economy won't be able to bounce back from this."

"It's all an intimidation tactic." Mr. Kelly's deep voice takes over the room as Daddy stands nobly beside him. "A setup. So he can play hero and put out a pretend fire."

"He's trying to terrorize us into submission!" Daddy yells.

"*Bastard.*" The word shoots from Mr. Kelly's lips like venom as the entire room goes into an uproar.

"What exactly *is* a state of emergency?" I whisper to Christopher, embarrassed for not fully understanding.

"It means the army can detain anyone suspicious . . . and the more JCG supporters he can get them to arrest before election day, the fewer votes we get," Christopher says through the commotion. "It changes everything."

I nod as it all dawns on me.

"If Morris wants a fight, then we'll wage a *war.*"

Rage drips from Winston Kelly.

"**BLOOD** for blood. *Fire for fire.*"

27

———

Irie

I pedal as fast as I can through the battered streets of Papine.

IT'S been four days since Daddy and Siarah were taken. Four days of sleepless nights trying to devise a plan to find my sister and bring her back.

And now, we've run out of food.

I rip down the street toward the record store. I have to go and get money from the register, but my heart is in my throat as I ride through the morning heat.

Military presence is *everywhere.*

The daunting sound of their engines fill the roads, and I hear them before I even see them. Jamaican soldiers are all over. As I ride on the backstreet that runs parallel to the main road, I see groups of men are lined up, their arms handcuffed behind their backs as they lie shirtless on the hot pavement. Guns to their heads, drawn by soldiers.

Keep pedaling. I focus my attention forward. But the streets are ominous as soldiers on green army trucks roll through with heavy weaponry. They stand on guard, ready to shoot.

I keep my head low.

My mind is a tornado with ideas and schemes. I'm willing to

get Siarah back by *any means necessary,* and I know there's only one person who can help me.

I have to figure out how to get in contact with Ace.

I swing a right into the square, and avoiding the police, I slowly pull up behind the record store. As I hop off the bicycle, tears instantly well in the backs of my eyes. *I can do this,* I tell myself. *But I have to be quick.*

My hands are clammy, and I wipe them on my black shorts as I slowly make my way over to the back door. If I can get to Daddy's address book, I can call Ace from the shop phone.

I can ask him to help me.

I make my way up to the door, unlocking the grille before turning the lock and pushing it open. The entire place is dark, and chills come over me as I make my way through the back hallway. I brace myself, holding on to the wall as I step down into the shop.

The entire place is destroyed.

Records are everywhere, and the shop has been turned upside down. Bloodstains cover the floor, and it takes everything I have not to burst into a million tears.

Stay focused, Irie, I scold myself. At least for now, I know where Daddy is.

But every second I waste could cost Siarah her life.

I zone in on what needs to be done, scurrying over to the front of the shop and making my way behind the counter. I use the key to open the register and take out what's left—*a few coins.* It's only enough to buy bread for a couple of days, but at least for now, it's something.

I stuff the money into my pocket and close the register before dashing across the shop floor. As I make my way down the hall, I approach the office door and go inside.

I'm stunned when I'm met with the sound of a man's voice.

"Jamaica is being destabilized by foreign and domestic conspirators!" Joshua Morris's brooding voice comes over the radio on low volume. The sound is eerie and unexpected as it statics through the room. I quickly turn it off.

"*Think, Irie,*" I whisper to myself as I scan the small dark office. *Where would Daddy keep his address book?* I make my way behind his desk, taking a seat in the wooden chair as I pull out his drawers. *Receipts, papers, and inventory slips.* I kneel down to the bottom drawer.

"Yes!" I say a silent thank-you when I find his pocket book staring back at me. I yank it open, desperately searching for the page. And then I see it, scribbled in messy black writing.

Ace's number.

I grab the phone from the hook. My fingers tremble as I dial each number. In seconds, the phone begins to ring.

Riiing, riiing.

But suddenly, I'm frozen in the chair.

Because I hear a noise coming from inside the shop.

I tremble as I take the phone from my ear, looking up at the doorframe. And then, from around the corner, Ace appears in front of me.

I slam the phone down.

"Irie," he says calmly. "I've been lookin fi yuh."

"Ace," I say, shocked. "Oh my god. When did you . . ."

But I'm speechless. I use all the strength I have left to dash out of the chair and race toward him. I thrust myself into his arms, collapsing as he holds me up. *I'm so grateful to see a familiar face.*

"Ace," I sob into his chest. It all pours out of me at once.

"I heard about what happened." His deep voice soothes me as he bundles me up in his arms. "Demons are lurking di streets, Irie," Ace whispers into my ear. "Babylon has ignited a war. It's not safe."

His words chill me as I pull away from him. "When . . . *when did you get here*?" I sob, confused as I wipe my face.

"Just now. Di back door was open. I thought someone had broken in."

"I was callin' yuh, just now." I heave. "I-I was coming to look fi yuh today. I need yuh help. They took Daddy to Up Park Camp."

"Up Park? There's no way he's getting out of there—"

"I know," I stop him. "But I have to find Siarah. I know it was di Tower Posse that took her. The JCG—"

"That's what I wanted to talk to yuh about," Ace stops me. The look on his face is strained as he takes a step closer to me. "I know where they took her."

"*What?* What do yuh mean? *Who?*"

"My boy said the crime boss might be holding her." Every inch of my body turns to stone.

"*What?*" I blurt out. "Like, the PLM Don?"

Ace nods. "A few guys who run wit' me said they saw her going into di go-go club. The Don brings new girls there to work di private rooms."

"But . . . but that doesn't make any sense." I shake my head in confusion. "None of this makes any *sense*, Ace," I say again firmly. "Why would the PLM do that? Daddy supported them! Why would the Power Posse take Siarah? Or *my fada*."

"Me nuh know, Irie." Ace's eyes go dark. "It nuh make sense to me, either. It could be that the soldiers paid di PLM gang to carry out the job. All sorta conspiracy ah gwaan around election time. But it's a question only di crime boss can answer."

My world goes from day to night in the span of seconds. Everything I said about the JCG.

I was wrong.

"Yuh *cyaan* tell nobody, Irie. We *haffi* be smart." His tone is chilling. "I swear to God, if any of the guys I work with find out I told you, it won't end well for me."

My heart hammers in my chest. "Ace, I *have* to get her back." My eyes flood with tears. "My sisters are all I have."

"I know." He nods. "I'm going to help you. I can get you in."

"Get me *in*?"

"As a performer. The go-go club usually has entertainment. Girls go up and dance, sing, and strip. The Don goes every Friday, and dem always ask us to bring in new girls, new talent."

"Friday?" My heart drops. "That's the night of the election."

Ace nods, his eyes chilling. "The Don will be there while they wait for the results to come in."

"Ace, I—" I shake my head as I try to process the information. "That's a death wish. I can't go on election night. That's—"

"Yuh only choice."

My knees go weak.

He's right.

"Now, di only thing is yuh cyaan go up there and sing nuttin' revolutionary, Irie. It would haffi be suh'um dark." He eyes me. "Yuh have suh'um yuh could perform? Suh'um yuh could dance to?"

The song I wrote a few days ago blasts back to me. I nod in a daze.

"Good. Then I can get yuh onstage. But yuh haffi bring another girl. Runners are expected to bring at least two or three for entry. It's nonnegotiable."

"I . . ." But I'm speechless as I rack my brain. "But I don't . . . I don't know anyone." I grip my forehead as I try to process. "I *cyaan* bring Tandi, Ace. She's my likkle sista, and she's all I have left. There's no way I can ask her to do that."

"What about yuh likkle friend?"

"*Jillian?*" I look at him, puzzled. "There's no way in hell. She would never say yes."

"If she's yuh real friend, she will."

I tense my jaw.

"I can help you, Irie." Ace puts his hand to my chin, steadying my breathing. "I know this is a lot, but I promise I can help you get yuh sista back."

A tear streams down my cheek.

Ace wipes it away.

"Make *no* mistake, I'm risking a lot fi you. If the PLM gang ever found out I went against them, it could cost me everything. My life included."

The danger looms in between us as Ace's eyes grow intense. "If we ah go do this, Irie, *we haffi do it right.*"

"I'm so *angry,* Ace." The truth tumbles out of me and into the palm of his hand. "I'm *done* being *irie.* I want *revenge.*"

Ace nods slyly, his brown eyes cool, calm.

Collected.

"**SO** come mek we go get it, then."

28

———

Irie

BEEEEEEP!

HORNS rage as I bolt through the streets of Kingston. I zoom down alleyways, passing bloodstains and bullet casings as I bite down on my bottom lip. It torments me to think about it for too long. *The truth*. So instead, I just pedal.

I just ride.

My heart slams against my chest as I skillfully maneuver the back roads, avoiding the soldiers at all costs.

I have to get to Jillian's.

I don't think long about what I'm going to say. In fact, I barely have a plan at all. All I know is I have no one else. I need Jillian's help more than ever, and every part of me wants to believe that it will mean something to her. It *has* to. Because what I'm facing is so much bigger than any fight.

Jillian is my *only* hope.

I rip down the corrugated roads, taking a right into a side gully. But just as I turn the corner, I bring my bicycle to a screeching halt. I'm revolted at the sight—right in front of me, mongrels gnaw at the remains of a dead body.

Rotting in the midday sun.

"Oh my god." I try not to gag at the horror as I turn my bicycle in the opposite direction. "*Stay focused, Irie. Stay focused,*" I whisper to myself as I turn onto a side street. "*It's okay . . . It's okay.*" I pump my thighs as hard and fast as they can go.

I don't stop until I reach Jacks Hill.

I use all the strength I have to turn into Jillian's neighborhood, zooming past the estates that are buried in the bushes. My heart rattles in my chest as I reach the front gate. I hop off my bicycle, and just as I go to press the buzzer, I see the car coming down the long driveway. I make out Lloyd's face through the front window.

Shit.

I step to the side, and in seconds, the gates automatically open. I stand with my bicycle as Lloyd slowly makes his way through, stopping when he notices me. The car is still for a moment, and then the door opens.

And Jillian steps out.

She wears a cream baby doll, and her hair is pressed straight down her back. She wears blush on her freckled cheeks and a distressed look on her face. "What are you doing here?" She storms toward me, looking back at the car.

My mouth is dry, and suddenly, I'm blank. Jillian steps in front of me, her hands folded as she keeps her voice a whisper, trying not to cause a scene.

"Irie, are you *insane*?" she whispers.

But my voice is caught in my throat.

"Irie, I'm speaking to you. *What the fuck* are you doing here?"

"I . . . I've been calling you."

"Yuh cyaan just show up at my house!" Her eyes go wide. She looks at me like she doesn't know me at all.

And then her mother winds down the window in the distance. "What the hell is going on here, Jillian?" she demands.

"One second, Mummy!" she calls back over her shoulder.

"Please, can we talk?" Tears fill my eyes, and my voice is desperate.

"I can't," she says firmly. "I'm headed out."

"Just, *please*, Jillian," I plead. "It's really important."

Jillian looks at me, weighing her options as she turns back around. "Mummy, Irie forgot something in my room. Can I please take her upstairs to get it?"

"Absolutely not, Jillian," her mother scolds. "Your father is due at the gala in twenty minutes."

"But it's urgent."

"Have Amala get it."

"She won't be able to find it, Mummy. I'll have to search the room."

"Please, Mrs. Casey," I say, my voice shaky.

Her mother's eyes are cutting as she looks away, disgusted.

And then her father's brooding voice comes through the window. "I can't afford to be late, Jillian. If you head back in, we'll have to leave without you."

"That's fine, Daddy." Jillian puts on her best front.

"This can't happen again." His tone is threatening as he watches me. Jillian takes a step closer to the car, lowering her voice as she negotiates with her parents.

"I'll talk to her. I promise," she whispers.

My stomach tightens as I look to the ground, biting back my anger.

My shame.

I can't stop my body from shaking as they inaudibly go back and forth. And then, after what feels like an eternity, Jillian's mother winds up the window.

And the black car drives off.

Jillian pauses before turning around. "Come on," she says, not looking at me as she marches her way back up the driveway. I trail behind her, through the entryway and up the stairs toward her bedroom.

She doesn't say a word to me the entire time.

A wave of emotions come over me as I enter her bedroom. She moves delicately, clearly gathering her thoughts as she makes her way to her bottom drawer. She uses the key to unlock it and digs inside, pulling out Bob Marley's "No Woman, No Cry." She places it on the player, attempting to drown out our conversation. The track begins to spin.

Jillian turns around to face me, her eyes glossy.

Betrayed.

"What the *hell* are you thinking?" Frustration fills her tone, taking me by surprise. "Irie, yuh cyaan just *come here* without asking."

"I had no choice, Jillian! Yuh haven't returned any of my calls."

"I've been *busy*, Irie. Yuh know this was a big week for me."

I temper my anger at the irony as I search myself for the right words. "Look, I really need your help."

"That's rich." She folds her arms. "You show up uninvited, without so much as an apology, *and* you need something from *me*?" The expression on her face is blank. "Irie, do yuh understand *how much trouble* I'm about to get into for this? I invited you here *one time*! That doesn't mean you can show up whenever you so choose."

Her words stun me.

"We're under a *state of emergency*! Yuh shouldn't even be here."

I'm silent as I take her in.

This was the worst idea.

"Well?" She looks at me, impatient. "What is it?"

I take a deep breath.

"They kidnapped my father. Shot him and hauled him out of the shop." It leaves my mouth void of emotion. "The police or the PLM gang. I don't know which." The tears begin to form, and I blink them back as my voice shakes. "They took my sister too. They raided the shop, and . . . and I guess it turns out you were right. About di PLM . . . about the ghetto . . . about everything."

Jillian's face goes completely white. "Oh my god." She looks at me in disbelief. "Irie—I . . . I don't even what to say."

But the pity in her eyes is enough to make me sick. "I need your help, Jillian." It leaves my mouth as an order and not a request. "I *need you* to help me get Siarah back. You're the only one that can."

"Wait, *what?*" She looks at me, puzzled. "What exactly do you want me to do?"

"I need you to come with me. Ace knows where she is. The PLM Don has her. They bring the girls they kidnap to dance at his go-go club, right off Crossvale Road. Ace said he can get me in as a performer, but runners are required to bring at least two girls with them to get in."

"*Runners?*"

"Ace, he . . . works for the Don. Low-level stuff, like drugs."

"Irie."

"I *can't* ask Tandi. There's no way she would even let me go. It's this Friday and—"

"*Friday?*" Jilly makes a face. "Irie, that's election night."

"I know," I say grimly. "But I *need you,* Jillian. The clock is ticking, and I . . . I have no other choice."

Jillian looks away from me and to the floor.

"*Please, Jilly,*" I plead. "Please. I promise I will never ask you for anything again as long as I live."

"I *can't,* Irie." Jilly shakes her head in disbelief. "I mean, yuh cyaan seriously be asking me to risk my life *again*? Don't you remember what just happened? You *cyaan* seriously expect me to say yes. I almost *died.*"

"But I *need you,*" I say again between gritted teeth. "I have to save Siarah. You're my only hope, and I would do it for you in a heartbeat."

"Please, don't do that." She shakes her head, dismissive as she looks away from me. "That's not fair. I would never put you in that position."

"You would never *have* to put me in that position!" I argue. "You think I want to be here? Asking you to help me *rescue my sister*? I didn't ask for this, Jilly."

Jilly looks away from me as the silence between us grows bigger.

"Wow . . ."

"Don't do that," she says firmly. "Don't make me the bad guy."

"*The bad guy?*" I yell. "Jillian, you haven't returned my calls in over a week! My life has turned upside down and . . . and I'm supposed to be yuh *best friend*!" It comes pouring out of me as the Bob Marley record goes round.

No woman, no cry . . .

"Everything we shared together, yuh just thew it all in my face!"

"Would you lower *your friggin' voice*?" Her tone is urgent. "*For Christ's sake,* Irie. Someone might hear you!"

"Why are yuh treating me like this?" I sob. I feel like a child as the tears come crashing down, echoing the words of the song. "Why are you treating me like yuh don't even know me? Like we didn't . . . like we didn't *do* things to each other."

"Can you *stop*?" Her eyes go wide. "I know you're hurting, but—"

"Don't give me that *bullshit*, Jillian!" I yell, coming undone. "Just tell me *the truth*. For once, tell me the truth about *why* you're throwing our friendship away."

I'm desperate as the question leaves my lips. I need to understand.

"Is it because *yuh liked it*?" I search her face for the answers. "Is it because it *felt betta than yuh thought it would*?"

"*Stop,*" she says between gritted teeth.

"Just tell me the truth," I demand. "Tell me the real reason why you're upset at me." I'm on pins and needles as I wait for her answer. As I wait for the truth. "You told me you loved me."

"*As friends,*" she says harshly as she meets my gaze. "Look, Irie. We *have* to be honest with ourselves. I'm getting *married.*" She holds up her hand to show me the ring. I nearly collapse at the sight of it. "*Think* about what you're *saying* to me right now. It doesn't make any sense. I mean, could you *really* see yourself with a woman?"

Her question takes me by surprise.

The truth is I hadn't thought about it before.

"I don't know," I say quietly. "But I could see myself with *you.*"

I tremble as the admission leaves me. Jilly's face goes blank as she watches me.

The silence between us is vulnerable as we both stand speechless.

"Me nuh know, Irie." She shrugs, shaking her head as a tear pours down her pale, freckled skin. "This whole ting between us just got *really* complicated, really fast."

"Jilly."

"I love you. *A lot.* And I'm *so sorry* about yuh fada and yuh sista, but this is *Jamaica,* Irie. It's not like we could ever *be* together. *It's a crime.* You're a *girl.* And so am I."

I feel my heart leave my chest as Jillian's hazel eyes go glassy. Cold.

"What happened between us . . . ," she continues, looking at the floor as she fiddles with her hands. "What happened between us was just supposed to be *fi us.* It was a one-night thing. We were foolin' around. Havin' fun . . . getting closer *as friends.* And I'm not saying I regret it." She shrugs. "But it just wasn't supposed to come with all this *consequence.* All this *pressure.* It was supposed to relieve it."

Her words nearly take me out.

"Put yuhself in my shoes, Irie." Her tone is distant as she tries her best to reason with me. "I already have *so much* to think about. I'm leaving Jamaica in less than a month, and who knows when I'll even be back. I *cyaan* jeopardize my future."

"But I can jeopardize mine, because I don't have one, right?"

Jillian wilts. "I don't know what you want from me." She shakes her head. "You expect me to hold myself back in life for this friendship? *We're friends, Irie.* We're not in a relationship!"

"But you *want to be,* right?" I drill into her. "You want to be with me *just* as badly as I want to be with you. I made you *feel things* yuh never felt before, and what we shared that night . . . *that's* the freedom you really want. *That's* the freedom you're longing for. Because you like *girls,* Jillian Casey. Admit it."

"Stop it!" she says abruptly. "I'm not doing this with you! I see myself with a *man,* Irie. That's the truth. I want to be *married* to one. *In love with one.* I want to have a family . . . with Christopher."

Her words go through my heart like a dagger.

"I hate you."

"Irie."

"I really, *really* do." My hand trembles as I wipe the tears from my cheeks. The rubies glitter as I snatch them from my wrist. "You're a liar. And you're as fake as they come. You think I haven't noticed you haven't worn yuh silly bracelet since you gave me mine?" I sob as I hold it up. "What is this? *A fucking collar?*"

I throw the bracelet straight at her chest.

"I'm not your *pet,* Jillian! Or your *dolly.* You *used me!*" I scream. "You used me to feel better about yuhself! I was just the *ghetto girl* yuh brought home fi a night to distract Mummy and Daddy, nuh true? To take the attention offa yuh *miserable* fuckin' face fi a night!"

"Fuck you."

"Fuck *you!*" I scream. "You and your stupid fucking sign!" I rage as I stare up at the *Out of Many, One People* poster. The irony has never been more infuriating.

"Are we *really* one people, Jillian?" I burst. "Are we really sharing the same fucking poverty? The same *fucking crime*? Are we even living in the same *fucking Jamaica*?" I come undone as I rip into her. "Or are people like *you* just setting up shop in a land that was never even yours to begin with? Stealing all the wealth and taking all the resources! Living in paradise while people like me are forced to rot in hell! *I'm not your maid, here to wipe your crocodile tears.*"

"Whatever, Irie," she says bitterly, tears streaming down her face as she turns away from me. "Just remember that every time yuh point fingers, there are *three more* pointing back at you."

"And what di hell is that supposed to mean?"

"Look around!" she explodes, turning back to me. "Are you blind? The entire island is under attack! And yet all you do is run around and act like *your people* are the heroes! When di JCG are the only ones *actually* trying to fix things! All you do is play victim! *Every fucking time!* Yuh never want to take any responsibility for *your government*. The PLM are destroying Jamaica, and you want to come in here and blame me for what's happened to yuh sister?"

"How dare you!"

"How dare *you*!" she erupts. "Just because *I'm rich* does not make yuh problems *my fault*! Stop blaming *me* for *your life*!"

I'm stunned as she comes undone.

"Yuh think I'm a *dunce*, Irie?" she continues. "I see the way you look at me! You like me for how I look, just like everyone else! *My life, my things!* You put me on this pedestal just so you can *judge* me when I fall from it! Just so you can resent me *even more*!" she cries. "I didn't choose my life, but just like everyone else, you never wanted to know the *real me*! You never even cared!" she sobs. "Yuh wanna talk about being someone's dolly? *I was yours, Irie Rivers!* Your high yellow, light-skinned dolly! And now what? I'm not Jamaican enough for you? Not Black enough to be yuh friend? *Give me a fucking break.*" She shakes her head. "I saw the way you looked at me when yuh came around my house. The

310 ★ ASHA ASHANTI BROMFIELD

same reason yuh never wanted to come up here in di first place. *You're judging me!* You're *always fucking judging me!*"

Her words kick me straight in the gut.

"If I'm *so* horrible, then why were you ever my friend?" she cries. "Did you *ever* really like me? Or just that I come from money?"

"Of course I liked you!"

"No you didn't!" she says firmly. "I was a sounding booth for you, Irie. Validation points. Someone to pat you on the back so you could feel like your life was going somewhere too. But it's not my fault that *it's not*! *I'm not the one to blame for your life!*"

I'm numb as she stands in the center of the room. Her medals and trophies line the shelves, and I want to smash every single one.

I want to destroy her, just like she's destroying me.

"Right," I say. "I think we're done here."

And just like that, I've lost my father, my sister, and my best friend all in the same week.

Jilly winces. "I think so too."

We stand across from each other, both in disbelief.

Both unable to take it all back.

"You think I like you for the way you look, but the truth is you *hide* behind it. I'm the only person who *actually saw you for who you are,* Jillian. I see the real you! And I fell in love with what I saw." I'm vulnerable as the emotion leaves me. "If you want to throw away our love, *then fine*. But I have news for you. It doesn't matter how many *cool new records* you buy or how much fancy perfume you spray on your *snow-white skin*. Befriending a girl from di ghetto *cannot* buy you a soul."

"Would you quit?"

But I can't.

I look over at her shiny new record player.

"*Of all people,* you put on Bob Marley." I laugh at the audacity. "The *one* light-skinned, commercially accepted Rasta."

"What does skin color have to do wit' any of this?"

"What about Peter Tosh? Bunny Wailer? Toots Hibbert? Dennis Brown?" I drill into her as I step in her face. "What, *too dark fi yuh*? Or yuh just let those records collect dust too? *Yuh dutty likkle secret just like me.*"

"What the hell is yuh problem?" she barks.

"My *problem* is, do you even *know* what this song *means*?" I march over to the record player and snatch the vinyl, holding the "No Woman, No Cry" record up to her face. "Do you even understand fi a *second* what Bob is *actually* singing about?"

"It's just a song."

"It's not *just* a fuckin' song, Jillian! Don't you *get* that?" I scream. "Yuh nuh *undastand* wha' me ah say to yuh? Or me haffi chat *Patois* fi yuh to undastand?"

I step into her face, ready to fight. Ready to *blow*.

"He's singing about *suffering*, Jilly!" I snap the vinyl in half. "*Suffering!* Something you haven't had to do a day inna yuh *fuckin' life*!"

"Get out of my house."

It leaves her lips in a whisper as a tear rolls down her porcelain skin.

Victim tears.

Because once again, her tears are supposed to matter more than mine. It takes everything in me not to combust.

But she doesn't need to tell me twice.

I throw the record pieces at her face before barging out of the room. I sprint down the stairs, blasting right by Amala and out through the front doors, slamming them shut.

I pedal out of Jacks Hill and never look back.

ONE WEEK LATER

29

———

Jilly

Fuck Irie.

I sit at the vanity, staring into my own reflection as Amala runs the hot comb through my hair. It's the night of the election, and the house is buzzing with staffers running around just outside my bedroom door. The smell of burning hair wafts through the room as Amala parts another section, laying the warm pieces down my back.

The smell alone is enough to make me nauseous.

The house is a whirlwind as everyone prepares for the big night. I'm completely zoned into my own world as Irie's words haunt me, creeping back into my psyche. I replay the situation over and over as I wait impatiently for Amala to finish. But I'm brought to only one conclusion.

Fuck.

Irie.

She was *never* my friend. She never truly cared about me. *About the real Jillian Casey.* How could she have if she could spew those nasty words at me? Those vicious *lies* about who she *thinks* I am. And now, in the aftermath of *her* wrath, *I'm* the one who must process the pain she left behind. *I'm* the one who's left to wrestle with myself.

With my own identity.

Fuck her.

I should have never let her inside. Not just inside my home, but *my heart.* I should've never called her my best friend, and I should've told her to go home when she showed up at the gate. Because now, I'm left to grapple with myself over everything we shared.

It was one night, I try to convince myself. *A moment between friends.* It doesn't have to be more than it was. And just because I *love* Irie doesn't mean I like girls—and it most certainly doesn't mean that I have to be with one.

Or that I ever could.

What we shared together was special—*magical*—but it didn't mean anything. And even if I did like it, *everything about it,* being with another woman is a crime in Jamaica.

What's the use in torturing ourselves? In thinking about it for too long? Why make me the villain?

Nothing other than Irie's own selfishness comes to mind. She assassinated my character and crucified me with her words. And now, I'm forced to replay the vile things she said to me like a broken vinyl. I'm forced to wonder if everything she said was true.

Could I really be in love with a girl?

No, I stop myself as the thought begins to infiltrate my mind. *That's not fair.*

But it's also not wrong.

"You okay?" Amala asks softly. I nod, giving her a polite smile.

But the truth is, I'm not.

What Irie and I shared together is a mere memory. A blip in time. And the truth is, when I leave this island, she's not going to be worried about my life beyond hers. When this election is over, Irie will go back to the shop and focus on music—the very thing she loves more than she loves me. She'll go back to following her dreams.

Because singing is *her* saving grace.

So fuck her for being mad at me. For blaming me. *And fuck her for making me fall in love.*

"*Ah!*" I yelp as Amala accidentally burns me with the hot comb.

"Oh—I am *so* sorry, Miss Jillian." Amala scurries for the oil, rubbing a little bit onto my scalp. "I was lost in my thoughts. There's so much to be done for tonight." She smiles nervously as she parts another section. "Your mother has me running around doing a million things."

"I can imagine." I sigh. "Everyone's on edge."

"How was voting today? It was yuh first time."

"It was pleasant," I say. "A lot of military around, but I voted for the JCG, of course."

"Well, let's just hope we get the results we're waiting for."

"Yeah," I say, my voice trailing as I study Amala in the mirror. "Let's hope so."

Just then, Mummy comes through the door. She wears a lavender ball gown with long white gloves, her pin-straight hair in an updo, held into place by crystal pins.

"You're not finished that yet?" Mummy scolds, a critical look on her face as she waltzes into the room. "Amala, I thought you would've finished that hours ago."

"It's not her fault," I say quickly, looking at Mummy through the mirror. "She was waiting on me."

"*Jesus,* Jillian. You're not even dressed yet." She notices as she marches over. "We're leaving here in less than an hour."

"I *know,* Mummy." I grit my teeth. "I'll be ready. It takes me two seconds."

"You know, when I was your age, girls wouldn't dare speak to their mothers in that tone," she says as she examines herself in the mirror. She stands in front of Amala like she doesn't even exist, before peering back over at me. "I see you got some sleep last night. Your face looks much less puffy than it did yesterday."

I tense.

"Amala, may I have a word with my daughter?"

"Of course, madam." Amala nods, placing down the hot comb. She scurries out of the room as Mummy places her hands on the back of my chair.

I brace myself.

"It's a big night, Jillian. For all of us." Mummy's tone is dry. "But I want you to know that your father and I are very proud of you. Getting into Cambridge is no easy feat." I squirm as her green eyes watch me in the mirror. "You've been expected to balance a lot this past month . . . with the engagement and the election. But I'm happy you're finally coming around. And it looks like you've lost a little weight." She gives me a pensive smile. "How have you and Christopher been getting on?"

"Well, I guess . . ."

"Good." She smiles. "I'm happy to hear that, darling. I know your father's vision is big, but we all make sacrifices, Jillian. We all have to give something—"

"For the greater good . . . I know."

She gives me a tight-lipped smile. "I expect you downstairs in forty minutes." She turns to leave.

"What did you give?" It slips out.

"I beg your pardon?" Mummy turns sharply on her heel.

"I just meant—"

"Are you insane?" Her tone drops as she lashes out. "I nearly *died* on that hospital bed giving birth to you. All for your father and his family to *ridicule me every day* for not being able to give them a son. *A real heir.*" Her tone is cutting as she drills into me. "I had to *fight* for you, Jillian. I nearly gave my *life* to give you the precious one you have now. So don't you ever question my sacrifice to this family."

I wither underneath her gaze.

"*Legacy,* Jillian. *That* is what you now carry. The same way I had to carry it when I married into this family. Because all of this—" She gestures to the room. "It doesn't come for *free*." Her eyes are seething as she leans over my shoulder, speaking to me through the mirror. "Whatever *your father needs,* it's our job as women to support him. That's our *role*." She tucks my hair behind my ears as she looks at me, villainous in the mirror. "It's a woman's *duty* to be of service to the men around her. Do I make myself clear?"

I cringe. "Yes, Mother."

"Good. Now, hurry up." She stands up straight, taking a breath as she gathers herself. "I want you dressed and downstairs."

And with that, she waltzes back through the door.

TWENTY minutes later, silky hair falls pin straight down my back. I adjust my long gown in the mirror as Amala finishes up, scurrying about and putting the tools away.

Moments later, I descend the spiral staircase as people rush about their duties. As I approach the final steps, I notice Daddy standing in the entryway with a man I've never seen before; he has smooth dark skin and cornrows, and Daddy shakes his hand just as he's about to usher him out the door. The man notices me and smiles, flashing a gold tooth as he makes his way through the door. *That's odd,* I think—I'm not used to seeing someone who looks like that in the house. I step down into the entryway just as Daddy turns around.

He's surprised to see me, the look on his face militant.

"Hey, Daddy." I muster a smile. "Big night."

"Indeed." He nods as he looks at my dress. "You look great."

"Thanks." I smile, happy to be approved of.

"You ready to go?"

"Yeah." I nod, glancing out the door. "Who was that, though? The man you were talking to."

"No one, Jillian," Daddy says firmly. His tone makes it clear not to ask again. "Hurry up and put your shoes on. I can't afford to be late."

"Okay."

"And where's Amala? I need her to adjust my tie."

"Right here, sir," says Amala, who happens to be breezing by. "My apologies." She starts to fiddle with my father's tie as he stands in front of the grand entryway mirror.

"Grab your stuff, Jillian," Daddy instructs. "Your mother's already in the car."

"Sure." I nod, deciding to drop it. I follow instructions, turning for my shoes. Before I can give it a second thought, one of the older housekeepers rushes up to me and helps me slip into my heels.

"Thanks," I say, steadying myself with her shoulder as I slip into the white kitten heels.

Just then, another housekeeper drapes a shawl around my shoulders.

"Oh, thank you," I say, politely nodding at them.

"You're welcome, Miss Jillian." They smile dutifully at me.

They all step back as I gather myself in the mirror and Daddy makes his way through the door.

"Good luck tonight, Mr. Casey!" one of them calls as Daddy continues through the door. He doesn't respond, and I nod apologetically at them as I follow behind him.

"Have a great night, Miss Jillian."

"Thank you, ladies." I smile politely.

As they close the door behind me, it takes everything I have not to kick myself. *I really should know their names.*

WE pull up at the Kelly residence thirty minutes later.

The estate is fully lit up when we arrive, and the *extravagant* mansion illuminates in the night as a sea of expensive cars line the circular driveway. The energy is bustling as Jamaica's wealthiest elite pile out and make their way up the long staircase toward the grand doors.

I make my way past the staffers, and once inside, I drift away from Mummy and Daddy. They mix and mingle as I search the room for Christopher or Monica, in desperate need of someone my age.

Or at the very least, a glass of champagne.

I roam around the party as people mingle all about the rooms. There's a tension in the air, and through fake smiles, everyone is on pins and needles. In the main space—an open entertainment room—a giant television is tuned to the JBC news channel as they begin counting votes. Waitstaff work the room with trays of shrimp and caviar, and champagne floats all about the space. I take a glass from one of the servers when I feel a tap on my shoulder. I spin around and lock eyes with Christopher.

"Just when I thought you couldn't get any more beautiful." He takes a sip of the champagne in his hand with his other hand in his pocket. "You look ravishing, Jillian," he says as he eyes me. "Welcome back to my home."

"Thank you," I say coyly. "Nice to see you."

He raises his glass, and I do the same. *Clink.*

Christopher holds my gaze as we both take a sip. I give him an awkward smile, looking away as the room buzzes behind us.

"May I interest you in a round of pool?"

"Pool?" I raise an eyebrow. "I would've thought you'd be on edge tonight. Eyes glued to the television, kind of thing."

"Ah, you mean on my third glass of scotch, drunkenly yelling profanities at the big screen, just like our fathers will be doing in thirty minutes?"

"Yeah." I smile. "Exactly."

Christopher laughs. "I usually take about an hour or so to work my way up to that," he teases. "But I'm not free of nerves, if that's what you're asking. I just prefer to quell them by distracting myself with a beautiful woman instead."

I nod, trying my best to feel flattered. "I'm excited to see the pool room, then."

Christopher smiles. "Right this way." He offers me his hand. I take it.

He leads me through the party and toward the back of the house. I've never seen the entirety of the inside, but the Kelly mansion is *huge*. They have double the number of staff, and the house is spotless and shiny as guests move about. I marvel at the artwork on the walls, impressed by the immaculate fixtures and chandeliers. Everything about the estate is grand and regal, and for a second, I wonder if this is how the halls of Cambridge will feel.

We pass party guests, saying polite hellos before Christopher leads me down a hallway off to the side. He opens a double door, and we make our way into a moodily lit room with brown leather couches and dark green walls. There's a bar off to the side, and a record player and sound system sit in the corner. In the center, there's a giant pool table with the balls perfectly lined up. The space is warm, secluded, and *private*. Far off from the party, the sound of guests begins to drown out. I stand in my gown as I take in the space.

Christopher makes his way over to the wall and grabs two sticks that hang from hooks.

"You really think we're going to win the election tonight?" I ask curiously.

"I have a lot of money riding on it, so we'd better."

"You're *betting* on the election?"

"I'd be a fool not to." He smirks as he makes his way toward me. I take the stick from his hands. "Would you like to listen to anything?"

I shrug. "Depends on what you have. You don't strike me as much of a music guy."

"Judging a book by its cover?"

"Perhaps."

"Okay. Let's see . . ." He makes his way over to the glass cabinet that holds an array of brand-new vinyls. "Carole King. James Taylor. Elvis?"

"Oh, come on." I make a face. "You've got to be kidding me."

"Simon and Garfunkel?" He laughs as he holds up the record. "Okay, you caught me. So, I don't know too much about what's popular, but I do know what I like to hear."

"How about reggae?"

"*Music?*" He screws his face.

"Yeah," I say boldly, suddenly missing Irie. The records I threw away.

"Yuh *really* don't like it that much?"

"Nah." Christopher shakes his head in disinterest. "Not at all. To be honest, I've yet to figure out what even draws people to that kind of stuff."

"You don't like to *dance*?" I ask, not fully believing him. "I'm sure you get the urge to . . . *let loose a little.*" I take another sip of the champagne, feeling bold. "Not even *Bob*?"

Christopher shakes his head. "It's not about how it *sounds* for me," he says as he leans over the pool table, removing the triangle. "I don't separate the music from the artist. And reggae artists are making a fool of Jamaica on a world stage."

"Oh, come on, Christopher," I say tipsily. "You can't seriously believe that."

"I do," he says firmly. "Everything about how those Rasta men present themselves is just so . . . *unkempt.*" He makes a face in disgust. "They're embarrassing us as an island."

"Okay, so they're not the most refined."

"It's more than that," he says passionately. "They go on *national television* boasting about smoking ganja with knotted dreads. It's *buffoonery.*" Christopher lets out a stifled laugh. "They sing about peace, yet they have *no* solutions." He shakes his head. "The few control the many. *That's just how the world works.* And the people representing us on a global stage should reflect the Jamaica we want to *become,* not the Jamaica we want to leave behind."

His words are vicious as he leans down and shoots.

"Wow," I say, suddenly feeling defensive. "A likkle harsh. You don't think that's sort of an outdated perspective? A bit of Stockholm syndrome."

"What do you mean?"

"I don't know." I shrug, remembering Irie's words. "Ideas left behind by the Brits. The colonizer that *enslaved* Black people and all of Jamaica? I mean think about it—what's wrong with knotted locks? Black Africans loving themselves as they are—"

"Whatever. I'm just saying what everyone's thinking, Jillian." He shrugs. "I'm not going to sacrifice my morals for some catchy beat. And I'm most *certainly* not going to change the way I speak or the things I listen to depending on what room I'm in."

I furrow my brow, suddenly feeling attacked. "And what's that supposed to mean?"

"Nothing, just—" He looks away from me in frustration. "What do you love so much about that music, anyway? Is it just to get a rise out of your parents?"

"No," I say defensively. "Not at all." I lean down, frustrated as I shoot the pink ball.

"So, what is it, then?" Christopher pries.

I stand back up as he watches me from across the table. "I like how it makes me *feel,* Christopher. Is that not a good enough reason for everyone?" I say, frustrated. "I know you think I'm just some spoiled rebellious brat, but I have *feelings.* And sometimes, I just want to be able to let them out." I shrug. "When it comes to reggae music, it's spiritual. You know the truth by the way it feels. And Reggae music . . . I feel it. I've never felt anything so visceral. Something so real . . . when I listen to the words, I feel like someone understands me."

"Understands you?"

"My desire to escape from this miserable ass life."

I regret the confession instantly. I raise my flute, downing the remainder of my champagne.

"So, that's what it makes you feel?" Christopher studies me. "A brief escape?"

"No." I place down my glass and look at him. "It makes me feel freedom." The answer leaves me without question.

"I don't know, Jillian." Christopher shakes his head. "I'm not fully convinced. But maybe the more time I spend around you, I might be." He leans down to take another shot.

The question pops into my head as I watch him. "Can I ask you something?"

"Sure," he says, leaning over the table. "Anything."

"There was a man in my house tonight." It dawns on me. "I mean, there were a *lot* of people in my house tonight, but for some reason, this man stood out to me. He had cornrows and a gold tooth."

Christopher looks up at me.

"Not that there's anything wrong with that—having cornrows. I guess I'm just not used to seeing my father have people like that over. *In our house.* Especially not on election night."

"And why do you find it surprising?"

"Yuh must not know my fada." I can't help but laugh.

"Evidently, neither do you."

"I beg your pardon?"

"Jillian, some of the *biggest crime bosses* in Jamaica are on your father's payroll."

I freeze with the stick in my hands.

"I know you don't know much about politics, but surely you must know that. The Dons in Jamaica work for your father."

"What are you talking about?"

"You didn't know that?" Christopher stares at me as I stand, dumbfounded. "Jillian . . . Why exactly do you think your father got a promotion?"

"Um . . . because he *auctioned* my hand in marriage?"

"As flattering as that is—and trust me, I'm flattered—that wasn't the sole reason," Christopher says matter-of-factly. "My father hired yours because he wants to *win* tonight. And on the campaign trail, your father is known for implementing some of the more . . . how shall I say it?" He pauses. "*Ruthless* strategies."

"*Ruthless?*" I furrow my brow. "What the hell are you talking about?"

"Don't play daft, Jillian." Christopher says it as if I must be joking. "Politics is a dirty game. You *must* realize that by now."

The room starts to spin, and I can't tell if it's the champagne. "I don't . . . I don't understand what you're saying."

He looks at me, confused. "You *do* know that America is one of the JCG's *biggest* campaign backers?"

"*America?*"

"They don't want us doing business with Cuba. Morris cozying up to Castro is a *huge* threat to the United States because they want to bring their corporations to the island—the big business conglomerates and such. And that can't happen if Morris turns Jamaica into a socialist or communist island. So, the Americans have been interfering with our election."

There's no way I could have heard him correctly. "*What?*" I stand, shocked. "What exactly does that mean?"

"It *means* that the CIA has a major hand in Jamaican politics." Christopher shrugs. "They want to bring in a bunch of American businesses. If they can turn Jamaica into a capitalist economy, the U.S. will make a lot of money. And so will we." Christopher leans down to shoot. "I scratch your back, you scratch mine. It all comes down to the dollars and cents, Jillian," he says, smiling smugly. "Always remember that."

"But . . . that's *wrong*. That's cheating."

"Not when you think of how much money Jamaica could make. I mean, we *were* the top tourist destination for the world's elite before Morris started spewing all that socialism crap all over the ghettos. Empowering poor people and destroying the economy. It's our fathers' jobs to implement strategy."

"*Strategy?*"

"Sabotage. I told you this already." Christopher's words are grim. "Oh, come, Jillian. How do you think *all those guns* get into the ghettos? *AK-47s and M16s?* You think they just fell from the sky?" He chuckles. "How else do you think the poor get access to that type of machinery?"

"I . . ." But I'm silent. Completely dumbfounded. "I guess I never really gave it much thought."

"Well, you should. We funnel weapons into the ghetto—your father's orders. All thanks to the U.S. and the CIA, of course. They provide the weapons, we distribute them to the Dons, the Dons distribute them to the people."

"The *Dons?* What is this, some kind of *Mafia movie?*"

"Where do you think we get our inspiration?" He smirks. "All this cowboy-style shooting. We're influenced by American exports, you know. Movies included."

I'm dazed as he continues.

"Our fathers are in business with both the JCG and PLM Dons, because the Dons control the ghettos. We *have* to have a good relationship with them in order to control the masses."

"Oh my god."

"If we can make Jamaica *look* like it's under a war under the Morris administration, they'll vote for the JCG by default." He shrugs. "A necessary evil."

The room starts to spin.

"You can't be okay with this," I whisper. "It's not right."

"I'm not," he says grimly. "But I don't make the rules, Jillian. I just pay attention to them a little more closely than you do." He shrugs. "People do it every day. Convince themselves that they're *good,* despite doing *evil.* No one's hands are clean."

He steps to the other side of the pool table as my entire world comes crashing down.

"*I can't believe that.*" Tears well in my eyes. "*I can't believe Daddy would*—"

"Your *daddy's* hands aren't only dirty, Jillian"—Christopher eyes me—"they're *drenched* in the blood of the Jamaican people."

I'm a flurry of emotion as my heart races in my chest.

"Oh my god." It dawns on me. "*Irie was right.*"

"Who?" Christopher looks up at me. "Your little friend?"

I nod, dazed.

Could Daddy have something to do with her father's and sister's kidnapping?

"This island is only as strong as its weakest link." Christopher's voice is low as he examines me. "And the weakest link will *always* be the poor."

"And so, the answer is to *kill* them?" I cry. "That's *horrible.*"

"Don't be foolish, Jillian. Murder is a crime." Christopher smirks, resuming the game. "*They* kill themselves. We just supply the weapons."

He draws back his billiard stick and strikes.

POW.

30

———

Irie

I race down the back roads of Kingston toward the shop.

I ride past barbed-wire fences and abandoned homes made of concrete. Broken glass and bullet casings litter the dirt roads as I navigate my way through the dark. It's nights like this that I'm grateful Daddy taught me all the shortcuts to the store. *For emergencies,* he would say.

It's nights like this I'm grateful I paid attention.

Headlights beam in the distance, illuminating me as I move through the shadows. I stay just out of sight from the soldiers who man the roads. Slum dwellers walk aimlessly—the only other souls brave enough to be out on a night like this.

Election night.

The only other souls without a choice.

I grip my handlebars tightly, pushing any trepidation to the pit of my stomach. I still have no idea what I'm going to tell Ace about not bringing a friend tonight. I couldn't bring myself to ask Tandi—she's all I have left. *Jillian* was supposed to be here. She was supposed to be my friend. But just because she let me down doesn't mean I won't be victorious.

I'll get Siarah back myself.

I shudder as sirens wail in the black of night. The noise cuts through the eerie thickness that looms over the tense city. Mongrels holler to the moon as the sound of tank engines drown them out. The island feels ready to erupt.

Like a bomb, just *ticking*.

The sound of gunfire keeps me on my toes as I ride sneakily through Papine. I have no time to consider what lies ahead of me. *What tonight might hold.* I only have one shot, and I focus all my attention on it—replaying the lyrics to my new song over again in my head. I practiced all day, perfecting the dance moves and lyrics from sunup to sundown until the routine was embedded in my body. I have no choice but to make it believable.

I'm dancing for the Don tonight.

The anticipation jolts me as I turn down the back road to the shop. I slow down, hopping off as I approach. It's pitch-dark, and I fight to see through the night as I carefully walk my bicycle toward the back entrance. But then someone sparks a light.

It's Ace, standing in the shadows, spliff in hand.

"Perfect timing," he says when he sees me, taking a draw. "I jus' reach."

"Hey," I say as he makes his way toward me. The nerves pool in my stomach.

"Where's yuh friend?" He looks at me, confused.

My mouth goes dry as I stare at the ground. "She, um . . . she said no."

"*No?*" Ace screws up his face. "Irie, wha' yuh mean, *no? I told you* we haffi walk in wit' at least two girls."

"I know, I know," I say remorsefully. "I'm sorry, Ace. But I—"

"Wha' 'bout yuh sista?"

"Tandi? I couldn't bring myself to ask her, Ace. And there's no way she would have said yes."

"Lawd, Irie. We had a *plan*. We *cyaan* afford fi look suspicious."

"She's my *baby sista,* Ace. *My likkle sista.* Yuh haffi understand."

My eyes are desperate as I whisper. "They already took my fada *and* my sista. I cyaan afford to lose another one."

Ace looks away from me, frustrated. "I swear to God, Irie, if dis nuh work out—"

"It will," I say adamantly, desperately needing him to believe it too. "Please, Ace."

He sighs, giving me one last skeptical look as he takes the bag from his shoulder. "Put this on." He reaches inside and pulls out two skimpy orange pieces of fabric. "I'll wait here while yuh change."

"Wait, I cyaan wear this?" I look down at my tank top and shorts. "What's wrong with what I have on?"

"Dem nah go let you in wearing that." Ace's tone is disapproving, "Yuh haffi look di part." He hands it to me, and I take it from him. "I'm not telling you again, Irie. We *haffi do this right.* I need you to listen to me from now on."

"Okay," I say, giving in as I place down my bicycle. "I will."

I walk toward the dark corner and slip out of my tank top and shorts, before slipping into the bra and tight, skimpy batty riders. I shove my clothes into the backpack with my gun, and when I turn around, Ace is standing by with a big T-shirt.

"Wear this until we get there."

I slide into it, preparing myself for the inevitable as Ace finishes up with his spliff. After a few seconds, he chucks it and takes my hand. My heart beats as he draws me closer.

"We got this. Y'hear?"

I nod.

And then we slink off into the night and out into the ominous streets of Kingston.

AN hour later, we arrive at a warehouse that sits just on the outskirts of town. From the outside, the building looks shabby and abandoned, located off the beaten roads. But as we get closer, I see armed men moving through the night. Ace holds my hand tightly as we maneuver through the dark streets with caution. He pauses before we approach the doors, pulling the T-shirt over my shoulders. He balls it in his hands, taking one final look at me.

"Yuh look good," he says as he watches me.

"Not exactly what I want to hear right now."

"But it's wha' yuh *need* fi hear," he challenges, bringing his hand to my jaw. "Own yuh power tonight, Irie. *Own that stage.* Mek dem believe yuh. Every note. Every move. And when yuh finished, we ah go leave here wit' yuh sista. I can promise you that."

I nod, believing every last word. "Thank you, Ace," I whisper as the gravity of what we're about to do pummels me. "Thank you for doing this wit' me."

Ace holds my gaze, his dark brown eyes deep and intense. He brings my face to him and kisses me gently on my forehead, before moving down to my lips. His lips are fluffy and soft. My stomach drops.

"You're a star, Irie," he whispers. "Come light it up."

It's the exact surge of confidence I need.

Ace grabs my hand, leading the way just as he did that night at the open mic. I'm on edge, trying my best to keep it together as we approach the doors. A tall, slender man in black clothes stands outside, manning the door with an M16 strapped to his side.

"Password?" His voice is dark and ominous.

"Gully creepa," Ace says.

The man nods before looking at me.

"She's wit' me," Ace says, holding my hand tightly.

"Yuh cyaan come inside wit' jus' one gyal."

"It's cool," Ace says calmly. "I talked to my brejin 'bout it."

"I said, *yuh nah go come in wit' one girl.*" The man puffs up his chest. "Unless yuh wan' deal wit' di boss."

"So mek me talk to him, nuh," Ace says confidently.

I freeze.

The moment between them is tense as the man considers. "Stay here," he instructs before turning to talk to the man behind him.

After a few strained moments, the other man opens the door. "Follow me."

It almost sounds like a threat.

"Come," Ace says, not letting go of my hand as we follow behind him.

I feel the bass in my chest the very moment we step inside.

Holy. Shit.

The entire place feels sinister. Fear stabs at me, gnawing at my insides as we make our way through. The club is dark and menacing, with deep red lights and a thick dub that bleeds through the walls. The bass is so heavy that I can feel it with every step that I take, and once we get into the main room, Ace releases my hand.

Predators are everywhere.

Men watch me, peering over as we make our way through. A slowed-down version of "Uptown Top Ranking" echoes off the walls as snipers, machetes, and machine guns stack the room. Power Posse members fill the space as if in a gentlemen's club, their eyes grazing me as I walk through.

Fresh meat.

I keep my eyes low as I follow Ace, noticing the cocaine and array of drugs laid out on tables. Dazed and delirious girls in slinky outfits parade around the room, and I watch them give lap dances to the men who pass through, revealing themselves as they grind onto their laps. Without drawing more attention to myself, I do my best to search the faces for Siarah.

Nothing.

The room is too dark, and it's too hard to make out faces. Before I can give it a second look, the man leading us inside stops at the stairs that descend to a lower floor. At the front of the club on the bottom floor sits a stage, a giant pole in the center, where a girl dances topless in a G-string. The men watch on with leering and dangerous eyes.

"See di boss down desso." The guy gestures down below to a man with cornrows.

"Tanks," Ace says as the man stands back. He turns to me. "Wait here."

"But—"

"Me say *don't move*," Ace whispers, looking me dead in the eye.

I follow instructions.

I try my best to blend in, tucking myself into the corner as I watch Ace descend the stairs. The man who walked us inside watches me suspiciously, but I avoid eye contact, looking straight ahead. I'm a nervous wreck as Ace makes his way down to the front stage area where the group of men sit. The demeanor of one of them tells me this is the man running the show.

The Power Posse Don.

I start to panic as I fight the urge to scour the room for my sister. All I want to do is find her. *Know that she's okay.* But I resist the urge to have my head on a swivel.

They're watching me. I can feel it. And I can't afford to seem too suspicious.

I watch as Ace takes a seat, talking to the man for a few minutes. Every second feels like an eternity. The Don keeps his back to me as he sits and listens, spliff in hand. And then I see him hand Ace a wad of cash. Ace shakes his hand and shoves it into his pocket before standing up.

My stomach drops.

I quickly look away as Ace makes his way back toward the stairs.

What the fuck was that? I pretend not to notice as he ascends the top step.

"It's all good wit' di boss," he says to the man who stands

beside me. The man nods before making his way back to the front of the club.

Ace looks at me, his voice low. "Yuh ready?" he asks me. "You're up next."

"But what about Siarah?"

"I'll search fi her." He looks me in the eyes. "While you're up on stage. I have a feeling she ah work di private rooms. That's where they usually bring the new girls."

I wince, taking in the magnitude of the operation.

Trafficking.

Ace scans the club, doing his best not to seem suspicious.

"I'll bring yuh up to where di dancers go."

I shudder, following behind him as another young woman takes the stage. She rocks her hips steadily to the booming bass, her voice a whisper as she growls into the mic. I watch in a rapture as she seduces the stage, grinding her pelvis into the dirty black floors as she tries her best to capture the attention of the room— the attention of the Don. She couldn't be more than seventeen, and her voice is hollow as she sings a soft and spellbound tune.

I'm lost in her performance as I follow Ace down a side set of stairs to the bottom floor. We stay out of the way as we move toward a long red curtain that drapes down. I peel my eyes away from the young performer, mustering up the last ounce of courage that I have left. Ace takes my hand, giving me one final look before ushering me inside a brown door.

"I'll search di back rooms fi Siarah. Meet me *right here* when yuh done. Yuh undastand?"

I nod, breathing deep. I feel my heart about to beat from my chest. "Okay."

"And, Irie?" He locks eyes with me. "I believe in you. Yuh got this."

"Thanks." I exhale.

And then, he closes the door.

I spin around to find a slew of girls down the hall behind me. They stand in their panties, littering the dark hallway as they wait for their turn to go up on stage. They talk among themselves, dazed, waiting drunkenly to step onto the stage and perform. I fight the panic that creeps up as I start to make my way through them. There's no time to think.

Only time to move.

Stay cool, Irie, I tell myself as I search the sea of faces for Siarah. But I'm overwhelmed by the magnitude.

Girls.

So many of them.

Taken.

Lost.

Stolen.

I try to catch my own breath, but it's no use. I'm a wreck as I try hard to make out features in the low-lit hallway. They all look around my age—as old as twenty-five and as young as fourteen. They scatter around the area, half-naked as they prepare and practice their routines.

All of them drugged.

Out of it.

"Siarah?" I whisper, my voice shaky as I slowly part my way through. "*Sisi?*"

No response. My cheeks burn as the tears begin to creep up.

"*Please . . . Siarah?*" I touch a girl on her shoulder. But it's not my sister, and she shrugs me off. I don't stop. I continue to call into the abyss, but the young women barely hear me over the bass that shakes the thin walls. Everything becomes hazy as the music inhibits us from hearing our own thoughts. All of us, in a rapture—under the spell.

I tremor as I move in and out of bodies.

"*Yow!*" A deep voice stops me dead in my tracks, calling to me from up ahead. My entire body seizes when we lock eyes.

Piercing and direct. His energy is pensive as he guards the entrance to the side of the stage. He points to me, ushering me over.

With no other choice, I move toward him.

"Who yuh come wit'?" he demands.

"Um . . . I was . . . I was brought here." I clear my throat. "I'm a performer . . ."

The man watches me with seething eyes. And then he yanks my wrist, his tone cutting.

"**YUH** up next."

31

———

Jilly

"The PLM and JCG are neck and neck as the votes continue to trickle in. Island officials predict the results will be in within the hour."

THE radio statics through the car as I dig my nails into my sweaty palms. I look up to the driver's seat at Lloyd, whose silence speaks volumes in the black of night.

"I really appreciate this, Lloyd."

I smile nervously as Lloyd looks at me through the rearview with an unfamiliar trepidation in his dark brown eyes. My entire body shakes as the car rattles over the rubble of the dirt roads. We make our way deeper down the path and into the dark forest.

Never in my life have I been this far out of town.

"I know this area's not the greatest, but I'm sure Irie will be thrilled to get a good night's rest somewhere more . . . *kept*." I try my best to keep up the pretense calm in my voice.

But I'm panicking.

"Are you sure this is where she lives, Miss Casey?" Lloyd's skeptical as his eyes scan the route. "Seems a ways off from Papine."

"She lives much farther out than her father's shop," I lie as

I look down the dark, barren roads. "It should be somewhere around here . . . right off Crossvale Road is what she told me."

I fight to see through the dark as Lloyd grows quiet.

"Miss Jillian . . ." His voice tremors. "Are you certain your father knows where we're heading?"

"I told you *a million times,* Lloyd." I grow frustrated as my pulse races. "He said Irie could sleep over tonight after the election. He told me to have you pick her up."

Lloyd goes quiet, clearly picking up on my lie. "I'm just surprised he didn't give me the order himself."

"On a night like tonight?" I look at him in the rearview. "Don't be daft, Lloyd. Daddy's got other things on his mind."

"I'm just worried for your safety, Miss Casey." The fear in his voice is contagious as he navigates the unfamiliar roads. "These shantytowns are incredibly dangerous."

Wham.

We're jolted as he presses on the brakes. My heart leaps to my throat as a stray mongrel dashes across the road. Lloyd looks back at me, the wrinkles in his brown skin pronounced in the shadows of the night.

"I'm going to turn around, Miss Casey. Your parents would never forgive me if something happened to you."

"And I'll never forgive *you* if you don't *drive,* Lloyd." My tone is stern as I give out orders. "It's not up for discussion. We pay you to follow orders. Not question instructions."

There's a moment of strained silence.

Lloyd nods obediently before continuing down the road.

I feel guilty speaking to him like that, but I can't take that on right now. *I need to get to Irie.* I have to make this right. I don't care about my parents or the repercussions—not after what they've done. What they're *a part of.*

There's blood all over their hands.

Lloyd reluctantly guides the car farther down the path. And

then, in the far-off distance, I see a building hidden in the bushes. A group of men hang out around the front.

"Stop here!" I lean to the front and tap Lloyd on the shoulder. "Turn off the headlights."

Lloyd listens without question as he brings the car to a halt.

"I'm going to get her. I'll be right back."

"Miss Jillian." He stops me. "Miss Jillian, I don't mean to pass my place. But I beg of you to reconsider."

"*Please,* Lloyd." My tone goes desperate. "Just let me do this. Okay?"

Lloyd's eyes begin to water, the look on his face pained.

"I'll be quick." I grab the door handle before glancing back at Lloyd one last time. "I promise."

And for the first time in my life, I see fear all over Lloyd's aged brown skin. He returns forward, dutiful and obedient, as dread drops to the pit of my stomach. He doesn't ask any more questions, and even though he doesn't say it, I know we both sense it.

THIS is bigger than me.

32

———

Irie

"I*'m going to be sick.*"

THE room starts to spin as my knees go weak. The man towers over me, ushering me to the stage as a dooming feeling sinks to the bottom of my stomach. I'm nauseous as what I'm about to do sinks in, and terror gets the best of me.

What if I'm making the biggest mistake of my life? What if Siarah's not even here?

"I'm sorry." My head is woozy as I stumble backward. "I just . . . I need a second."

"Me say *yuh up next, gyal,*" he demands, pulling on my wrist.

"Can I please just use di bathroom?" I whimper, hunching over. "They gave me something, I think . . . I . . ." The lie slips out as the man towers over me. "I just . . . need a minute. I feel like I'm goin' to throw up."

He glares at me, clearly untrusting as he flings my wrist back. And then he points to the drugged-out girl behind me who sloppily practices her routine in her bra and panties.

"*Ay, gyal!*" he barks at her. "Yuh up next. Di Don nuh have time we waste."

I sink into relief as I slowly move away from him.

"You," he growls, stopping me with menacing eyes. "Follow me."

"Okay." I do as I'm told, keeping myself small as he leads me back down the dark hallway. We weave in and out of the girls as I fight to see through the smoked-out haze and dark red lights. The man leads to a door far off to the side.

"Gwaan. And hurry up. Nuh badda fuck around."

I nod obediently. Using all the strength I have, I push open the heavy door and slip inside the dark space. I close the door, resting my forehead on the metal before taking a deep breath. I turn around to take in the cramped, dirty space.

Holy shit . . .

A girl lies by the toilet, completely dazed. It takes everything I have not to scream out.

Siarah.

"Oh my god." I gasp as I rush to her side, falling to my knees.

Her body is sprawled out on the floor, half-conscious as I pull her into my lap. Her face is sunken and worn, almost unrecognizable. Tears pool in my eyes as the booming bass shakes the walls.

"Siarah," I whimper, shaking her face. "Siarah, please, *wake up.*"

I cradle her head, rocking her in my lap until, soon, she opens her eyes. I'm a wreck as her brown eyes stare back at me.

"Irie . . ." Her voice is weak as she recognizes me.

"Oh my god, Sisi. *What did they do to you?*" I pull my sister into my arms as the tears begin to pour. Bruises cover her body, and her lip is split open. "It's okay, Sisi. I'm here now."

She grabs on to me, fading in and out of consciousness as my adrenaline takes over. I have to get her out of here. I panic as I look around the dark space, but then high up in the corner, I see it—

A small window.

I rise and start to pull her to her knees. "We have to go through the window."

"It's too high," Siarah slurs.

"I'll hoist you up on my shoulders. Come on. We *have* to try."

"No," Siarah whimpers, helpless. "They'll kill me, Irie."

"*We have to go, Siarah.* I need you to use everything you have. You have to fight."

Our eyes lock as I grip my sister. I watch as the energy comes back to her face and she grabs on to me tightly. Together, we make our way over to the corner of the bathroom, and using all the strength I have, I hoist Siarah up on my shoulders.

"It's locked," she says as I balance her on my back.

"Break it."

"I can't."

"*You can,* Siarah," I tell her. "*Break it.*"

She balls a fist and punches the window. "Ah!" she cries out. "Irie—"

"Break it, Siarah!" I say urgently. "Give it *everyting* yuh have."

SMASH!

Siarah breaks through the old glass as the thin shards shatter all around us. Blood drips from her fist as she uses pure adrenaline to clear the shards. And then I give it everything I've got and shove her small frame through the window. She slides through the jagged opening and out onto the grass above. Blood drips from her knees as she makes her way out.

"I'm not leaving yuh, Irie," she cries as she reaches back down.

But the distance is too far.

I think quickly, searching around the cramped space.

Nothing.

And then it hits me.

I race over to the sink, and running along the dark walls are old rusting industrial pipes that connect to the sink. I put my foot against the wall for stability, and without a second thought, I use all of my strength to pull on the old pipes.

After a few tries, one of them pops right off. I race back to the window with the long pole, giving the other end to Siarah.

Bam, bam, bam.

I jump from my skin as the man from earlier pounds on the wall.

"Fuck ah tek yuh so long?" His brooding voice comes through the door as the bass continues to boom.

"Pull me up," I whisper to Siarah, tears of desperation streaming down my face. "Brace yuh foot pon di wall. Yuh can do it, Siarah." My voice shakes. "I believe in you."

The look on Siarah's face is doubtful as she panics.

Bam, bam, bam.

I'm seconds away from life or death as Siarah positions herself and uses all her might to pull me up. I hold on to the rusting pipe for dear life as I climb the wall with my feet.

"Don't let go!" I cry out as she pulls me higher. I grab onto the ledge of the window and wince in pain as my hand cuts on the ridged edges of the glass. I fight back tears, but there's no time to think—only time to move. I grab onto Siarah with everything I have left as half my body dangles from the window.

BUT just as my adrenaline kicks in, he kicks in the door.

33

———

Kojo

"Load up di truck!"

MY commander's voice blares in the distance. It's just past midnight as we man the roads, bracing ourselves for the election results to come in. All the men around me rush toward the truck as we run underneath the dim streetlights, militant with our guns under our arms.

We're all tense as we begin to race off into the night.

"Wha' gwaan?" I call out to my friend Romi, who runs ahead of me down the battered rubble.

He slows, turning back around. "Yuh neva hear?" He slows down so I can catch up. "The call jus' came in from up top. PLM took victory. Won di election."

"*Ah lie . . .*" I take in the news. "Over di *JCG*?"

"Yeah. And Winston Kelly is *not* happy about it. Gave us a lead on where di Power Posse Don is going to be tonight."

I'm stunned.

"*Dudley?*" I look at him in shock. "*The crime boss?*"

Romi nods, clutching his gun tighter. "Betta gear up. They're sending us in first."

My stomach knots. *They always send the road boys in first.*

"A raid on election night." I shake my head in disbelief. "That's mod."

"Nuh badda question orders."

I nod as we approach the packed-up truck. If we catch the Power Posse Don the same night the PLM is taking victory, Jamaica will war.

I keep a brave face, but my heart pounds. *What if this gets me closer to Siarah?*

"*GO, GO, GO!*" our sergeant barks, militant as we load up on the truck. I look around at the group of boys and men who surround me. We line up, taking our seats as everyone wears a brave face. The truck engine is loud, but we remain diligent, focused as we begin to speed off into the black of night. The truck rattles along the red rubble as we all sit quietly, lost in thought as we mentally prepare for what's to come.

For the war we're about to fight.

"Yuh all right?" Romi peers over at me, noticing that I'm tense.

"Yeah." I exhale. "Just . . . thinking about my sister."

"I'm sorry again, mon."

"Iz all right." I sigh quietly, keeping my voice low. "Yuh really think tonight makes di most sense fi dis?"

"It's not our job to question it," Romi says firmly, his eyes sure. "It's our job to answer di call. We follow orders. That's what soldiers do."

"Course." I nod, feeling ashamed for asking.

It's our job to protect and serve.

We ride for another thirty minutes, pulling through back roads as we pass by abandoned vegetation. After a while, we make our way down a dark, beaten trail into the underbelly of Kingston.

Trenchtown—one of the most dangerous garrisons.

"Gear up!" the sergeant calls as we pull closer to our destination. I hold my gun at attention, preparing to hop out when the truck stops. They always send the younger boys in first.

But Romi's right; it's not our job to question it.

I try to calm my breathing as the truck slowly rattles down the beaten trail. The night is haunting and dark, making it hard to see ahead of us. And then, they turn off the engine and everything goes quiet.

The young guys hop out first.

We stay in formation as we scan the area, creeping our way closer to the property—a seemingly abandoned building right off the road. We crouch in a straight line, staying low to the ground as we approach the building from behind. The bass gives it away—*this has to be it.*

The Don's go-go club.

It makes sense that he would be here on election night. Tonight, of all nights, while the entire island is on edge. A smile creeps onto my face as adrenaline shoots through me.

We might just be victorious tonight.

I'm going to prove to Irie she was wrong about me. I *am* a hero. And I'm going to find Siarah.

A surge of courage moves through me as all the young men around me hold their guns at attention. My mind moves a mile a minute as the music grows louder. I nod at Romi as we surround the back of the building.

Romi counts down as we draw our weapons. "Five, four, three . . ."

And then, from out of the corner of my eye, I see it.

Flying through the night sky like a shooting star.

A *grenade.*

TWENTY MINUTES EARLIER

34

———

Jilly

Alarm bells sound in my head as I round the building.

BUT there's no time to think. I have to keep moving. I creep through the bushes, slinking behind palm trees as I search for a way in. I can barely see through the dark when I spot it.

A broken window.

By the grace of God.

It sits just above the grass at the side of the building. I count to ten, and then I step out into the night and race toward the club. I crouch low when I reach the window, removing my dress. There's no way I could go inside wearing it, so I use the material to cover the shards. Wearing only my undergarments, I slip inside, putting my legs through before falling to the floor with a hard thud.

"Shit!"

I wince in pain as I fall to the floor. A stabbing sensation shoots up from my ankles as I hit the floor. Tears fill my eyes as I take a moment to gather myself, biting down on my lip to distract me from the pain. As the music bathes the club, I rise from the dirty floor. I make my way to the door and turn the handle.

I step out into the dark hallway, and at the end, I spot a sea of girls—lost, delirious, and half-naked just like I am. My pulse races as I start to make my way toward them. And then I hear the cocking of a gun being drawn from behind me.

Oh my god.

I freeze with my hands in the air.

"Turn 'round." A man's deep voice orders.

I follow instructions, locking eyes with him as a chill moves down my spine.

"Who di fuck are you?"

"I . . . I came to dance." I tremor, trying my best to act naive. "Fi di Don." I hold my breath as he eyes me, disbelieving. He steps closer to me, lowering his gun from my chest.

"Yuh nuh look like nuh dancer."

"I'm one of Ace's girls. I was . . . I was jus' runnin' behind."

He scans me up and down before pointing the pistol down the dark red hallway. "Gwaan."

I waste no time, making my way deeper into the club as he trails behind me. I make my way over to the rest of the girls, falling in with the crowd. I keep my head low as he watches me.

I search the faces for Siarah. For Irie. For anyone who can save me from this moment.

But not a soul comes to my rescue.

"Gwaan to di stage." The man looms behind me, his menacing tone crawling up my skin as he points to the steps with the pistol. *"Me wan' see yuh dance."*

It's an order.

"Okay." I tremble, doing as I'm told. I'm completely vulnerable as I fight to see through the hazy, dark red lights. My knees quiver as I step up the side of the stage. I watch as a girl around my age slithers on the dirty floors, drunk and naked as she dances to the slowed dub that bleeds through the club. In the audience, the Don sits center stage.

You can do this, Jilly.

The red light instantly floods my vision, and from where I stand, the entire club is dark, making it hard to see *out*. As I step out onto the stage, the girl scurries past me as she holds her bra to her chest.

The music doesn't stop, spinning on rotation as the dub permeates the dark room. I start to move slowly, catching the melody as I nervously make my way onto the stage. I vibe with the track, trying my best to relax as I move my hips around. I can feel the sinister eyes of men undress me as I move in time to the tempo.

Commit, Jilly, I tell myself.

So, I decide to give them a show.

I drop to the floor, giving it all that I have as I roll my waist in time with the heavy dub beat. I'm under a trance as the rhythm takes over. As the music slinks and coils through my body, I decide that this is my sacred protest. I'm not going to cower.

I'm going to fight.

I'm lost in the rhythm as I give it all to the stage. *For Irie.* The Don can't take his eyes off me as I offer my body to him on a platter. I groove to the music, seducing the drunken eyes that watch me in a rapture. *In confusion.* Hate might be their weapon, but tonight, I will be the remedy for their spell.

As I merge with the dark,
I wonder if I have always been
The dark.
I whine my hips as the Don leans forward in his seat
Consuming me.
But I don't break for a second.
With all eyes on me, hopefully this will buy Irie more time.
Wherever she is.
I lock eyes with the Don, commanding all his attention. The power of a woman rises in me, and I dare him to look away. I will commit to this performance. I will help my friend.

I will pay for my family's sins.

The melody crashes down around me as the song comes to an end. I fight to control my breathing as I come back to myself.

As I come back into my body, ready to face the consequences. The entire club goes quiet. The Don grins ever so slightly, and then I see it.

The gold tooth.

My heart catapults as I recall the man in my house earlier tonight.

"*Holy fuck,*" I whisper as the club falls silent.

But silence only lasts for a second.

SMASH!

I'm jolted by the sound of shattering glass.

We hear it before we see it.

And then . . .

BOOOOM!

Everything around me explodes.

Glass rains like a million tiny angels fluttering through dark red sky. In a second's notice, heat encapsulates the club, and soon, I am facedown on the stage, surrounded by a sea of flames.

The building implodes as *blood spills* from my chest.

POP! POP! POP! POP! POP!

All I can hear are the sounds of bullets as they blare through the nightclub.

All around me girls are

Yelling and screaming,

And yelling and screaming,

And,

Red leaks from me and out onto the floor.

I don't know how or when.

But suddenly, it is my heart that soaks the ground.

Smoke fills my lungs, but my cries are muffled—drowned in the devastation of the frenzy of girls around me. The entire club is ablaze, and I watch paralyzed in position as bullets fly left and right, piercing through the night like hummingbirds trying to find their way home.

Trying to find freedom in disaster.

I let my eyes close.

But maybe it was only a matter of time.

A brush of Fate.

A wheel of Fortune.

I cry as the bass blares through me

Except this time

I disappear

The smoke clouds my vision, encompassing my hell as flames rip through the club.

All I can feel is the heat from the fire.

And then it happens.

I let go.

The smoke takes over my lungs as I melt into an unfamiliar rhythm.

At last,

Freedom merges with my bones

The sound of peace,

THE only music I hear.

FOURTEEN YEARS LATER

35

————

Siarah

"Sorry I'm late!"

I'M in a haste as I burst through the guest room door in the Pegasus Hotel. Tandi stops cleaning and looks over at me, a scolding look on her face. "Look who decided to show up . . ."

"My bad, Tan." I give her an apologetic look. "I had to stop and do suh'um dis mawnin'."

"*Yuh lucky.*" Tandi makes a face as I settle in. "Boss just passed by asking fi yuh."

"Yuh cover fi me?" I ask as I start spreading the unmade bed.

"Course I did, bighead. What are sisters for?" She playfully tosses a pillow at my head. "But I left the bathroom just for you. Me nuh in di mood fi scrub no toilet."

"How thoughtful." I stick out my tongue. She smiles.

"So, yuh nah go tell me which part yuh ah come from? Not like you to be so late."

I stop spreading the sheets and look up at her. *I'm way too excited to keep this to myself.*

"You'll neva believe it." A smile creeps onto my face. "I met up wit' U-Roy dis mawnin'."

"U-Roy?" Tandi's face drops. "*Daddy Roy?*"

"Yup. 'Memba him from all those years back?" I burst. "He gave me the record. *Irie's record.* The one she recorded."

"Siarah."

"*I know.*" I laugh, the excitement pouring out of me. "Can yuh believe it? He still had it. After all this time."

"Does Irie know you went to see him?"

"Not yet." I shift as the question catches me off guard. "Me nuh know how me ah go tell her, either. Yuh know how she stay when it come to di music ting."

"Yeah." Tandi nods, understanding. "So, wha' yuh ah go do wit' it?"

"Bring it down ah dat new station, IRIE FM." I beam. "I heard these ladies talking about it on the bus. Apparently, it's going to be di first radio station in Jamaica that plays twenty-four-hour reggae."

"Wait, *what?*" Tandi stops, dropping the sheets. "Siarah, are you insane? Yuh cyaan put Irie pon di radio without her permission."

"I have to at least *try,* Tandi. She'd never say yes if I asked her."

"That's *my point.*"

"She needs to let the past *go,*" I say, growing frustrated. "We've all been through a lot, but how long is Irie going to spend feeling bad about what happened? She didn't *kill* her, Tandi. She can't just give up her passion. She *has* to sing again."

Just then, the door opens, and Irie walks in.

"Mawnin'!" Irie's oblivious as she enters, a smile on her face as she ties her apron around her. "Sorry I'm late. I missed that stupid bus again. Dem bus driver nuh wait fi *nobody.*"

"It's all right, Irie." Tandi smiles, trying to cover for our conversation. "Don't worry about it. The only thing left to clean is the bathroom."

"You always save the best for last." She's sarcastic as she takes out her gloves.

"Unu lucky I saved anything at all," Tandi says playfully. "Next time I want triple pay."

I decide to drop it as Tandi pulls out the mop. We both know better than to discuss this in front of Irie.

Ever since Jilly's death all those years ago, she stopped singing and writing songs. She lost her passion for the music, and whenever we bring it up, she gets sensitive about it. She doesn't like to discuss that time in her life, but I don't think it's because the music reminds her of Jilly—I think it's because it reminds her of who she used to be.

I know deep down Irie wants to sing again.

Her heart deserves to be free. And I'm going to help her to do just that.

I turn back to my duties, picking up the radio and cleaning underneath. After shining the nightstand table, I turn on the radio for some background noise before opening the curtains.

A woman's voice moves through the room. *"Tuesday marks the anniversary of the Crossvale Street bombing. The infamous tragedy, known for taking place the night of Jamaica's 1976 election, gained worldwide coverage for taking down infamous PLM crime boss Dudley."*

We all freeze in position as the woman continues, *"The bombing is also marked by the death of political heiress Jillian Ca—"*

"Turn it off." Irie's voice is stern. The color drains from her face. *"Please."*

"I'm so sorry, Irie." I rush over to the nightstand table and grab the radio, switching it off. "I didn't realize . . . I forgot what week it was—"

"It's fine." She kills the conversation.

But her entire mood changes in an instant. She's sullen as she heads over to the cleaning products. She fumbles with them, and then her eyes start to water.

The room goes quiet as Tandi and I stop cleaning.

"Are you okay?" Tandi asks.

Irie says nothing, gathering herself. She makes her way over the bed and plops down, her demeanor suddenly defeated. Tears stream down her warm brown skin.

"Oh, Irie, I know this time of year is tough for you," I say as I move in closer, taking a seat beside her. "It's tough for all of us."

"But we're here for you," Tandi adds. "We mean it. If you ever want to talk . . ."

Irie sighs, wiping the tears from her cheeks. "I appreciate you both." She looks up at us. "But sometimes there's just not much to say."

"That's *exactly* why I think you need to sing again." My passion gets ahead of me as I take her hand. "Start writing music, Irie. It used to bring you *so* much joy. Maybe it's exactly what you need to do to finally heal from this."

"Please don't start, Siarah." She shrugs me off. "Music . . . it was a lifetime ago."

"No, it wasn't. It was *this lifetime,* Irie." Tandi takes her hand. "I know that time took a lot from us . . . Daddy . . . Kojo . . . Junior . . . *Jilly.* But all those people, they would want you to carry on, Irie. They would want you to keep singing."

"Can you stop?" Irie shakes her head. "I don't want to talk about music right now."

"But maybe you need to. Have yuh ever thought about that?" I look at her. "You'll always be a star, Irie. Yuh cyaan run from yuhself. Yuh have to remember who you are."

"You don't get it, Siarah." Irie shakes her head. "That was years ago. A completely different me. I was younger back then. So much has changed."

"We made it *out of there* that night, Irie," I remind her. "Yuh cyaan keep yuhself locked in that building. We made it out alive."

"But Jilly *didn't.*" Irie's voice breaks. "And I'm the *only one* to blame for that, Siarah. I walk wit' dat guilt *every single day* of my life. Jillian had no reason to be out there."

"And neither did we," I say sternly. "Yuh cyaan spend your whole life suffering. *God gave you a second chance.*" My baby sister's brown eyes go glossy as I study her. "You deserve to let this go, Irie. You deserve to be free and you deserve to make music again."

I watch as tears stream down Irie's soft brown skin.

"I was such a horrible person to her."

"You were *not* a horrible person to her, Irie." Tandi sits down on her other side. "How could you ever think that? You were a great friend to Jilly."

"You weren't there that night, Tandi. You don't know the horrible stuff I said to her . . . and the things she said about *me.*"

"*Weren't true,*" I say passionately. "And you can't keep carrying them, Irie. You *have* to remember who you are . . . the things you *love.* You have to come home to yourself." I take her face in my hands as I look into her starry brown eyes. "I told you from the beginning—I always had a feeling that friendship would bring crosses to yuh life, but *you* get to decide how long you want to carry it for, Irie. *And you deserve to put it down.* You deserve to sing what's in your heart again."

Irie says nothing, crying as she falls into my arms. I pull her into a hug, and soon Tandi joins in. The memories that haunt her show themselves to the light of day as we hold her, mourning the lives we all leave behind.

"We're here for you, Irie," I whisper. "Always will be."

AFTER I finish work, I take the long bus ride to IRIE FM.

I tell my sisters I'll meet up with them later, and soon I find myself squished like a sardine in the sun as I ride in the hot, over-crowded taxi. People spill out of the windows, cramped as we all hold on tightly. I hold Irie's record in my hands as the taxi driver rips through the roads.

I know this is what Daddy would have wanted.

I wonder where he is—if he's dead or alive. I wonder if he

knows the day he dreamed about *actually came true*. A twenty-four-hour reggae station in Jamaica. Who could have imagined that change would come gradually but the price would be so steep.

I refuse for Daddy's life to be in vain. For *our lives* to be in vain. The music must live on.

When I reach my destination, I stumble out the doors and into the hot sun.

Finally.

You got this, Siarah, I tell myself as I set my sights on the palm trees and the paved roads that lie ahead of me. And then, clutching the vinyl, I begin the trek down the road.

After about twenty minutes, I find myself at the doors of a new, bright yellow building. IRIE FM is spelled out in colorful block letters across the front. The coincidence isn't lost on me as I say a silent prayer, tucking the record under my arm. I open the front door to find a receptionist sitting behind her desk.

"Hello." I smile.

The woman looks up at me, confused by my presence as I make my way over to her. "May I help you?" she asks, although her tone doesn't seem like she wants to.

"Um, yeah. I . . . um . . ." I pull the vinyl from under my arm. "I'm here to see Kevin . . . I mean, Mr. Young," I awkwardly correct myself. "Mr. Kevin Young."

The woman eyes me suspiciously as the phone next to her begins to ring. She places her hand on top, preparing to pick it up. "I'm sorry, do you have an appointment?"

"No." I shake my head regretfully. "But I heard your station was doing some test transmissions this week. I was just hoping that he might have some time to see me."

"Kevin is by appointment only." Her tone is scolding, and suddenly, the whole thing starts to feel like a bad idea. "What is this concernin', exactly?"

"A record," I say mustering up some courage. "One I think he'll really love."

She gives me a doubtful look.

"*Please.* I traveled really far."

The lady considers for a moment, sighing before nodding to the empty chairs. "Have a seat."

"Thank you *so* much." I'm relieved as I follow instructions.

I wait patiently, twiddling with my thumbs. After what feels like an eternity, she calls out to me.

"He'll see you now." She files through papers as I rise from the chair. "Room 202."

I scurry down the long hallway, scanning the numbers, and at the end, I approach door 202. Beres Hammond's "Last War" bleeds through the adjacent door. I peek inside to find a man with brown skin sitting behind a desk as he goes through a stack of cassettes. I knock.

"Hello?" I peek in as he looks up from his desk. "Mr. Young? My name is Siarah . . . Siarah Rivers."

"Come in." He gestures for me to sit down. "Nice name."

I nervously make my way inside. "Thanks." I flush. My eyes trail the sign over his head, a large yellow banner that reads the radio slogan: *IRIE FM: Your #1 Station for Songs of Irie.*

"What can I do for you, Miss Siarah Rivers?" He looks up at me. "I don't usually take meetings that aren't by appointment."

"I understand that, sir, and I *really* appreciate yuh time. I also want to say congratulations on all of this." I gesture around to the office at the array of cassette tapes. "My father was a *big* lover of reggae music. Played it before its time. He owned a shop back in the seventies, and . . . and I know he would be *so glad* to see that Jamaica finally has a station. One that honors reggae *at home,* not just abroad."

"Yuh fada has a shop?" He raises an eyebrow.

"*Had.* In Papine Square many years ago. Ricky's."

"Records?" He smiles, taking me in. "Your father was a trail-blazer. Bought a few records there when I was a boy."

"Wow." I laugh, stunned. "That's incredible."

"Ricky was truly one of a kind. I'm sorry about what happened to him." His tone is empathetic. "Did they ever release him?"

"No," I say, looking away. "We don't really know what happened after they took him into custody."

His smile fades. There's a strained moment of silence as he looks at me.

"I'm sorry, dear. A lot of casualties from that time. Certainly not Jamaica's finest hour. The seventies . . . We're still paying for those sins."

"Yeah." I clear my throat, trying not to get too emotional. "Well, I actually came here because I have something I think yuh *really* ah go love. *From* the seventies. Recorded during the height of the war." I pull the record from under my arm and place it on the table. "It's a song written and performed by my likkle sista . . . *real roots reggae* stuff."

"A female reggae singer? What's her name?"

"Irie."

"Wow." He smiles. "Serendipitous."

"Right? She actually recorded this song with Daddy Roy a few years back." I'm nervous as he takes it from my hands. "I heard on the radio the other day that your station is looking to promote local reggae artists, so . . . here I am." I smile awkwardly. "Hopefully with your next hit record."

"On vinyl?"

"I wasn't too sure how to get it printed onto cassette." I shift. "Things are changing so fast. It's hard to keep up."

"Well, I'm just glad to know that Ricky's love of reggae continued in his daughters. Would've been a shame if all that passion went to waste." He considers as he holds it up. "You said Daddy Roy produced this?"

"Yes, sir." I nod. "And I really think it has the potential to be Jamaica's next big hit. Maybe even compete in the American markets."

He places the record down onto his desk. "I'll give it a listen."

"*Really?*" I stare at him in shock.

"Why not? We already have enough people telling us this station isn't going to work. Some of the biggest reggae artists are hesitant to send their catalogs." He leans back in his chair as he looks at me and sighs. "People don' think an all-reggae station can survive in Jamaica. Can you imagine? Critics think reggae can only survive abroad. It's ludicrous." He shakes his head. "The truth is, we're in need of fresh voices. Especially from a woman."

"Wow." A giant smile covers my face. "So, yuh *really* ah go play it? Pon di *actual* radio?"

"I never said all that, Miss Rivers," he retracts. "I'm not making any promises. But I will give it a listen."

"Okay." I shift, unsure of how to feel.

"Is that all?" he asks as he resumes sorting through the pile of tapes in front of him.

"Yeah." I nod, trying not to get my hopes up. "I guess that's it."

He gestures to the door as I rise from my seat.

"Thank you, Mr. Young. And good luck. You know, with the station."

Just as I turn to go, he stops me.

"Miss Rivers, does the record have ah name?"

I pause, unsure of the answer. I look up at the banner over his head.

IRIE FM: Your #1 Station for Songs of Irie.

"'Sounds' . . . or, um." I rack my brain. "'*Songs*' . . . 'Songs of Irie.'"

He nods. "Your sister is very lucky to have you."

I pause, never having considered it.

"I actually think it's the other way around," I say softly. "She saved my life once. I just hope I can return the favor."

SIX YEARS LATER

36

———

Irie

"Who should I make it out to?"

I can't stop smiling as I sit at the table of my dressing room vanity. Two giddy schoolgirls stand across from me, reminding me exactly why I do what I do. They couldn't be more than twelve—*thirteen at most.* Their smiles are bright as I hold the marker in my hand.

"*Lily.*" The brown-skinned girl with pigtails beams. "And Kyra. Spelled wit' ah *K*."

"Lily and Kyra." I smile, doing my best handwriting across the poster. "Those names are beautiful. I really appreciate you girls comin' out."

"*Are yuh kidding, Irie?* We could *neva* miss di chance fi come see *you!*" Lily squeals. "I'm literally *yuh biggest fan.* I have yuh posters all ova ma room. Ask Kyra."

"We even skipped class fi come here." Kyra's so excited I think she might burst. "When we won di meet-and-greet contest on di radio, there was no way we could pass it up. We sing yuh songs *all* di time at school. We even mek our own dance routines."

"Wow." I'm humbled as I take it in. "You have no idea how much that means to me."

"Yuh mean the world to *us*." Lily's ecstatic, and her energy is contagious. "When I grow up, I wanna sing reggae music just like you, Irie. Inspire di world wit' ma songs."

"I have no doubt that you will."

I'm touched as I pull her in for a hug. Her brown eyes dance, reminding me of my school days, when being a star was only a dream inside my heart.

A twinkle in my eye.

"All right, girls, Irie haffi start get ready fi go pon stage." Tandi's voice is kind as she makes her way over. "But maybe after di show, you can come spend some time with her."

"*Seriously?*" Kyra explodes with joy.

"Seriously." I laugh. "I would love that. Yuh can sing me one of yuh songs."

The girls are elated, doing a happy dance as Tandi escorts them to the door.

"See you girls after the show."

"I'll take them to their seats." Tandi opens the door. "Yuh have an hour till showtime. I'll come get yuh in a bit," she calls back over her shoulder. "*Light it up, girl!*"

"Thanks, Tan." I'm emotional as I watch them go.

And then, it's just me and my reflection in the mirror.

I adjust my locs, adorning them with shells and trinkets. They fall long down my back, and I marvel at how much they've grown in such a short space of time. My brown skin glows, illuminated by the warm bulbs around the mirror, and I'm reminded of the days I prayed for moments like this.

To finally see my own reflection.

The nerves start to creep up as I imagine just how packed the stadium will be today. I always get so nervous before shows. No matter how many times I do this, the anxiety always takes over before I hit the stage. The tour has been completely sold out, and I'm exhausted from spending the last few months traveling. I've been all over the world—but I saved the best for last.

I'm finally performing back home in Jamaica.

I can hear the bustling of the crowd all the way from my dressing room as the anticipation mounts. My stomach drops as the nerves start to kick in. Thousands of people.

All out there waiting for me.

Breathe, Irie. I calm myself down, reaching for the box of fan mail that sits nearby on the dresser. It's one of hundreds of boxes that I still have to go through, letters written to me from fans all over the world.

I've made it my goal to read every single one.

I spend the next ten minutes shuffling through letters, allowing the love to overwhelm me and calm me back down. To ground me in the present moment and help me give thanks. As I dig through the box, a bulky red envelope catches my eye. I pick it up and read the cursive on the front. I'm stunned when I see the name on the return label.

Amala Wilkins.

I freeze.

No way. It couldn't be . . .

My pulse starts to race as I open the envelope.

A white handkerchief and a note fall out.

Dearest Irie,

Congratulations on your massive success. You are a trailblazer, and the whole of Jamaica is so proud to watch you follow your heart.

I found this buried in one of Jillian's old boxes. I know she would have wanted you to have it. You were a great friend to her . . . and I know she was deeply grateful.

Love,

Amala

Tears well in my eyes as I stare down at the faded cursive. I read the letter again and again, processing the note. And then I carefully unfold the cloth. I'm shocked when it falls out:

The ruby bracelet.

"Oh my god . . ."

I push back tears as I stare down at it in shock.

Just then, there's a knock on the door.

"Come in!" I call out as Ace makes his way inside.

"There's my supastar." He beams when he sees me. "Just wanted fi check pon yuh before di big show. Everyone's so excited. Looks like di whole ah Jamaica is out there."

"Don' say that." I shift in my seat. "I'm nervous enough."

"Fi wha?" He smiles. "You've got this, Irie. Yuh always do."

I nod, biting down as I put the letter away. "It just feels so different from the rest of the tour," I confess as Ace takes a seat on the vanity. "Being back here feels so . . . *surreal*. I know so much time has passed, but there's so many memories, Ace. It's hard to shake. I couldn't have imagined this for myself years ago."

"That's not true, Irie," Ace reminds me, cupping my chin. "You always did."

"I guess." I'm overwhelmed by my emotions as tears form again. "I just . . . I guess I just thought things would be different, yuh nuh? I thought Daddy and Junior would be here." I meet Ace's gaze, vulnerable. "And Jilly and I . . . we had so many plans."

Ace nods, empathetic as he watches me. He knows exactly what's on my mind without me having to get into it. He knows me better than anyone. He's used to the ghosts I carry.

"I feel so guilty all the time . . . fi dat night." I shake my head as I put the ruby bracelet on the counter. "Jillian's words . . . *what she thought of me* . . . It still haunts me. And sometimes I struggle with letting it go." I look up to meet his gaze. "Sometimes I wonder why I got to live and she didn't."

Ace pauses, taking me in before moving in closer. His voice

goes low. "Yuh hear all dem people out desso ah chant yuh name?"

I pause, breaking away from my melancholy. I listen carefully to the faint sound that bleeds through the walls.

IRIE! IRIE! IRIE! IRIE!

"Irie, yuh *worldwide,*" Ace says passionately, bringing me back to the present moment. "Do yuh understand yuh cyaan even turn on di news without hearing about you?" He kneels down to my level, serious as day. "We survived that night *fi a reason,* Irie. *Guilt nah serve you.* It never has," he says softly, stroking my palm. "Your life is ahead of you. Not behind."

His words calm me down as he rises.

"I tell you all di time—life is all about *choices.* Some choices, we choose. But some choices . . . *they choose us.*" He touches his hand to my chin. "You weren't meant to stay stuck in that building that night because *God had more fi you.*"

I'm emotional as his words land.

"Dem can kill a revolutionary, but dem cyaan kill a revolution."

"Maybe," I whisper, staring down at the ruby bracelet in my hand. "It's just so hard to lose my best friend like that."

"Yeah." Ace nods. "But it's even worse to lose yourself."

His words send a chill down my spine as he makes his way toward the door.

"Music is yuh gift, Irie. *Gwaan go light it up* . . . they need you out there."

Time stops as I take him in.

"They can kill a revolutionary, but they can never kill a revolution. If yuh believe in freedom, yuh cyaan rest, Irie. Yuh haffi lead with the love an' light the way . . . Yuh only get one life." Ace winks. "Don't mek it pass yuh by, Stargirl."

And with that, he makes his way back through the door.

Before I can process his words, Tandi comes bursting in. "Irie!" She beams, clipboard in hand. "We ready fi you!"

I give myself one final look in the mirror.

"*I got this,*" I whisper.

I take a deep breath, clipping the ruby bracelet around my wrist.

And then, I rise from my seat.

In a matter of minutes, I'm surrounded by my team as they usher me backstage and around the side of the venue. My stomach knots as I look out of the size of the crowd—it's *massive,* and it's pandemonium as the crowd roars. I'm in a daze, shot with nerves as a few women fuss over my makeup, fixing my hair and smoothing my outfit. My mind is a whirlwind as the crowd's cheers grow louder.

IRIE! IRIE! IRIE! IRIE! IRIE!

It's showtime.

I feel the love of a thousand soldiers go before me as I step out onto the stage. The crowd erupts, and goose bumps race down my spine as I dance my way up toward the mic. The energy is infectious, and laughter spills from my lips as the band plays me on. I give the audience a giant wave, grabbing the mic as my power comes back to me.

Finally.

"Wha' gwaan, Jamaica?" I yell.

The monstrous crowd explodes. The drums and horns flood the air as I start to groove.

Freedom courses through my veins

And suddenly it dawns on me

That maybe I have always been the miracle,

Waiting on a miracle.

As the band plays on, I dig deeper than I ever have before.

Gathering my fire, I channel the force within me

Because Love is the conquering Lion

And it shouldn't be for our keeping.

"I wrote this song for a friend of mine." I scan the beautiful array of black and brown faces as they scream my name, cheering me on with a vigorous passion. "I made a promise to him years back that I would always hear di music . . . that I would *always sing the song in my soul.*"

The crowd goes wild as the band comes to a crescendo.

And when the beat drops, I feel no pain.

I keep the fire burning,

AND I set myself free.

IRIE FM *was the first all-reggae radio station to launch in Jamaica in 1990, decades after reggae music had made a global impact abroad in the U.S., in the UK, and around the world.*

The months leading up to Jamaica's 1980 election are considered some of the most violent, horrific times in the island's history, with thousands of lives lost.

SONGS OF IRIE *was written in honor of those lives, and the countless reggae artists, revolutionaries, Rastafarians, freedom fighters, and trailblazers who paved the way for peace to reign on the island and around the world. We are forever changed by your music, your art, and your activism.*

Thank you for your courage.

Thank you for your voice.

And in the midst of war and injustice,

Thank you for your Songs of Irie.

ACKNOWLEDGMENTS

Thank you, JAH.

It's amazing the way your fire keeps blazing. You are my Eternal Light, and I am so thankful for the way your love has reigned supreme over my life. The journey has not been easy. I have cried an ocean's worth of tears. But I will follow your Love throughout dimensions, universes, and lifetimes, and in every iteration, I pray that my art is a reflection of your endless unfolding. I pray that your eternal Love shines down onto those of your children whom for so long have not been seen or cherished by humanity. May your light illuminate the darkness so that they may shine freely and sing joyfully. May they have the spotlight they have deserved for so long. I pray that your love liberates and inspires truth, healing, and compassion in mankind. May we be brave enough to hear the music and humble enough to know that we are All children of Creation.

One Love means All of us.

Thank you to my Father—I love you endlessly, till Kingdom come. Thank you for imparting your wisdom onto me and teaching me about this important, critical time in our history. Thank you for my African consciousness. You are my Jamaican Sunrise and

Sunset. Your wisdom goes beyond this life, and I am so thankful I was born to be your Rasta pickney. It was destiny, nuh true? All praises to the Most High for choosing you to be mi Fada, forever and eva and eva. Love you bad, Pupa. Love you nuff.

Thank you to my Mother—My source of Love and my endless well of Inspiration. Mummy, you make life brighter. Your spirit is contagious. Your laugh is infectious. You are Irie's greatest inspiration, and I pray you feel a piece of yourself on the page with this story. Thank you for sharing the stories that live in your heart with me. You light up the universe with your smile alone. I could write a lifetime of stories about you. You are my greatest muse. My earth angel. You give my life meaning. Thank you for teaching me it is always about the Art.

The fragments of Love we leave behind.

This book is dedicated to Kendall, Mila, and Veronica—My sweet, whimsical Stargirls—and all the little black girls with a dream inside their hearts.

Dream far, big, wide, and endlessly.

You are the future, and the now. Write, sing, dance, play. Create. Offer Love to life and it will come back to you in ten folds. You are a work of art—cherish your life so that others may learn the way. You are stronger than you know, more creative than you could imagine. I pray your creativity roams and is never be bound by the illusion of fear. You are worthy of all you can conjure up. Your art is sacred—so share your song with the life. You are the Medicine.

The gift is You.

Thank you to my Family. My Tribe.

Ulett, Cliff, Makeda, Clayton, Trisha, Luka, Amani, Xavier, Siya, Symone, Veronica, Rosalee, Rosemarie, Ingrid, Kuya, Shernette, Arlene, Daphne, Kendell, Mila, Khai, Jahleem, Jaheem,

Nikita, Tenea, Triniti, Tafari, Burge, Jamel, Tina, Vanessa, Shan-Tai, Doreen, Joy, Justice, Tenisha, Kemisha, Serena, Rachel, Nasa, Jahlani, Shaka, Mama Winnie, Alex, Renee, Kyra, Zulu, Pele.

You are my home and my greatest joy. I met God in your arms. I am grateful beyond measure for the ways you have up-lifted me and kept me during the hardest times in my life. For the ways you have wiped every tear and held onto every bit of hope. Thank you for seeing the light in the times when I couldn't. There is no me without you. No love without your grace. You are my family. My home and the strength of my creativity.

It is the greatest honor of my life to love you all back.

To my amazing agent, Emily Van Beek—You are a light and a powerhouse agent. I am so grateful to you and the entire team at Folio Literary for believing in my voice and my work. Thank you for your love, guidance, and wisdom. Thank you for believing in the power of this story.

An endless Thank You to Sara Goodman—My fearless editor with a heart of pure platinum gold. I thank the moon and stars every day that I get to work with you. Your belief in my work has transformed my life. Thank you for seeing my message, champi-oning my purpose and my words. Thank you for believing in Irie and Jilly and for helping me shape this book into a masterpiece! I am honored to work alongside you and I'm so grateful I get to learn from you with each story. You have made me a stronger artist with each draft. My gratitude to you!

Thank you to my incredible team at Wednesday Books, of which none of this is possible without. Your love and care are felt within every inch of this book, and I am forever grateful. Thank you to the following creatives:

Editorial Assistant: Vanessa Aguirre

Jacket and Mechanical Designer: Kerri Resnick

Designer: Kelly Too

Managing Editor: Eric Meyer

Production Editor: Merilee Croft

Production Manager: Diane Dilluvio

Copy Editor: Sara Ensey

Proofreader: Megha Jain

Publicist: Meghan Harrington, Mary Moates

Marketing: Rivka Holler, Brant Janeway

Audio Producer: Elishia Merricks

Audio Marketing: Maria Snelling

Audio Publicity: Amber Cortes

And finally, an eternal Thank You to my grandfather, Daddy Burge—Who owned the *boddest* record store in all of Kingston. Your love has given me strength and deep, deep courage. I am so thankful for the promises we made. I am so grateful to be your granddaughter. I know you are flying high with the best of them.

True Kings never die.

"But every now and then, I say to myself—it'll all come out in the wash. History is the great leveler of artists and activists alike."

—*Michael Norman Manley*